MYSTERY WRITERS OF AMERICA
presents

ICE COLD

Tales of Intrigue from the Cold War

MYSTERY WRITERS OF AMERICA
presents

ICE COLD

Tales of Intrigue from the Cold War

EDITED BY

JEFFERY DEAVER

and

RAYMOND BENSON

GRAND CENTRAL
PUBLISHING

NEW YORK   BOSTON

Grand Central Publishing
Hachette Book Group
237 Park Avenue
New York, NY 10017
www.HachetteBookGroup.com

Printed in the United States of America

RRD-C

First edition: April 2014
10 9 8 7 6 5 4 3 2 1

Grand Central Publishing is a division of Hachette Book Group, Inc.
The Grand Central Publishing name and logo is a trademark of Hachette Book Group, Inc.

The Hachette Speakers Bureau provides a wide range of authors for speaking events. To find out more, go to www.hachettespeakersbureau.com or call (866) 376-6591.

The publisher is not responsible for websites (or their content) that are not owned by the publisher.

Library of Congress Cataloging-in-Publication Data
Mystery Writers of America presents ice cold : tales of intrigue from the Cold War / edited by Jeffery Deaver and Raymond Benson. — First edition.
     pages cm
     ISBN 978-1-4555-2073-2 (hc) — ISBN 978-1-4555-2072-5 (ebook)   1. Spy stories, American.   2. American fiction—21st century.   3. Cold War—Fiction.   4. Spies—Fiction.   I. Deaver, Jeffery editor of compilation.   II. Benson, Raymond, 1955– editor of compilation.   III. Mystery Writers of America.   IV. Title: Ice cold.
     PS648.S85M97 2014
     813'.0872083582—dc23
                                                                        2013030532

ISBN 978-1-4555-2071-8 (pb)

CONTENTS

Much of this is mediocre slush, when it isn't downright unreadable

CONTENTS

dreadful

left-wing lecture not a story

very bd flaws

unreadable

INTRODUCTION
BY JEFFERY DEAVER AND
RAYMOND BENSON

RAYMOND: Hey Jeffery, I'm really pleased to be coediting this MWA anthology with you. I think we've got some great authors and terrific stories that explore many aspects of what we commonly refer to as the "Cold War." The process has been great fun.

JEFFERY: Hi, Raymond. Yes, this project has been a big treat for me. And you've hit on one of the most compelling elements of the book—the many different takes our contributors have on that era. The stories range from classic espionage to subtle psychological drama of the decades that saw huge change in America...and the rest of the world.

RAYMOND: Seeing that we're both around the same age—meaning we're old farts—we can actually remember that tense period in the early 1960s when the Cold War was really causing some anxiety. I recall doing the "duck and cover" drills in elementary school and not totally understanding what they were for. I thought they were fun—you got to take time out from class to practice jumping underneath your desk a few times.

JEFFERY: And how reassuring to learn that six inches of fiberboard and metal could ward off the overhead blast and radiation from a thermonuclear bomb. Your comment brought back a very real memory of the Cuban Missile Crisis standoff. I was in middle school outside of Chicago and a teacher told my class to be particularly diligent in ducking and covering, since we were not far from Argonne National Laboratory in DuPage County—sure to be targeted by the Soviets. You're a Chicagoan, too; do you also remember the Nike missile sites in the area?

RAYMOND: I didn't come to Chicagoland until the early nineties; I grew up in West Texas, where everyone would have rather been dead than Red. But I'm sure my experience in the classroom was similar to yours at that time. And, yes, there is an old Nike missile site not far from my current home in Chicago's northwest suburbs. It looks like the remains of a forgotten World's Fair. Seriously, one of the structures resembles a broken-down amusement park ride. I think, though, my full realization and understanding of the Cold War came with my discovery of James Bond—first through the films, which really didn't address the Cold War much, and Ian Fleming's novels, which did.

JEFFERY: Apart from a few *Twilight Zone* TV series episodes, Bond was my first fiction exposure to the Cold War. I was more a fan of the books than the movies and so, yes, I had a real sense of how the Cold War could set the stage for a thriller. *From Russia, With Love* is the quintessential Cold War Bond novel for me. Of course, it's a bit ironic that you and I, as the only two American authors to write James Bond continuation novels, chose not to set our 007 tales during the Cold War. That's one of the reasons I was delighted to participate in this project, *Ice Cold*.

RAYMOND: I agree with you about *From Russia, With Love.* Actually, my directive from the Fleming people was to make my books "more like the current movies," which, at that time, were the Pierce Brosnan action extravaganzas. But back to America's reaction to the Cold War...You know, it seems to me that the U.S. was much more freaked out about it than other countries, even England. There were some serious over-reactions to the situation. Senator Joe McCarthy's rhetoric in the fifties, and the Hollywood blacklisting in the late forties and all through the fifties, were terribly misguided. When you look at the list of Hollywood actors, writers, and directors who *were* blacklisted, your jaw drops. I actually played around with the idea of writing a blacklist story for this anthology, but ultimately rejected it because I couldn't shape it into a mystery or thriller—it was, simply, pure tragedy.

JEFFERY: Yes, that insanity ruined lives forever. I remember my disappointment at learning that some musicians and film-makers whom I admired turned in their colleagues at Congressional hearings; I never looked at them the same—but since I wasn't in their shoes, it's easy to cast judgments, I suppose. It's curious how we think of the Cold War in terms of nuclear or conventional military confrontation, which was certainly true (just ask anyone in Eastern Europe or who lived within missile-range of Cuba), but the blacklist is a reminder that there were more subtle consequences, like paranoia, anxiety, and derailed or destroyed political and social movements. I think our authors tapped into these two sides of the Cold War era very well.

RAYMOND: There were also a bunch of "Red Scare" movies made in the late forties and the fifties...Ever seen *I Married a Communist* or *Invasion USA*? Today they're wonderful and unintentionally humorous relics of the era. But the ultimate

INTRODUCTION

Cold War movie—and one that puts everything in perspective today and which was amazingly ahead of its time (1964), is Stanley Kubrick's *Dr. Strangelove*. It captures the paranoia, the insanity, and the *absurdity* of the Cold War long before intelligent and sensible people in this country accepted it as such. Alas, we don't have any black comedies in our collection, but we do have some exciting mysteries and thrillers that paint varied portraits of that significant time in world history. I'd like to thank Barry Zeman for the idea of bringing the two of us together to coedit the anthology, Larry Segriff at Tekno Books for initial copyediting, Lindsey Rose at Grand Central, Margery Flax, all of the MWA members who worked hard to submit stories—and I'm sorry we couldn't use everyone's—and all the authors who have contributed to the collection.

JEFFERY: *Dr. Strangelove* is my favorite Kubrick film (yes, even over *2001*!). And take a look at the YouTube of Tom Lehrer, the comic songwriter (and mathematician), performing his "We Will All Go Together When We Go." It's further proof that irony and wit were alive and well during that dark time…Ah, Raymond, I think we could continue this dialogue forever but I suppose we better get on to some other projects. Let me add my heartfelt thanks to all of those you mention above—especially our contributors, whose stories truly bring to life a complex and edgy time in world history.

MYSTERY WRITERS OF AMERICA
presents

ICE COLD

Tales of Intrigue from the Cold War

COMRADE 35

BY JEFFERY DEAVER

Tuesday

To be summoned to the highest floor of GRU headquarters in Moscow made you immediately question your future.

Several fates might await.

One was that you had been identified as a counter-revolutionary or a lackey of the bourgeoisie imperialists. In which case your next address would likely be a gulag, which were still highly fashionable, even now, in the early 1960s, despite First Secretary and Premier Khrushchev's enthusiastic denunciation of Comrade Stalin.

Another possibility was that you had been identified as a double agent, a mole within the GRU—not proven to be one, mind you, simply *suspected* of being one. Your fate in that situation was far simpler and quicker than a transcontinental train ride: a bullet in the back of the head, a means of execution the GRU had originated as a preferred form of execution, though the rival KGB had co-opted and taken credit for the technique.

With these troubling thoughts in mind and his army posture well in evidence, Major Mikhail Sergeyevich Kaverin strode toward the office to which he'd been summoned. The tall man was broad shouldered, columnar. He hulked, rather than walked.

The Glavnoe Razvedyvatelnoe Upravlenie was the spy wing of the Soviet Armed Forces; nearly every senior GRU agent, including Kaverin, had fought the Nazis one meter at a time on the western front, where illness and cold and the enemy had quickly taken the weak and the indecisive. Only the most resilient had survived.

Nothing culls like war.

Kaverin walked with a slight limp, courtesy of a piece of shrapnel or a fragment of bullet in his thigh. An intentional gift from a German or an inadvertent one from a fellow soldier. He neither knew nor cared.

The trek from his present office—at the British Desk, downstairs—was taking some time. GRU headquarters was massive, as befitted the largest spy organization in Russia and, rumors were, the world.

Kaverin stepped into the ante-office of his superior, nodded at the aide-de-camp, who said the general would see him in a minute. He sat and lit a cigarette. He saw his reflection in a nearby glass-covered poster of Lenin. The Communist Party founder's lean appearance was in marked contrast to Kaverin's: He thought himself a bit squat of face, a bit jowly. The comrade major's thick black hair was another difference, in sharp contrast to Lenin's shiny pate. And while the communist revolutionary and first Premier of the Soviet Union had a goatee that gave him—with those fierce eyes—a demonic appearance, Kaverin was clean shaven, and his eyes, under drooping lids, were the essence of calm.

A deep pull on the cigarette. The taste was sour and he absently swatted away glowing flecks of cheap tobacco that catapulted from the end. He longed for better, but couldn't spend the time to queue endlessly for the good Russian brands and he couldn't afford the Western smokes on the black market. When the cigarette was half smoked, he stubbed it out and wrapped the remainder in a handkerchief, then slipped that into his brown uniform jacket.

He thought of the executions he'd witnessed—and participated in. Often, a last cigarette for the prisoner. He wondered if he'd just had his.

Of course, there was yet another fate that might await, having been summoned to this lofty floor of headquarters. Perhaps he was being *rewarded*. The Comrade General, speaking for the Chairman of the GRU or even the Presidium itself—the all-powerful Politburo—could be recognizing him for furthering the ideals of communism and the glory of the Union of Soviet Socialist Republics. In which case he would receive not a slug from a Makarov pistol, but a medal or commendation or perhaps a new rank (though not, of course, a raise in pay).

Then, however, his busy mind, his *spy's* mind, came up with another negative possibility: The KGB had orchestrated a transgression to get him demoted or even ousted.

The soviet civilian spy outfit and the GRU hated each other—the KGB referred to their military counterparts contemptuously as "Boots," because of the uniforms they wore in their official capacity. The GRU looked at the KGB as a group of effete elitists, who trolled for turncoats among the Western intelligentsia, men who could quote Marx from their days at Harvard or Cambridge but who never lived up to their promise of delivering nuclear secrets or rocket fuel formulas.

Since neither the KGB nor the GRU had exclusive jurisdiction in foreign countries, poaching was common. On several occasions in the past year Kaverin had run operations in England and the Balkans right under the nose of the KGB and turned an agent or assassinated a traitor before the civilian spies even knew he was in country.

Had the pricks from Lubyanka Square somehow put together a scandal to disgrace him?

But then, just as he grew tired of speculation, the door before him opened and he was ushered into the office of the man who was about to bestow one of several fates.

A train trip, a bullet, a medal, or—another endearing possibility in the Soviet Union—perhaps something wholly unexpected.

"You may smoke," said the general.

Kaverin withdrew a new cigarette and lit it, marshaling more escaping sparks. "Thank you, sir."

"Comrade Major, we have a situation that has arisen. It needs immediate attention." The general was fat, ruddy and balding. The rumors were that, once, he had set down his rifle and chosen to strangle, rather than shoot, a Nazi who came at him with a bayonet on the outskirts of Berlin in 1945. One look at his hands and you could easily believe that.

"Yes, sir, whatever I might do."

So far, this did not seem like a death sentence.

"Did you know Comrade Major Rasnakov? Vladimir Rasnakov?"

"Yes, I heard he suffered a heart attack. Died almost instantly."

"It should be a lesson to us all!" The general pointed his cigarette at Kaverin. "Take the baths, exercise. Drink less vodka, eat less pork."

The man's rasping voice continued, "Comrade Rasnakov was on a very sensitive, very important assignment. His demise has come at a particularly inconvenient time, Comrade Major. From reading your dossier, you seem like a perfect replacement for him. You can drive, correct?"

"Of course."

"And speak English fluently."

"Yes."

This was growing more intriguing by the moment.

The general fixed him with a fierce gaze of appraisal. Kaverin held the man's eyes easily. "Now, let me explain. Comrade Rasnakov had a job that was vital to the cause of communist supremacy. He was in charge of protecting the lives of certain people within the United States—people who we have deemed indispensable to our interests."

Because they were all trained soldiers, GRU agents often served as undercover bodyguards for valuable double-agents in enemy countries.

"I will gladly take over his tasks, sir."

The vodka bottle thudded onto the middle of the desk. Glasses were poured and the men drank. Kaverin was moderate with alcohol—which put him in the minority of men in Russia. But, just like not uttering certain thoughts aloud, you never declined the offer to share a drink with a superior officer. Besides this was real vodka, good vodka. Made from corn. Although as a soldier and a member of the GRU, Kaverin had some privileges, that meant simply potatoes without frostbite, meat once a week instead of every other, and vodka that, while it didn't poison you, came in a corked bottle with curious flecks afloat. (Unlike the KGB, whose agents, even those in the field, had the best liquor and food and never had to queue.)

The general's voice diminished nearly to a whisper. "Intelligence was received from a trusted source in America about a forthcoming occurrence there. It is necessary that the man behind this event remains alive, at least until he completes what he intends."

"Who is this person? An agent of ours? Of another service?"

The general stubbed out his cigarette and lit another. Kaverin noted he left a good inch and a half unsmoked. The ashtray was filled with such butts. Together they must have made up a full pack.

"No..." His voice was even softer now. And—astonishing—the comrade generally actually seemed uneasy. He tapped the top secret file before him. "As you'll see in here, this man—Comrade Thirty-five, the code name we've given him—is not motivated by any overt desire to help the Soviet Union but that's exactly what the effect of his actions will be—*if* he succeeds in his mission." The general's eyes were far more intense than his whispered voice as he said, "And it is up to you to make sure that he remains alive to do so."

"Of course."

"Now, Comrade Rasnakov learned that there are two men who intend to take the life of our American comrade by week's end. That cannot happen. Now, read this file, Comrade Major. Study it. But make sure it does not leave the building. It is for your eyes only. It is perhaps the most sensitive document you will ever come in contact with."

"Of course."

"Learn all you can about Comrade Thirty-five and the two men who wish to harm him. Then make plans to leave immediately for America. You'll meet with Comrade Colonel Nikolai Spesky, one of our GRU agents in place. He can provide weapons and updated intelligence."

"Thank you for this opportunity, Comrade General." Kaverin rose and saluted. The general saluted in return then said, "One more thing, Comrade Major."

"Yessir."

"Here." The man handed him a packet of French cigarettes. "You must learn to smoke something that will not set fire to the carpet of your superior officers."

Kaverin returned to his own small office, which offered a partial view of the airport; he would sometimes sit and look at airplanes on final approach. He found this relaxing.

He opened the file and began to read. He got no more than halfway through the first paragraph, however, then sat up with a start, electrified as he read what the mission would entail and who was involved.

Oh, my God…

Kaverin lit a cigarette—one of the new ones—and noted that for the first time in years his thick fingers were actually shaking.

But then, soldier that he was, he put aside his emotions at the momentous consequences of the assignment and got to work.

Wednesday

The flights were carefully planned to arouse the fewest suspicions of the enemy intelligence services.

For the trip Kaverin was dressed Western—a black fedora, a fake bespoke suit and white shirt and narrow black tie, like a funeral director, he thought. Which in a macabre way seemed appropriate. His route took him from Moscow to Paris on an Aeroflot TU-124, then to Heathrow. He connected there to a Trans-Canada Air Lines DC-8 bound for Montreal. Finally he flew from Canada into the United States, first port of call, Idlewild Airport in New York City.

Four hours later he disembarked in Miami.

Whereas New York had seemed hard as steel, edged and unyielding, the Floridian metropolis was soft, pastel, soothed by balmy breeze.

Kaverin walked from the airport terminal, inhaling deeply the fragrant air, and hailed a taxi.

The car—a huge Mercury—bounded into the street. As they drove, Kaverin stared at the palm trees, the bougainvillea and plants he'd never seen. He blinked to observe a flamingo in the front yard of a small bungalow. He'd seen the birds in Africa and believed they were water dwellers. He laughed when he realized the creature was a plastic decoration.

He regretted that dusk was arriving quickly, and soon there was nothing to see but lights.

In a half hour he was at the address he sought, a small, one-story office building, squatting in a sandy lot filled with unruly green groundcover. On the front window was a sign.

COMRADE 35

East Coast Transportation Associates.
Nick Spencer, Prop.

As good a cover as any for a spy operation, he reflected. After all, the company *did* do some transporting: stolen secrets and occasional bodies. And the proprietor's pseudonym was a reasonable tinkering with the real name of the GRU agent who worked out of the facility.

Kaverin found the door locked and knocked. A moment later it flew open and there stood a round, broad-shouldered man in a short-sleeved beige shirt—with black vertical stripes of a chain design—and powder blue slacks. His shoes were white.

"Ah, Comrade!" Nikolai Spesky cried, warmly pumping his hand.

Kaverin frowned at the word, looking around at the other office buildings nearby.

Ushering him inside and locking the door behind them, Spesky laughed, and wrinkles rippled in his tanned face. "What are you worried about, Comrade? Microphones? It's a different world here."

"I suppose I am."

"No, no, no. See here, to eavesdrop, the government must get the courts to approve it."

"Which they surely do."

"Ah, Comrade, not necessarily. You'd be surprised. And, what's more, the CIA has no jurisdiction here."

Kaverin shrugged. He took off his heavy jacket—the temperature was about 75 degrees.

"Sit!" Spesky said jovially.

The men lit cigarettes. Spesky seemed delighted Kaverin was the agent chosen to take over for Comrade Rasnakov. "You are quite famous," Spesky said, though without the awe that would have made his comment awkward. "The vile traitor Penkovsky... The people owe you quite a debt, Comrade."

Penkovsky was a GRU agent who spied for the British and

Americans, his most valued contribution being providing information that helped Kennedy stand up to the Russians during the Cuban Missile Crisis in 1962. He was, as Kaverin had learned, less motivated by ideology than by a desire to lead a decadent life in the West. Which he had—until caught by the Soviets and executed.

"I was merely one of a number of people who found the traitor."

"Modest, modest…a good trait for a spy. We must remain unseen, anonymous, subtle. Only in that way can the exultant cause of Mother Russia and the ideology of *Herren* Marx and Engels, as espoused by our noble progenitor Comrade Lenin, be furthered for the glory of our cause and the people!"

Kaverin remained silent at this pronouncement. But then, as if he could not control himself, Spesky exploded with laughter. "I do a very good impersonation of the Premier, do I not?"

Khrushchev was notorious for his bombastic speeches, but Kaverin wouldn't think of answering the question affirmatively, though Spesky was in fact spot on.

The man scoffed good-naturedly. "Ah, relax, relax, Comrade! We are field agents. The rules don't apply to us." His smile faded. "It's a dangerous job we do and we are to be entitled to some indulgence, including poking fun at the people and the institutions taken far too seriously at home." He patted his large belly. To Kaverin it resounded like a timpani. "I missed my lunch today, Comrade. I must eat something." Squinting at his guest, the man asked, "Now, do you know of CARE packages?"

"Yes, indeed. They were a propaganda tool created by the West after the War for the purpose of exploiting the unfortunate and winning them to the cause of capitalism and imperialism."

Spesky waved his hand impatiently. "You must learn, Comrade Major, that in this country not every comment is an invitation to a political statement. I was merely inquiring if you know the concept. Because I have received a CARE package, of sorts—from my wife in Moscow, and I have been waiting for your arrival to indulge." He lifted onto his desk a large cardboard carton, labeled

"Accounting forms," and, with a locking-blade knife, sliced open the lid. He removed a bottle of good vodka—Stolichnaya—and tins of paté, smoked fish and oysters. He unwrapped a loaf of dark bread and smelled it. "Not bad. Not too moldy yet."

They drank the vodka and ate the bread and paté, both of which were excellent. The bread didn't taste the least moldy to Kaverin, and he had quite some intimate knowledge of bread in its final stages.

Tossing down a third small glass of vodka, Spesky said, "I will tell you the details of this assignment." His face clouded over. "Now, our Comrade Thirty-five, the man you are to protect, is not a particularly likable fellow."

"So I have read."

"He acts impulsively, he speaks out when he should listen. Frankly I believe he is a cruel man and may be unstable. Accordingly he has made enemies."

"The Comrade General told me there are two men who present an immediate threat."

"Yes, that's correct. They are U.S. citizens, though of Latin American extraction. Comrade Rasnakov learned that they plan to kill him sometime on Friday." He slid a slim file across the battered desk. "Your job is to intercept them. Then communicate with them."

"Communicate?"

"Yes, exactly. With one of these." Spesky removed two pistols from his desk, along with two boxes of ammunition.

"You're familiar with these?"

One was a Colt Woodsman, a small caliber, .22, but very accurate, thanks to the long barrel. The other was a large 1911-style Colt .45. "And you will need a car, Comrade," Spesky told him. "I understand you can drive?"

A nod.

"Good. In the file you will find an address, an abandoned house. There's a garage behind it, off an alley—'garage' they say here to mean not a repair station but a separate place to keep your car in, like a stable."

"I'm aware of that."

"In the garage is a Chevrolet Bel Air. The keys are hidden up under the front seat...Ah, I see you know not only guns but automobiles too, Comrade."

Spesky had apparently noticed that Kaverin was smiling at the mention of the Bel Air.

"Now these are your targets." Spesky opened the file and tapped the documents.

Kaverin read through the file carefully, noting facts about the two men whose mission was to kill Comrade 35—Luis Suarez and Carlos Barquín, both in their mid-thirties. Dangerous men, who were former prisoners. They had murdered before. Their round faces—both bisected with thick mustaches—looked sullen, and Barquín gave the impression of being stupid.

Kaverin, though, knew it was a mistake to underestimate your enemy; he'd seen too many soldiers and agents die because they had done just that. So he read carefully, learning every fact he might about the men.

According to Rasnakov's sources, the two were presently traveling—whereabouts unknown—but would arrive in Texas day after tomorrow. The plan was to kill Comrade 35 that day. Spesky explained that Rasnakov had planned to lie in wait and kill them when they arrived at the boarding house. This would be Kaverin's job now. He pushed the file back and placed the guns and ammunition in his attaché case.

Spesky then handed him an envelope. It contained one thousand dollars U.S. and another airline ticket. "Your flight's tomorrow morning. You'll stay at a hotel near the airport tonight."

After calling for a taxi, Spesky poured more vodka and they ate the rest of the paté and some smoked oysters. Spesky asked about life back in Moscow and what were the latest developments at GRU headquarters. There was gossip about who had become nonpersons and an affair at a very high level, though Kaverin was careful not to mention any names. Spesky was delighted nonetheless.

Neither man, however, had any hesitation in sharing stories about the latest KGB cock-ups and scandals.

When the taxi arrived, Spesky shook Kaverin's hand. Suddenly the brash spy seemed wistful, almost sad. "You will enjoy certain aspects of life here, Comrade. The weather, the food, the plenty, the women, and—not the least—the absence of spies and informers dogging you everywhere. Yet you will also find such freedom comes at a price. You will be alone much, and you will feel the consequences of that solitude in your soul. There is no one to look out for you, no one above to care for you. In the end, you will long to return home to Mother Russia. I know this for a fact, Comrade. I have eight months left here and yet already I am counting the days until I can fly back to her bosom."

Thursday

The flight the next morning, on a propeller-driven DC-7, was turbulent as the plane fought its way west through strong winds. The journey was so bad that the stewardesses, who were quite beautiful, could not serve breakfast. Kaverin, more irritated at that fact than scared, at least had managed to secure a vodka and he took comfort in sipping the drink and smoking nearly half a pack of Chesterfield cigarettes, which were marvelous, during the flight.

The weather broke and, as they descended, he could look down and see flat sandy earth for miles and miles, grass bleached by the season, occasional groves of trees. Cattle, lots of cattle.

The aircraft landed uneventfully and the passengers disembarked.

He took his attaché case, containing his guns and ammunition, from the plane's overhead bin and walked down the stairs onto the tarmac.

Pausing and inhaling the petrol- and exhaust-laced air, Mikhail Sergeyevich Kaverin found himself content. Here he was in a country very different from that portrayed by the great propaganda mill of the Soviet empire. The people were friendly and courteous, the food and cigarettes plentiful and cheap, the workers content and comfortable, not the least oppressed by greedy capitalist robber barons. And the weather was far nicer than in Russia this time of year. And nearly everyone owned an automobile!

Kaverin strode into the lobby of Love Field in Dallas, Texas. He glanced at the front page of today's morning newspaper, Thursday, November 21, 1963.

Kennedy to Visit Dallas Tomorrow

President and First Lady Join Governor for Fund-Raiser at Dallas Trade Mart

Feeling the weight of the guns and ammunition in his case, Kaverin now felt an unabashed sense of pride to think that he alone had been selected for this critical mission of helping the USSR extend its reach throughout the world and further the glorious goals of communism.

As he waited for his bus, at a weedy stop in Dallas, Lee Harvey Oswald was troubled.

People had been following him. He knew this for a fact.

People who wanted to do him harm.

The skinny, dark-haired man, in his mid-twenties, looked around him again. Was there someone watching him? Yes!

But no. It was just a shadow. Still, he wished he had brought his pistol with him.

He awakened early in his boarding house on Beckley Avenue in Oak Cliff and taken a bus to a stop near the Dobbs House Restaurant for breakfast. The food had been bad and he'd complained.

He wondered why he kept going back there. Maybe I'm a creature of habit, he reflected. He'd heard the phrase on a TV show.

Was it *Ozzie and Harriet*? He'd wondered. He liked that show, partly because it echoed his nickname in the Marines. *Ozzie Rabbit.*

When he thought this, he remembered his days in the service and recalled the fight he'd gotten into with a sergeant and that made him angry once more.

As angry as he'd been with the waitress over the food.

Why do I keep going back there? he thought again. Looked around once more. He didn't see any overt threats but he still had to be careful. Considering what he had planned for tomorrow. And considering that he knew people were after him, smart people. Ruthless ones.

The bus arrived and Oswald boarded it and rode to the place he worked, the Texas Book Depository on Elm Street and North Houston, across from Dealey Plaza. He climbed off the bus, and gazed about him once more, expecting to see one of the sullen faces of the men who he was sure were following him.

FBI maybe. Those bastards had been harassing Marina and their friends again.

Oh, he'd made some enemies in his day.

But in morning glare—it was a beautiful autumn day—he saw only housewives with perambulators and a few salesmen, a retired couple or two. Ranchers. Some Hispanic men...

Killers?

It was possible. Oswald grew alarmed and leapt into the shadows of the depository building to study them. But they showed no interest in him and strolled slowly to a landscaping truck, pulled out rakes and headed into the park across the street.

Despite the bristling of nerves up and down his back, Oswald noted that no one seemed to have much interest in him. He shivered again, though this was from the chill. He was wearing only a light jacket over his T-shirt, and he had a slight frame with little natural insulation.

Inside the depository he greeted fellow workers, nodding and smiling to some of them. And he got to work. It was while he was filling out paperwork for a book order that he happened to look down at a scar on his wrist. He was thinking of his attempt to become a Soviet citizen several years before. He was about to be deported but had intentionally cut himself to prolong his stay after his visa expired, and convince the Russians to accept him.

Which they had and they welcomed him as a comrade. But there was a lot of important work to do in this hemisphere and, with his Russian wife, he'd returned to the United States, where he'd resumed his procommunist and anti-American activities. But now, he wanted to return to Russia, for good, with Marina and their two baby girls.

There'd been a setback, though. An incident had occurred that had put his plans—and his life—at risk. After he finished his task tomorrow he wanted to go to Cuba for a while and then back to Russia. Just last month he'd gone to the Cuban consulate in Mexico City to get a visa to allow him to travel to Havana, but the bastards had given him the runaround. The officials had looked over his records and said he wasn't welcome in Cuba. Go away. None of them understood what an important man he was, more important than his five-foot-nine, 135-pound frame suggested. None of them understood his great plans.

The rejection in Mexico City had sparked his terrible temper, and he'd said and done some things he shouldn't have. The Cuban security force had been called and he'd fled the capital and eventually made his way back home.

Stupid, he told himself, making a scene like that. Like fighting with the waitress at the diner. He'd lost control and made a spectacle of himself.

"Stupid," he raged aloud.

He shivered once more, this time from pure fury, not fear or from the chill. And gazed out the window of the depository, looking for people spying on him.

Fucking Cubans!

Well, start being smart now. He decided it wouldn't be safe to go back to the boarding house. Usually he spent weekdays at the boarding house. Tonight he'd return to the Paines in Irving, stay the night. Considering what he was about to do tomorrow, he couldn't afford any complications at the moment.

His serenity returned—thanks largely to a memory of his time in the Marines in 1954, specifically the day his firearms instructor had looked over his score on the rifle range and given him a nod (the man never smiled). "You did good, Ozzie. Those scores? You just earned yourself the rank of sharpshooter."

Anthony Barter swung his slim frame out of the car.

He stretched.

The thirty-one-year-old was tempted to light a Winston, *needed* one bad, but his employer wouldn't approve. It wasn't like drinking—that was wholly forbidden—but even taking a fast drag could get you in hot water.

So he refrained.

An old Martin 4-0-4 roared overhead and skewed its way onto the runway at Love Field.

He straightened his narrow tie and his dark gray felt fedora, from which he'd long ago removed the green feather—very bad form, that.

Barter looked around, oriented himself and went to the Eastern Airlines luggage claim area. His long hands formed into fists, relaxed and contracted once more.

He found a supervisor, a heavyset, balding man, sweating despite the pleasantly cool temperature. He displayed his identification.

The man drawled, "Oh. Well. FBI."

Barter was from New England; he'd been assigned to Texas,

though, for ten years and recognized an accent from much further south, probably El Paso.

He explained he needed to find out about a passenger who'd arrived that morning from Miami. The supervisor almost seemed amused at the idea that luggage handlers could recognize a passenger, but he went off to gather his employees.

The Bureau's New York field office had informed their colleagues in Dallas-Fort Worth that a man believed to be a Russian military intelligence agent had arrived in the country yesterday or today and continued on to Dallas. There'd been debate in New York and Washington about the purpose of the agent's trip, if he was indeed an agent.

There was, of course, the question of Presidential security. Kennedy was coming to town tomorrow, and lately the threats against him had been numerous—thanks largely to the U.S.'s aiding Cuban rebels at the Bay of Pigs invasion, as well as Kennedy's and his brother's support for civil rights. (He'd kicked some Soviet ass last year, too, of course, with the missile blockade, but no one in national security believed that the Russkies were stupid enough to attempt to assassinate the President).

No, more likely the spy's mission was pure espionage. The GRU was the intelligence organ specializing in stealing technology secrets—specifically those dealing with nuclear weapons and rocket systems—and Texas was home to a number of defense contractors. Barter's boss, the special agent in charge of the office here, immediately assigned him to the case.

The only lead was a photograph of the purported spy, entering the country as a Polish businessman. All individuals coming in from Warsaw Pact countries were surreptitiously photographed at Customs at Idlewild airport. The image was crude but functional. It depicted a sullen man, blond and large, wearing a fedora not unlike Barter's. The man was about forty years of age.

After viewing the picture of the Russian, however, the baggage handlers reported that they hadn't noticed anyone resembling him.

Barter thanked them and stepped outside into the low November morning sun. Speaking to the cabbies was more productive. It took him only a half hour of canvassing to find the Prompt Ride taxi driver who recognized the man in the photo. He'd taken him to a boarding house off Mockingbird. The man remembered the number.

Barter climbed back into his red and white Ford Galaxie. He headed in the direction of the place and parked up the block. He approached cautiously but noted it was abandoned. Barter found a neighbor, a retiree, it seemed, who was washing his car. He showed his ID and asked about the house.

After the typical blink of surprise at the credentials, the man said, "Yessir, been closed up for months now. Bankruptcy. Foreclosed on. Damn banks. All respect."

Barter stifled a frown of frustration, fists clenching and relaxing. "Well, I'm trying to find someone who might've been here several hours ago." He displayed the picture.

"Yup. Saw him. Got outa a taxi cab. I was impressed. Them cost money. Taxis. Anyway, that fella picked up a car from the ga-rage and drove off."

"Car?" Barter's heart beat a little faster.

But the man had only heard the engine, not seen the make or model.

They walked to the small detached structure. Barter opened the unlocked door. The place was empty.

"Sorry I can't be more help."

Barter sniffed the air and bent down to examine the floor of the garage.

"You've been plenty helpful, sir."

"So was I right? Bank robber? He looked plum like one."

"You have a good day, sir."

Mikhail Kaverin had checked into the Dallas Rose Motel, left his luggage and was enjoying piloting the Chevrolet Bel Air through the spacious streets of Dallas.

What a wonderful car this was!

A Bel Air! How Kaverin loved cars. He'd always wanted one, though in truth not a Russian make. For one thing, you waited forever and then you had to take whatever the government had on hand to sell you—for an exorbitant price (where was communism when you needed it?). And the best you could hope for was a temperamental, boxy AZLK or the slightly more stylish and popular GAZ Volga (whose manufacturer's hopes for a handsome income stream by sales to the West never materialized—since the vehicles' sole decoration was a big red Soviet star).

Guided by the map, and instructions from a helpful service station attendant, Kaverin found the Old East Dallas portion of town. The neighborhood was filled with private residences close together, many with front porches dotted with rockers and from whose roofs hung swings. He noted too inexpensive shops and a few small companies. He parked in front of the boardinghouse where Luis Suarez and Carlos Barquín would arrive tomorrow on their mission to track down and kill Comrade 35. It was a one-story, nondescript place, just a notch above shabby. He carefully studied doors and windows and sidewalks. And which neighbors seemed to be home now, during the day—potential witnesses.

He planned out the shootings. He would be waiting here in front of the house when they pulled up, with the trunk of the Bel Air open, pretending to be changing a tire. When they climbed out of their own car, he would shoot them and throw the bodies and their luggage in the trunk.

He drove slowly up and down the street, scanning, scanning. A spy's primary weapon is the power of observation. His first handler at the GRU, a man who later became a nonperson under Stalin, had insisted that Kaverin and he take long walks through the streets of Moscow. After they returned to headquarters the mentor would interrogate the younger agent about what he'd noted. The initial trips yielded a half dozen vague observations. The later ones, hundreds of impressions, all rendered in acute detail.

Sergei had been pleased. Kaverin pictured the man's unsmiling yet kind face and could almost feel the affectionate arm on his young shoulders. Then he tucked the hard thought away.

The peculiar circumstances of this assignment made Kaverin particularly cautious. He drove through the neighborhood again, looking for anyone who might be a threat. After fifteen minutes, he was satisfied he had a good sense of the place and of the risks he might face. He piloted the expansive Chevy out of this part of town and onto a main road. In ten minutes he pulled into the parking lot of a large grocery store. As he climbed out and walked toward the front door he thought: This place has the most ridiculous name I've ever heard of in a retail establishment.

The Russian spy was shopping in a Piggly Wiggly.

FBI Special Agent Anthony Barter sat in his Galaxie, which was parked in the far end of the lot, and watched the spy walk toward the store.

Picking up the spy's trail had been less daunting than he'd expected. He'd deduced by smell and an examination of the significant oil slick on the garage's floor that the spy was driving a car that leaked and burnt oil. So Barter had driven to the nearest gas station, a Conoco, and flashed a picture of the man. Sure enough, the attendant said that the man, who spoke English fine, but with an accent, had come in driving a bright turquoise Chevy Bel Air, bought a couple quarts of Pennzoil.

The Russian had also picked up a map of the area. He'd asked about the best way to get to Old East Dallas, then motored off in that direction in his oil-guzzler.

Barter had headed over to that neighborhood himself and cruised the streets until he found the Bel Air, which was paused at a stoplight. It was hard to tell for certain, but he believed the driver was the man in the surveillance photograph.

The FBI man almost smiled as he watched the spy stop in his tracks at the entrance of the grocery store—probably astonished by the multitude of plenty spreading out in the aisles. When he disappeared inside, Barter climbed out of his car and, hoping that the Russian would spend some time browsing the aisles, hurried to the Bel Air.

The vehicle was registered to a company in Plano, which Barter suspected would be phony. The Russian's jacket and hat were sitting in the back seat. In the pocket of the sport coat he found a key to room 103 of the Dallas Rose Motel, on East Main Street in Grand Prairie, about ten miles away.

Barter returned quickly to his Galaxie and pulled out of the lot before the Russian left the store. He knew this was a gamble but he was worried about continuing to follow his subject. J. Edgar Hoover had required all the agents in the bureau to study communist spies. The message was that the GRU operatives were the best of the best. Barter was afraid he'd be spotted. So he left and drove to the parking lot of a gas station across the street from the Dallas Rose Motel.

He waited nervously. What if the spy had checked out of the motel, and simply forgotten to return the key? What if it wasn't even his jacket? Had Barter lost his only lead?

If he ever needed a cigarette, it was now.

But he managed to refrain, nervously clenching and unclenching his sweaty hands.

Five minutes passed.

Ten.

Ah, thank you...

The brashly colored Bel Air rocked into the driveway and pulled up in front of room 103.

Barter's car was parked facing away from the motel and he was hunkered down, observing through his rearview mirror.

The Russian climbed out, looked around suspiciously but not Barter's way. He lifted a large grocery sack from the floor of the passenger seat. He disappeared through the door of his room.

Barter went to a pay phone and called his office. He asked a fellow agent about the company to which the Bel Air was registered.

The man called back five minutes later. Yes, it was fake. Barter then ordered a surveillance team put together.

In twenty minutes, four FBI agents arrived, in two cars— personal ones, as Barter instructed. One vehicle pulled in front and one in the rear of the motel.

Whatever the Russian's game might be, it was now doomed to failure.

Kaverin was truly enjoying his time in the motel, which was a word that he had never heard before. It was, charmingly, a hybrid of "motor" and "hotel." How very clever.

While the décor was rough around the edges, the place was a million times better than the "posh" resorts on the Black Sea— those unbearably shabby shacks, featuring useless plumbing, stinking carpet, dirty sheets and the worst examples of cheap furniture Russian factories could disgorge.

Yet here? The linens were clean, the air fragrant, towels plentiful. The soap was even wrapped; it wasn't decorated with body hairs from prior guests. No vermin prowled the floors.

And in the middle of the room was a television set! He flicked it on.

He opened his attaché case, removed the guns and cleaned them, eyes shifting from the screen to weapon and back.

A handsome newscaster was speaking into the camera.

"President Kennedy will arrive at Love Field in Dallas around noon tomorrow to attend a sold-out luncheon at the Dallas Trade Mart. More than two hundred thousand people are expected to greet the President as his motorcade makes its way through the city. Governor and Mrs. John Connelly will accompany the President and the lovely first lady, Jacqueline."

She is indeed lovely, Kaverin reflected, noting a film clip of her waving to people outside the White House.

He put the weapons away and perused the menu card on the bedside table. He lifted the beige receiver of the phone, reflecting how curious it was to make a call—even one as innocuous as this—and not worry about being listened to.

He smiled as he tried to understand the cheerful but heavily accented voice of the woman who took his order. He chose a large T-bone steak, a "Texas-sized" baked potato and a double helping of green beans. To drink, a large glass of milk.

It was decadent, yes, but Mikhail Kaverin had learned that as a spy—in the field or even at home—you could never be sure if any given meal was your last.

Friday

At 6 a.m. Special Agent Anthony Barter pulled his Galaxie into the far end of the Dallas Rose's parking lot.

More or less refreshed after three hours' sleep, he climbed out of the car and walked casually toward the sedan containing the FBI surveillance team. Crouching, he asked the agent on the passenger side, "Anything?"

"Nup," drawled the man. "Nobody came or went."

"Any outside calls, in or out?"

That too was negative. Nor had the spy used the pay phone in the lobby. He hadn't left his room since his return from Piggly Wiggly.

Barter found his hands making fists, then relaxing. He looked over at the Bel Air.

"What do we do, Tony?"

"We wait till he exits, then follow him to see who he's rendez-vousing with."

Barter's hope was that the spy was working with employees of LTO Inc. or one of the other big defense contractors here, whose engineers were designing sophisticated weaponry for the army and air force. He was hoping to bring down a whole cell of traitors spying for the Soviets.

He returned to his Galaxie, blinking as he noted a black sedan speed toward him and skid to a stop nearby. Barter was irritated; the Russian wouldn't have a view of this spot from his window but the squealing stop might have put him on his guard.

The driver leapt out and sprinted through traffic.

"The hell're you—?" Barter got no further than that. The young agent from his office was thrusting a telex into his hand.

TOP SECRET

Urgent.

   Russian who entered country illegally two days ago identified as Mikhail Kaverin, GRU agent. Specialty reported to be close-in assassination of double agents and other enemies.

Hell! He's not a spy. He's a killer!

And Barter suddenly understood why Kaverin had come to town—not to steal secrets, but to assist in an assassination attempt. It was too much of a coincidence that a trained GRU killer was here just prior to the President. True, the Soviets would never risk an international incident by being directly involved in an assassination. But one of their agents could easily have come here to protect someone *else* whose mission was to kill Kennedy, someone private, without a direct connection to Russia, most likely a U.S. citizen.

Oh, Jesus Christ…

He explained his thinking: "Kaverin's here to back up an assassin. Maybe he's providing guns or acting as a bodyguard for the trigger man, or helping him with escape routes. I don't care if we break every bone in his body but we're going to find out who he's helping. Move *now!*

With guns drawn, the agents ran to the door of Kaverin's room and kicked their way in.

Somehow, in his heart, Barter wasn't very surprised to find that the room's sole occupant was a bag of untouched groceries from Piggly Wiggly.

Nor was it any shock that the back window was unlocked.

Kaverin looked out the window of his room in the Skyline Motel, in north Dallas.

The parking lot and road were clear. The agents who'd been on his trail were, of course, still at the first motel he'd checked into, the Dallas Rose in Grand Prairie.

He'd become aware of a possible tail yesterday as he'd driven through the neighborhood of Old East Dallas, assessing risks, looking for anyone who might be unusually interested in him. He'd noted a Ford Galaxie—red body and white top. The car had been driving the opposite direction when he'd first seen it, but moments later it reappeared, following him.

Kaverin had left that area immediately and driven along commercial roads until he found the Piggly Wiggly and pulled in. The Galaxie followed. It too parked and the driver sat there alone, not smoking, not reading. All he was doing was ostentatiously *not* looking toward the Bel Air.

Clearly, this was suspicious: A man alone in a grocery store parking lot, who was not waiting for his wife?

He'd decided to find out the identity of his pursuer. So Kaverin left his jacket, containing the Dallas Rose room key, on the backseat and had gone into the grocery store and he'd slipped out the back, circling around to the parking lot. Yes, there was the man who'd been tailing him, wearing a suit—an official-looking one. He'd sidled up to the Bel Air and, looking around casually, too casually, eased the door open and went through the interior.

Kaverin himself had hurried to the man's Ford Galaxie—and found the registration. Anthony Barter. He found nothing of the man's affiliation but he'd hurried back to the Piggly Wiggly and used one of the store's pay phones, which—unlike in Russia—actually worked. He had had to make only three calls—to the Dallas Police, to the Texas Rangers and to the FBI, asking for an Anthony Barter. The secretary at the last of the three had started to put him through to Special Agent Barter's office. He'd hung up, bought a sack's worth of random groceries and returned to his Bel Air.

The agent had left by then but when Kaverin had returned to the Dallas Rose he saw that, yes, the Galaxie was parked across the street. Kaverin had taken the groceries, gone inside, put on the TV and then quickly gathered his belongings and climbed out the back window. He'd made his way through a field to a bus stop and had ridden a mile then gotten off near a car dealership. He'd bought a four-year-old DeSoto Firedome coupe, huge and with impressive rear fins, with some of the thousand dollars Spesky had given him in Miami. He'd driven north until he found another motel, the Skyline. It was here that he'd spent the night, watching television, cleaning his weapons again and enjoying the sumptuous steak dinner.

Now, it was time to complete his mission. According to Rasnakov, Luis Suarez and Carlos Barquín would be arriving at the boardinghouse soon, to prepare for the killing of Comrade 35. Kaverin left the hotel and was at the boardinghouse in twenty minutes. He parked the DeSoto across the street, slipped the smaller of the guns—the Colt .22—into his waistband. He got out and opened the trunk, set the jack and tire iron on the grass beside the car and rested the spare tire against the bumper.

And he waited.

Fifteen minutes later a yellow Chrysler pulled slowly down the street, two men in the front seat. Men with mustaches and observant eyes.

Yes, they were his targets.

Kaverin's hand eased into his jacket, gripped the handle of his pistol. It didn't make much noise, just a pop, like a bigger gun with a silencer, but it was much more accurate.

He was breathing steadily, focusing on finding that unique place within you where you had to tuck your soul away when you took a human life. He murdered for his country, for the cause of what was just, for communism, for his own self-preservation. He was efficient at this dark task, even if he didn't enjoy it.

He knew he was ready. And flicked the safety catch off the gun as he crouched down, watching the Chrysler in the reflection of his car's chrome bumper.

It was then that a voice from behind startled Kaverin.

"Need some help there, sir?"

Still facing the Chrysler, he looked back to see a Dallas police officer standing on the sidewalk. Hands on his hips.

"I'm sorry?" the spy asked evenly.

"Have a flat? Need some help?"

"No, I'm doing fine, thank you, Officer." Kaverin was speaking over his shoulder, with his back to the officer. His jacket was open and the pistol obvious.

"Don't mind helping, really," the man drawled.

Kaverin casually fixed buttons, but as he did he looked across the street and saw his two targets staring his way. Perhaps they thought the police and he were working together, looking for them. Or maybe the officer's voice had simply caught their attention and they'd seen the pistol. In any event, the driver—it was Luis Suarez—aborted the parking maneuver, put the car in forward and eased into the street. He didn't speed away—not just yet. But once the Chrysler turned the corner, Kaverin heard the big engine accelerate fast.

He turned back to the policeman and gave an appreciative smile. "I've gotten everything taken care of, Officer. Thank you, though."

"Any time," the man said and returned to his beat.

*   *   *

At around 8:30 a.m., Lee Harvey Oswald was being driven to work at the Texas Book Depository by a friend. He often did this, bummed rides. He didn't have a license and, in fact, didn't enjoy driving.

He had mixed feelings about his decision to spend the night at the Paines' house in Irving. It was smart because it provided a good hiding place from those bastards who wanted to kill him. He'd looked forward to seeing Marina and their two daughters, one of whom was only a month old; they were staying permanently with the Paines. But that turned out to be a disappointment. He'd hoped to reconcile with Marina after a recent fight but it hadn't happened. The bickering resumed, the night had turned to shit and he was upset.

"Whatcha got back there?" his friend asked as they nosed through morning traffic. He was nodding toward the long, paper-wrapped bundle in the backseat.

"Just some curtain rods."

"Ah."

Oswald continued to be cautious, shifting his gaze around the surrounding streets and sidewalks. Yes, some people seemed to be watching him, wary, suspicious, as if they knew exactly what he was going to do today. He reflected that he had told too many people about his contempt for Kennedy. And, hell, he'd just written an angry letter to the FBI, warning them to leave his family alone... That wasn't too bright.

And *curtain rods*?

Jesus. No, it's a 6.5-mm Carcano model 91/38 rifle. That's what was wrapped up in the paper. How could anybody believe the bulky package was curtain rods? You need to think better. Be smarter.

And be cautious. He had a sense that his enemies were getting closer and closer.

He had the chance to make an indelible mark on history. He'd be famous forever. He had to make absolutely sure nothing would prevent that.

He looked around the streets of central Dallas, partially deserted now. There'd be crowds later, that was for sure, right there along Elm Street. Thousands of people. He knew this because the local newspaper had conveniently reported the exact route the President's motorcade would take. The vehicles would come west on Main, then north briefly on Houston, then turn west again on Elm, passing right under the windows of the Texas Book Depository where he would be waiting in a sixth-floor window.

"You okay there, Lee?" his friend asked as he eased to a stop at a light.

"What's that?"

"You didn't hear me, I guess. I just asked if you'd be needing a ride back to the Paines' tonight?"

Oswald didn't answer for a minute. "No. I'll probably just take the bus."

"There. That's a good place to shoot." Luis Suarez said.

Carlos Barquín was examining the intersection where his partner was pointing—the sidewalk in front of the side door to the Texas Book Depository. "Looks like the *only* place to shoot. Good or bad, we don't have any choice. Where else could we do it?" He seemed impatient.

Suarez nodded, though he didn't much care for the man's attitude. "Not very private, though."

"Well, we don't have the luxury of private. Not with a paranoid asshole like him."

They had parked their Chrysler on North Record Street in downtown Dallas and were looking over the sidewalk in front of the Texas Book Depository. The morning was chill but they kept their jackets buttoned up because of the guns in their waistbands.

"I think it'll work. All the buildings, they'll cover the sounds of the shots."

"Cover them?" Barquín asked.

"I mean the sounds'll bounce around. Nobody will know where they came from."

"Oh."

"Nobody'll know it was us. We'll shoot him, drop the guns and walk back to the car. Walk slowly." The pistols were wrapped in a special tape that didn't hold fingerprints.

Barquín said defiantly, "I know what to do. I've done this before."

Suarez didn't say anything. He and Barquín shared both a certain ideology and a love of liquor. They'd even shared the same woman once or twice. He really didn't like the man, however.

As they continued through the cool morning, Barquín asked, "That man, back there at the boarding house? In the suit, talking to the cop. He was police too, you think?"

"I don't know." Suarez had pondered who he'd been. He'd been armed and had been talking to that patrolman but it would have been odd for a cop to be there changing the tire of his own unmarked car—and an old DeSoto? No, the man was trouble but he couldn't figure out how he fit into the picture.

They had some effects back at the boardinghouse, which they'd stashed there last week, but they'd have to abandon them now. Not that it mattered; they could pick up whatever they needed on the road as the Underground spirited them out of the country and back to Havana.

As they walked up Houston toward Elm, they passed a dim alley. A car was parked there, rear end facing them, the engine running and the trunk open. What was familiar about it?

"That car, haven't we—?"

And Suarez realized it was the same DeSoto parked in front of the boardinghouse earlier when they'd seen that man changing the tire. The big, blond man. It was his car! Which meant—

He turned quickly, Barquín too. And both instinctively reached for their weapons, but the man was approaching fast from across Houston Street, already aiming his own gun at them.

The two Cubans froze.

Without a hesitation, without a blink, without breaking stride, the hulking blond man fired twice, hitting Barquín in the forehead. *Pop, pop.*

He dropped to the ground like a discarded doll.

Suarez decided there was no choice. He continued to draw his gun, and hope he could get a round off in time.

The weapon wasn't even out of his waistband when saw a tiny flash, then felt a tap between his eyes, a burning.

Which lasted less than a second.

Kaverin got the bodies into the trunk of the DeSoto quickly.

This was effortless. They were slight, weighing half what he did.

He fired up the DeSoto—he liked the Bel Air better—and pulled into Houston Street and then made his way out of downtown.

The search to find the men had been tense, though he'd known in general where they would be going—the most likely place to shoot down Comrade 35. Once there, central Dallas, he'd cruised the streets, looking for a yellow Chrysler. Finally he'd spotted it, near North Record Street. Suarez and Barquín were just getting out and walking south.

There were too many people to kill them there but Kaverin had noted the route they were taking and he'd pulled into an alley several blocks ahead of them. Once again he'd opened the trunk, then slipped into a doorway across Houston Street and waited. The men strode up the avenue and when their attention turned to the DeSoto he'd stepped across the street, drawing his gun.

Pop, pop...

Kaverin now drove out of the downtown area, parked and walked up the street to the Western Union office he'd located earlier.

There the spy spent some moments with a cipher pad writing a telegram reporting his success. He sent it to a safe house in Washington, D.C., where someone with the Russian consulate was waiting.

In fifteen minutes the response came back. It referred to shipments of wheat and truck allotments. But after deciphering:

Have submitted to the Special Council of the Presidium the report regarding your successful elimination of the threat to Comrade 35. Please proceed to any locations where the two counterrevolutionaries had contact in Dallas and secure any helpful information.

The people of the Soviet Union thank you.

Kaverin returned to the boardinghouse in the Old East Dallas part of town, opened the trunk of the DeSoto after making sure no one could see him—and no beat police officers were nearby—and emptied the pockets of the men he'd just shot. He found a fob containing the key to the front door of the boardinghouse and one to room number 2. He walked slowly up to the front door, checked to make sure he was alone, and then entered their room.

The men had not been inside that morning—after the scare with the police—but they had apparently stored some things there: several suitcases, containing clothes, money, ammunition, binoculars and Spanish to English dictionaries. He pulled out a penknife and began to look for secret compartments. He found none.

At about 12:45, he heard a commotion from the hallway, voices speaking urgently. He thought at first it might be the police, that he'd been tracked here, or that someone had seen an unidentified man entering the boarders' room.

His hand on his pistol, he walked to the door, leaned close and listened.

"Did you hear? Did you hear?" a woman was calling, the words sliced by hysteria. "The President's been shot! They think he's dead!"

"No! Are you sure?" A man's voice.

Someone began to sob.

Kaverin released his grip on the Colt, looked around the room and walked to the television set. He turned it on and sat in a creaking chair to wait for the device to warm up.

Saturday

The time was 2 a.m., the day after the worst day of his life.

Special Agent Anthony Barter was trudging along the sidewalk to his apartment in Richmond, Texas. He'd been up for nearly twenty-four hours and he needed a little sleep—just a nap, really—and then a shower.

Then he'd return to the hunt for Lee Harvey Oswald's assistant or savior or bodyguard or whatever he was: the Russian spy, Mikhail Kaverin.

The fallout was bad. Barter had kept his own superiors at the FBI and the Secret Service informed of every fact he'd learned about the spy from the moment he'd gotten the report from New York. But it was finger-pointing time now and Washington wanted to know exactly, minute by minute, what he knew and when he knew it and why he wasn't more vocal about the threat to Kennedy.

"Because it wasn't a threat at first," he'd explained to the assistant director of the FBI in Washington. "We thought he was after classified weapons information. His behavior was suspicious but he didn't seem dangerous."

The assistant director had barked, "Well, the President of the United States is now *suspiciously* dead, Barter. I thought you were tailing him."

Barter had sighed. "I was. He evaded me."

He didn't say "us." Barter didn't shift blame.

"Jesus Christ." The man told him that J. Edgar Hoover personally would be calling him at some point tomorrow. And slammed the phone down. At least that's what Barter imagined. He heard only a click, then static.

So this is what the demise of a career looks like, he thought. His heart clutched. Being a special agent was the only job that had ever appealed to him, the only job he'd ever wanted. His passion for the FBI went back to seeing newsreels about G-Men, to reading comic books about Elliot Ness, to watching movies like *Gang Busters* over and over again at Saturday afternoon matinees, while munching popcorn and sipping fizzy grape soda pop.

But his future wasn't the first thing in his mind at the moment. All he cared about was finding Lee Harvey Oswald's accomplice, finding Kaverin. For a moment he was flushed with anger and he hoped that, if he found the man, the Russian resisted arrest so Barter could put a bullet in his head. Even as he thought this, though, he knew it was an unreasonable, passionate reflex; the reality was that he would arrest the man, following procedure to a T and interrogate him firmly but respectfully.

The problem, of course, was *finding* him. Since he'd been Oswald's protector, and the assassin was now in custody, Kaverin was probably long gone. Barter guessed he was probably on a steamer headed back to Russia. Still, Barter was doing everything possible to find the man. The instant he'd heard of the shooting, he had sent the Russian's picture to every law enforcer in Texas and neighboring states and made sure the nearby airports and the train and bus stations were being watched. The automobile rental agencies too (ironically the Texas Book Depository was crowned with a huge Hertz billboard, touting Chevrolets). Roadblocks were set up, as well, and the docks along the Texas coastline were being searched by local police, FBI and the Coast Guard.

As every minute passed without word of a sighting, Barter grew more and more angry with himself. Oh, hell, if he'd only done more digging! Oswald had been under investigation by agents in his own office! The man had tried to defect to Russia, he was actively procommunist and had recently been in Mexico trying to get visas to Cuba and Russia. If that investigation had been better coordinated, Barter might have put the pieces together.

Now approaching his apartment, Anthony Barter paused, fished out his keys and stepped to his door, thinking: Okay, I'll have one Lone Star beer. Yes, agents were not supposed to drink. But considering that tomorrow Mr. Hoover would tell him that he was soon to be an *ex*-agent, liquor was one vice that he wouldn't have to worry about keeping secret any longer.

Barter walked inside, closed the door and locked it. He was reaching for the light switch when he heard, behind him, a floorboard creak. Special Agent Anthony William Barter's shoulders slumped. He thought of his failure to the Bureau, to his country—and to his President. He was almost relieved when the Russian agent's pistol muzzle touched the back of his head.

"How the hell did you find me?" Anthony Barter asked.

Mikhail Kaverin briefly studied the FBI agent, whose hands were shackled with his own cuffs. The Russian was impressed that the man seemed merely curious, not afraid. He returned to his task, which was using a penknife to slice open the lining of his attaché case.

Barter noted this surgery but seemed uninterested in it. His gaze was fixed ruthlessly on his visitor.

"How did I find you," Kaverin mused, slicing away. He explained about observing the agent's surveillance at the grocery store.

"You saw me?"

"Yes, yes, we're trained to notice that. Aren't you?"

"Not many people follow FBI agents. It's usually the other way around."

This made some sense.

He explained about his ruse at the Piggly Wiggly. The FBI man squinted his eyes shut in disgust. Then he sighed. "Okay, you didn't kill me," Barter said evenly. "So you're going to kidnap me. Negotiate my life for safe passage out of the country." He then said in a low, defiant voice, "But that isn't going to work, my friend. We don't negotiate with scum like you. Assassination's the most cowardly act imaginable. You and your countrymen're despicable and whatever you do to me, that won't stop our entire law enforcement apparatus from finding you and making sure you're arrested—and executed. And there'll be sanctions against your country, you know. Military sanctions." He shook his head in seeming disbelief. "Didn't your superiors think through what would happen if the President was killed?"

Kaverin didn't respond. He turned his attention to the agent. "We have not made introductions. I am Major Mikhail Kaverin of the Glavnoe Razvedyvatelnoe Upravlenie."

"I know who you are."

Kaverin wasn't surprised. He said, "Well, Special Agent Barter, I have no intention of kidnapping you. Nor of killing you, for that matter. I found it necessary to come up behind you and relieve you of your weapon so that you would not act rashly—"

"Shooting an enemy of the country, a spy, is not acting rashly."

Kaverin said. "No, but shooting an *ally* would be."

"Ally?"

"Agent Barter, I am going to tell you some things you will undoubtedly find incredible—though they are true. Then, after we make some formal arrangements, I will give you your gun back and I will give you my gun and I will surrender to you. May I proceed?"

Warily Barter said, "Yes, all right." His eyes shifted from the pistol to the documents extracted from the lid of the attaché case.

"Earlier this week I was called into the office of my superior at GRU headquarters. I was given an assignment: to protect an individual in the United States who would further the interests of the Soviet Union. A man we have code named Comrade Thirty-five."

"Yeah, yeah, that son of a bitch, Lee Harvey Oswald."

"No," Kaverin said. "Comrade Thirty-five was our code name for John Fitzgerald Kennedy."

"*What?*" Barter squinted at him.

"'Thirty-five,'" Kaverin continued, "because he was the thirty-fifth President of the United States. 'Comrade' because he shared certain interests with our country." The Russian pushed forward the documents he'd extracted from his case. "Can you read Russian?"

"No."

"Then I will translate."

"They're fake."

"No, they are quite real. And I will prove to you they're real in a moment." Kaverin looked down and scanned the documents. "'To Comrade Major Mikhail Kaverin. Intelligence received from sources in Washington, D.C., has reported that in October of this year President John Fitzgerald Kennedy signed an executive order, initiating the reduction of American advisory and military forces in Vietnam.'"

"Vietnam?" Barter was frowning. "That's that country near China, right? A French colony or something. Sure, we've sent some soldiers there. I read about that."

Kaverin continued his reading. "'Our sources have reported that Charles de Gaulle told President Kennedy that it would be very detrimental for the United States to become enmeshed in the politics of Southeast Asia. Kennedy went against the advice of his generals and established the goal to have all American troops out of Vietnam and neighboring countries by 1964. After the Americans are gone, the communist regimes in Vietnam, Laos and Cambodia will surge south through Malaysia and Singapore, establishing governments with true Marxist values throughout Southeast Asia. Our Premier and the Politburo will form an alliance with that bloc. Together we will stand firm against the wrong-minded Maoist cult in China.'

"'If anything were to happen to Kennedy, our intelligence assessment is that his successor, Lyndon Johnson, will drastically *increase* the U.S. military presence in the region. This would be disastrous for the interests of the USSR.'"

He put down the documents, shook his head and sighed. "You see, Agent Barter, the mission of the agent who preceded me and of myself was to do whatever we could to uncover any threats to your President Kennedy and stop them. Our job was to protect him." Barter snapped, "That's bullshit! You knew about Oswald but you didn't report it! If you'd really been concerned, you—"

"No!" Kaverin replied angrily. "We knew *nothing* of Oswald. That's not why I was sent here. There was *another* threat to your President. Completely unrelated to the assassin. Do you know of Luis Suarez and Carlos Barquín?"

"Of course, we've been on the look-out for them for months. They're Cuban Americans under orders from Fidel Castro to kill Kennedy because of the Bay of Pigs invasion. We haven't been able to find their whereabouts."

"I can produce them."

"Where are they?"

"They're in the trunk of my car."

"Are you joking?"

"Not at all. *That* was my assignment. To find and eliminate them. We knew they were going to attempt to assassinate Kennedy, possibly on his visit here. When I shot them they were on Houston Street—at a place where your President's motorcade would pass by. Undoubtedly they were looking for vantage points to shoot from. Both of them were armed."

"Why didn't you tell us that you had a lead to them?"

Kaverin scoffed. "What would you have done?"

"Arrested them, of course."

"For what? Have they committed a crime?"

Barter fell silent.

"I thought not. You would have put them away for a few months for threatening the President or for having a weapon. Then they would have been released to try to assassinate him again. My solution was far more efficient and...far more permanent." Kaverin grimaced. He said passionately, "No one was more shocked and upset than I to hear the terrible news today of your President's fate."

Kaverin fell silent, noting that Barter, who until now had been looking him straight in the eye, had grown evasive. The Russian said, in a whisper, "You knew about Oswald."

No answer for a moment. Then: "I'm not at liberty to talk about investigations."

Kaverin snapped, "You *knew* he was a threat and yet you were not watching him constantly?"

"We have...limited resources. We didn't think he'd be a threat."

Silence flowed between the men. Finally Kaverin asked softly, "Well, do you believe me, Special Agent Barter?"

After a moment the FBI man said, "Maybe I do. But you haven't told me what you want out of all this."

Kaverin gave a laugh. "It's obvious, no? I want to defect. I have failed in my mission. If I return home I will become a nonperson. I will be killed and my name and all record of my existence expunged. It will be as if I never existed. I had hoped to marry, even at this age, to have a son. That is a possibility if I remain here." He gave a faint smile. "Besides, I must tell you, Agent Barter. I've been in this country for only several days but I already find it rather appealing."

"What's in it for us?"

"I can give you a great deal of information. I have been a GRU officer for many years. And I can offer something more. Something to, as your card players here say, sweeten the pot."

Barter said, "And what's that?"

"What I can offer you, Agent Barter—excuse me, *Special* Agent Barter—is a real, living, breathing KGB agent."

"KGB?"

"Indeed. You can arrest him and interrogate him. Or your CIA could run him as a double agent. You Americans *love* KGB spies, do you not? Why, your citizens know nothing of the GRU or the Stasi. But the KGB? Pick up a James Bond novel or go to the cinema. Wouldn't it be a fine national security coup to land a fish like that?"

Kaverin put just the right tone into his voice to suggest that the arrest would be fine for Barter's career personally too.

"Who is this man?"

"He is in Miami, operating undercover as the head of a transportation company. His real name is Nikolai Spesky. He purports to be a GRU agent, but in fact his employer is the KGB."

"How d'you know that?"

"For one thing, because of your presence on my trail."

"Me?"

Kaverin said, "I assume you learned of me through an anonymous tip, correct?"

"Yes, that's right. Received by our New York office."

"Perhaps *through* New York, but it originated from Comrade Spesky in Miami. He informed on me. You see, neither Customs officials or any airline in New York knew that my final destination was Dallas. Only Spesky did. I didn't receive my ticket until I was in Florida. In fact, I wasn't wholly surprised when you appeared; I was suspicious of Spesky from the beginning. That is one of the reasons I was looking for surveillance—and spotted you."

"Why did you suspect him?"

"Top-brand vodka and paté and smoked oysters and bread with very little mold."

Barter shook his head.

Kaverin continued, "Spesky told me his wife had sent him such gifts from Moscow. No GRU field agent's wife would ever be able to afford such delicacies, only the wife of a KGB agent could."

"But why would he betray you? Wouldn't the KGB have the same interest you would—to keep the President alive so he'd withdraw the troops from Vietnam?"

Kaverin smiled again. "Logic would suggest that, yes. But in truth the essential interest of the KGB is in furthering the interest of the KGB. And that cause is advanced every time the GRU fails."

"So your security agencies spy on each other, for no other purpose than sabotaging their rivals?" Barter muttered, his tone dark.

Kaverin fixed him with a piercing look. "Yes, shocking, isn't it? Something that could *never* happen here. Fortunately you have Mr. J. Edgar Hoover to uphold the moral integrity of your organization. I know he would *never* illegally wiretap politicians or civil rights leaders or members of other governmental agencies."

Anthony Barter offered his first smile of the evening. He said, "I can't make any deals myself. You understand that?"

"Of course."

"But I think you're telling the truth. I'll go to bat for you. You know what that means?"

Kaverin gave a broad frown. "Please. I am a fan of the New York Mets."

Barter laughed. "The Mets? They had close to the worst season in major league history this year. Couldn't you pick a better team?"

Kaverin waved his hand dismissively. "It was their second year as a team. Give them some time, Agent Barter. Give them time."

The Russian then slid the photographs of the top-secret documents toward the agent, along with the keys to the DeSoto. He uncuffed the agent and, without a moment's hesitation, handed over both of the pistols.

"I'm going to make some phone calls, Major Kaverin. I hope you won't mind if I put the handcuffs on *you*."

"No, I perfectly understand."

He slipped them on, albeit with Kaverin's hands in front of him, not behind his back. Before he reached for the phone, though, he asked, "Would you like to have a beer?"

"I would, yes. In Russia we have vodka but we don't have beer. Not good beer."

The agent rose and went to the refrigerator. He returned with two bottles of Lone Star, opened them and handed one to the spy.

Kaverin lifted his. "*Za zdorovie!* It means, 'To our health.'"

They tapped bottles and both took long sips. Kaverin enjoyed the flavor very much, and the FBI agent regarded the bottle with pleasure. "I'm not supposed to be doing this, you know. Mr. Hoover doesn't approve of drinking liquor."

"No one will ever know, Special Agent Barter," Kaverin told him. "I'm quite good at keeping secrets."

Tuesday

TOP SECRET

NOVEMBER 26, 1963

FROM: OFFICE OF THE SECRETARY OF DEFENSE, THE PENTAGON, ARLINGTON, VIRGINIA

TO: SECRETARY OF THE ARMY

SECRETARY OF THE NAVY

SECRETARY OF THE AIR FORCE

SECRETARY OF THE JOINT CHIEFS OF STAFF

Be advised that President Lyndon Baines Johnson today issued National Security Action Memorandum 273. This order reverses NSAM 263, issued by the late President Kennedy in October of this year, which ordered the withdrawal of U.S. troops from Vietnam and the transfer of responsibility in countering communist insurgency in Southeast Asia to the Vietnamese and neighboring governments.

NSAM 273 provides for maintenance of existing U.S. troop strength in Vietnam and sets forth a commitment to increased American military and advisory presence in combating communism in the region.

POLICE REPORT

BY JOSEPH FINDER

The incident in the small Cape Cod town of Westbury began on an evening of dismal weather. A freakishly early snow mixed with sleet had closed most of the roads off Route 6, the Cape's main artery, and knocked out power and telephone service throughout much of Barnstable County. By some stroke of luck, though, Westbury was spared.

So at 2:50 in the morning the phone rang in the bedroom of the house belonging to Westbury's police chief, Henry Silva.

He rolled over and reached out in the darkness without looking and grabbed the touch-tone's handset. "Silva," he said.

"Chief, Melissa here at county dispatch."

He coughed, rubbed his eyes, switched on the lamp. On the nightstand were a pad of paper and a Bic pen. He uncapped the end of the pen with his teeth. "Go, what do we got?"

"A fatal shooting. Vladimir Polowski of 14 Old King's Highway."

"The old guy? Christ. Where's Jeff Crane?"

"His cruiser's stuck in a drainage ditch off Long Pond Road. Says he should be freed up just as soon as Tucker Towing gets him out."

"Oh, jeez," Henry said. Jeff Crane was Silva's only officer. "All right, who called it in?"

"Ray Richardson."

"Don't know him. Is he a neighbor of Polowski's?"

"No. He's not from around here. Says he's been living up at the Westbury Motel for the past couple weeks or so."

Henry scribbled a note. "Where is this Ray Richardson now?"

"Says he's in the victim's kitchen."

"Huh. He say what he's doing in there?"

A pause. "Yeah. He says he's the one that killed him."

That jolted Henry wide awake. "Say again?"

"When he called it in, he identified himself, gave the address, and said he shot Vladimir Polowski. He also said he'd be sitting in the kitchen with his hands up whenever the cops arrived. I asked him why he did it, but he wouldn't say. He said he'd only tell the chief of police."

Henry fell silent for a long moment.

"Chief?"

"Sorry," he said. "Okay. Tell Jeff Crane to haul ass over to Vladimir Polowski's house soon's they get him out of the ditch. Then call the county district attorney's office, get a hold of the assistant D.A. on duty, and alert the State Police. Medical Examiner's too, while you're at it."

"Got it, Chief."

"All right, I'm getting dressed and heading out there."

"Okay," Melissa said. "And Chief…?"

"Yeah," he answered, dreading what she was about to say.

"Sorry about your wife. Carol was good people."

"She sure was," he said, and hung up the phone.

Fifteen minutes later he was sitting in his police cruiser, waiting for the engine and the interior to warm up. The 1978 Ford LTD was sheeted with ice. He turned the windshield defroster all the way up. While he waited for the car to thaw out, he listened to the AM radio, catching WBZ out of Boston, with its strong signal.

It was one of those all-night talk shows. He sat listening with folded arms and a scowl. They were arguing about a tragedy that had happened a few weeks ago and a half-world away. The Russians had shot down a Korean Air passenger jet over Sakhalin Island in the North Pacific. The two hundred and sixty-nine people on board had all been killed. Unbelievable. The plane had been en route from New York to Seoul, South Korea, carrying sixty Americans, a U.S. congressman and—most terrible of all—twenty-two children.

Henry remembered arguing about it with his officer and the owner of Al's diner, Al Perry, over coffee at the counter not long ago.

"You need any more proof those bastards are the evil empire?" said Al, a giant, ruddy-faced, potbellied guy whose father, Big Al, had opened the diner right after the war. Al—Little Al, as he was sometimes still called—was hand-wiping a stack of dishes hot from the dishwasher's station. "A civilian airliner happens to stray a little bit over into Soviet airspace and they shoot it down in cold blood. I mean, for the love of God."

"Not how I heard it," said Jeff Crane, by far the youngest of the three men. Jeff was lanky and sharp-jawed and had a buzz cut so close you could see the pink of his scalp. "I heard it was a spy plane."

"Horse crap it was," Al spat back. "All those civilians on board?"

"Yeah," Jeff persisted. He seemed to like tweaking Little Al. "The Pentagon puts, like, spy equipment, radar or whatever, on passenger planes all the time to spy on the Russians. I think that was in the *Globe*."

Henry took a swig of coffee.

"You don't know what the hell you're talking about!" Al said. His face had turned crimson. "Hank, you were in the Air Force, tell this kid he's full of it."

Henry set down his mug. "You're both wrong," he said. "I was just talking to a buddy of mine who's pretty high up in the Pentagon. We went through Skyraider training together in Florida, back in the day. He said don't listen to the news, it's all propaganda, both sides."

"What, it's propaganda that two hundred and sixty-nine innocent souls were killed?" Al said.

Henry traced a pattern on his place-mat with the tines of a fork. "Oh, no. They got killed by the Russians, all right."

"Exactly!" said Al.

"So what're you saying, boss, the plane wasn't really in Soviet airspace?" said Jeff.

"Oh, no," said Henry evenly. "It strayed into Soviet airspace, all right. By accident, I'm sure. I'll bet the pilot programmed the nav system wrong. It happens. You'd be surprised."

"So what the hell did the Soviets shoot it down for?" Al demanded.

"My buddy says the Russians thought this Boeing 747 was a big old Boeing RC-135 reconnaissance aircraft. An intruder."

"Oh, come on," said Al. "I bet they don't look anything alike."

"You're saying the Russians screwed up?" said Jeff.

"Big time," said Henry.

"So how come they don't just say so?"

"And admit their Air Force is so incompetent it couldn't tell a Boeing 747 from an RC-135? Yeah, right. It's the Cold War, man. Us versus Them. Can't let the facts get in the way."

Now, listening to the argument on the radio, Henry shook his head in disgust, got out of the cruiser and reached into the back for a snow scraper. He broke up a big ice sheet on the windshield. Meanwhile the freezing rain kept on splattering against the glass, big fat slushy drops.

He cast a longing glance back at the house. Usually on nights like this, no matter how late, Carol would be up as well, swathed in her baby-blue bathrobe, pouring freshly brewed coffee in a travel mug for him. She'd always hand him the mug with a sweet kiss and the same whispered words: "Stay safe out there, honey."

But the house was dark now, and quiet. He opened the car door, tossed in the ice scraper, got into the cruiser, and backed slowly down the driveway. At the first stop sign, the cruiser fishtailed and slid straight through the intersection. He cursed aloud, pumped the brakes to bring the car careening to a stop. The windshield wipers thumped rhythmically.

It was a dangerous night to be out and about, and as he carefully crossed Route 6 toward Old County Road, he wondered what might make a guy go out on a night like this and murder an old man.

Old County Road was a narrow winding country lane with no guardrails, lane markings, or streetlights. He slowed down and switched on the side spotlight, and as he maneuvered the steering wheel with one hand, he shone the spotlight with the other, illuminating the mailboxes on the side of the road, one by one.

There it was. Number fourteen. On the left.

He turned and advanced slowly down the dirt drive. Up ahead, surrounded by sand and a spiky sea-grass lawn, was a white single-story double-wide, no doubt planted right on top of a concrete slab. On one side of the modest house was a pickup, blanketed with snow and ice. It looked like it hadn't been used in days. Next to it was a Subaru all-wheel-drive sedan with Ohio plates. It looked like it had been there no more than a few hours. He edged in the cruiser and parked behind the two vehicles. Grabbing the handset to the Motorola police radio, he said, "Dispatch, this is Westbury C-One, off at the scene."

"Ten-four, Westbury," Melissa said. "FYI, your P-One is still stuck."

"Got it," he said. Poor Jeff.

He switched off the engine, got out, and took his handheld radio. The freezing rain was coming even harder now. He pulled out his .38-caliber Smith & Wesson revolver and kept it at his side as he slowly climbed the short stoop.

The front door was open. He could see through the storm door right into the house. He saw a tidy living room. A tired-looking

couch and matching chairs and a television. A color TV set in a
console with rabbit ears. Beyond the living room was a well-lit
kitchen.

Seated on a stool in the kitchen was a scruffy middle-aged man
in jeans and sneakers and a gray sweatshirt.

The man saw him and slowly raised both hands.

With his free hand, Henry pushed open the storm door. He strode
in, raising the revolver in a two-handed grip. "Don't move," he
called out. "Keep your hands up."

"Absolutely, officer," the man said calmly. He smiled. "Good
evening." On second glance he looked younger than middle-aged.
He appeared to be in his mid-thirties. He had shaggy blond hair
and several days' growth of beard.

When Henry reached the kitchen threshold, he saw the body.

Lying on the linoleum floor was an elderly white-haired man in
gray pajamas and bedroom slippers. In the center of his chest were
two sizable entry wounds. Dark crimson blood stained a large oval
area around the wounds and pooled on the floor.

Henry looked quickly around. "Is anybody else in the house?"

"No, sir," he said. "Just me and the deceased."

"Where is your weapon?"

"On the counter." He gestured with his chin. Next to the toaster
oven on the white speckled Formica counter was a steel-framed
Colt .45 1911 with wood grips, plain and powerful.

Henry advanced a few steps farther. "Who are you?"

"Ray Richardson."

"All right, now, Ray, I'm going to ask you to slowly—and I mean
slowly—stand up and rotate, with your arms still up in the air. Do
you understand?"

"Yes, sir." The man obediently got off the stool, hands up, and
turned around. Henry stepped up, slid his left foot between Richardson's legs, and smoothly handcuffed the man. Only then did he
holster his revolver. He frisked the man and was satisfied. Then,

grabbing the stranger's left elbow, he guided him into the living room and sat him down on the couch.

"Sit, and don't even think about moving," he said.

"I understand," Ray Richardson said quietly, even pleasantly. Henry backed into the kitchen, keeping his eyes on the living room, then peered more closely at the body on the floor. Vladimir Polowski, all right. Retired dairy farmer from Vermont, still spoke with a thick accent from his native Gdansk. He'd moved to Westbury a decade or more ago because he missed seeing the ocean. He liked to hang out at Crane's Hardware and the Westbury Diner. He'd come here after selling his cows in Vermont because he was weary of getting up early every day for the milking.

Yes, those were some serious entry wounds. The Colt .45 packed a serious punch. One bullet would have done the job. The old Pole's face had grayed out, nearly matching his white hair and handlebar mustache. Only a birthmark on his cheek stood out, an angry-looking purplish scimitar. His eyes were open, staring.

Henry looked back at the living room. Richardson sat quietly on the couch.

"All right, now, what happened here?"

"I shot him."

"I can see that. Care to tell me why?"

Now an expression came over the man's face, a twist of contempt. "That son-of-a-bitch killed my dad."

Henry looked back at the dead dairy farmer. "I find that hard to believe. When do you say he killed your father?"

"In 1958."

"That's, what, twenty-five years ago."

Ray Richardson nodded once.

"You want to explain?"

He shook his head. "Not here."

"Huh?"

"I can't tell you here. Take me back to my motel room, I'll explain everything."

Henry waited with the suspect in silence for another forty-five minutes. Then a flare of headlights spread across the living room wall.

The rest of the Westbury Police Department had arrived.

Henry opened the door for Jeff Crane, who was dripping wet and profusely apologetic. Henry held up his hand. "You can tell me about it later."

"Okay, Chief," Jeff said, removing his police hat, shaking water on the living room carpet. "Holy shit, that's really Polowski over there, huh?"

Henry suspected Jeff Crane had never actually seen a dead body before. He'd been on the force for less than a year, and was the son of George Crane, owner of Crane's Hardware and chairman of the board of selectmen. From talking to other small-town chiefs on the Cape, Henry knew what a minefield it could be to hire local. But Jeff had been a pleasant surprise. Once he'd even given his own mother a speeding ticket, and he hadn't told Henry about it until the story appeared in the *Cape Cod Times*.

"Jeff, the Staties and the D.A. should be coming up here in a bit. You secure the scene. Don't let anybody in, and I mean anybody, until they show up. That body's leaving the kitchen only when the medical examiner says so. Got it?"

"Got it."

"I'm going to take our suspect here back to the station, print and process him. You need me, gimme a holler. Otherwise, hang tight here and wait."

Jeff wiped his hand over his face. "Yeah, about that, Chief, I got a message from county dispatch just before I got here. Seems like Route 6 is flooded around Cahoon Hollow. The Staties and the county attorney are going to be delayed some."

Henry shrugged. "No matter. Your job's still the same. Keep the place secure. Questions?"

"Nope." He hesitated a moment. "Oh, hey, Chief, I wanted to let you know my Aunt Clarisse, in Falmouth, she sent a big donation to the American Cancer Society. You know, in honor of Carol."

"So no questions?"

"I'm good."

"Then Mr. Richardson and I will be off."

The Westbury Motel was right on Route 6, a one-story structure with a modest office building at one end, and a series of connected motel rooms extending off to the left. Out front was a small swimming pool, covered with a vinyl tarp for the winter. Underneath the Westbury Motel sign, a VACANCY light flickered.

He parked the cruiser in front of the office underneath an overhang. Leaving the confessed killer in the back seat, secured and cuffed, he got out and pressed the buzzer. Eventually Tommy Snow answered the door, yawning, scratching at his bald head, clutching his tattered brown bathrobe with his other hand.

"Shit, Chief, what's up?"

"I need you to open up a room for me. Rented by a guy named Ray Richardson."

"Something happen to him?"

"You could say that."

"Well, he's an odd duck, I'll tell you that. Been here about two, three weeks, and you know what? He won't let anybody clean his room. Even pays me an extra fifty a week to keep out of it. I leave him fresh towels and sheets outside the door. He's a strange one."

Tommy ducked back into his office and came out with a key. "Hey, Chief, sorry about your wife."

"Thanks for the key," Henry said.

He drove the cruiser around to unit 9. The rain seemed to be slowing. He left the engine running to keep the headlights on. Henry got out of the cruiser and opened the rear door for Ray Richardson. Then he unlocked the motel room door and switched on the light.

A shabby room with a double bed against one wall. A cheap

veneer nightstand with an ugly lamp. An open suitcase rested on a folding luggage stand.

And the walls...

They were covered with newspapers and magazine clippings and photocopies, many of them yellowed and marked up. Strung here and there in jagged lines, weaving this way and that, was red yarn, connecting one photo with another, connecting maps with clippings...

He'd seen such scenes on TV and in movies. The serial killer's wall of death. The paranoid obsessive's charting of some loony conspiracy theory. An intricate web of madness.

He felt a wash of acid at the back of his throat.

A roomful of crazy.

The tortured work of a lunatic.

Ray Richardson stood handcuffed in the doorway.

"All right," Henry said. "Talk."

"The whole story's up here, left to right. I'll talk you through it if you'd like."

"Yeah," Henry said. "I'd like."

Richardson stepped into the room. Henry looked closer at the bizarre collage. On one side of the room were photos of an Air Force aircraft, circa 1950s, with four propellers and a shiny fuselage, some parked on an airstrip, some airborne. There were photos of uniformed airmen gathered in front of the parked aircraft for a group shot like they'd just graduated from high school. Headshots of one particular Air Force officer. Ray Richardson's father, Henry guessed. He could see the resemblance. A large map of Turkey and Central Asia. Blurry photocopies of newspaper articles.

Ray stood gesturing with his chin like a demented museum guide. "That's my dad, on the left. Back in 1956, '57, when he was in the Air Force. Lieutenant Andrew Richardson."

A yellowed clipping from the *Cleveland Plain Dealer* with a photo of the same man, with a headline: AIR FORCE PILOT LOST OVER RUSSIA—LOCAL MAN WAS 36.

"You know what the government told my mom after my dad was shot down? That it was a routine weather reporting flight. So my poor mom...when she'd had one too many martinis in the afternoon, she'd say my dad had been killed to measure winds and clouds. What a waste, she said. And when I got older, I decided to find out the truth."

Richardson nodded in the direction of the wall. "That's more than ten years of research up there. I even interviewed a couple of guys from my dad's unit. That's when I found out what they were really doing. I knew my dad flew in the Korean War. What I found was, he later volunteered to fly special intelligence missions for the Air Force, for the National Security Agency. He was based at Adana, Turkey."

Henry peered closely at one of the photos. "That's a C-130..."

"You know your aircraft, huh?"

"I was a flyboy too."

"Well, then, you know those things were jammed full of electronic surveillance equipment. To intercept radio transmissions, radar frequencies, other electronic signatures. They'd fly right up to the border of the Soviet Union, trigger their antiaircraft radar, then measure the frequencies. That way they could let the bombers down the road know how to spoof the radar. Let 'em slip through to hit Moscow or Minsk or Pinsk."

"Who the hell are you? A researcher? Military historian?"

He shook his head. "John Deere salesman from Ohio."

"So you want to explain what this is all about, all this...this..."

"It's my attempt to cut through the lies, the bullshit, everything that was slopped our way the past couple of decades."

"I see."

"Once I found out who my dad really was, and his mission, I wanted to find out who had ordered his plane shot down." Another nod to the wall. "And that's the guy."

There were fewer photos and newspaper clippings on the other half of the wall. Most of them were in Russian. A few headshots of a Soviet military officer. The photos looked like they'd been photocopied from library books.

"And this is...?" he asked.

"General Dmitri A. Kunayev, head of the *PVO Strany* district, where my dad was shot down in Soviet Armenia."

"The *PVO* who?"

"It's an acronym," Richardson explained. "Stands for *Protivovozdushnaya Oborona Strany*, which translates into Anti-Air Defense of the Nation. It took me ten years to find out, but he was the son-of-a-bitch who ordered four MiG-17s to shoot down an unarmed surveillance craft."

A gust of wind splattered rain against the room's window. Henry felt colder. He turned to Richardson and said, "You got to be kidding me."

The handcuffed man shook his head. "Vladimir Polowski. Vermont dairy farmer maybe. But he was really Kunayev. And he murdered my dad."

"Uh huh. So poor old Vlad Polowski was actually a Soviet general living under an assumed name right here in Westbury, Massachusetts? Do I have that right?"

"Exactly."

"You do all this... research... on your own?"

"Wasn't easy," Richardson said, a tinge of pride in his voice. "Took a hell of a lot of digging. I found a little news clip in the *International Herald Tribune*, back in 1971. Said a General Kunayev had been killed in a car accident in Tehran while on a military exchange mission. Body burned in the wreckage. I figured, well, at least the old bastard met a fiery death. Until last year, when I went to the Big E."

"You're talking about the Big E Agriculture Fair, in West Springfield? That Big E?"

"Yep. I was staffing the John Deere booth. Just doing my job... and then I saw him walk by. The son-of-a-bitch walked right by me... That big ole birthmark—Christ, I nearly jumped him right then and there and strangled him."

"So why didn't you?"

"Because I wanted to make absolutely sure of it, that's why. I followed him around for a while, followed him right out to the parking lot. And then—then I wimped out. I didn't have the guts to do it. Not yet, anyway."

Henry glanced again at the photos. An ugly birthmark on the man's face, a long dark blotch that looked sort of like a scythe or a scimitar. If you took that general and aged him and slapped a handlebar moustache on the face...

Vladimir Polowski. Yep, that was him, all right.

"So how'd you make sure?"

"Wrote down his license plate number. Made a bunch of calls and eventually turned up his name and address. Kept on digging. His records said he'd been a dairy farmer in Strafford, Vermont, before moving to Cape Cod. So I took some vacation time, and went to Vermont, and you know what I found out?"

"What's that?"

"Absolutely nothing. Nobody in Strafford remembered him. Nobody remembered any Polish émigré who owned a dairy farm around there. No one."

"Okay." His handheld radio at his side crackled to life: "Chief? Chief?"

"So then I got it," Richardson said. "That alleged car crash in Tehran was a cover story engineered by the U.S. government. Kunayev didn't die. He defected. The CIA must have debriefed him and resettled him with what they call a 'legend'—a fake biography and identity. It was a perfect cover. Except for one thing."

"What?"

"One obsessed John Deere salesman."

* * *

Henry stepped outside. The air had gotten colder. All the slushy crap on the ground would soon be freezing into deadly ice. He picked up his handheld.

"Jeff, go."

Another burst of static, and he made out *"... They're here."*

"What's that? Repeat, Jeff."

"Chief, I said, the State Police are here. Along with the medical examiner."

"How about the D.A.?"

"He's about half-hour out still. They're processing the scene now...but there's a Detective Peyton from the State Police, wants to see you and the suspect. Are you at the station?"

"No," Henry said. "I'm at the Westbury Motel. Send him over here, okay?"

"You got it."

For the next ten minutes he stood quietly in the motel room, with an equally quiet Ray Richardson. His kept on glancing back at the wall, wondering what kind of demons would possess someone to go so far, to do so much. To risk so much. To go happily to prison for the sake of long-delayed vengeance.

Finally he turned to Ray and said, "Let's say you're right, and this old dairy farmer really was a Soviet defector living here under deep cover. Let's just say for the sake of argument you're right. Don't you think the guy deserves at least an arrest and a trial?"

Ray shrugged. "You think they'd ever let this go to trial? No way, José. I even called the FBI. Told them about this guy. No one wanted to take my call. They all but hung up on me. Finally I got through to this assistant special agent in charge of something or other. Know what he told me?"

Henry shook his head.

"Guy said, 'Just live your life.' But I couldn't. Thing had got its hooks in me. The idea that the guy who ordered my dad to be

killed was just living the good life on Cape Cod. My wife left me
six months ago. Thought I was unhinged."

"Huh."

"Then a couple weeks back I heard about all those poor people
on the Korean airliner who got shot down over Japan? Like two
hundred some? Know what I'm talking about?"

"Oh, yeah."

"And that kinda flipped a switch in me. Those people—they
were innocent. They just got caught in the crossfire. Just like
my dad."

"I see."

"That's why I waited for you. Now there *has* to be a trial."

Outside, a car door slammed. Henry looked outside. A big black
official-looking Chevy Suburban with tinted windows pulled in
next to his cruiser.

A short, squat man knocked at the open door, and Henry let him
in. The man was wearing a soaked tweed cap and a black cloth
raincoat, gray slacks, and black shoes. He held out a leather wallet
with his photo and badge from the Massachusetts State Police.

"Warren Peyton, State Police Troop D," the man said. "You're
Chief Silva?"

"I am," he said. "You made good time."

"We're the state. We get the Suburbans." He gave a perfunctory
smile. "So what do we got?"

Henry spent the next fifteen minutes describing the events of the
evening so far, beginning with the phone call from the county dispatch, right up to Ray's remark about "crossfire." The state police
detective nodded and grunted and took a lot of notes. He had a
somber look about him and seemed older than the usual Statie who
might have the bad luck of catching a call like this in the middle of
the night. "Okay, tell you what," he said. "Why don't I drive this
gentleman over to your station so you can get him booked and all
the paperwork taken care of?"

"Makes no difference to me who takes him over."

"Since he's waived his rights, maybe he'll tell me a story on the way over that makes a little more sense."

"He's all yours." The Staties were going to bigfoot him anyway. They took over most homicide cases in Massachusetts. His job was done. And frankly, Henry was relieved to be just about rid of the man and the whole bizarre story.

"How about I go with the chief instead?" said Ray Richardson.

Peyton shook his head and smiled and took Richardson's elbow gently. He guided him out to the dimly lit parking lot and into the black Suburban. It had a couple of whip antennas in the back.

Another big black Suburban pulled up the steep drive.

"C triple-S," the detective said. He meant the state police Crime Scene Services Section.

Henry nodded. "Want to follow me over?"

"I'll find my way, no problem," the detective said.

"How about I go with the chief instead?" Ray Richardson said.

Henry shook his head. "He's got the nicer ride," he said.

Henry caught a last glimpse of Ray Richardson, sitting in the back of the Suburban. His eyes were darting around, a panicked expression on his face. For the first time he looked scared.

After the Suburban pulled away, Henry stood there for a moment, staring at the crazytown walls of the motel with an increasing sense of disquiet.

Then it hit him.

Abruptly, he hustled out to his cruiser. The Suburban had turned left on Route 6, he'd noticed, not right. Wrong way.

The Suburban was far off in the distance, the taillights disappearing. Heading away from Westbury. Heading off-Cape.

Two miles down Route 6, the cruiser slid and slithered and the wheels locked and it spun out onto the shoulder. He sat there with the engine ticking and his heart racing.

It was no use. Route 6 was a sheet of ice. No way he was going to chase down the Suburban. That beast of a sport-utility vehicle with its V8 engine and four-wheel drive was probably halfway to the Sagamore Bridge by now.

He heard faint voices and static crackle on the two-way. Melissa from county dispatch. "County to Westbury C-One," she said.

"I'm here, County, go."

"Update from the State Police, chief. They're on their way, but they said to give 'em another twenty minutes or so before they get to you. The roads are really bad."

He nodded, rubbed the hard plastic of the microphone against his forehead. "County, tell them to turn around and go home. There's nothing here."

"You mean, false report?"

"Yeah, I guess you could say that."

He sat in the cruiser for another minute or so, enjoying the blast of hot air from the heater. A couple of other beefy black Suburbans barreled past, headed off-Cape.

It took him a good ten minutes to maneuver the cruiser off the shoulder and back onto the treacherous highway, where he made a U-turn.

He smiled to himself, but it was an ugly smile.

When he got back to the Westbury Motel, he found the door to unit 9 slightly ajar.

Henry pushed it open with his shoulder and switched on the overhead light.

He wasn't surprised. Not really.

The place had been thoroughly cleaned out. Not a photo or a newspaper clipping remained. No suitcase. No trace of a man named Ray Richardson.

The room smelled faintly of bleach.

It was almost sunrise.

When he got back to the Westbury police station, he found Officer Jeff Crane sitting at a typewriter, punching the keys so hard it looked like he might break the damned thing. Open on his desk at his elbow was an old black briefcase lined with jars of fingerprint powders and brushes and transfer tape and other tools.

"The Staties took the body away, Chief," Jeff said. "Even arranged for a tow truck to haul the shooter's car. Plus lots of boxes of evidence."

"So what're you up to?" Henry asked.

"Writing up the police report," Jeff said. "I got some good latents right here. I'll drive them over to Yarmouth first thing in the morning." He glanced at his Timex. "Actually, it's almost six o'clock, isn't it? Good morning."

Henry looked at the earnest young officer, at the resolve in his face, his sharp jaw. Then he reached over, grabbed the envelope of latent prints and tossed them into the steel trash basket.

"Chief, what—what—?"

Henry pulled the set of triplicate carbon-paper forms from the platen of the typewriter. He tore it in half, then in quarters, and then dropped the scraps into the trash.

"Let's head over to the diner and grab a cup of coffee," Henry said.

Little Al set down plates of pancakes and bacon. "Top off your coffee, gentlemen?" he asked.

Henry smiled and nodded and held out his mug. Jeff shook his head. "I'm good," he said.

"So you're just gonna let it drop?" Jeff said. "I don't get it."

"How much did you know about my wife Carol?"

"Not much," he admitted. "I know you guys met in the Air Force. I know she was pretty sick with cancer for a long time, right?"

"Carol was what they call a Radiological Safety Officer. Went places and did things I couldn't even know about...except for one thing. A number of years ago there was this incident down in Arkansas. A Titan II nuclear missile silo caught fire and exploded. The warhead separated. Flew out of the silo. And Carol was part of the recovery team. They went in there and saved the day. Got everything cleaned up. Official story was, no problem, warhead wasn't damaged, nothing to look at here, everything's hunky dory. Real story was, she and the others sacrificed themselves so the nearby towns didn't get nuked into a sheet of flat glass."

Jeff was quiet. Henry went on. "Papers were signed, oaths were given. No one ever heard any more about it. Carol's medical file at the V.A. hospital said she'd contracted lung cancer from smoking. I called up the Pentagon and got through to someone senior and said Carol never touched a cigarette in her life. I just wanted them to acknowledge what happened."

"Yeah?"

"The lieutenant colonel I talked to said I had a choice. I could keep making noise and lose Carol's medical coverage and the rest of Carol's life would be a living hell. The medical bills would bankrupt us. Or else I could keep my mouth shut and she'd get the best care available. So I thought about it. Carol didn't have much time left." Henry's eyes were moist. His eyes were probably just irritated from being up all night. "I knew I was going to lose her. I just didn't feel like doing something that would make me lose her that much quicker."

Jeff toyed with his fork for a moment. "So who really took Polowski's body? And Ray Richardson? And who was Detective Peyton really?"

Henry shrugged. "O.G.A."

"Huh?"

"Other Government Agency. Take your pick. There's about a half-dozen three-letter agencies could have pulled something like this off. We'll never know."

"What do you think's going to happen to Ray?"

"Oh, they have a thousand ways of making you disappear. Maybe there'll be a week of secret interrogation. Then a corpse will turn up on a back road somewhere. Single-vehicle accident. The coroner will say the guy's blood alcohol level was sky high. He'd been going through a rough patch after his wife left him. It'll all be in the police report."

"But...why?"

Henry shrugged. "Couple of weeks back, a civilian airliner was shot out of the sky by a Soviet aircraft. Now the Russians are on the front page, day after day, being portrayed as heartless monsters. But suppose this little story from Cape Cod got out—that a Soviet air defense general who defected had been secretly living here all these years? A general who gave an order to shoot down an American plane in 1958. An order that sounds kinda like another order another Soviet general just gave two weeks ago. Only we protected one general because we wanted to know his secrets. Wouldn't look so good, would it? Especially with all our shouting about the Evil Empire. See, the thing is, Jeff—no government likes to be embarrassed."

"Holy crap," Jeff whispered. He blotted maple syrup on his fingers with a paper napkin. Little ribbons of white napkin stuck to his palm like feathers. "So what do we do about it?"

Henry lifted his cup of coffee and took a long swig. He shook his head. "Stay out of the crossfire."

THE LAST CONFESSION

BY JOHN LESCROART

They didn't call it Asperger's Syndrome in those days, but my younger brother Julian probably had it.

Certainly, everybody who remembers him agreed that he was not quite normal and probably had some highly functioning version of autism. When he was very young, he was silent, withdrawn, and clumsy much of the time, although excellent at almost all mental games, and blessed with a sly sense of humor that was all the more surprising for his lack of verbal skills. He is the one, for example, who put the Saran Wrap over the toilet bowl in my parents' bathroom, although I think that to her dying day, in spite of my denials, my mother thought it was me.

I was the firstborn, a baby boomer in 1948. Julian and I were "Irish twins," eleven months apart in age to the day. I guess big brothers can go one of two ways with awkward siblings, especially if they are close in age. I could either ignore the difficult little rat who was taking so much of my parents' time and energy, or as a dutiful first child I could become my parents' ally as his protector, playmate, and friend. I don't remember actually choosing, but by the time he started school, I had fallen into and was completely committed to the latter role.

We were a good Catholic family, which meant we belonged to St. Benedict's parish and went to Mass every Sunday, and confession at least every two weeks. I was an altar boy from second grade on, and amazingly to everyone (except me, who tutored him relentlessly), Julian followed me one year later. He couldn't always get out what he knew in English, but he could memorize and spew Latin as well as or better than anybody.

Of course, being a good Catholic family also meant that my parents followed the rhythm method for birth control, which in turn meant that the other kids followed along on a regular schedule. Michelle arrived twenty-one months after Julian, then in short order followed Paul, Louise, Marian, and Barbara. With each new child, and my parents' commensurate lack of time for any individual one of us, my responsibility to Julian became greater. I understood his moods, I could entertain him, translate for him, and occasionally, very occasionally, I would let him win at some physical contest—hoops, ping-pong, mini golf.

And then, when he was in sixth grade, Julian suddenly changed in a fundamental way. And perhaps more remarkably, some of the other kids stopped treating him like a freak. Astoundingly, and maybe because the director wanted to make a point that whom so many called the "retard" actually had a good brain, he was cast as Rolfe in the school musical, *The Sound of Music*, and it turned out that he had a beautiful singing voice. The rehearsed words in the play came out with a natural ease that somehow carried over to his day-to-day speech. Still in sixth grade, he later won the school's Spelling Bee, and went on to place second in the entire county. Kitty Rice, the prettiest girl in his class at St. Benedict's, got a crush on him and they actually walked around the school yard holding hands for a couple of months.

In short, Julian had become "normal"—though of course not in all ways. And not to someone who knew him as well as I did. Not to his protector and confidante and best friend.

The basic problem, and it was a paramount issue for a preadolescent young man in the late 1950s, was that in spite of his achievements and advances in apparent normalcy, he suffered from a medical condition over which he had little control. He was, in fact, different, even as he improved in his day-to-day coping with the Asperger's.

He felt things more than other people did.

That was simply a fact.

When Kitty Rice broke up with him, for example, he went into a brooding silence that went on for over a month. Another time, our younger brother Paul had shot a really beautiful bird out in the backyard with his BB gun, and when he'd brought it inside to show it off, Julian took the little broken thing into his hands, petting it, breathing on it, trying to will it back to life. Afterward, exuding silence like a black miasma, he hid himself away in his secret place in our unfinished attic and slept up there until the next morning.

And some kids still teased him. Friendly and trusting by nature, Julian was sometimes smart enough to realize that people were having fun at his expense, but unfortunately he lacked the gene for irony. Consequently, he could be led a long way down the primrose path before he realized that he was the butt of a joke. All too often, being a year ahead of him, I wasn't around to cut things off and shut the bullies up before he got hurt.

These not-infrequent episodes would always leave him demoralized, depressed, and silent, and they drove me to near-homicidal rage that I only rarely acted on. But I was a good Catholic, and anger was one of the deadly sins, so I generally offered my anger up to the poor souls in Purgatory, and life went on.

But sometimes, it almost didn't.

By the time Julian was in eighth grade, I'd moved on to Mother of Mercy ("MOM") High School in Burlingame, just south of San Francisco, and so for the very first time in Julian's life, he was on his own back at St. Benedict's without my protection at school. It wasn't a good time for him, as the hazing and general abuse kicked up a big notch or two. Doubly upsetting to me, though, was his reaction to it. Instead of fighting back or lashing out, as I would have done, he reverted back into his silent shell.

And then the big event: another one of the girls, Andrea, in his class asked him to the first dance of the year and instead, without canceling with Julian, went with another guy. As it happened, I was at MOM's homecoming dance that same night and got home around midnight. The rest of the house was asleep, but in our shared room, Julian wasn't in his bed. I waited for him, figuring he was late getting home from his own dance, but all too soon it was near one o'clock, and that was just plain wrong.

(Times were different then. My parents tended not to wait up and felt no guilt about it. When my own daughter went out on dates through high school, Bonnie and I would never sleep until she got home.)

On my way to wake up my parents to see if they knew something about Julian being gone, I thought to check the attic hideaway and found him there.

"How you doing?"

No answer.

"Did something happen?"

He just looked at me for a long time.

"Come on out," I said finally. "Let's go downstairs and get a Coke."

He shook his head. "No Coke."

"Okay, no Coke." I sat down across from him, Indian-style in the tiny enclosure. One bare dim bulb glowed from the low ceiling. Julian's face looked empty and lost.

"What happened?" I asked again.

He stayed silent for a long time. Then: "It's not worth it," he said.

"What's not worth what?"

"Life."

"What are you talking about? Of course it is."

"Maybe for you. You've got a future."

"So do you."

Staring at some place behind me, he shook his head. "No." Gradually he told me about his night—my Mom driving him by Andrea's house to pick her up and being told by her mother that there must have been some misunderstanding. Andrea had been going steady with Kevin Jacobs for months now—surely Julian knew about that.

This was bad enough, but on top of Julian's super sensitivity…

Just as he was finally finishing up, I saw the pistol.

My father was a cop in our town and he had a few guns that he normally kept in a dresser drawer next to his bed. (Another huge difference between then and today, when I have my three guns in a locked safe at all times.) But beyond his service weapons, he also had a target practice .22 revolver that he kept—unloaded to be sure, but with easily available bullets in the nearby drawer—hanging from a peg in an old-fashioned quick-draw holster down in the garage.

"What's that doing here?" I asked.

No answer.

"Julian. Give me a break. Let me have that thing."

He stared at me for a long time, then finally picked it up by its barrel and passed it across to me. It had one bullet in it.

"Don't tell Mom and Dad," he said. "I wasn't going to do anything."

"Julian. She's just a dumb girl with an even dumber boyfriend."

"I know. It's not her."

"No? Then what else was it?"

"Everything," he said. "Everything. Life. Like I told you."

Much to my everlasting regret, I didn't mention anything about the gun incident to my parents. That was the ethic among brothers with secrets—and who among us didn't have them?—and I bought into it entirely. I must say, though, in my own defense, that even if I had gone to my parents, they probably would not have done anything. The idea of seeking professional help for psychiatric or psychological distress was not in the range of solutions my parents would have pursued.

Let's remember, Julian had always been difficult and different... and he'd gotten progressively "better" over time. So I viewed this as a setback, certainly, but not as a true crisis, not as a warning about his future behavior.

At all-men's Mother of Mercy, we started every school year with a two-day retreat, which was supposed to be a time for all of us young sinners to examine our lives and renew our commitment to prayer, to the Catholic Church, to spirituality, and especially to the love of Jesus Christ. These retreats were usually hosted by a priest from one of the missionary and/or teaching orders. In my sophomore year, a Maryknoll priest, Father Aloysius Hersey, was back after a truly thrilling performance the previous year, when he had talked about his own history of self-flagellation and then removed his cassock on the last day, folding it down over his waist, to reveal the scars on his back to prove that he practiced what he preached. While conceding that this form of self-torture wasn't absolutely necessary either for salvation or for leading a holy life, Father Hersey was also unmistakably proud of the sixteen young men who came forward at the end of the second day to volunteer to take the lash—over their shirts, of course, in deference to those possibly squeamish mothers who might have objected if they found out, and if any of their sons' skin had actually been broken.

Seven of those sixteen flagellants quit MOM before the year was out to enroll in the seminary. This was seen as further proof of Father Hersey's charisma and power. And in truth, I must say that even among those of us who started the retreat as skeptics, Father Hersey had induced a powerful kind of religious hysteria among all of us. And this, in turn, heightened expectations about what would be in store for this year's retreat.

Contributing exponentially to the volatile mix was an accident of history: on October 22, 1962, the Tuesday two days before the retreat was to begin, President John Kennedy had addressed the nation on television and announced the presence of offensive missile sites in Cuba. The Cuban Missile Crisis was well underway. In response to that presence, he directed U.S. military forces go to DEFCON (Defensive Condition) 3. By the next day, U.S. ships had set up a blockade of Soviet shipping headed to Cuba, to be enforced at the 800-mile perimeter. On the day the retreat began, in the face of Soviet intransigence (or ambiguity) about the blockade, the President pulled the quarantine back to 500 miles and announced DEFCON 2, the highest level in U.S. history. Driving into school in our carpool (Julian was now a freshman at MOM), we had been transfixed by the news on the radio that all of the Soviet ships en route to Cuba had slowed or turned around—except for one.

After homeroom, we all dutifully filed into the Assembly Hall, which comfortably held all four years of MOM's students—800 young men—and the entire faculty. The stage had been cleared except for a podium front and center, where Father Hersey would address us, and in the back an altar, where Mass would be celebrated later on.

After I was at my seat in about the middle of assembly, I saw Julian enter and take a seat to my right on the aisle in one of the front rows. He was talking to some of the guys around him, which I took to be a good sign. He seemed to be fitting in well in his new school environment, and I didn't give him any more thought.

At last, our Principal, Monsignor Tully, strode onto the stage and up to the podium and gave us the usual ground rules for general assemblies—show respect for the speaker(s), no unnecessary talking, no rough-housing, no bathroom breaks, and so on. And then he introduced, fresh from a mission to China and Indonesia, Father Aloysius Hersey.

The cleric cut a somewhat exotic figure—and not only because he'd just arrived fresh from the Far East. In contrast to the black cassocks worn by our faculty priests, he wore a brown monk's robe, with sandals and no socks. (At MOM, our dress code forbade white socks, to give you an idea of how novel this seemed to all of us.) He also sported a shaggy beard and, pre-Beatles, hair down over his ears. From where I sat this year, I couldn't make out his eyes, but from the year before I knew that they were a striking and intense shade of blue in an almost shockingly sunburned face. Tall and thin, with a toothy smile and a gentle manner, he seemed to exude holiness, a true ascetic for the modern world.

A consummate showman, Hersey appeared just off the wings and, stepping out into full view, stood with his hands pressed together in a prayerful gesture. As more of the students saw him and recognition kicked in, a round of applause began and grew until it had become a full-blown standing ovation of the entire student body.

When the applause died down, Hersey bowed with a show of humility, walked to the middle of the stage, bowed again, then turned back toward the altar, where he knelt and made an elaborate sign of the cross. In a large room full of teenage testosterone, a person is lucky if they can command five seconds of quiet attention. But Hersey knelt there praying for at least a minute and there wasn't a sound in the room. Finally, he crossed himself once more, turned, and came back up to the podium.

"God bless you," he said. "Let us pray. Our father, who art in heaven..."

As the prayer went on, suddenly Monsignor Tully appeared again in the wings, a few steps onto the stage. As though uncertain about what he should do, he waited until the "Amen" had resounded through the room, at which time he came up next to Hersey and whispered something in his ear.

Hersey's shoulders noticeably gave under the weight of what he'd been told.

Turning away from the podium, he went back to the altar, where he genuflected, blessed himself yet again, and hung his head.

The silence this time was profound.

Slowly, haltingly, he returned to the podium. "My brothers," he said. "God bless you. God bless us all."

Appearing to struggle for control, he drew a breath, raised his eyes to heaven, then settled them upon us. "As I'm sure all of you are aware, the U.S. Navy has been running a blockade on Cuba for the past couple of days. All of our ships have been on highest alert, and have been stopping Soviet ships bound for Cuba in order to enforce the blockade that President Kennedy has ordered.

"Well, this morning, just a few minutes ago really, the captain of one of these Soviet ships refused to allow one of our Navy vessels to send officers to board and search his ship. Words and radio signals were evidently exchanged and then some hothead in charge of one of the navy guns fired on the Russian ship.

"We have just learned that in retaliation, Russia has launched several nuclear-tipped intercontinental ballistic missiles from its bases in Siberia, just across the Bering Sea from Alaska. Preliminary analysis indicates that these missiles have been fired on targets along the West Coast, including San Francisco, where the first of them can be expected to explode sometime in the next fifteen to twenty minutes.

"I am afraid, my dear brothers, that this is the end of our world."

Although time for me seemed to stop, it must have only taken a few seconds for the reaction to set in, and that reaction ran the gamut from stunned silence to swearing to screaming. A few of the guys, probably for reasons they didn't understand, stood up and starting charging from their seats, knocking other classmates out of their way, breaking up or down the aisles, heading for whichever exit was nearest. I remained numb, stuck to my seat, my heart pounding, trying and failing to find an acceptable location to put the knowledge that within a half hour I would in all probability be dead. I would never see my parents or brothers or sisters again, never see Maggie, my girlfriend.

Nothing I had ever hoped for would come to pass.

Dead, immolated, at sixteen.

Oh my God. Oh my dear sweet God. Have mercy on me, the sinner. (I remember the exact phrase that came into my mind. I'm now forty-eight years an atheist, and such was my upbringing and brainwashing that that phrase still shows up in times of overwhelming stress.)

The hysterical, panicked, even violent reactions started to gain the upper hand in the pandemonium that now threatened to engulf the whole student body. Hersey, still up on the stage, slammed his fist against the podium. "Gentlemen! Gentlemen, please. I need your attention right now!"

Such was Hersey's air of authority, so impeccable his timing on knowing exactly when to rein in the rampant flow of emotions, that almost immediately he had restored order and gained everyone's attention.

"Listen to me! Listen to me!" He paused, soaking the moment for all it was worth. "What I've just told you is not the truth. I repeat, it is *not* the truth." The energy in the hall subsided like a tide going out, as we all hung there in frenzied anticipation.

What was he saying? Could it be that we would escape Armageddon after all?

Hersey showed his horsey teeth in a triumphant grin. "I just wanted to scare the *Hell* out of you."

What an asshole!

But of course, I didn't think that at the time. No, at that moment, like almost all the rest of school, all I could feel was a sweeping sense of relief. I literally felt blood rush back into my face. A gradual wave of nervous laughter began in the back of the hall and soon, growing and growing, swept over the entire assemblage.

But there was one glitch ruining the brilliant piece of theater that Hersey had orchestrated, and that was my brother Julian, who shortly after the initial announcement of our imminent death had fainted and even now lay gripped in some kind of seizure in the aisle next to where he had fallen.

The knot of students who had gathered around him called

attention to the problem. Seeing where the commotion was taking place, I knew immediately that it was Julian, and though I don't exactly remember how I managed it, soon I had gotten myself out of my row and was next to him before any of the faculty had made it down. Pale as a ghost, he lay half on his side in an unnatural pose, his teeth clenched, his arms and legs curled up in the fetal position.

I gathered him up against me, his head on my lap, not really having any clue what to do in a medical sense, but somehow knowing I needed to protect him. As I held him, he opened his eyes, shivered violently, and then vomited just as the first of the faculty arrived and took control. Over the next couple of minutes, as he came back to full consciousness, I stayed close by and finally helped walk him out of the assembly and into the nurse's room, where we covered him with some blankets and called my parents.

Astoundingly, after my parents heard what had happened, they did not blame Hersey, Tully, or anybody else. They thought the priest had made a pretty good point that had worked with the vast majority of other students, who'd surely gotten the Hell scared out of them. My Dad, I think, actually admired the scam. In his view, anything that made you tougher was better. He never expected Julian to be tough, but the more he could deal with in the real world, the better off he was going to be.

Both of them agreed that what had happened to Julian was unfortunate to be sure, but not really that big a deal. Somebody among the faculty who had known about his "condition" might have warned him about Hersey's prank and saved him some misery and embarrassment (embarrassment!). But Julian had only been at the school for less than a month, so no one really knew except me. And there simply wasn't much if any understanding of "special needs" in that strict, Catholic environment in 1962. Indeed, my parents had succeeded in getting Julian accepted into MOM by producing documentation from St. Benedict's grammar school that he had his condition under control, that he wouldn't disrupt classes, that he was "normal."

But after that October 24, Julian wasn't the same. After dinner every night for the next four days, he retired to the attic hideaway. I went up the first two nights, but he simply wouldn't say a word to me, no matter what blandishments I offered him. This time, I did tell my parents how worried I was. In response, they both talked to Julian and were sure he would be all right. He'd had setbacks in the past, and he'd always pulled out of them. He'd just have to process what he'd been through and he'd be back to normal in no time.

I should just be patient.

Meanwhile, though, I took the .22 off its peg in the garage and hid it in a crawl space under the back of the house.

On the next Monday, Julian went back to school. Evidently, some of the guys in his class—not particularly any more Christ-like than they'd been before that weekend's retreat—heckled him pretty relentlessly about what a wimp he'd been at the assembly. What's the matter, couldn't the guy take a little joke?

Later, police pieced together what they believe happened. Julian simply walked off campus after lunch on Monday and caught a bus to San Francisco. At the city bus terminal, he asked directions at the information booth for the bus that would drop him off closest to the Golden Gate Bridge. On the bridge itself, a tourist couple from Chicago stopped and, seeing a solitary young man at the rail gazing out over the Bay, asked if he was all right. He had assured them that he was. They identified him by his school picture. They had stopped to admire the view a hundred yards farther on and, much to their horror, had seen him jump.

Missionaries such as Father Hersey, when not on assignment, often got put up as guests in local rectories. During the retreat, he had made a big point of announcing that he would be hearing confessions for all of the next week. He wanted us all to understand that he was a regular guy with a great sense of humor; he promised light penances—no more than three Hail Marys—no matter how grave your mortal sins or how numerous your sins of the

74

flesh—this latter to much laughter. He would be at MOM's chapel before school, during lunch, and after school hours, and then from 7 to 9 p.m., he would hear confessions at St. Benedict's every evening through Friday of the following week, when he would be shipping out to India.

On Thursday, we had the memorial service for Julian, which was held at St. Benedict's parish hall.

The next night, I announced that I was going over to visit my best friend, Frank Sydell. At this time, I had almost completely free rein over my activities. The basic rule for me, as the oldest, was that I should be home by 10:00, and if I was staying over at a friend's house, I should call just so my parents knew where I was. I dutifully went to Frank's, about a mile from our house, and at around 7:45 suggested that we go get a pizza at our local Round Table, located in the shopping center across from St. Benedict's, about halfway back to my place.

When we finished the pizza, I told Frank I wasn't feeling great—still totally bummed about Julian's suicide, I wasn't faking it—and told him I was going home.

I didn't go home.

Instead, I walked to the dark side of the shopping center's parking lot, where I'd hidden the .22 on the way over to Frank's, and crossed the street mid-block, away from any lights. The church itself was large, cavernous, and dimly lit, although as I had anticipated and hoped, at this time Friday night, it was empty of worshippers. Friday was not a normal confession night, and I didn't really expect any of my fellow retreat members to be taking advantage of Father Hersey's offer on what was every teenager's date night.

There were four confessionals, but only the one at the back on my left had the little white light over the confessor's door that indicated a priest was inside. The doors to the cubicles on either side of the priest's had green lights over them, indicating that they both were empty.

I pulled the revolver from my belt where I'd hidden it under my letter jacket. Cocking the hammer, I opened the door and knelt down on the padded riser just in front of the sliding window that separated the penitents from the confessors.

That window slid open.

For a long beat, I could not force myself to move. I had been to confession at least twice a month for the past ten years, and every time I had begun with the words "Bless me, Father, for I have sinned."

This night, though, I was mute.

The figure on the other side of the screen leaned forward and came into my field of vision.

"Father Hersey?" I asked.

"Yes, my son." No doubt he placed me correctly among the MOM students who'd taken part in his retreat. He came closer to the window. "It's all right, whatever it is," he whispered.

"I know."

I put the muzzle of the gun against the screen of the window— three inches from his head—and pulled the trigger.

After spending most of a lifetime on the bench working in the criminal justice system, I should perhaps be surprised at how cleanly I got away with my one homicide. After all, my father himself was a cop. I was there the whole time he was investigating the case, and neither he nor his colleagues even once looked at me crooked, much less questioned me about my activities on that Friday night. Someone, it seems to me, should have had the instinct or intelligence to put together the ICBM moment at the retreat, Julian's reaction to it and subsequent suicide, and Father Hersey's murder, and at least come to ask me some questions. Especially since it was the only gunshot murder in our little town of Belmont during that entire year.

But no one did.

I finished high school at Mother of Mercy, went on to Santa Clara University, then Boalt Hall for my law degree. At thirty-six, I got appointed to the Superior Court in San Francisco, and four years ago, Obama made me a federal judge. Bonnie and I have raised four good young atheists of our own, and two of them have gone into the law as well. The other two are artists—a musician and a painter. Go figure.

Last week, I received my own nonprank death sentence—Stage Four pancreatic cancer—far enough advanced that they have sent me home for hospice. My doctor is a good guy who didn't want to get my hopes up. He told me I might last another twenty days, tops.

One of the last remnants of my long-dead faith is a stubborn belief in the healing power of confession. I've seen hundreds of criminals in the course of my career give in to this basic need to admit the wrongs that they have done. In my case, I find it highly ironic that I don't know what I would accept as the definition of "wrong." All my life, I've acted and ruled as though murder was the ultimate crime, but I have committed murder and have no feelings of guilt about it. I would do it again tomorrow if the circumstances were the same.

And yet, something in me feels relief at this confession. I don't need or ask for forgiveness. But someone should know what I did and why I did it.

That seems important.

And so does this: Julian, you are avenged.

A CARD FOR MOTHER

BY GAYLE LYNDS AND JOHN C. SHELDON

At seven o'clock on an August morning, Fraulein Doktor Anna Klaas joined the crowds hurrying into Munich's Central Railroad Station. In her mid-thirties, she was a pretty woman, with glossy black hair, large black eyes behind steel-rimmed glasses, and porcelain skin that was a little too pale. She was dressed in a fitted brown jacket, a matching wool skirt, and sensible brown pumps. As if it were a talisman, she held her briefcase in both hands close in front of her. She walked purposefully.

The train station was the city's largest. Handsomely rebuilt in modern architecture by Krupp, it'd opened only two years before, in 1960. Like nearly half of Munich's buildings, its predecessor had been destroyed by Allied bombing. She could still feel the ground shuddering under her feet, hear the thunderous explosions in those last terrifying months.

Nervous, Anna glanced around the massive station. The spicy aroma of breakfast *wurst* drifted across the crowds. Long lines of commuters queued up for tickets. As the wood wheels of baggage carts rumbled across the floor, she headed down a short corridor, pushed into the ladies' washroom, and waited. When the second stall from the window was empty, she entered and locked the door behind her. Opening her briefcase, she took out a playing card sliced in half. It was the five of diamonds. She crouched, reached behind the stool, and lodged it between the pipes. She flushed the toilet, left the stall, washed her hands, and walked out of the station.

Promptly at 7:55 a.m., Anna strode down Sendlinger Strasse in the Alstadt, Munich's historic center. Tall cathedral spires loomed over her, gray against the cloudy sky. Tired and worried, she closed in on the eighteenth-century rococo building where she worked. The elegant brass sign announced Forschungszentrum Für Historische Landwirtschaft—Center for the Study of Historical Agriculture.

She climbed the granite steps and, forcing a pleasant smile, entered an expansive room, a library of some ten thousand books dealing with crops and practices of farming dating all the way back to the ancient Greeks. Passing antique reading tables and chairs, she skirted the carved wood counter.

A librarian was sorting through the card catalog. She looked up and smiled. "*Guten morgen*, Fraulein Doktor."

"*Morgen*, Frau Schröder."

Behind the librarian stood rows of floor-to-ceiling bookcases that extended to the back wall. Anna walked down the end aisle, opened a door labeled *Mitarbeiterstab* ("Staff") and entered a short corridor. At the end, she reached a door that had no sign and no knob. She stopped.

A moment later the door swung inward, and she stepped into a secret world of scientists and engineers, technicians and secretaries. The hum of voices and the tap of typewriters sounded from open doors along the hallway. The agriculture library she'd just left was used primarily by scholarly researchers—but it was also a front for the work that went on here. She liked the irony of it—the research library celebrated the past, while this hidden research institution focused on the future.

The duty guard looked up from his desk. "*Willkommen*, Fraulein Doktor." He pushed a button, and the door swung closed behind her. Encircling his desk were screens displaying the corridors throughout the library and the research facility. Anna's employer, Siemens AG, had pioneered the first closed circuit camera system, in 1946, so naturally the latest version was installed here.

"*Guten morgen*, Herr Steinbock." She heard a quiet *click* as the door locked.

He gestured. "*Bitte.*"

She handed him her briefcase. All purses, briefcases, and backpacks were inspected when employees arrived or left. It wasn't personal. Still, she felt a frisson of fear as he took it, wrapping his hand authoritatively around the leather handle. Opening it, he examined the journal articles, magazine clippings, and latest Siemens newsletter.

"*Danke.*" He returned the case.

Anna headed down the hall, nodding and greeting administrators, assistants, and fellow engineers.

The door to her office was open.

"Good morning, Fraulein Doktor." Her secretary, Helga Smits, held up a large white envelope bordered in black. "I have a Confidential for you." A "Confidential" was a controlled document. Only those with Class 2 security clearances, such as Helga, could handle them; only those with Class 1 clearances, such as Anna, were allowed to read them.

"Good morning, fraulein. Thank you." Anna raised the hand in which she held her briefcase and accepted the Confidential envelope with her thumb and forefinger. With the other hand she took the pen Helga offered. Helga pushed an acknowledgment-of-receipt form across her desk, and Anna signed it.

In seconds, Anna was inside her office. Closing the door, she hurried to her desk, dropped her briefcase at her feet, and sank into her chair. She opened the big envelope. Inside was a memo followed by five more pages. Leafing through them, she saw they were detailed diagrams and figures. She read the memo. It was from Herr Doktor Gunter Vogel: "How would you like to lose some weight?"

So droll, Gunter, Anna thought, but that was Gunter. An engineer's humor. By asking whether she'd like "to lose some weight," he was asking for help. The five technical pages illustrated the problem.

Anna picked up the phone. "So you're calling me fat, Gunter?"

"Would I dare? And risk a date with Germany's most beautiful PhD?"

"Check your fingers, Gunter. Is your wedding ring still there?"

"Wait a moment." There was a pause. "Nope, not there."

"Sudden transfer to your vest pocket, no doubt. Stop proposing bigamy and let's get down to business."

"If the Soviets ever attack, we've always got you—you can shoot down anyone." He was trying, poorly, to sound hurt.

"Talk to me about your other problem—your engineering problem."

Anna and Gunter were team leaders of a project to design new technology—a turbofan jet engine that would give the West a critical military edge over the Soviets. Conventional jet engines worked by sucking air into the compressor then driving it into the combustion chamber—"combustor"—where it was mixed with fuel and ignited. The resulting hot exhaust created the thrust that propelled the aircraft. What made the turbofan engine cutting-edge was that it diverted some of the air around the combustor, forcing it out the back of the engine cold. The combination of hot and cold exhaust produced more power without consuming more fuel. Such new engines would significantly increase the range of NATO's bombers and fighters.

Anna's team was designing the turbine, and Gunter's the combustor.

"We're having trouble with the inner combustor casing," Gunter told her. "It's too fragile at peak temperatures, so we have to switch to a heavier alloy."

"So you need a heavier casing," Anna said, "which means—just a wild guess here—you're asking us to reduce our weight to compensate. How much?"

"Two kilograms."

She sighed. Her team had spent months refining the turbine. They'd developed an exquisitely light and strong alloy for the blades and shaved every gram possible from the rotor and shaft. Now they were supposed to cut even more weight? Where? *Damn.* Weight versus budget, heat versus weight, weight versus thrust, thrust versus fuel efficiency, production schedules versus budget—Sisyphus had it easy.

Anna considered the situation. At last she nodded to herself. "How about I lend you our expert on heat dissipation, the good Herr Doktor Sterne."

Gunter laughed. "Hermann Sterne? Isn't he the one who told you a real German woman belonged in a kitchen making strudel? If I remember, you asked for the address of his cave."

"That's the guy," she said grimly.

"Sure, I'll take him off your hands—and you owe me."

"No, Gunter, Neanderthal or not, he's good at his job. He's yours for a month. Then I want him back."

The problem resolved for now, they ended the call.

The sudden quiet in her small office gave Anna relief. She gazed at her desktop—the telephone was set at the corner equidistant from both edges. Then at her file cabinet—the labels were perfectly horizontal. And at the stacks of working papers and blueprints— aligned like marching soldiers along the edge of her credenza. She prided herself on orderliness. It gave her a sense of decency, of control and purpose.

She stared around her immaculate office. Control and purpose—the very things she'd lost. She dropped her head into her hands. *What had she done? How could it have gone so far?* All she could think about was her mother. Her mind churned; her heart ached. With effort she pulled herself together. They would get through this crisis, she vowed. Taking a deep breath, she lifted her head and reached for the diagrams and notes Gunter had sent in the Confidential. Yes, this information would be useful.

She picked up her phone again and pushed a button. The noise of the buzzer on Fraulein Smits's phone was muffled by the closed door.

"*Ja*, Fraulein Doktor?" Fraulein Smits's voice sounded in Anna's ear.

"I'm working on some new specs. I don't want to be disturbed."

"Yes, of course."

Hanging up the phone, Anna reached for her briefcase. Using a razor-thin blade from her desk drawer, she popped open the leather handle. Inside, nestled in black felt, was a metal cylinder about two inches long and the width of a man's thumb—a miniaturized microdot camera.

Moving quickly, Anna unscrewed the camera's top, inserted film, and began photographing Gunter's diagrams.

For lunch, Ines Klaas sliced freshly baked rye bread, plump red tomatoes, and fine Emmentaler cheese, a Bavarian specialty. With care, she took out her favorite blue-and-white porcelain plates from the old days, before the war. She was a tall woman, taller than her daughter, Anna. Her long gray hair was parted in the middle and gathered back into a ponytail. At one time her hair had been as black as her daughter's, and in the old days it was said her smile could light up a banquet hall.

But much had happened since then. Her husband had been killed in the early years of the war, a Luftwaffe captain. Anna's fiancé had died in 1946, a teenage army private who'd survived the Soviet campaign but come home with end-stage tuberculosis. Now only the two of them were left, she and Anna. The story of her family's losses wasn't unusual.

Remembering better times, Ines went to the mirror in the sitting room and pulled her fine linen tunic close. It was pale yellow. Anna had given it to her, brought it home when she'd finished her studies at the California Institute of Technology—Caltech, she called it. With a critical eye, Ines studied her body. She'd lost fifteen pounds in the last month. The frames of her eyeglasses accented the thinness of her face. Her back hurt all the time now; she was always weary.

Still, as she returned to the kitchen to finish making the sandwiches, she began to smile. Anna would be home soon. She pinched her cheeks to bring color to them.

Anna and Ines shared a two-bedroom flat on the top floor of a nineteenth-century building overlooking Beethovenplatz. Sitting on their balcony, they enjoyed the views across Munich's church spires and red-tile roofs as they ate their sandwiches and drank their coffee.

"Simple, good food," Ines commented.

"Delicious. But I was going to make lunch for you." Anna's eyes searched her mother. "How do you feel today?" She saw how stiffly her mother held herself, how carefully she moved.

"Wonderful. Excellent. Better all the time."

Anna shook her head. Then she smiled. "You're impossible." But that was Mamma, upbeat, optimistic. From what the doctor had explained about Hodgkin's disease, Ines was probably in constant pain, but she never complained, in fact wouldn't even talk about it. Her bravery strengthened Anna's resolve. "I think I've found a way to send you to the Mayo Clinic in the United States." The renowned hospital was considered the preeminent treatment center for Hodgkin's. Nothing in Europe was nearly as good.

Ines shook her head. "Darling, don't bother. You can't afford it. I've had a good run, a good life." She changed the subject. "I heard a funny joke this morning from Frau Dingmann down the hall." Her eyes danced as she launched into it: "Two workers of the state were assigned to improve a street in East Berlin. One dug a hole, and the other came along behind and filled it. This went on all day, digging holes and filling them, with timeouts for the usual schnapps and cigarettes. Finally someone from around here, who was visiting relatives over there, asked what they were doing. One of the East Germans said, 'Just because the comrade who sticks the trees in the holes didn't show up, that doesn't mean the state is going to let us off work, too.'" Ines laughed hard, her eyes watering.

Anna laughed, too. Then she reached across the table and took her hand. "I love you, Mamma."

"When are you going to find a nice man and make your own life again? You mentioned a 'Hari.' Is he your beau?"

Anna felt a chill. "Hari?"

"You were talking in your sleep again last night. I was worried, so I went into your room. You were muttering the name Hari. It seemed to me you were having a long conversation with him."

"Oh, just someone I work with." Anna patted her mother's hand. "Speaking of which, I'm going to be a little late tonight. Don't cook. I'll bring you dinner."

Following a long afternoon at her desk, Anna arrived at Karlsplatz at 5:30 p.m., just as the bus pulled up. From the corner of her eye she saw Hari Bander sitting on a sidewalk bench reading a newspaper. She had signaled him she wanted a *treff*—a meeting—by leaving half of the five of diamonds in the ladies' toilet in the train station that morning. The suit—diamonds—meant the Karlsplatz bus stop. The number—five—meant five o'clock, and half of the card meant half past the hour. One of Hari's associates, undoubtedly a woman, would have picked up Anna's message and left it at another dead drop for him.

Anna hurried to the queue waiting to board. He stood up and ambled toward it, too. He was small and gangly, with a clean-shaved face and a ski-jump nose. He looked like a shop owner or perhaps a college professor, dressed as he was in a tweed sports jacket, brown silk tie, and fawn-colored homburg. He joined the queue three people behind her. She boarded and sat in front on the right side. Passing her, he sat in the rear on the left. The bus drove east, jostling through the traffic. After ten blocks, she disembarked and turned north, walking casually. She passed restaurants and pubs then went around the corner, heading east again, feeling the sun's warmth on her back. She stopped to peer into the display window of a dress shop. Soon he came around the same corner.

Hari had an easy walk, the gait of a confident man.

If he passed her, she'd know they'd been followed.

With the slightest smile, he tipped his hat to her. "I'll meet you at the macaws." And he was gone, walking off, lighting a cigarette.

Now that she had their final destination, she hailed a taxi.

In the middle of the city, Tierpark Hellabrunn was an oasis of serenity. A vast open space with a zoo and surrounding park, it was renowned for its grassy hills, specimen trees, and bright flower-beds. Following signs, Anna took a winding path past a picnic area to the macaw exhibit. A dozen colorful males and females sat on tree branches, preening.

An older couple paused at the display. They glanced at Anna, and she exchanged nods and smiles with them. Over the woman's shoulder, Anna saw Hari approaching.

With a flicker of his eyes, he took in the situation. "Hello, Anna," he called. "Is that really you?" With a large smile, he hurried over and shook her hand.

"How lovely to see you, Hari," she said, playing the game. "It's been a while."

The older couple moved on, her arm in his.

Glancing around, Hari lowered his voice. "Why did you want to meet?"

"Let's walk."

He nodded, and they headed off. There was something nice about Hari, something charming. Yet he carried a pistol, in a shoulder holster under his jacket, that he'd admitted to using. He'd told her he was the child of German artists who were members of the Communist Party. They'd believed communism was the only humane political system, and if Germans followed Marxist rules the nation would be set right. Instead, Adolf Hitler rose to power, and the family left, emigrating to southern Russia. Hari's father served in the Soviet Army, while Hari and his sister attended Russian schools. When the war ended, Hari was sent to Moscow University. Afterward the Soviet government assigned him to work in the German Democratic Republic—East Germany. Like his parents, Hari was a true believer in communism.

"I have something your bosses will want." As they walked, she took a gift-wrapped package from her briefcase and handed it to Hari.

He felt the package. "A book?"

"On page 37, the dot over the third *i* on the seventh line is a microdot. It shows a problem we're working out on our turbofan engine."

He frowned. "What's a turbofan engine?"

"It's a new jet engine design. It can increase the range of a bomber or a fighter up to twenty-five percent, which means NATO will have much deeper penetration into Soviet airspace."

Hari's eyebrows rose. "Shit!"

She gave a grim smile. "Exactly."

They paused to let a crush of locals pass them. Chatty and friendly, the group was exuberant, as if the world was theirs, but then the country was finally experiencing prosperity again. An awful taste gathered in her mouth. They were her people—and she was betraying them. She looked away. It had all begun six years earlier when she was writing her PhD dissertation. Since East German doctoral students weren't allowed to publish their theses, many sold them for much-needed cash to students in the West. The buyers felt safe that their professors or colleagues would never be able to identify the work as someone else's. Anna had bought one and hadn't attributed the portions she'd used. Then a year ago, East Germany's dreaded state security agency, the Stasi, had discovered her plagiarism and threatened to reveal it to Caltech, jeopardizing her degree, and to Siemens, jeopardizing her career.

"I always liked Goethe." Hari had opened the package—*Selected Poetry* by Johann Wolfgang von Goethe.

Anna took a deep breath, collecting herself. "You'll like him even more now. What I've given you is only a sample. Your engineers will salivate over the prototype data. You're going to be a hero, Hari."

He assessed her. "You've always resisted giving us anything we asked for. But now you seem to be offering technological gold. It doesn't make sense. In fact, it makes so little sense I'm inclined not to believe you."

Keeping her tone even, she said, "My mother has Hodgkin's disease. It's a form of cancer. We only found out a few days ago, when I finally convinced her to go to a doctor." She paused, controlling her emotions. "The cancer is advanced. The best treatment is in Minnesota, in the U.S., and it's expensive. Siemens won't give me a raise or a loan. So that leaves the Stasi." She told him the lump sum she needed. "That's to fly her there and begin treatment. We don't know how long she'll stay. It may take more money."

Saying nothing, Hari stopped at a railing and leaned on it, apparently thinking as he peered down a steep hill into a stand of birches. He clasped his hands in front of him, the book solidly between them.

She stood beside him, anxiously waiting for him to say something.

His gaze was solemn as he glanced at her. "I'm sorry about your mother."

She nodded. "Thank you."

But then he looked away again. "We operate on a small budget. Most of our assets believe in the better world we're trying to build. They work for free. We give a small stipend to others. You're one of the lucky few who gets some money. We want you to enjoy the extra deutschmarks, even become dependent on them. But that's all there is for you." His voice grew low, too quiet. "Be realistic, Anna. You're in a precarious position." He turned toward her and enunciated each word clearly: "We have standards of pay. We don't exceed them. There are no exceptions. No one negotiates with the Stasi."

Anna felt as if she'd been gut-punched. She gripped the rail and saw in her mind's eye her mother turning on her heel, a butcher knife in her hand. It'd been the first winter after the war, the harshest in living memory, so deadly it became known as *Der Elendswinter*, The Winter of Misery. Temperatures plummeted to twenty-five below zero Fahrenheit. Their house was a bombed-out hulk, little protection against the biting cold. Anna's fiancé died. Every day she and her mother went off to join the army of grandmothers, housewives, and girls cleaning up the rubble of the town with their hands and whatever tools they could find. They were called *Trümmerfrauen*, rubble women. They were paid in food and the equivalent of ten cents an hour. Anna was fifteen years old; her mother forty. They were hungry all the time.

Anna's mother heard about an old Nazi food depot that others were raiding. Insisting Anna stay home, she left at midnight and returned two hours later with a gunny sack of canned meats and vegetables, enough to get them through the month. Anna was crouched, shoving the canned goods into a hole they'd dug under the house, when she sensed motion and looked up just as her mother whirled around and jammed a long-bladed butcher knife into the belly of a man. "I knew I was being followed," was her only comment. Her expression hard, she'd dragged him out to the street and left him there. People died in the street all the time then, from the cold, from violence. Anna had tried to talk to her about what happened, but Ines had only smiled and shrugged. Nevertheless, Anna understood: Without her mother, she wouldn't have survived.

Now it was her turn. She wasn't going to let her mother die. "Don't try to play that game with me, Hari. There's nothing 'precarious' about my situation. If you tell anyone about me you'll get the exact opposite of what you want—I'll be arrested, probably go to prison, and you'll lose your source for the turbofan engine and whatever other state-of-the-art technologies Siemens develops."

For an instant she thought she saw concern, perhaps even fear, in his eyes. Encouraged, she gave her head a firm shake. "Tell your Stasi bosses they need to make an exception for my mother."

He looked away. "You'll have our answer shortly, Anna."

"Good. I think we're done here." She turned on her heel and walked away.

The call came at 4 p.m. the next day.

Anna was at her desk at work, double-checking equations with her slide rule, when Fraulein Smits knocked on her door, cracked it open, and peered around it, her eyes wide with fear.

"The *polizei* are on the phone." She whispered "police" as if she could hear jackboots on pavement. She had crossed over from East Berlin a year earlier, escaping to her relatives only a week before the Berlin Wall went up.

"*Danke.*" Anna gave her a reassuring smile. "I'll handle it."

Fraulein Smits nodded and vanished, closing the door softly.

Puzzled, Anna reached for the telephone.

"Fraulein Doktor Klaas?" The man's voice was strong.

"Yes, and you are?"

"Police Lieutenant Dominique Harbeck. I'm afraid your mother's had an accident."

Anna went rigid. "She's all right, isn't she? Did you take her to the hospital?"

"One of your neighbors said she had cancer. Is that right?"

"Yes, but we were getting her treatment. She was worried about how much it would cost, but I was managing it." Her heart seemed to stop. "You said *had*—"

"Fraulein Doktor, you should come home. Your mother fell off your balcony. I'm afraid she didn't survive."

Tears streaming down her face, Anna ran the eight blocks from work. A police car and ambulance were parked in front of their apartment building. The neighbors stood in clumps, watching as policemen detoured the traffic. Wiping her eyes, Anna gazed up the six stories to the balcony where she had shared so many happy meals with her mother. Before she could stop it, she saw in her mind's eye her mother plummeting down through the air, helpless, knowing she was going to die. Anna wanted to scream, to shake her fists at the heavens, to hold her mother tight in her arms.

"Fraulein Doktor," a man called.

She turned.

A handsome man in a sleek black suit was walking toward her. "I'm Lieutenant Harbeck. I'm the one who called you."

"Where's my mother?"

"This way." He led her to the ambulance, opened the doors, and pulled a sheet back from the covered figure lying on a gurney.

"Is this Ines Klaas?" he said. "Sorry, but we have to make it official."

Her throat thick, Anna forced herself to look. Her mother's strong-featured face was smooth, waxen, her dark eyes closed. Her long gray hair was matted with blood.

"Yes, it's her." Anna reached for her mother's hand. It was still warm. For an instant, she could almost believe Ines was alive. She burst into tears.

"Come, Fraulein Doktor." He handed her a large white handkerchief and led her away.

Losing her mother was like losing herself. In her mind she could see her mother laughing, see her stab the man who wanted to steal their food, see her dance in the years afterward as Anna got her degrees and they slowly reached a comfortable standard of living in their pretty apartment overlooking the city.

"The super let us into your apartment," the lieutenant told her. "Forgive us, but we had to look for a note. We didn't find one. If you do, please contact us. We'll need to add what it says to our records."

She nodded.

"Your mother was well liked," the lieutenant went on sympathetically. "Had she been talking about killing herself?"

"No. She was cheerful. She was...as much as anyone can be under the circumstances...herself. She never discussed her illness."

He cocked his head and raised his eyebrows sympathetically. "Sometimes, something as devastating as cancer can lead to deep depression."

Anna walked into the silent apartment. What had once been soothing in its quiet orderliness was now lifeless. There's nothing worse than emptiness, she thought. She looked around the living room and kitchen then went down the hall to her mother's bedroom and peered inside. It was a lovely room, done up in pale blue. She inhaled the scent of face powder and closed her eyes, remembering her mother's zest, her vibrancy. Why would she have killed herself? She'd been through hell during the war. It was her personality to be optimistic, to be happy.

Crossing the hall, Anna went into her own bedroom and sat in the corner chair where her mother used to settle when she came in to chat. She gazed around the room, at her smooth bed quilt, her jewelry box square atop her dresser, the simple wooden frame of the mirror.

The mirror. She stared. Stood and ran to it. Lodged in the lower right corner was half of a playing card—the five of diamonds. She saw the corner was bent, the same corner that she had jammed between the toilet pipes in the train station. A trickle of sweat ran down her spine. She recalled Hari's words: "No one negotiates with the Stasi." She snatched the card. "You'll have our answer shortly," he'd said.

Horrified, she smashed the card between her hands. Then she looked up and saw in the mirror's reflection her bedroom doorway behind her, and the hallway beyond that, and then her mother's bedroom. The emptiness, and the silence.

OK until this conclusion

MISS BIANCA

BY SARA PARETSKY

A bigail made her tour of the cages, adding water to all the drinking bowls. The food was more complicated, because not all the mice got the same meal. She was ten years old, and this was her first job; she took her responsibilities seriously. She read the labels on the cages and carefully measured out feed from the different bags. All the animals had numbers written in black ink on their backs; she checked these against the list Bob Pharris had given her with the feeding instructions.

"That's like being a slave," Abigail said, when Bob showed her how to match the numbers on the mice to the food directives. "It's not fair to call them by numbers instead of by name, and it's mean to write on their beautiful fur."

Bob just laughed. "It's the only way we can tell them apart, Abby."

Abigail hated the name Abby. "That's because you're not looking at their faces. They're all different. I'm going to start calling you Number Three because you're Dr. Kiel's third student. How would you like that?"

"Number Nineteen," Bob corrected her. "I'm his nineteenth student, but the other sixteen have all gotten their PhDs and moved on to glory. Don't give the mice names, Abby: you'll get too attached to them, and they don't live very long."

In fact, the next week, when Abigail began feeding the animals on her own, some of the mice had disappeared. Others had been moved into the contamination room, where she wasn't supposed to go. The mice in there had bad diseases that might kill her if she touched them. Only the graduate students or the professors went in there, wearing gloves and masks.

Abigail began naming some of the mice under her breath. Her favorite, number 139, she called "Miss Bianca," after the white mouse in the book *The Rescuers*. Miss Bianca always sat next to the cage door when Abigail appeared, grooming her exquisite whiskers with her little pink paws. She would cock her head and stare at Abigail with bright black eyes.

In the book, Miss Bianca ran a prisoner's rescue group, so Abigail felt it was only fair that she should rescue Miss Bianca in turn, or at least let her have some time outside the cage. This afternoon, she looked around to make sure no one was watching, then scooped Miss Bianca out of her cage and into the pocket of her dress.

"You can listen to me practice, Miss Bianca," Abigail told her. She moved into the alcove behind the cages where the big sinks were.

Dr. Kiel thought Abigail's violin added class to the lab, at least that's what he said to Abigail's mother, but Abigail's mother said it was hard enough to be a single mom without getting fired in the bargain, so Abigail should practice where she wouldn't disturb the classes in the lecture rooms or annoy the other professors.

Abigail had to come to the lab straight from school. She did her homework on a side table near her mother's desk, and then she fed the animals and practiced her violin in the alcove in the animal room.

"Today Miss Abigail Sherwood will play Bach for you," she announced grandly to Miss Bianca.

She tuned the violin as best she could and began a simplified version of the first sonata for violin. Miss Bianca stuck her head out of the pocket and looked inquiringly at the instrument. Abigail wondered what the mouse would do if she put her inside. Miss

Bianca could probably squeeze in through the F hole, but getting her out would be difficult. The thought of Mother's rage, not to mention Dr. Kiel or even Bob Pharris's, made her decide against it.

She picked up her bow again, but heard voices out by the cages. When she peered out, she saw Bob talking to a stranger, a small woman with dark hair.

Bob smiled at her. "This is Abby; her mother is Dr. Kiel's secretary. Abby helps us by feeding the animals."

"It's Abigail," Abigail said primly.

"And one of the mouses, Abigail, she is living in your—your—" the woman pointed at Miss Bianca.

"Abby, put the mouse back in the cage," Bob said. "If you play with them, we can't let you feed them."

Abigail scowled at the woman and at Bob, but she put Miss Bianca back in her cage. "I'm sorry, Miss Bianca. Mamelouk is watching me."

"Mamelouk?" the woman said. "I am thinking your name 'Bob'?"

Mamelouk the Iron-Tummed was the evil cat who worked for the jailor in *The Rescuers*, but Abigail didn't say that, just stared stonily at the woman, who was too stupid to know that the plural of "mouse" was mice, not "mouses."

"This is Elena," Bob told Abigail. "She's Dr. Kiel's new dishwasher. You can give her a hand, when you're not practicing your violin or learning geometry."

"Is allowed for children working in the lab?" Elena asked. "In my country, government is not allowing children work."

Abigail's scowl deepened: Bob had been looking at her homework while she was down here with the mice. "We have slavery in America," she announced. "The mice are slaves, too."

"Abigail, I thought you liked feeding the animals." Dr. Kiel had come into the animal room without the three of them noticing.

He wore crepe-soled shoes which let him move soundlessly through the lab. A short stocky man with brown eyes, he could look at you with a warmth that made you want to tell him your secrets, but just when you thought you could trust him, he would become furious over nothing that Abigail could figure out. She had heard him yelling at Bob Pharris in a way that frightened her. Besides, Dr. Kiel was her mother's boss, which meant she must never EVER be saucy to him.

"I'm sorry, Dr. Kiel," she said, her face red. "I only was telling Bob I don't like the mice being branded, they're all different, you can tell them apart by looking."

"*You* can tell them apart because you like them and know them," Dr. Kiel said. "The rest of us aren't as perceptive as you are."

"Dolan," he added to a man passing in the hall. "Come and meet my new dishwasher—Elena Mirova."

Dr. Dolan and Dr. Kiel didn't like each other. Dr. Kiel was always loud and hearty when he talked to Dr. Dolan, trying too hard not to show his dislike. Dr. Dolan snooped around the lab looking for mistakes that Dr. Kiel's students made. He'd report them with a phony jokiness, as if he thought leaving pipettes unwashed in the sink was funny when really it made him angry.

Dr. Dolan had a face like a giant baby's, the nose little and squashed upward, his cheeks round and rosy; when Bob Pharris had taken two beakers out of Dr. Dolan's lab, he'd come into Dr. Kiel's lab, saying, "Sorry to hear you broke both your arms, Pharris, and couldn't wash your own equipment."

He came into the animal room now and smiled in a way that made his eyes close into slits. Just like a cat's. He said hello to Elena, but added to Dr. Kiel, "I thought your new girl was starting last week, Nate."

"She arrived a week ago, but she was under the weather; you would never have let me forget it if she'd contaminated your ham sandwiches—I mean your petri dishes."

Dr. Dolan scowled, but said to Elena, "The rumors have been flying around the building all day. Is it true you're from Eastern Europe?"

Dolan's voice was soft, forcing everyone to lean toward him if they wanted to hear him. Abigail had trouble understanding him, and she saw Elena did, too, but Abigail knew it would be a mistake to try to ask Dr. Dolan to speak more slowly or more loudly.

Elena's face was sad. "Is true. I am refugee, from Czechoslovakia."

"How'd you get here?" Dolan asked.

"Just like your ancestors did, Pat," Dr. Kiel said. "Yours came steerage in a ship. Elena flew steerage in a plane. We lift the lamp beside the golden door for Czechs just as we did for the Irish."

"And for the Russians?" Dolan said. "Isn't that where your people are from, Nate?"

"The Russians would like to think so," Kiel said. "It was Poland when my father left."

"But you speak the lingo, don't you?" Dolan persisted.

There was a brief silence. Abigail could see the vein in Dr. Kiel's right temple pulsing. Dolan saw it also and gave a satisfied smirk.

He turned back to Elena. "How did you end up in Kansas? It's a long way from Prague to here."

"I am meeting Dr. Kiel in Bratislava," Elena said.

"I was there in '66, you know," Dr. Kiel said. "Elena's husband edited the Czech *Journal of Virology and Bacteriology* and the Soviets didn't like their editorial policies—the journal decided they would only take articles written in English, French, or Czech, not in Russian."

Bob laughed. "Audacious. That took some guts."

Abigail was memorizing words under her breath to ask her mother over dinner: perceptive, editorial policies, audacious.

"Perhaps not so good idea. When Russian tanks coming last year, they putting husband in prison," Elena said.

"Well, welcome aboard," Dr. Dolan said, holding out his soft white hand to Elena.

She'd been holding her hands close to her side, but when she shook hands Abigail saw a huge bruise on the inside of her arm:

green, purple, yellow, spreading in a large oval up and down from the elbow.

"They beat you before you left?" Dr. Dolan asked.

Elena's eyes opened wide; Abigail thought she was scared. "Is me, only," she said, "me being—not know in English."

"What's on today's program?" Dr. Kiel asked Abigail abruptly, pointing at her violin.

"Bach."

"You need to drop that old stuffed shirt. Beethoven. I keep telling you, start playing those Beethoven sonatas, they'll bring you to life." He ruffled her hair. "I think I saw your mother putting the cover over her typewriter when I came down."

That meant Abigail was supposed to leave. She looked at Miss Bianca, who was hiding in the shavings at the back of her cage. *It's good you're afraid*, Abigail told her silently. *Don't let them catch you, they'll hurt you or make you sick with a bad disease.*

Rhonda Sherwood's husband had been an account manager for a greeting card company in town. His territory was the West Coast. When he fell in love with a woman who owned a chain of gift shops in Sacramento, he left Rhonda and Abigail to start a new life in California.

It was embarrassing to have your father and mother divorced; some kids in Abigail's fifth-grade class made fun of her. Her best friend's mother wouldn't let her come over to play any more, as if divorce were like one of Dr. Kiel and Dr. Dolan's diseases, infectious, communicable.

When her husband left, Rhonda brushed up on her shorthand and typing. In May, just about the time that school ended, she was lucky enough to get a job working for Dr. Kiel up at the university. Rhonda typed all his letters and his scientific papers. Over dinner, she would make Abigail test her on the hard words she was learning: *Coxiella burnetii, cytoblasts, vacuoles.* Rhonda mastered the odd concepts: gram staining, centrifuging. Dr. Kiel was not a kind

[handwritten margin notes: anachronistic — form not known in 1968 or 1971]

man in general, Rhonda knew that, but he was kind to her, a single mom. Dr. Kiel let Rhonda bring Abigail to the lab after school.

There were eight scientists in Dr. Kiel's department. They all had graduate students, they all taught undergraduate classes at the university, but Abigail and Rhonda both knew that none of the other scientists worked as hard as Dr. Kiel. He was always traveling, too, to different scientific conventions, or overseas. Rhonda hadn't been working for him when he went to Czechoslovakia three years ago, but she was making travel arrangements for him now. He was going to Washington, to San Francisco, and then to Israel.

Even though Dr. Kiel had an explosive temper, he had a sense of camaraderie that his colleagues lacked. He also had an intensity about his work that spilled over into the lives of his students and staff. His students and lab techs were expected to work long hours, do night shifts, attend evening seminars, but he took a personal interest in their families, their hobbies, took his male students fishing, brought his female students records or books for their birthdays. When he went to New York in August, he brought Rhonda back a scarf from the gift store in the Metropolitan Museum of Art. Dr. Kiel had a wife and five lumpy, sullen children: Abigail met them when Dr. Kiel had everyone in the department out to his house for a picnic right after school started. He never seemed to think about his children the way he did about his staff and students.

It was Dr. Kiel who suggested that feeding the animals might make Abigail feel that she was part of the team. He seemed to sense her loneliness; he would quiz her on her classes, her music. He knew better than to tease a ten-year-old girl about boys, the way Dr. Dolan did.

When Rhonda worried about the diseases the animals were infected with, Dr. Kiel assured her that Abigail would not be allowed in the contamination room. "And if some Q fever germ is brave enough to come through the door and infect her, we keep tetracycline on hand." He showed Rhonda the bottle of orange pills in one of his glass-doored cabinets. "I've had it, and so has Bob Pharris. Watch out for a high fever and a dry cough, with aching joints; let me know if either of you starts having symptoms."

"High fever, dry cough," Abigail repeated to herself. Every day when she went in to feed the animals, she checked Miss Bianca for a fever or a cough. "Do your joints ache?" she would ask the mouse, feeling her head the way Rhonda felt her own head when she was sick.

Elena Mirova's arrival unsettled the lab. She was quiet, efficient, she did whatever was asked of her and more besides. She worked with Bob and Dr. Kiel's other two graduate students, often giving them suggestions on different ways to set up experimental apparatus, or helping them interpret slides they were studying.

"Czech dishwashers know more science than ours in America," Bob said one day when Elena flipped through the back pages of the *Journal of Cell Biology* to show him an article that explained apoptosis in *Rickettsia prowazekii*.

Elena turned rigid, her face white, then hurriedly left the room, saying she heard the autoclave bell ringing.

"It's the communists," Rhonda explained to her daughter, when Abigail reported the episode to her.

"It was so weird," Abigail said. "It was like she thought Bob was accusing her of a crime. Besides, she was lying, the autoclave bell didn't ring."

"The Russians put her husband in prison," Rhonda said. "She's afraid that they'll try to find her here."

That frightened Abigail. Everyone knew how evil the communists were; they wanted to take over America, they wanted to take over the whole world. America stood for freedom and the communists wanted to destroy freedom.

"What if they come to the lab to get Elena and kill you instead?" she asked Rhonda. "Are the mice safe? Will they want the mice?"

Dr. Dolan came into Dr. Kiel's office at that moment. "Of course they want the mice; the mice are our most important secret."

Abigail rushed down to the animal room to make sure Miss Bianca was still safe. The mouse was nibbling on a piece of food, but she came to the front of the cage as soon as Abigail arrived. Abigail was about to take her out when she saw that Bob was in the contamination room.

Instead, she stroked the mouse's head through the cage door. "I wish I could take you home, Miss Bianca," she whispered.

When Bob came out and went into the back room to scrub himself down in the big sink, Abigail followed him.

"Do you think Elena is a communist spy?" she demanded.

"Where do you come up with these ideas, short stuff?" Bob asked.

"Dr. Dolan said the communists want our mice, because they're our most important secret."

"Dr. Dolan talks a lot of guff," Bob said. "There's nothing secret about the mice, and Elena is not a communist. She ran away from the communists."

"But she lied about the autoclave. She didn't like you saying how smart she was."

Bob stopped drying his arms to stare at her. "You're as small as the mice, so we don't notice you underfoot. Look: there's nothing secret about our mice. We get a grant—you know what that is? Money. We get money from the Army, so we do some work for the Army. The disease Dr. Kiel works with can make people very sick. If our soldiers got sick in Vietnam, they wouldn't be able to fight, so Dr. Kiel and I and his other students are trying to find a way to keep them from getting sick."

"But he has that drug, he showed my mom," Abigail said.

"That's great if you're already sick, but if you're in the middle of a battle, it would be better not to get sick to start with. It would be hard for the Army to get enough of the drug to our soldiers out in the jungles and rice paddies while the Vietcong were firing rockets at them."

"Oh," Abigail said. "You're trying to make a shot, like for polio."

"And the mice are helping us. We give them some of Dr. Kiel's disease, and then we study whether we've learned any way to prevent them from getting sick."

After Bob went back to the lab, Abigail took Miss Bianca from the cage and let her sit in her pocket, where she had a lump of sugar. "Even if the mice can help win a war with the communists, I think it would be better if you didn't get sick."

She practiced her violin for half an hour. The scratchy sounds she got from the strings sounded more like the squeaks the mice made than Bach, but neither she nor the animals minded. When she finished, she took Miss Bianca out of her pocket to ride on her shoulder. When she heard voices outside the animal room door she crouched down, holding Miss Bianca in her hand.

"Mamelouk is here," she whispered. "Don't squeak."

It wasn't Mamelouk, it was Dr. Kiel with Elena. Elena's face was very white, the way it had been when she first came into the lab. She fumbled in her handbag and produced a jar with something red in it that Abigail was sure was blood.

"I hope is sterile. Hard job doing self. *Myself*," Elena said.

Abigail bent her head over her knees, so Miss Bianca wouldn't have to see such a dreadful sight. After Dr. Kiel and Elena left the animal room, she stayed bent over for a long time, but finally went up to the floor where the labs and offices were.

Her mother wasn't in the outer office, but the typewriter was still uncovered, which meant she was either taking dictation from Dr. Kiel or in the ladies' room. The door to Dr. Kiel's inner office wasn't shut all the way; Abigail walked over to peer through the crack.

Dr. Dolan was there. He had a nasty look on his face. The vein in Dr. Kiel's forehead was throbbing, always a bad sign.

"I got the library to order copies of the Czech *Journal of Virology and Bacteriology*, and no one named Mirov is on the editorial pages." Dr. Dolan said.

"I didn't know you could read Czech, Patrick," Dr. Kiel said. "I thought you moved your lips when you read English."

Abigail wanted to laugh, it was such a funny insult. Maybe she could use it the next time Susie Campbell taunted her about her parents' divorce.

"Don't try to change the subject, Kiel," Dr. Dolan said. "Are you or aren't you harboring a communist here? What kind of background check did you do on your protégée before you let her into a lab doing sensitive work for the government?"

"I met her husband in Bratislava three years ago," Dr. Kiel said coldly. "We were correspondents until the tanks rolled in last year and the Soviets put him in prison as an enemy of the state. Elena came here in danger of her life."

"Correspondents? Or lovers?" Dr. Dolan sneered.

Abigail put a hand over her mouth. Lovers, like her father and the new Mrs. Sherwood out in California. Was Elena going to turn Mrs. Kiel into a single mom for the five lumpy Kiel children?

"Maybe you grew up in a pigsty," Dr. Kiel said. "But in my family—"

"Your communist family."

"What are you, Dolan? A stooge for HUAC?"

"The FBI has a right to know what you were really doing in Bratislava three years ago. You work with a weapons-grade organism, you speak Russian, you travel—"

"The operative word here being *work*," Dr. Kiel said. "If you worked on *listeria* as energetically as you do on spying on my lab you'd have won the Nobel Prize by now."

Mother came into the outer office just then and dragged Abigail to the hall. "Since when do you eavesdrop, young lady?" she demanded.

"But, Mom, it's about Elena. She's lying all the time, her husband didn't work for that magazine in Czechoslovakia, Dr. Dolan said. He says she's stealing Dr. Kiel away from Mrs. Kiel, like that lady who stole Daddy from us. And Elena just gave Dr. Kiel something funny in the animal room. It looked like blood, but maybe it's a magic potion to make him forget Mrs. Kiel."

Rhonda stared down at her daughter in exasperation, but also in sadness. "Abigail, I'm not sure it's such a good idea for you to come here after school. You hear things that are outside your experience and then you get upset by them. Elena is not going to break up Dr. Kiel's marriage, I promise you. Let's see if I can find someone to stay with you after school, okay?"

"No, Mom, no, I have to come here, I have to look after Miss Bianca." *Stop with the bloody robot already*

Elena came into the hall where they were standing. She'd been in the lab but they hadn't seen her. Rhonda and Abigail both flushed.

"Sorry," Elena murmured. "I making all lives hard, but I not understanding, why is Dr. Dolan not like me?"

Rhonda shook her head. "He's jealous of Dr. Kiel, I think, and so he tries to attack the people who work for Dr. Kiel. Try not to pay attention to him."

"But Dr. Dolan said your husband's name wasn't in—in the Czech something, the magazine," Abigail piped up, to Rhonda's annoyance.

Elena didn't speak for a moment; her face turned white again and she clutched the door jamb for support. "No, he is scientist, he reading articles, deciding is science good or not good? He telling editor, but only editor have name in journal, not husband."

Dr. Dolan stormed out of Dr. Kiel's office, his round cheeks swollen with anger. "You were quite a devoted wife, Elena, if you studied your husband's work so much that you understand rickettsial degradation by lysosomal enzymes," he said sarcastically.

"I married many years, I learning many things," Elena said. "Now I learning how live with husband in prison. I also learn acid rinse glassware, forgive me."

She brushed past Dolan and went down the hall to the autoclave room, where the pressure machine washed glassware at a temperature high enough to kill even the peskiest bacterium.

Over the weekend, Bob and the other graduate students took care of the animals. On Monday, Abigail hurried anxiously back to the lab after school. Bob was in the animal room with a strange man who was wearing a navy suit and a white shirt. None of the scientists ever dressed like that: they were always spilling acids that ate holes in their clothes. Even Mother had to be careful when she went into the lab—once Bob accidentally dripped acid on her leg and her nylons dissolved.

"But she has access to the animals?"

Bob was shifting unhappily from one foot to the other. He didn't see Abigail, but she was sure the man in the suit was talking about her. She crept behind the cages into the alcove where the big sinks stood.

Bob was putting on a mask and gloves to go into the contamination room, but the man in the suit seemed to be afraid of the germs; he said he didn't need to go into the room.

"I just want to know if you keep it secure. There are a lot of bugs in there that could do a lot of damage in the wrong hands."

"You have to have a key to get in here," Bob assured the man, showing him that the door was locked.

When the two men left, Abigail went out to the cages. Miss Bianca's cage was empty. Her heart seemed to stop. She had the same queer empty feeling under her ribcage that she'd felt when Daddy said he was leaving to start a new life in California.

A lot of the cages were empty, Abigail realized, not just Miss Bianca's. Bob and Dr. Kiel had waited until the weekend so they could steal Miss Bianca and give her a shot full of germs while Abigail wasn't there to protect her.

Dr. Kiel had given Mother a set of keys when she started working for him. Abigail went back up the stairs to Dr. Kiel's lab. Mother was working on Dr. Kiel's expense report from his last trip to Washington. Abigail pretended to study Spanish explorers in the 1500s, sitting so quietly that people came and went, including Bob and the man in the suit, without paying attention to her.

Dr. Kiel was in his lab, talking to Elena as they stood over a microscope. The lab was across the hall; Abigail couldn't hear what anyone said, but suddenly Dr. Kiel bellowed "Rhonda!" and Mother hurried over with her shorthand notebook.

As soon as she was gone, Abigail went to the drawer where Mother kept her purse. She found the keys and ran back down to the animal room. She didn't bother about gloves and masks. At any second someone might come in, or Mother would notice her keys were missing.

There were so many keys on the key ring it took five tries before she found the right one. In the contamination room, it didn't take long to find Miss Bianca: slips of paper with the number of the mouse and the date of the injection were attached to each cage door. *139. Miss Bianca*. The poor mouse was huddled in the back of her cage, shivering. Abigail put her in her pocket.

"I'll get you one of those special pills. You'll feel better in a jiffy," Abigail promised her.

When she got back upstairs, Mother and Dr. Kiel were inside his office. He was talking to her in a worried voice. Elena and Bob were in the lab. Abigail got the bottle of pills from the cabinet. The bottle said four a day for ten days for adults, but Miss Bianca was so tiny, maybe one tablet cut into four? Abigail took ten of them and put the bottle away just as Mother came out.

While Mother was preparing dinner, Abigail made a nest for Miss Bianca in a shoebox lined with one of her t-shirts. She took a knife from the drawer in the dining room to poke air holes into the box, then used it to cut the pills into four pieces. They were hard to handle and kept slipping away from the knife. When she finally had them cut up, she couldn't get Miss Bianca to take one. She just lay in the shoebox, not lifting her head.

"You have to take it or you'll die," Abigail told her, but Miss Bianca didn't seem to care.

Abigail finally pried open the mouse's little mouth and shoved the piece of pill in. Miss Bianca gave a sharp squeak, but she swallowed the pill.

"That's a good girl," Abigail said.

Over dinner, Abigail asked her mother who the man in the suit had been. "He was with Bob in the animal room," she said. "Is he spying on the animals?"

Rhonda shook her head. "He's an FBI agent named Mr. Burroughs. Someone sent an anonymous letter telling the FBI to look at Dr. Kiel's lab."

"Because Elena is a communist spy?" Abigail said.

"Don't say things like that, Abigail. Especially not to Agent Burroughs. Elena is not a spy, and if Dr. Dolan would only—" she bit her lip, not wanting to gossip about Dolan with her daughter.

"But she did give Dr. Kiel a potion," Abigail persisted.

"Whatever you saw was none of your business!" Rhonda said. "Clear the table and put the dishes in the machine."

If Mother was angry, she was less likely to notice what Abigail was doing. While Mother watched *It Takes A Thief,* Abigail cleaned up the kitchen, then brought a saucer from her doll's tea set into the kitchen and put some peanut butter in it. Before she went to bed, she stuck some peanut butter onto another piece of the pill and got Miss Bianca to swallow it. When she brushed her teeth, she filled one of her doll's teacups with water. The mouse didn't want to drink, so Abigail brought in a wet washcloth and stuck it in Miss Bianca's mouth.

She quickly shoved the shoebox under her bed when she heard Mother coming down the hall to tuck her in for the night.

Abigail didn't sleep well. She worried what would happen when Dr. Kiel discovered that Miss Bianca was missing from the lab: she should have taken all the mice, she realized. Then the FBI might think it had been a communist, stealing their secret mice. What would happen, too, when Mother realized one of Abigail's t-shirts was missing.

In the morning, she was awake before Mother. She gave Miss Bianca another piece of pill in peanut butter. The mouse was looking better: she took the pill in her little paws and licked the peanut butter from it, then nibbled the tablet. Abigail took her into the bathroom with her and Miss Bianca sipped water from the tap in the sink.

All this was good, but it didn't stop Abigail feeling sick to her stomach when she thought about how angry Dr. Kiel would be. Mother would lose her job; she would never forgive Abigail. She put the mouse on her shoulder and rubbed her face against its soft fur. "Can you help me, Miss Bianca? Can you summon the Prisoner's Aid society now that I've saved your life?"

ugh

The doorbell rang just then, a loud shrill sound that frightened both girl and mouse. Miss Bianca skittered down inside Abigail's pajama top, trying to hide. By the time Abigail was able to extricate the mouse, she was covered in scratches. If Mother saw them—

The doorbell rang again. Mother was getting up. Abigail ran back to her bedroom and put Miss Bianca into the shoebox. She peeped out of her room. Mother was tying a dressing gown around her waist, opening the front door. Dr. Kiel was standing there, the vein in his forehead throbbing.

"Did you do this?" he demanded, shaking a newspaper in Mother's face.

Mother backed up. "Dr. Kiel! What are you—I just got up— Abigail! Put some clothes on."

Abigail had forgotten to button her pajama top. She slipped back into her room, her heart pounding. Dr. Kiel had come to fire Mother. Her teeth were chattering, even though it was a warm fall day.

She flattened herself against the wall and waited for Dr. Kiel to demand that Mother turn her daughter over to the police. Instead, Mother was looking at the newspaper in bewilderment.

" 'Reds in the Lab?' What is this about, Dr. Kiel?"

"You didn't tell the paper that the FBI was in the lab yesterday?" he demanded.

"Of course not. Really, Dr. Kiel, you should know you can trust me."

He slapped the paper against his hand so hard that it sounded like the crack of a ball against a bat. "If Bob Pharris did it—"

"Dr. Kiel, I'm sure none of your students would have called

the newspaper with a report like this. Perhaps—" she hesitated. "I don't like to say this, it's not really my place, but you know Dr. Dolan has been concerned about Elena Mirova."

Dr. Kiel had been looking calmer, but now his jaw clenched again. "Elena is a refugee from communism. She came here because I thought she could be safe here. I will not let her be hounded by a witch hunt."

"The trouble is, we don't know anything about her," Mother said. "She seems to know a great deal about your work, more than seems possible for a dishwasher, even one whose husband was a scientist."

Dr. Kiel snarled. "Patrick Dolan has been sharpening his sword, hoping to stick it into me, since the day he arrived here. He's not concerned about spies, he's studying the best way to make me look bad."

He looked down the hall and seemed to see Abigail for the first time. "Get dressed, Abigail; I'll give you a ride to school."

Dr. Kiel drove a convertible. Susie Campbell would faint with envy when she saw Abigail in the car. When she started to dress, Abigail realized her arms were covered with welts from where Miss Bianca had scratched her. She found a long-sleeved blouse to wear with her red skirt. By the time she had combed her hair and double-checked that Miss Bianca had water, Mother was dressed. Dr. Kiel was calmly drinking a cup of coffee.

Abigail looked at the newspaper.

The FBI paid a surprise visit to the University of Kansas campus yesterday, in response to a report that the Bacteriology Department is harboring Communists among its lab support staff. Several members of the department work on micro-organisms that could be used in germ warfare. The research is supposed to be closely monitored, but recently, there's been a concern that a Soviet agent has infiltrated the department.

The newspaper and the FBI both thought Elena was a spy. Maybe she was, maybe she really had given Dr. Kiel a magic potion that blinded his eyes to who she really was.

"Rhonda, we're going to have every reporter in America calling about this business. Better put your war paint on and prepare to do battle," Dr. Kiel said, getting up from the table. "Come on, Abigail. Get to school. You have to learn as much as you can so that morons like this bozo Burroughs from the FBI can't pull the wool over your eyes."

Abigail spent a very nervous day frightened about what would happen when she got to the lab and Bob Pharris accused her of stealing Miss Bianca. She kept hoping she'd get sick. At recess, she fell down on the playground, but she only skinned her knees; the school nurse wouldn't let her go home for such a trivial accident.

She walked from school to the bacteriology department as slowly as possible. Even so, she arrived too soon. She lingered at the elevator, wondering if she should just go to Dr. Kiel and confess. Bob Pharris stuck his head out of the lab.

"Oh, it's you, short stuff. We've been under siege all day—your mom is answering two phones at once—someone even called from the BBC in London. A guy tried to get into the animal room this morning—I threw him out with my own bare hands and for once Dr. Kiel thinks I'm worth something." He grinned. "Number 19 cannot get a PhD but he has a future as a bouncer."

Abigail tried to smile, but she was afraid his next comment would be that he'd seen that Number 139 was missing and would Abigail hand her over at once.

"Don't worry, Abby, this will blow over," Bob said, going back into the lab.

Dr. Kiel was shouting; his voice was coming up the hall from Dr. Dolan's lab. She crept down the hall and peeked inside. Agent Burroughs, the bozo from the FBI, was there with Dr. Kiel and Dr. Dolan.

"What did you do with her?" Dr. Dolan said. "Give her a ticket back to Russia along with your mouse?"

Abigail's heart thudded painfully.

"The Bureau just wants to talk to her," said Agent Burroughs. "Where did she go?"

"Ask Dolan," Dr. Kiel said. "He's the one who sees Reds under the bed. He probably stabbed her with a pipette and threw her into the Kansas River."

Agent Burroughs said, "If you're hiding a communist, Dr. Kiel, you could be in serious trouble."

"What is this, Joe McCarthy all over again?" Dr. Kiel said. "Guilt by association? Elena Mirova fled Czechoslovakia because her husband was imprisoned. As long as she was in Bratislava, they could torture him with the threat that they could hurt his wife. She was hiding here to protect her husband. Your jackbooted feet have now put her life in danger as well as his."

"There was no Elena Mirova in Czechoslovakia," Burroughs said. "There are no Czech scientists named Mirov or Mirova."

"What? You know the names and locations of everyone in Czechoslovakia, Burroughs?" Dr. Kiel snapped. "How did you get that from the comfort of your armchair in Washington?"

"The head of our Eastern Europe bureau looked into it." Burroughs said. "The Bratislava institute is missing one of their scientists, a biological warfare expert named Magdalena Spirova; she disappeared six weeks ago. Do you know anything about her?"

"I'm not like you, Burroughs, keeping track of everyone behind the Iron Curtain," Dr. Kiel said. "I'm just a simple Kansas researcher, trying to find a cure for Q Fever. If you'd go back to the rat hole you crawled out of, I could get back to work."

"Your dishwasher is gone, whatever her name is, and one of your infected mice is gone," Burroughs said. "I'm betting Mirova-Spirova is taking your germ back to Uncle Ivan and the next thing we know, every soldier we have below the DMZ will be infected with Q Fever."

Abigail's bookbag slipped out of her hand and landed on the floor with an earth-ending noise. The men looked over at her.

Dr. Kiel said, "What's up, Abigail? You think you can be David to all us angry Sauls? Play a little Bach and calm us down?"

Abigail didn't know what he was talking about, just saw that he wasn't angry with her for standing there. "I'm sorry, Dr. Kiel, I was worried about the mouse."

"Abigail is the youngest member of my team," Dr. Kiel told Burroughs. "She looks after our healthy animals."

The FBI man rounded on Abigail, firing questions at her: Had she noticed Elena hanging around the contamination room? How hard was it to get into the room? How often did Abigail feed the mice? When did she notice one of the mice was missing?

"Leave her alone," Dr. Kiel said. "Abigail, take your violin down and play for the mice. We have a lab full of fascists today who could infect you with something worse than Q Fever, namely innuendo and smear tactics."

"You signed a loyalty oath, Dr. Kiel," Agent Burroughs said. "Calling me names makes me wonder whether you really are a loyal American."

Dr. Kiel looked so murderous that Abigail fled down to the animal room with her violin and her bookbag. She felt guilty about taking Miss Bianca, she felt guilty about not rescuing the other mice, she was worried about Miss Bianca alone at home not getting all the pills she needed. She was so miserable that she sat on the floor of the animal room and cried.

Crying wore her out. Her head was aching and she didn't think she had the energy to get to her feet. The floor was cool against her hot head and the smells of the animals and the disinfectants were so familiar that they calmed her down.

A noise at the contamination room door woke her. A strange man, wearing a brown suit that didn't fit him very well, was trying to undo the lock. He must be a reporter trying to sneak into the lab. Abigail sat up. Her head was still aching, but she needed to find Bob.

The man heard her when she got to her feet. He spun around, looking scared, then, when he saw that it was a child, he smiled in a way that frightened Abigail.

"So, Dr. Kiel has little girls working with his animals. Does he give you a key to this room?"

Abigail edged toward the door. "I only feed the healthy mice. You have to see Bob Pharris for the sick mice."

As soon as she'd spoken, Abigail wished she hadn't; what if this man wrote it up in his newspaper and Bob got in trouble?

"There aren't any foreigners working with the animals? Foreign women?"

Even though Abigail was scared that Elena was a spy, she didn't feel right about saying so, especially after hearing Dr. Kiel talking about witch hunts.

"We only have foreign witches in the lab," she said. "They concoct magic potions to make Dr. Kiel fall in love with them."

The man frowned in an angry way, but he decided to laugh instead, showing a gold tooth in the front of his mouth. "You're a little girl with a big imagination, aren't you? Who is this foreign witch?"

Abigail hated being called a little girl. "I don't know. She flew in on her broomstick and didn't tell us her name."

"You're too old for such childish games," the man said, bending over her. "What is her name, and what does she do with the animals?"

"Mamelouk. Her name is Mamelouk."

The man grabbed her arm. "You know that isn't her name."

Bob came into the animal room just then. "Abby—Dr. Kiel said he'd sent you—what the hell are you doing here? I thought I told you this morning that you can't come into the lab without Dr. Kiel's say-so and I know damned well he didn't say so. Get out before I call the cops."

Bob looked almost as fierce as Dr. Kiel. The man in the brown suit let go of Abigail's arm.

He stopped in the doorway and said, "I'm only looking for the foreign woman who's been working here. Magdalena, isn't it?"

Abigail started to say, "No, it's—" but Bob frowned at her and she was quiet.

"I *thought* you knew, little girl. What is it?"

"Mamelouk," Abigail said. "I told you that before."

"So now you know, Buster. Off you go."

Bob walked to the elevator with Abigail and called the car. He stood with a foot in the door until the man got on the elevator. They watched the numbers go down to "1" to make sure he'd ridden all the way to the ground.

"Maybe I should go down and throw him out of the building," Bob said. "He was here when I opened for the day. Elena took one look at him and disappeared, so I don't know if he's someone who's been harassing her at home, or if she's allergic to reporters."

He looked down at Abigail. "You feeling okay, short stuff? You're looking kind of white—all the drama getting to you, huh? Maybe Dr. Kiel will let your mom take you home. She didn't even break for lunch today."

When they got to the office, Bob went in to tell Dr. Kiel about the man in the animal room, but Rhonda took one look at Abigail and hung up the phone mid-sentence.

"Darling, you're burning up," she announced, feeling Abigail's forehead. "I hope you haven't caught Q Fever."

She went into Dr. Kiel's office. He came out to look at Abigail, felt her forehead as Rhonda had, and agreed. "You need her doctor to see her, but I can give you some tetracycline to take home with you."

Rhonda shook her head. "Thank you, Dr. Kiel, but I'd better let the pediatrician prescribe for her."

Mother collected the bookbag and violin where Abigail had dropped them on the floor of the animal room. "I never should have let you work with the animals. I worried all along that it wasn't safe."

In the night, Abigail's fever rose. She was shivering, her joints ached. She knew she had Q Fever, but if she told Mother, Mother wouldn't let her stay with Miss Bianca.

Mother put cold washcloths on her head. While she was out of the room, Abigail crawled under bed and got the mouse. Miss

Bianca needed more of her pills, but Abigail was too sick to feed her. She put Miss Bianca in her pajama pocket and hoped she wouldn't make the mouse sick again.

Mother came and went, Abigail's fever rose, the doorbell rang.

Abigail heard her mother's voice, faintly, as if her mother were at the end of the street, not the end of the hall. "What are you doing here? I thought it would be the doctor! Abigail is very sick."

An even fainter voice answered. "I sorry, Rhonda. Men is watching flat, I not know how I do."

She was a terrible spy; she couldn't speak English well enough to fool anyone. Abigail lay still, although her head ached so badly she wanted to cry. She couldn't sleep or weep; Mother might need her to call the cops.

"You can't stay here!" Mother was saying. "Dr. Kiel—the FBI—"

"Also KGB," Elena said. "They wanting me. They find me now with news story."

"The KGB?"

"Russian secret police. I see man in morning, know he is KGB, wanting me, finding me from news."

"But why do the KGB want you?"

Elena smiled sadly. "I am—oh, what is word? Person against own country."

"Traitor," Rhonda said. "You are a traitor? But—Dr. Kiel said you had to hide from the communists."

"Yes, is true, I hiding. They take my husband, they put him in prison, they torture, but for what? For what he write in books. He write for freedom, for liberty, for those words he is enemy of state. Me, I am scientist, name Magdalena Spirova. I make same disease that Dr. Kiel make. Almost same, small ways different. Russians want my *Rickettsia prowazekii* for germ wars, I make, no problem. Until they put husband in prison."

Rhonda took Elena out of the doorway into the front room. Abigail couldn't hear them. She was freezing now, her teeth chattering, but she slid out of bed and went into the hall, where she could hear Elena.

Elena was saying that when she learned the authorities were torturing her husband, she pretended not to care. She waited until she could take a trip to Yugoslavia. She injected herself with the *Rickettsia* she was working on right before she left Bratislava to go to Sarajevo. In Sarajevo, Elena ran away from the secret police who were watching her and hitchhiked to Vienna. From Vienna, she flew to Canada. In Toronto, she called Dr. Kiel, whom she had met when he came to Bratislava in 1966. He drove up to Toronto and hid her in the backseat of his car to smuggle her to Kansas. He gave her tetracycline tablets, but she didn't take them until she had extracted her infected blood to give to Dr. Kiel. That was the magic potion Abigail had seen in the animal room; that was why her arm was all bruised—it's not easy to take a blood sample from your own veins.

"Now, Dr. Kiel have *Rickettsia prowazekii*, he maybe find vaccine, so biological war not useful."

The words faded in and out. Miss Bianca had a bad Russian germ, now Abigail had it, maybe she would die for thinking Elena-Magdalena was a communist spy.

The front door opened again. Abigail saw the brown suit. "Look out," she tried to say, but her teeth were chattering too hard. No words would come out.

The brown legs came down the hall. "Yes, little girl. You are exactly who I want."

He put an arm around her and dragged her to her feet. Mother had heard the door; she ran into the hall and screamed when she saw the brown suit with Abigail. She rushed toward him but he waved an arm at her and she stopped: he was holding a gun.

He shouted some words in a language that Abigail didn't understand, but Elena-Magdalena came into the hall.

"I am telling Dr. Spirova that I will shoot you and shoot the little girl unless she comes with me now," the man said to Rhonda. His voice was calm, as if he was reading a book out loud.

"Yes, you putting little girl down." Elena's voice sounded as though her mouth were full of chalk. "I go with you. I see, here is end of story."

Elena walked slowly toward him. The man grinned and tightened his grip on Abigail. It took Rhonda and Elena a moment to realize he was going to keep Abigail, perhaps use her as a hostage to get safe passage out of Kansas. Rhonda darted forward but Elena shoved her to the ground and seized the man's arm.

He fired the gun and Elena fell, bleeding, but he had to ease his chokehold on Abigail.

"Miss Bianca, save us!" Abigail screamed. *bathos*

She dropped the mouse down the man's shirtfront. Miss Bianca skittered inside in terror. The man began flailing his arms, slapping at his chest, then his armpits, as the mouse frantically tried to escape. He howled in pain: Miss Bianca had bitten him. He managed to reach inside his shirt for the mouse, but by then, Rhonda had snatched the gun from him. She ran to the front door and started shouting for help. *really ??*

Abigail, her face burning with fever, fought to get the mouse out of his hand. Finally, in despair, she bit his hand. He punched her head, but she was able to catch Miss Bianca as she fell from his open fist. *just like that ?*

The police came. They took away the KGB man. An ambulance came and took Elena to the hospital. The doctor came; Abigail had a high fever, she shouldn't be out of bed, she shouldn't be keeping mice in dirty boxes under her bed, he told Rhonda sternly, but Abigail became hysterical when he tried to take Miss Bianca away, so he merely lectured Rhonda on her poor parenting decisions. He gave Abigail a shot and said she needed to stay in bed, drink lots of juice, and stay away from dirty animals.

The next morning, Dr. Kiel arrived with a large bouquet of flowers for Abigail. Rhonda made Abigail confess everything to Dr. Kiel, how she had stolen Miss Bianca, how she had stolen tetracycline out of his office. She was afraid he would be furious, but the vein in his forehead didn't move. Instead, he smiled, his brown eyes soft and even rather loving.

"You cured the mouse with quarters of tetracycline tablets dipped in peanut butter, hmm?" he asked to see the pieces Abigail had cut up. "I think we're going to have to promote you from feeding animals to being a full-fledged member of the research team."

A few months later, Dr. Dolan left Kansas to teach in Oklahoma. Later still, Bob did get his PhD. He was a good and kind teacher, even if he never had much success as a researcher. Magdalena recovered from her bullet wound and was given a job at the National Institutes of Health in Washington, where she worked until the fall of the Iron Curtain meant her husband could be released from prison.

Miss Bianca stayed with Abigail, living to the ripe old age of three. Although Rhonda continued to work for Dr. Kiel, she wouldn't let Abigail back in the animal lab. Even so, Abigail grew up to be a doctor working for Physicians for Social Responsibility, trying to put an end to torture. As for the five lumpy Kiel children, one of them grew up to write about a Chicago private eye named V. I. Warshawski.

Absolutely dreadful Shameful performance by a "best-selling" writer [sic]

THE ESSENCE OF SMALL PEOPLE

BY GARY ALEXANDER

Ho Chi Minh City, Socialist Republic of Vietnam, is home now, but my first conscious sensation was of our village in the Mekong River Delta, not far from Can Tho. The sweet stink of night soil. Mist drifting off the paddy in the morning. Utter silence but for birdsong.

The first memory that burned into my brain was me clinging to my mother's legs, pressing with all my might. I was the second youngest of four. My baby brother was in her arms. We were standing in shade cast by an enormous American officer, an unjolly green giant. He reeked of butter and gunpowder. He had more hair on his arms than on his head.

My mother chanted over and over, "Me no VC. Me no VC. GI number one. GI number one."

That was her only English, and she was trembling so hard I could barely hang on. My father was nowhere to be seen. Where was Father?

There were helicopters above us, hovering, bristling with guns and rockets, going *whoompa whoompa whoompa*. Dragonflies from hell, hovering above water buffalo that moved as slowly as the village pace.

A South Vietnamese Army interpreter spoke for the American. He said our village was a suspected Vietcong sanctuary.

"Me no VC. GI number one," my mother replied.

The interpreter slapped her face hard. We swayed together, managing to keep our feet. Nobody moved to help her. Not the giant. Not the villagers who stood at our rear.

The American officer said that we harbored the enemy. He said we were communist sympathizers. He said we were ungrateful. He said we did not love our country. He said we were traitors. He said we were lower than snake shit. He said that he was declaring a free fire zone.

He gave us ten minutes to pack up and go. He gave us ten minutes to leave our home of ten centuries. The bones of our ancestors were in this ground. They could not leave. What would become of them? When the village was gone, they would be nowhere.

We carried what we could and watched the helicopters vaporize our village. Huts turned fiery orange and bubbled black into the sky. The smoke seared my nostrils with earth, life, and death. I saw faces in that smoke, old old faces that stretched in sooty agony as they rose and diffused in the air. The faces screamed, and so did I.

My mother took us to Saigon. This was before the city was named in honor of Uncle Ho. Our Saigon was not the leafy and elegant colonial Saigon, the Saigon of fine cafés and shops. Our Saigon was a shantytown, 100,000 of us per square kilometer. We had mud and rotted planks for roads. We had lazy rivers of piss and turds and garbage and typhoid. Our roofs were corrugated tin, hot as a stove. Our walls were printed cardboard, with the logos of Coca-Cola and Sony.

Let me tell you, my mother was a beauty. I remember most her aroma, how her perfume overwhelmed the rancid air. She wore makeup and Suzy Wong skirts. She went out at night.

My father never joined us in the city and she refused to discuss him. Years later, my older sister confided that he was working in the paddy that day and had lifted a hoe out of the muck. A jumpy helicopter gunner saw it as an AK-47. That was what happened to Father and why our village came to be a Vietcong sanctuary.

In 1975, when the North Vietnamese rumbled into Saigon in their tanks, my mother scrubbed the paint from her face and threw away the tight dresses. She wore black silk pajamas when she went out at night. We still had to eat.

By 1980, the Americans and their guns and their dollars were long gone. It was the time of the Carter-Reagan embargoes, when we had less to eat than ever. We moved in with Uncle Thanh, a widower with two grown children, a son and a daughter. He lived in an apartment on Yen Do Street, in a crumbling, stuccoed relic of a building. It had wooden shutters, a ceiling fan, and a water closet. Uncle Thanh and our family shared two rooms.

His house seemed like a French colonial mansion.

Uncle Thanh was stooped. He wore a perpetually bewildered look. He was ancient to me, although he was only in his fifties. Uncle Thanh sold food and drink from a wheeled cart, of which he was immensely proud. It was made of hardwood that he polished with a rag until it shone like glass. On the scrap-metal canopy not a speck of rust was tolerated, even during the monsoons when rain fell as if from a faucet. In joking tones, the Americans had nicknamed his cart and the thousands in Saigon like it as "Howard Johnsons." Uncle Thanh neither knew nor cared what they had meant.

Every predawn, Uncle Thanh went to the Central Market for his merchandise—bread, meat, produce, pastries, whatever was available that he could afford. My mother helped him cook the meats and prepare sandwiches. Later in the day, he cooled bottles of soda and beer in the lower compartment with chunks of ice bought from men who pedaled their wagons in a furious race against the vertical sun.

I begged my mother to let me go with Uncle Thanh. Once a week she relented and permitted me to miss school to do so. I think she was relieved that I became attached to him. I regretted that my mother and I were not closer. It was not for lack of love. It was because she had so many other worries. Of her children, I could fend for myself the best.

Times were difficult, not that they had ever been easy. Food and drink were scarce, customers scarcer. Instead of the Americans and the French who preceded them, we had the Soviets, plump and unhappy, the color of lard. They were known as Americans Without Dollars.

Suddenly Uncle Thanh's business improved. He had new merchandise to sell: American cigarettes. Vietnamese-made Ruby Queens tasted like asphalt and smelled like a car fire. Diplomats, journalists, and Party officials would pay 200 dong for a package of Salems or Winstons. To put that in perspective, my schoolteacher earned 600 dong per month.

Thanks to his newfound income, Uncle Thanh could afford to pay a few dong per week to a policeman for the privilege of moving his cart to an improved location, half a kilometer from home but very near Dong Khoi, the avenue of the rich.

During the French war, this elegant strip of bars, restaurants, and shops was Rue Catinat. In the American War it was Tu Do, or Freedom Street. Now it was Dong Khoi, the Street of Simultaneous Uprisings.

When Uncle Thanh thought my ears were old enough to hear such language, he said that since the flesh and sin trade had not diminished, Dong Khoi was commonly referred to as the Street of Simultaneous Erections. This was an unimaginable street where an evening of nightclub fun would cost six months' wages for a laborer.

Uncle Thanh worked at the side of a theater. The cinema was out of business, doors nailed shut, pictures of Sabu on the marquee plastered over with posters of Ho Chi Minh and Vo Nguyen Giap, commander of the People's Army and hero of Dien Bien Phu. Uncle Thanh could see Dong Khoi and customers could see his cart.

It was there that Comrade Vo approached him.

"Comrade Thanh," he said. "I am happy to meet you. I am pleased you are so prosperous."

Uncle Thanh presented a broad, jittery smile. Vo was our neighborhood political cadre. He was a northerner, dark and rat-faced and not much taller than I. Vo had simply moved into the home of Uncle Thanh's friend, Minh, an office clerk. There had been whispers about Vo, hushed fears. Uncle Thanh avoided the stories as he sought to avoid the cadre himself.

"I came to see you," Vo went on, "for I have wondered why I do not see you at political discussion meetings, either you or your lovely sister."

Uncle Thanh replied so quietly that I could barely hear him. "I humbly think I am too old to be of value."

"You are too old for improvement?" Vo asked incredulously. "You have lived under the puppet boot of imperialist decadence and you cannot change your thinking through education and self-criticism?"

Uncle Thanh lowered his eyes. I had never seen him so frightened and this frightened me.

"How is your son, Pham?"

Uncle Thanh looked up. He maintained his silence. I knew it hurt him to speak of Pham, whose crime had been to rise in the South Vietnamese Army to the rank of captain. After Liberation, he had been sent to the countryside for reeducation. Other officers in Thieu's army had been reeducated and released. Pham had not.

"Your son fought bravely but wrongly, Thanh. Reports indicate that Pham is not receptive to new ideas."

Uncle Thanh shrugged. "We receive few letters from him and I do not understand politics."

"Perhaps I could contact his instructors. I can inquire of his progress and tell them he would be coming home to a family with proper revolutionary attitudes."

Uncle Thanh bowed. "Thank you, Comrade."

"Your daughter, Thi. She concerns me too."

Uncle Thanh's head came up with such a start that I flinched. I didn't know Pham. Thi either. But I did know Thi had been a typist at USMACV Headquarters. She had many American friends, spoke their language, read their books, and wore Western clothing. She had escaped in one of the last helicopters to lift off the roof of the U.S. Embassy in 1975.

Thi married a Vietnamese man in San Francisco. They had good jobs and plenty of money. The Winstons and Salems came from Thi.

"I have little contact with her," Uncle Thanh lied.

Comrade Vo smiled, looking through him. "Yes, of course. It is sad, not your fault that she was contaminated and corrupted. Nonetheless, those of mean spirit could say you are influenced by her cowardice and counterrevolutionary path."

Uncle Thanh said, "I harm nobody."

Vo walked around his cart. He slid open the lowest drawer and took from the compartment two packages of Salem cigarettes. Just helped himself.

"The road to socialist purity is arduous," Vo said. "The end of the journey will not be reached until everyone is equal. In Ho Chi Minh City, this journey has proven especially grueling. Neocolonial reactionaries here cling to their decadent ways.

"However, patriotic sacrifice does not require that pleasure be shunned altogether. Our neighborhood citizens meet to learn the joys of revolutionary socialism after a long day of toil.

"Perhaps if I provide good cigarettes, the people will be more relaxed and amenable to improvement."

Vo frowned at the Salems. "California tax stamps on the seals. Is that not the American province where many of the bad elements resettled?"

Uncle Thanh shrugged again.

Shaking his pinhead, Vo walked off. Was there anything about Uncle Thanh and his family Vo had not learned? When Vo was out of sight, I ran to the corner and peeked. The political cadre had lit up and was puffing like a chimney.

Uncle Thanh and my mother faithfully attended the political

discussion meetings. They would come home, and we children expected if not revolutionary fervor at least a recounting of what they'd been taught. They were as silent as stones. I am certain Vo would regard the silence as a bad attitude, but Vo was not told. Uncle Thanh and my mother were not raising rodent informers.

It did not take me long to figure out why Uncle Thanh was not talking; the meetings made him angry. I made him smile when I asked if Comrade Vo was really giving out cigarettes at the meetings. It was a tight cold smile issued without comment.

Uncle Thanh did not appreciate being told what to do. I loved him for that alone. I almost convinced myself that I had inherited the trait from him. But I could not have, for Uncle Thanh was no more my mother's brother, my biological uncle, than Uncle Ho.

When six share two rooms, you learn the facts of life at an early age. In the nights when the moon was fat, I would peek through a crack in the curtain that separated their bed from ours. I saw my mother straddling Uncle Thanh, rocking and gyrating, biting a knuckle so she did not cry out.

They never explained the complexities of their love to us children. I always believed they were waiting until we were older, though I doubt we would ever have been old enough. The passion of an older gentleman and a lady he met through less than proper circumstances surely embarrassed them.

I developed big eyes and ears. I spied as Uncle Thanh and my mother spoke in tense whispers of things they did not wish us children to hear. Their secret discussions usually concerned Comrade Vo.

"Minh's wife complains about Vo," my mother said. "He pays nothing for his food and expects his laundry done. Quoc the tailor mends trousers for Comrade Vo. He did not pay Quoc. Vo told him that in an ideal proletarian society, there is no money and everybody is equally wealthy. What does that mean? I am afraid that Vo will continue to take cigarettes from you."

Uncle Thanh nodded. "If I refuse, he will have me arrested for being against the Revolution and harboring greedy imperialistic tendencies."

"Does he have any word on Pham?"

"He says I must be patient."

"Is there nothing we can do?"

Uncle Thanh shook his head. "There will always be a Comrade Vo. There have always been governments that tell us what to do and what not to do, to tell us what to believe and how to behave. We are small people who must bend with the slightest breeze. That is the essence of small people. We can no more change these events than we can change the direction of the wind."

My mother said, "It is a foul-smelling wind."

There were other times when the discussions were arguments, a glassy-eyed, stammered code I was unable to break, other than that Uncle Thanh was dead set against and my mother was for, as there was no choice. It was too sad to watch. I could not guess then what this terrible thing was, though there was no question in my mind that Vo was the cause.

I began skipping school regularly, accompanying Uncle Thanh nearly every day. That was our secret from Mother. I promised to do my arithmetic tables and grammar, and he allowed me to pursue my practical education on the street. Comrade Vo was taking from us three packages of cigarettes per day. Mail service was erratic and customs officials at the airport stole with both hands. Shipments from Thi were unpredictable.

I took the packs that Thanh did not sell and Vo did not steal. I made them multiply. I traded them for cans of gasoline, which I traded for bottles of Johnnie Walker Red Label (their USMACV PX seals intact), which I traded for tins of cooking oil (unopened, with the USAID clasped-hands label), which I traded for bags of Thai rice, which I traded for American cigarettes. On an average day I returned with a ratio of two packs to one, partially compensating for Vo's thievery, but that did not make the cadre any easier for us to stomach.

On a soggy night soaked by the spring monsoon, my mother closed the shutters. One by one, our neighbors crept in, creating puddles where they stepped. I was puzzled about who called this dangerous meeting. It may have been my mother. Her eyes had been red throughout the day. It may have been Uncle Thanh. Say anything to him lately and you would have to say it again. It was as if his body was on Earth and his thoughts on Mars.

Actually, any of our guests might have called the meeting. Everybody was angry. Everybody had a story about Vo.

Minh, an office clerk, started. "Comrade Vo has not paid us a single dong. He lives in our home like it is his and he eats more than two men. I hint at payment and he repeats the stupid things he says at his meetings we are afraid not to attend. Revolutionary joy is sufficient payment and that we all must endure sacrifice, and so forth. He endlessly reminds me that I was a clerk for the Thieu puppet regime. Then he says that my cooperative attitude may earn me a promotion at my present job. He threatens and promises in a single breath."

Quoc the tailor said, "I repair his clothes and I am sewing him a new shirt. He said I incompetently repaired a seam. A sleeve tore while he was at an important Party conference. He lost face. The sleeve came apart because Comrade Vo is getting fat from Minh's food. He knows that before Liberation I altered South Vietnamese Army uniforms and sewed insignia on them. He promises to have my cloth ration increased, but as yet he has not."

Phu, a mechanic, was next. "When Saigon was choked with cars and motorbikes, I repaired them and sold parts. Comrade Vo says I was a running-dog lackey of the bourgeois. My customers today are bicyclists. I gave Vo tires for his bicycle. His tires were worn out and he had to get around for vital Party business. He lied. I saw his bicycle. The tires are good. He sold my tires on the black market. You must stand in line for hours to buy a tire at a government store, if they have any in stock at all. Comrade Vo says he knows somebody who can supply me all the tires I want. I have not seen this 'somebody.' "

Lan the barber spoke. Nguyen the fishmonger spoke. Canh, a cyclo driver, spoke. Their stories were different but the same. Comrade Vo had his hair cut free, ate free fish, and rode for free in a pedicab.

"You have the most to lose, Thanh," Quoc said. "Vo has power over your son. Can he really have Pham released from the camp?"

"I have no idea," Uncle Thanh said bitterly.

Minh said angrily, "Having him in my home is unbearable. We must do something!"

"We cannot," Canh answered. "Vo is but a strand of hair on the monster."

"What if we pluck the hair?" said Thanh. "Rip it out by the roots."

"If we remove the hair, it may grow back even coarser. That is stupid talk that will get us jailed or even killed," my mother blurted. "Will somebody please talk to Thanh? He will not listen to me when I tell him that he cannot touch Vo."

The room fell silent. It was then that I *knew* my mother had arranged this gathering. My thoughts were drifting to the incineration of our village and our ancestors. Either my nose filled with the hot stench of smoke my mind generated or with dust. I sneezed.

They dragged me from under the bed where I was hiding. My sandal had gotten hooked around a twine-wrapped cardboard box, and it came out with me. I was chastised by Uncle Thanh for not being elsewhere with the other children and gently cuffed by my mother. Everybody had a good laugh at my expense and the tension diminished.

Then Uncle Thanh undid the twine and lifted the lid. A smile radiated across his face.

"I had forgotten these things Thi did not have room or time to take with her. I could swear I destroyed everything incriminating the day the communists arrived," he said, removing the contents with loving care, one item at a time.

My mother looked at me oddly, then Uncle Thanh, swiveling her head. "What are you two thinking?"

Thanh was smiling, knowing what I was thinking.

Uncle Thanh and I went right to work on our plan. Other major players were Minh and his family, who got Vo out of Minh's house on a pretext. Canh and Phu and Nguyen reported Vo's suspiciously counterrevolutionary behavior to four different revolutionary committees. I was a burglar in reverse, who gave rather than took.

Comrade Vo pleaded his innocence mightily as unhearing soldiers prodded him out of Minh's house with bayonets. Other soldiers examined the treasonous material as they loaded Vo into a truck.

These were the belongings abandoned by Thi, the belongings found in Vo's room:

1. A novel, *The Quiet American*, by Graham Greene.
2. A schoolbook devoted to the study of democracy.
3. A volume of English-language poetry.
4. The framed photograph of a former American leader.
5. A *Time* magazine.

Uncle Thanh and I had carefully cut out the picture of the former American leader from the *Time* magazine cover and mounted it in a nice brass and glass frame. It was the American president who was forced to leave office—in the manner that the last Americans had fled Saigon in 1975 from the U.S. Embassy rooftop—by helicopter.

One week to the day after Comrade Vo was taken away, Pham came through our door. He was thin and his clothes were ragged, but to Uncle Thanh he had never looked better.

Following hugs and kisses and tears and laughter, Pham said, "It is a miracle. A man from this neighborhood arrived, a counterrevolutionary traitor of the worst sort. We were ordered to avoid him whenever possible. He was put to work in the paddies, doing the hardest stoop labor at the hottest time of the day. The camp commissar came to me and said the traitor had denounced me. Therefore I must have chosen the correct path. My rehabilitation was complete. Can anybody explain what this means?"

"We changed the direction of the wind," Uncle Thanh said.

CHECKPOINT CHARLIE

BY ALAN COOK

YOU ARE LEAVING THE AMERICAN SECTOR.
The chilling words were printed in black block letters on the large white board in four languages: English, Russian, French, and German. It should have also said, "Abandon hope all ye who enter here," Dante's inscription at the entrance to Hell. For Hell was on the other side of Checkpoint Charlie.

It was a gray Hell, with gray buildings and gray people, made grayer on this particular day by the gray clouds and the rain that fell steadily on everything. Gerhard Johnson had a knot in his stomach the size of a basketball as he showed his papers to the American soldier at the newly painted white guardhouse made of wood that looked out of place in this drab setting, partly because he was afraid the East German guards wouldn't let him through—and partly because he was afraid they would. But he had to go.

He was waved through the American side as he had expected he would be. He approached two of the East German guards with their long coats and unsmiling faces in his borrowed Volkswagen Beetle. One stood in front of the car and motioned for him to stop. The other came to his window and took his passport and visa.

Gerhard tried to look casual, as if he did this every day. However, he hadn't crossed the border for over a year. That was before the Wall was erected, when people could pass freely back and forth between East and West Berlin, before the brain drain of highly educated and skilled East German citizens fleeing to the West had become a rushing torrent, threatening to bring the economy to a standstill.

The guard stared at the visa for a long time, as if trying to find something wrong with it. It was perfectly legal. Gerhard had jumped through the proper hoops to get it. As an American citizen he carried a U.S. passport, and the visa had been issued to him by the American Embassy in West Germany.

The guard spoke to him in broken English. "Why you go to GDR?"

Gerhard phrased his answer carefully. "My aunt lives here. I'm going to visit her." He wasn't about to mention that he had a one-year-old daughter here. That would surely raise a red flag.

"How long you stay?"

"Two days."

It was all the time he had. He was in West Berlin on business for the import-export firm he was employed by, and the vacation days had been reluctantly granted him by his boss to use before he had to fly back to the U.S. Business was booming in Europe, and the company needed his ability to speak German.

The guard suddenly spoke to him in German. "Do you know what we do to spies in the GDR?"

In spite of having prepared for this situation, it was all Gerhard could do not to react to the statement. If they found out he spoke perfect German they would never let him in. Young foreigners passing through Checkpoint Charlie were automatically suspected of being spies. He looked at the guard in what he hoped was a questioning and uncomprehending manner.

The guard watched him. Had an eye blink given him away? His heart pounded and the basketball in his stomach grew larger. The guard looked at the other guard, who motioned for him to pop the hood, which was the storage space for the rear-engine VW. It contained only a small suitcase with clothes and toilet articles, unlocked. Meanwhile, the first guard peered into the backseat, which was empty.

The guard with the suitcase took his time looking through it, while Gerhard hoped the sweat he was feeling on his back wouldn't show up on his face. He had considered leaving a pile of West German marks on top of his clothes. They were valuable in the black market here. But he didn't know how they would react. A bribe could be taken as an indication of guilt, and he wasn't guilty of anything.

The guard closed the hood and walked up to the window. The two men spoke together in German about whether Gerhard was a spy, keeping an eye on him for a reaction.

Perhaps his German first name had spooked them. His mother had been German. He had learned to speak German before he learned English. His father had met her when he was studying in Germany, and he had asked her to marry him. She was part of an upper-class family in the city of Halle, where she grew up, and she never adjusted to life in the U.S., being married to an itinerant minister who had trouble holding a job. She took Gerhard and his sister back to Germany several times when they were young, and on one occasion his father had to come over and take them home.

She became a psychological cripple during the war, partly because her brother was in the German army. He died somewhere in the frozen expanses of Russia. She died soon after, perhaps from a broken heart.

The guards stopped talking, and one of them handed Gerhard his passport and visa. He motioned for Gerhard to go on. It happened so quickly he was unprepared, and it took him a few seconds for his shaking hand to get the car into first gear. Then he had to be careful not to drive away too fast. He looked in his rearview mirror and saw they had turned their attention to the next car.

The autobahn to Halle was bumpy and potholed. It even had a speed limit, although few cars observed it, at the risk of their tires and suspensions. Gerhard did, however. The VW wasn't his, and he wanted to return it in one piece.

He had no trouble negotiating the streets of Halle with its churches and double spires, and a population approaching 300,000. He had been here many times while stationed in West Berlin with the military, first to visit his aunt, who was his mother's sister, and then to visit Inga, a friend of Brunhild with whom he fell in love.

Inga. Gerhard had beseeched her to come and live with him in West Berlin until his tour of duty was over, and then to go to America with him. She said she would, but she had to take care of her grandmother, who was in failing health. His pleas had increased in volume when he found out she was pregnant. Still she put it off. Then the East Germans closed the border in 1961 to prevent the exodus of the freedom-loving, and it was too late. Inga was trapped inside.

Inga had died giving birth to Monika. Her doctor had been smart enough to head for the West while the border was open, leaving Inga in the bumbling hands of the mediocre medical people who remained. If she had made her escape while it was still possible, she would be alive today. Gerhard could never stop thinking about the "what ifs." He reflected that he had good reason to equate East Germany with Hell.

Gerhard looked at the blue-eyed, blond miniature of Inga, and couldn't believe he had helped to create this beautiful creature who was smiling at him and picking his teeth with her fingers. He had left Germany before she was born, his army career ended, not being able to bear living fairly close to Inga but not with her. There was no way he would ever live in East Germany.

He had seen pictures of Monika, but the reality was far superior. If only he could take her with him. That was impossible. The tales of people who had tried to escape and failed were legend. Peter Fechter, a teenager who had made the attempt, had been shot and left to bleed to death beside the Wall in full view of both sides, while the soldiers of neither side went to help him.

Some people had escaped successfully, going over, under, or through the Wall, but how did you get a baby out?

"Would you like to give Monika her bottle?"

Gerhard's Aunt Brunhild handed the bottle to Gerhard. Monika's eyes lit up when she saw it; she snatched it out of his hands and started noisily sucking on it.

Gerhard laughed. "Greedy little thing, isn't she?"

"Well, hungry, anyway. She likes you. I knew she would. She likes Gunter too."

Gunter was the man who took care of the apartment building where Brunhild lived.

They spoke in German. Brunhild's knowledge of English was infinitesimal. She was too thin, had graying hair pulled back severely into a bun, and wore a patterned housedress that was clean but repaired in several places where seams had ripped. The thread used for the repairs didn't match the color of the original.

When Inga died, Brunhild agreed to take Monika. Inga's parents had died in the war, and she had no other close relatives. It was a brave thing for Brunhild to do, and Gerhard honored her for it. She didn't have much to live on, and raising a child was a strain for her. Of course, everyone was under a strain in this land of shortages and make-dos, planned by a tone-deaf government. Brunhild worked as a nurse at a retirement home. Fortunately, her job allowed her to keep Monika with her while she was at work.

In contrast to the dingy hallways of the building, her small apartment was clean. The lace curtains on the windows were white. She was doing the best she could. If Monika had to stay in East Germany, Gerhard was glad Brunhild was here to take care of her. Maybe someday the Wall would come down and Gerhard could take Monika to the U.S. But there was no sign that this was going to happen any time soon.

Brunhild and Gerhard chatted about all the things Monika had accomplished recently. She was crawling and even trying to walk. They kept in touch by mail, but international delivery was slow, and by the time Gerhard received a letter noting Monika's accomplishments it was out of date. How much better it would be if he could watch her progress on a daily basis.

During a pause in the conversation, Brunhild said, "I want you to meet Gunter."

She looked at her ornate grandfather's clock, a family heirloom. The hands showed 5 p.m.

"At this time every day he is in his apartment listening to the world news. Let's go and see if he's there. And by the way, you can trust him."

An interesting statement, Gerhard reflected as he stood, holding Monika, who was still working on her bottle. Implying there were people one couldn't trust. He wasn't surprised that in a totalitarian state amateur spies would be everywhere, thirsting for tidbits of information about their neighbors they could pass along to petty functionaries.

The other thing occurring to Gerhard was that Brunhild must know this Gunter quite well if she knew what he was doing at a certain hour. Well, she had never married, and she deserved some male companionship, if that's what was happening here. Gunter's apartment was on the ground floor, two floors below Brunhild's. As they walked down the staircase past peeling paint, Gerhard saw a stout woman laboriously climbing the stairs from below. She didn't appear to be undernourished.

Gerhard shot a quick glance at Brunhild, and watched a look of distaste highlight her face for a moment, but then it was gone and she smiled at the lady and spoke in a musical voice.

"How are you today, Mrs. Rudolphi?"

The lady stopped, huffing and puffing, and looked at the three of them, and then shrewdly appraised Gerhard. "So, you are the child's father?"

There was no point in Gerhard pretending he didn't know

German, so he responded in that language, as politely as he could. "Yes I am. My name is Gerhard. I'm pleased to meet you, Mrs. Rudolphi."

"So you are Brunhild's nephew. I haven't seen you here before. Where do you live?"

He was trying to decide whether to tell the truth when Brunhild said, "He lives in the United States. He was in the army, stationed in West Berlin. He met Inga when he came to visit me—"

"And you thought nothing about getting the poor girl pregnant and then deserting her. A girl who is now dead. You Americans are all alike. I am surprised you bothered to come back and see your child."

Gerhard didn't know how to respond to this. He didn't want to start an argument. If he said he'd loved Inga she wouldn't believe him. He was still dithering when Brunhild spoke for him.

"He came to Germany on a business trip. He was able to take two days from his busy schedule to visit Monika and me. I am very happy to see him, and Monika is too."

Monika had finished her bottle and was busily examining Gerhard's teeth again. Mrs. Rudolphi frowned. Gerhard suspected she went through life with a chip on her shoulder.

She said, "So you are leaving the day after tomorrow?"

Gerhard nodded and was about to say something when Mrs. Rudolphi started up the stairs. She shouldered her way between Gerhard and Brunhild, and continued on in a determined manner.

"It was nice to see you," Brunhild called after her, but she didn't respond.

When Gerhard and Brunhild came out of the stairway on the ground floor, Brunhild half-whispered to him. "I don't like her."

It wasn't hard to understand why. They walked along a dimly lit corridor. Brunhild knocked on a door near the front of the building. Gerhard thought he heard a voice coming from the other side. The voice stopped.

After perhaps thirty seconds a loud voice just on the other side of the door asked who was there. Brunhild identified herself. After a few clicks the door opened. A stocky man with a big head appeared in the doorway. He must be in his fifties. When he saw Brunhild he smiled.

"Come in. Come in."

Gerhard followed Brunhild into the apartment, which was small, like Brunhild's, but not as well decorated. It did have a bookcase against one wall packed with old and nicely bound books.

Brunhild said, "Gunter, this is my nephew, Gerhard."

Gerhard moved Monika to his left arm and he and Gunter shook hands with a European handshake, one quick up and down, and said how do you do. Gunter backed up a step and looked at Gerhard, just as Mrs. Rudolphi had.

"Brunhild has told me about you. She said you are a fine young man. You will make a good father for Monika."

"Unfortunately, I am only here for two days."

"Yes."

Gunter paused and looked at Brunhild. Some kind of communication seemed to pass between them.

"Please sit down."

Gerhard sat on a small sofa covered with a threadbare blanket. Brunhild sat beside him. Gunter went into the next room and brought back a wooden chair that he set down facing them. He sat in it.

"When you knocked on the door I was listening to the news of the world beyond the GDR. Not everybody would be happy I can do that."

He looked at Gerhard again.

"A person has to be very careful living here. This is not a good place to raise a child." He looked at Monika who was babbling and apparently practicing her talking. "A child should be free to discover the world without always looking over her shoulder."

Gunter paused again, and Gerhard felt he should say something.

"I agree. I would love to take Monika to live in America."

Gunter nodded as if that was what he wanted to hear. "Brunhild told me you were driving a Volkswagen. Is that correct?'

"Yes. It belongs to a friend of mine in West Berlin."

Brunhild had asked him in her last letter if he could drive to East Berlin in a Volkswagen. He considered that a curious request at the time, especially the way she'd phrased it, as if it would be a fun thing to do. She had to be careful what she wrote; there was no guarantee someone wasn't reading her mail. Gerhard figured she might have a hidden meaning. Fortunately, a friend from his army days who lived in West Berlin was willing to lend him his VW.

Gunter said, "I am a mechanic. I have worked on a lot on Volkswagens. I would like to look at your car."

That was a strange request too. After all, one Volkswagen was like another. That was part of their beauty.

"It's parked outside on the street."

"There is a garage under the building that only I have the key for. We will drive your car in there."

Apparently, judging from the equipment in the garage, Gunter was running a business here, fixing cars. A Trabant, a car of questionable quality produced in East Germany, was sitting with its engine exposed, but there was room for the Volkswagen beside it. After Gerhard drove it in, Gunter closed the door and said he wanted to check something. He used his tools to take out the bottom of the luggage storage area under the hood, while Gerhard watched and wondered what was going on. Brunhild stood by and smiled at him. She had said to trust Gunter.

Gunter motioned for Gerhard to look at the space below the luggage area. Gerhard handed Monika to Brunhild and peered down at the wires, axle, steering mechanism—the stuff that made up a car. Cars to him were a method of getting from point A to point B. This was a jumble. He looked at Gunter, puzzled.

Gunter nodded as he made some measurements using his hands. He glanced at Gerhard. "If we are careful we can build a small compartment that would fit under the place where you put your suitcase. It could not be spotted."

Gerhard still wasn't comprehending. "It would be very small. What would be the purpose of it? ... Oh."

Gerhard suddenly understood. He looked around, half expecting to see an eavesdropper. Then he looked at Brunhild.

She said, "This is no place to raise a child. Monika should grow up in America."

"But ... Would she fit in there? She would suffocate."

Gunter shook his head. "That is the beauty of the Volkswagen. All the exhaust goes out the rear. She is small enough to fit. Now is the time to do this before she grows. If she is wrapped in a warm blanket, she will be fine."

"What if she cried?"

Brunhild said, "I will give you a pill that will make her sleep right through it."

Shivers went up and down Gerhard's spine. Could he really get Monika out of here? What if he failed? What would happen to him? He didn't want to rot in an East German prison. What would happen to *her*? What would happen to Brunhild and Gunter? Surely it would be traced back to them. But Brunhild and Gunter had planned this together. They trusted him to do it. Even in the military, he had never done anything this dangerous. Or, if it worked, glorious. He looked from one of them to another.

"It is a tremendous risk for you."

Brunhild spoke for both of them. "This is our way of protesting against an intolerable government. We have to do something. We have to draw a line somewhere."

Gunter nodded.

Still, Gerhard couldn't commit. It was too much to swallow.

"It's not my car."

Gunter said, "The alterations will not damage the car in any way. The compartment will be easy to remove."

"I have to think about it."

"There isn't time to think about it. I have to start working on it now."

Gerhard liked to weigh his decisions carefully. But for once in his life he had to act decisively. This might be the most important thing he ever did.

"If you think this can be done, I'm willing to do it. How do we start?"

Gunter nodded approvingly. "I will build the box."

"Can I help you?"

"No. Better I do it myself. I know how. I am also a carpenter. I will start right now."

Brunhild said, "First, come and join us for dinner. You need to have something to eat."

Gunter shook his head. "It is better if we are not seen so much together. I am fine. Go now and let me get started."

Gerhard took out his wallet. "I will pay you for materials."

He took out a wad of East German bills he'd bought on the black market in West Berlin, and handed them to Gunter. It was money he'd been planning to give Brunhild. Gunter shook his head initially, but Gerhard persisted. Cash was difficult to come by here. Gunter reluctantly took the money.

Brunhild said, "Come, Gerhard. We will go and eat while Gunter gets to work."

Gerhard hardly slept that night. He tossed and turned and decided not to undertake this perilous task half a dozen times. He almost got up and sought out Gunter, who he was sure was working through the night. Then he thought of Brunhild's words: "We have to draw a line somewhere."

Gerhard could see the dinginess and the poverty and the pollution on an intellectual level, he could see the fear in people's eyes and watch them looking over their shoulders, he could read about the million ridiculous regulations that made doing anything productive next to impossible, but he didn't feel the weight of the tyranny on his back like Brunhild and Gunter did every day. He could leave. If they were willing to take the risk, he should be willing also. He slept a little just before dawn.

Gerhard awoke to the sun streaming in the window of the living room, where he'd slept on the sofa. It was too short for his long legs, and he was stiff and sore when he stood up. Perhaps the sunshine was a good omen. He noticed a piece of paper on the floor near the outside door. He picked it up and unfolded it. For a few seconds he couldn't read the scrawled German handwriting. Then he realized it was from Gunter. By concentrating he could make out the words: "Come to the garage door at 11. Knock three times." It was signed with a G.

Gerhard heard Monika fussing and Brunhild talking to her. That's right, babies were early risers. Brunhild wasn't working today. He went into the small kitchen, said good morning, and showed Brunhild the note. She read it quickly.

"I knew he could do it. He is a good man. I am making your breakfast. If you like you can feed Monika."

Monika was sitting in a highchair. When she saw Gerhard she banged her hands on the tray of the chair and burbled to him in her own language. Brunhild showed him how to spoon up the pureed food of indeterminate color and put it into her mouth. He tried it.

"She's spitting out half of it."

"Welcome to the world of babies."

But Monika was so good-natured about it that Gerhard couldn't help but love her. How could he even think of leaving her behind?

There was a loud knocking. Gerhard almost jumped out of his skin.

"Who do you think that is?"

Brunhild frowned. "I don't know. It's early, even for Mrs. Rudolphi. She sometimes 'checks up' on me, to see, I'm sure, if I'm hewing to the Party line. I will go. You stay here with Monika. I don't want her exposed to negative vibrations any more than necessary."

The Communist Party line, Gerhard assumed. Brunhild went to the door. Gerhard could tell it was Mrs. Rudolphi, speaking in a loud voice. Brunhild evidently wouldn't let her in, and he couldn't make out what the woman was saying. In a couple of minutes Brunhild managed to close the door on her and return to the kitchen. Her fists were clenched and she sounded angry when she spoke after Gerhard asked her what Mrs. Rudolphi wanted.

"She didn't want anything—that is, anything that made sense. She told me about a stinking new rule concerning trash collection. She was just spying on us, trying to figure out whether we are planning some kind of funny business, but I am convinced she doesn't have any idea what we are really doing. She asked again whether you were leaving tomorrow."

"It sounds like she's a suspicious type."

"Suspicion is her middle name."

They went out for a walk at ten. Brunhild had an ancient baby carriage. Gerhard carried it down the stairs while Brunhild carried Monika. They didn't meet Mrs. Rudolphi, which Gerhard was thankful for. He still felt jumpy. They blended in with the people on the street, most of whom didn't look at them or anybody else, and took a circular route that led them to the garage door just at eleven. The garage was facing a side street, and Gerhard didn't see anybody when he knocked three times on the door.

Within a minute the door was opened and a smiling Gunter swept them inside and quickly closed it again. He led them to the front of the Volkswagen.

"It is finished."

Gerhard and Brunhild looked at each other. That's what they had hoped he'd say. Gunter showed them what he'd done. It was ingenious. The compartment was a wooden box with a cover and a latch that would keep Monika from falling out but which could easily be opened. It had air holes and Gunter had padded it with pieces from an old quilt. He showed Gerhard how to put the floor of the luggage compartment in place over it using only a screw-driver. Nobody would guess that a baby was hidden underneath.

They congratulated Gunter on his workmanship, and Gerhard thanked him effusively. Gunter smiled and asked Gerhard when he wanted to leave.

Brunhild said, "Right now."

"So soon?"

"Mrs. Rudolphi is getting too suspicious. If Gerhard leaves now he should be able to get over the border in three hours, four at the most. It will still be daylight and the driving will be easy. I will stay away from here for that time so Mrs. Rudolphi can't find out that Monika is missing."

A thought suddenly occurred to Gerhard. "When she does find out you will be arrested."

Brunhild shrugged. "I can put her off for a while, and then I will make up a story that she is with her mother's relatives. If that doesn't work, so be it. But Monika will be safe."

Brunhild was willing to trade what was left of her freedom for that of Monika. Gerhard could only bow to her devotion and do his part. He took his small suitcase out of the baby carriage, where they had hidden it under a blanket. In addition to Gerhard's clothes, it contained some food and a blanket for Monika, and a couple of diapers. Of course, anything that belonged to her would have to be jettisoned before he crossed the border.

Brunhild hugged and kissed Monika and placed her on the front seat of the VW. It didn't have seatbelts, and Gerhard would have to protect her in case of any sudden stops. Brunhild had told him of a secluded park he could drive to just before he entered Berlin. There he would sedate Monika and place her in the compartment.

Gerhard hugged Brunhild and shook Gunter's hand, thanking him again. Gerhard got in the car, ready to drive out when Gunter opened the door. The door screeched upward on rollers that needed oiling. Gerhard was just about to start the engine when he saw a shadow and then a man in the doorway. The man, who was taller than Gunter, although not as broad, took in the scene inside the garage with a glance.

Gunter spoke to him. "Klaus, what are you doing here?"

"Mrs. Rudolphi told me she suspected all of you were up to no good. It appears that she was right. The police will be very interested to hear what's going on."

Klaus started to walk away. Gunter grabbed him by the arm and yanked him into the garage before he could resist. They started wrestling. Brunhild reacted just as fast, pulling down the garage door with one big screech. Gerhard opened the door of the VW and jumped out. It appeared Klaus was getting the better of the fight. He was trying to knock Gunter down.

Gerhard grabbed the first tool he saw, a wrench, and looked for an opening. The two men were weaving back and forth, and Gerhard was afraid he would hit Gunter. He maneuvered around until he was behind Klaus. He managed to grab the big man by the shoulder with one hand, but got elbowed in the jaw. In spite of the pain he was able to trip Klaus, who stumbled backward, separating him from Gunter.

Gerhard hit Klaus on the head with the wrench before he could recover his balance. He fell on the floor in a heap. His eyes were open and he started to get up. Gerhard hit him on the head again, as hard as he could. This time his eyes were closed. Blood oozed through his hair. Gerhard stood staring at him. He'd never attacked anyone with intent to injure, even when he was in the military.

"You must leave *now*." Brunhild's voice was urgent.

When Gerhard continued to stand in shock, Gunter said, "Please go. We will take care of Klaus."

"He may be hurt."

"We will deal with him." Gunter grabbed Gerhard's arm. "You must get Monika away from here."

"Mrs. Rudolphi—"

Brunhild said, "I'll handle Mrs. Rudolphi. Do this for Monika."

Gerhard overcame his paralysis and climbed into the car. Monika was crying. Brunhild opened the passenger-side door and gave her a quick kiss. Then she closed the door quickly. Gunter threw a tarpaulin over Klaus and opened the garage door.

Gerhard drove out of the garage and turned onto the street, holding Monika with his right hand so she wouldn't be thrown around by the g-force. He shifted gears and accelerated, wanting to get out of Halle as fast as possible.

Gerhard was off the autobahn, looking for the park Brunhild had told him about where he could put Monika in the compartment without being seen. At least now he didn't have to watch for the police in his rearview mirror, something he'd done ever since he left Halle. It was highly unlikely he would be spotted here on the narrow streets, even if the alarm had been sounded. He hoped Brunhild and Gunter had Klaus and Mrs. Rudolphi under control. He couldn't take time to worry what would happen to them when the authorities found out what they'd done.

He realized he'd passed this corner before. He was going in a circle. He didn't know where the park was, so he'd have to improvise. He had to get through Checkpoint Charlie as fast as possible, before the guards were told to look for a black Volkswagen.

Monika had long since stopped crying and seemed to enjoy the ride on the bumpy autobahn. She bounced up and down and sucked on a pacifier. She was a happy baby, which made her more lovable.

However, Gerhard was growing more and more frustrated at not finding the park. He turned onto a street that was being repaired. It dead-ended at a barrier a hundred yards from the intersection. No workmen were in sight. He stopped the car. This would have to do. He rolled down his window to get some air, because there was an odor in the car.

He said a few reassuring words to Monika and opened a jar of baby food. He took a pill from the small container Brunhild had given him and inserted it in a spoonful of the pureed food. Brunhild had assured him it was her favorite. He took her pacifier and offered her the food. She opened her mouth but promptly spit it out.

Gerhard was aghast. If she wasn't asleep there was no way he could get her through Checkpoint Charlie in the compartment. She would be bawling her head off. He had one more pill. Apparently, Brunhild had prepared for this contingency. But if this one didn't work they were lost. He almost yelled at Monika, but stopped himself when he realized that would make matters worse. She didn't understand that their futures depended on her taking the pill.

"Your baby is very cute."

Gerhard's head hit the roof of the car. He had been too preoccupied with Monika to see the older woman approaching. She was dressed in black and looked like a grandmother type. He got his heart under control and said, "Thank you."

"Are you trying to feed her?"

"Yes, but she spit it out."

"I raised six children. Perhaps I can help."

Gerhard rejected that idea. He had to get rid of her. But he couldn't just knock her unconscious and leave her here. Maybe he'd let her help for a minute. He thanked her again and got out of the car. He lifted Monika out and handed her to the woman who sat on a stone wall. She started spooning the mixture into Monika's mouth, and she was swallowing it.

The pill. Gerhard said, "Monika has a cough and I'm supposed to give her this pill with her food."

The woman nodded. "It's a small pill but it would be better if it were ground up."

She laid a cloth, which Gerhard used to wipe Monika's face, on a rock, and placed the pill on it, mashing it with the spoon. Then she combined it with a spoonful of food and fed it to Monika, who immediately swallowed it. Success. Gerhard could never have done it as well.

He appreciated her help, but now she had to go. However, she continued to feed Monika the rest of the jar. He wanted to yank it out of her hand. Time was wasting.

She said, "She needs to have her diaper changed."

Gerhard realized he couldn't place Monika in the compartment with a dirty diaper. The guards would smell it, as he had for some time now. He produced a diaper. He hadn't been looking forward to changing her. To his amazement, the woman deftly changed Monika's diaper, wiped her off, and handed him the dirty one, folded up.

"Thank you again. You've been very helpful."

Monika was getting sleepy. The pill was working. It was obvious she wasn't going to eat any more. Gerhard put her back in the car. He thanked the woman once again. She said what a beautiful baby Monika was and wished them well. He drove away.

Gerhard still had to hide Monika. He went around the corner and stopped again. This time he looked around more carefully. He didn't see anybody. He wrapped her in the blanket. She was asleep. He opened the hood. The floor of the luggage area was loose. He lifted it out and placed Monika in Gunter's box underneath it. She just fit. He touched her innocent cheek and then closed the box and replaced and screwed in the luggage floor. He took his suitcase from the backseat and laid it in the storage space.

Nobody could tell there was anybody underneath. Gerhard hoped she didn't wake up in there. He threw out everything that belonged to a baby, including the diaper. The smell lingered in the car. He opened the windows and drove away, hoping it would dissipate.

As Gerhard approached Checkpoint Charlie from the East German side he noticed the spot on the seat where Monika had spit up the food. Damn. He pulled a handkerchief out of his pocket and frantically rubbed at it. It was hardly noticeable—he hoped. He surreptitiously threw the handkerchief out the window as he came up to the guard shack.

He felt strangely calm as he handed his passport and visa to the guard. He'd done everything he could. He and Monika were in the hands of the fates.

"Step out of the car, please."

The guard spoke excellent English. Gerhard hoped this was a good sign. He popped the hood, as requested, confident the guard wouldn't find anything amiss. The young man opened the suitcase and gave the contents a cursory look. He also took a peek through the rear window at the backseat, which was empty. Gerhard thought he was going to let him go.

The guard stood in front of Gerhard and looked at him. "How did you get the bruise on your jaw?"

His jaw? Where Klaus had struck him with his elbow. Gerhard had been ignoring the pain and the fact that he couldn't open his mouth very wide.

"I-I..." *Stop stuttering.* "I was helping my aunt move some furniture down the stairs. I slipped and lost my hold on a dresser and it hit me in the jaw."

It sounded hokey. Would the guard buy it? He examined Gerhard's jaw from close range. Another guard came up to them and spoke in German to the first guard, telling him there was a phone call for him. Guard number two stood with Gerhard, while number one went into the guard shack. He didn't speak, and Gerhard didn't either.

Several minutes dragged by. When would Monika wake up? Was the phone call about a certain black VW they should be on the lookout for? Gerhard felt like jumping into the car and making a run for it, but the barrier in front of him had been strengthened since somebody had crashed through it, and after a couple of convertibles had managed to slip under it and escape. There was no way...

Finally, the first guard came ambling back, taking his sweet time. He had a serious look on his face. When he got close he spoke to the other guard in German. He said they had to go to a meeting. He waved Gerhard through. The barrier was raised.

Gerhard saw the path to freedom open. He jumped into the car and drove away before they could change their minds.

The letter was from a cousin of Gerhard who lived in East Germany. They had never met. He hurriedly opened it. He'd had no news of Brunhild in the two months since he'd brought Monika across the border and taken her to Buffalo, New York, USA. Brunhild hadn't answered his letters.

The letter was written in German. It said Brunhild had asked him to write. She was in an East German prison. So was Gunter. Klaus had died from his wounds. Brunhild wanted Gerhard to write to the cousin and tell how he and Monika were doing. The cousin would pass what he said on to her.

Gerhard sat for a long time, trying to absorb this information. It made him very sad. The plight of Brunhild and Gunter, not the fact he'd killed a man. There had been no other way. He called to Monika who was walking, or rather running, now, and asked her to come to him. She raced over and he sat her on his lap. She looked solemnly into his eyes, as if she knew this was serious. She was very intuitive that way. Gerhard was sure she was wise beyond her age. He showed her the letter.

"Honey, this letter has news from where you used to live. The people there who love you are in trouble. They gave up what freedom they had for us, and we will always be grateful for what they've done. We are going to help them all we can."

Monika smiled and seemed to nod. Then she slid off his lap and went racing after the kitten he'd brought home for her.

CRUSH DEPTH

BY BRENDAN DUBOIS

In the New Hampshire island community of New Castle, Michael Smith spent nearly a month conducting a surveillance op at an oceanfront park called the Great Island Common. It was small, with a tennis court, gazebo, and picnic tables and benches scattered on a scraggly green lawn. There was a stone jetty sticking out into the near channel, from where ships entered and left nearby Portsmouth Harbor to the Atlantic, and across the narrow channel was the state of Maine.

Near the stone jetty was a good downstream view of the Portsmouth Naval Shipyard, which had been building warships for the U.S. Navy since 1800.

It was now one year after the hammer-and-sickle flag had been lowered for the last time over the Kremlin, and sitting in a rented blue Toyota Camry, Michael thought it ironic that his work and the work of so many others was still going on, despite peace supposedly breaking out everywhere.

Cold war or hot war, there was always plenty of work to be done.

He stepped out of the Camry, started walking to the jetty. It was a warm day in late May. As with every previous Wednesday, his target was sitting on a park bench adjacent to the jetty, an old man with a metal cane balanced between his legs, looking down the channel, at the buildings, cranes, and docks of the shipyard.

Michael walked around the park bench, sat down, and gave a quick glance to the man about three feet away. He seemed to be in his late sixties, wearing a white cloth jacket, partially zipped up, a blue baseball cap with the U.S. Navy emblem in the center, dungarees, and black sneakers that had Velcro snaps. He looked over at Michael, then turned his gaze back to the shipyard. His nose was large with big pores, his face leathery and worn, white eyebrows about the size of butterfly wings.

"Nice day, hunh?" Michael asked.

There was a pause, and the man said, "Yeah, it sure is."

"But I bet fog can come up pretty quick, thicken everything up."

"You know it."

He sat still for a bit longer, not wanting to spook the man. All those months and weeks, poring over the dusty files, then making last-minute travel arrangements, and then ending up here. He had finally made it, and he didn't want to screw it up.

"Think the shipyard will close now that the Cold War is over?"

A shrug. "Beats the hell out of me. But somethin' that's been there for nearly two hundred years, it'd be a shame if it did."

"I agree," Michael said, putting warmth into his voice. "I mean, there are good-paying jobs over there, with a lot of skilled guys and gals, am I right? Working with their hands, having special knowledge, knowing how to build subs."

"Nobody over there builds subs," the man declared.

"Excuse me? It's a shipyard, isn't it?"

"Yeah, but all they do now is overhaul work or the occasional repair. Last time they built a sub over there was the *USS Sand Lance*. Launched in 1969."

"What kind of submarine was that?"

"An attack sub. Sturgeon class. Used to hunt Russian missile subs."

"Oh. I see."

Michael kept quiet, folded his hands in his lap. Looked back at the older man, said, "Excuse me for asking this, I get the feeling you worked there. True?"

A long pause. The old man rubbed his hands along the top of the cane. "Yeah. I did. A pipefitter."

Michael felt a small sense of triumph, tried to keep it out of his voice and expression. "You miss it much?"

"The people," he said quickly. "You miss the guys you worked with. A real smart bunch of fellas, could pretty much figure out how to solve any kind of problem, no matter what it was, no matter if it was welding or electronics or anything else. Most of the times, we finished the boat under budget and on schedule. A great, great group of guys."

"Sounds like it," Michael said. "Makes it good to know that the place might still stay open."

The old man kept quiet, and Michael stayed with him a few minutes longer, and said, "Lots of birds out there today."

"Mostly seagulls," the old man said. "More like rats with wings, not sure if they count as birds."

Michael spoke softly, "Ever see a kingfisher?"

"No," he said sharply. "Never have."

He let it be, and after a couple of minutes, got up and said, "So long," and walked back to his rental car.

Good ops were like going fishing. Getting that initial nibble was always encouraging.

Exactly a week later, Michael came back to the Great Island Common and once again found the old man sitting at the same park bench, like he had never left. He sat down and, when the guy glanced over, he put his hand out and said, "Michael."

The man took his hand. It was wrinkled and rough. "Gus."

"Glad to meet you, Gus."

They sat there for a while, and Gus said, "What brings you here?"

Michael sighed. "You know, Gus, sometimes I just need to sit outside and get some fresh air. I work in an office, and after a while, you realize, man, is this it? Is this your life? Moving papers from one pile to another. Going to lots of meetings. Moving some more papers around. Kissing the right ass. Go home, go to bed, get up and do it again. Blah."

Gus stayed quiet, and Michael said, "I know this sounds crazy, but sometimes, you know, sometimes I envy guys like you. Worked with your hands. Building things. Fixing things. Could point to something at the end of the day. Could say, hey, that submarine that just got launched, I had a part of it."

"Well . . . it wasn't easy work."

"Oh, man, yeah, I know that. I know it was hard, dirty, and maybe dangerous. But I'm sure you felt like you were helping out the country, you know? Helping defend it by making the Navy strong. Me? End of the day, end of the month, what do I get? I moved some papers around and made some middle-managers happy. So what?"

Gus cackled. "Yeah, managers. Always tend to get in the way, don't they. Paperwork, procedures, forms, checklists. If it wasn't for completed and filled-out forms, made you think whether they could breathe or not."

"They sure do. Man, so how many submarines did you work on?

Gus shrugged. "Lose track. Eighteen, maybe nineteen."

"So you were there when they went from diesel subs to nuclear?"

"That I was."

"Bet security was really something, back then."

Gus didn't say anything, and Michael wondered if he had gone too far. He waited, wondering what to say next.

The old man finally said, "Yeah, it was something. Had to be. We were in the middle of the Cold War, weren't we?"

Michael nodded. "People tend to forget that, don't they."

"Well, I don't."

"Neither do I."

Michael got up. "Tell me, you ever see a kingfisher fly by here?"

A firm shake of the head. "Nope, can't say I ever have."

The third time, the third Wednesday, it was overcast, with a steady breeze coming off the Atlantic, whitecaps making the channel choppy. But Gus was still sitting there, watching the gray buildings and cranes of the shipyard.

Michael sat down, having brought two cups of coffee with him. He passed one over to Gus, who took it and murmured, "Thanks, appreciate it."

"Not a problem."

A cargo ship was making its way slowly out of the harbor, being escorted by two tugboats. Michael watched it slide by and said, "Your dad work at the shipyard?"

"No, he was Navy."

"Oh. During World War II?"

"Kinda. He joined up just as it was wrapping up. Went to Japan as part of the occupation forces, right after the war ended."

"I see."

"Me, I got into the shipyard in the late 1940s, just as a kid."

"Bet your dad was proud of you."

"Yeah, you'd think," he said, speaking slowly. "But my dad... something in the Navy really changed him. Didn't talk about his duty for a long, long while. But he hated the fact I had anything to do with the military."

"Really? That sounds strange. I mean, you read all those books and see those television shows about 'The Greatest Generation.' It seems most guys were proud of their service. My grandfather, he fought the Nazis during the war. Said it was the best four years of his life. Nothing ever came close to giving him that close bond, of being part of something larger than him, fighting against fascism."

Gus took a noisy slurp from his coffee. "Yeah, but the war was pretty much over when my Dad joined up. No more fighting. Just occupation duty."

"Something must have happened to him, back then."

Michael sensed he had gone too far. It seemed Gus was staring at something very, very far away. His orders told him to do something, but he couldn't do it. Not yet.

He didn't know enough.

Finally Gus said, "This coffee is good. Thanks."

Michael sat with him for a little while, and then got up.

"Later, Gus."

The old man didn't say anything else.

In nearby Portsmouth, the Federal Building in the center of the city contained offices from the Post Office to the Armed Forces Recruiting Centers to the local office of the FBI. Michael parked nearby and walked for a bit, arriving to a room where he made a phone call to give an update.

His supervisor was brusque with him. "You should be wrapped up by now."

"I'm close. I don't want to spook him."

"This whole thing can blow up in our faces unless it gets handled right. So handle it."

"I will."

"You better."

And then his supervisor hung up.

The Wednesday next, Michael came to the park bench where Gus sat. In addition to bringing two coffees, he had brought a bag of doughnuts. Gus grunted when he saw the doughnuts. "My doc says I shouldn't eat this stuff."

"What do you say?"

"My doc should mind his own goddamn business."

The doughnuts came from a local bakery—not a chain shop—and they were tasty and filling as both men ate. Michael took in the channel, the bridges, the brick buildings of Portsmouth and the cranes and gray buildings of the shipyard.

"You said you worked on a lot of subs over the years," Michael said. "Any one of them stand out in your mind?"

Gus took a good mouthful of coffee. "No, not really."

"You sure? I think there'd be at least one that stuck out in your mind."

"Nope."

"Not even the *USS Thresher*? You sure?"

Gus paused, one hand holding the coffee cup, the other holding a half-eaten cruller. He coughed. "What do you know about the *Thresher*?"

"It was built over there, at the shipyard. Came back for some overhaul work in 1963. Went out one morning for a test dive, off Cape Cod. Something went wrong. It sank, all hands lost. One hundred twenty-nine crew members and civilians. Hell of a thing."

Gus lowered his shaking hands, let the coffee and the cruller fall to the ground. Michael said, "Went out on April 10, 1963. A Wednesday. Funny thing, hunh? Every time I come by here and you're sitting here, looking at the shipyard, it's a Wednesday. What a coincidence, eh?"

"Sure," Gus said. "A coincidence."

"Never a Tuesday. Or Friday. Or Saturday. Only Wednesday. Why's that?"

No answer.

Michael pressed on. "Tell me. You ever see an osprey out there?"

Gus turned to him, tears in his eyes. "Who the hell are you, anyway?"

Michael took out a leather wallet with a badge and identification, and held it up for Gus to look at. Gus looked at it, sighed, and sat back against the park bench. He seemed to age ten years from one heartbeat to another.

"How did you do it, Gus?" Michael asked. "How did you sink the *Thresher*?"

Michael waited, thinking he now knew this guy pretty well, and Gus didn't disappoint. He didn't argue, he didn't deny, he didn't try to get up and run away.

Gus just seemed to hold on to his cane tighter. "Wasn't meant to sink the damn thing. That wasn't the plan."

"What was the plan, then?"

Gus said, "You told me the code words, in the right sequence. You should have figured it out, you and the rest of the FBI."

Michael put his identification away. "You'd be surprised at what we don't know."

"You seem to know enough."

"No, not really," Michael said. "Biggest thing for me is, why didn't you bail out once I said 'kingfisher' that first day?"

Gus turned to him. "What? Where would I go? Shuffle off to my assisted living facility? Empty out my savings account and take a Greyhound to Florida? I didn't know who the hell you were...so I waited you out. Maybe you were a birdwatcher. Maybe not. I'm old enough now I don't really give a shit."

Michael knew his supervisor wanted him to wrap this up as quickly as possible, but he was patient. Maybe too patient, but he wanted to make sure he had this one settled before proceeding.

"So what can you tell me, Gus," he said. "How did it start?"

"You go first," he said. "How the hell did you find out about me, after all these years?"

Michael laughed. "What, you haven't been watching the news last year? In case you didn't get the memo, the goddamn Evil Empire has collapsed. The Communist Party's practically outlawed, peace is breaking out, and the Soviet Union is no more."

"So?"

"So when you got a country that's collapsing, the Army's being called out to harvest potatoes, and their Navy is sinking dockside, then everything's for sale. Everything! So we've had guys going over to Moscow and other places, passing out the Benjamins, getting files and dossiers. You wouldn't believe the old secrets that are being given up. We had special squads lined up to get answers to old puzzles...I put in for the JFK squad but I was assigned to naval matters. And we found your dossier...or parts of it. Got your real name, your job at the shipyard, and your assignment for the *Thresher.*"

Gus sighed. "I never got contacted after she sank. I thought I was in the clear. Thought they had forgotten me."

Michael said, "Then you don't know how they operated. The KGB had a seal they'd put on some of their more sensitive documents. *Dolzhny khranit'sya vechno.* Know what that means? It means 'to be kept forever.' That's how their minds worked. They thought they'd be victorious against us evil capitalists, so nothing would ever be burned or shredded. Their proud files would be kept forever."

Gus looked out at the channel, and Michael said, "But something was missing in your dossier, Gus. It's why you did it. Was it money? Were you that hard-pressed for money back in the 1960s? Was it gambling? Medical bills for a family member? Did the KGB promise you a ton of cash?"

"No, nothing like that. It wasn't for the money. Didn't get paid a dime."

"So why did you do it, Gus? Why did you betray your country? Sabotage a nuclear powered submarine, the first in its class, a sabotage that would sink it and kill everyone on board?"

The old man sighed. "You wouldn't believe me."

"Try me. C'mon, let me in on it."

"Why?" he shot back. "To make it look good on your arrest report?"

Michael laughed. "Who said anything about arresting you?"

* * *

Gus turned, shocked. "Then why the hell are you here? What's going on?"

"Didn't you hear what I said earlier? We're getting old questions answered, puzzles figured out. I didn't say anything about arrests, now, did I?"

The old man slowly turned his head back. Michael said, "Look, the JFK squad. They're compartmentalized, so I don't know what they're learning. But suppose they did find something out. Like somebody in the KGB ordered the hit on JFK. Or if Oswald really was sent over as a patsy to cover up for whoever really did it. What, you think the President will hold a news conference and say nearly thirty years of official history and explanations were wrong? And by the way, let's start a new Cold War to get revenge for what the Reds did back in '63?"

There was a siren sounding out by the shipyard, which eventually drifted silent. "Same thing with you, Gus. We just want to know how it happened, why it happened, and fill in those gaps in the secret histories. And once those gaps are filled, I'll leave you here and I promise, you'll never be disturbed, ever again."

Gus seemed to ponder that for a few moments, and his voice quiet, he said, "My dad."

"What about him?"

"It was his fault."

Michael was so glad he hadn't rushed things, because this was certainly a new bit of information. Gus sighed. "My dad. A gentle guy. Never once hit me. Was a deacon at our local Congregational Church. Didn't really belong in the military at all. But they were calling everybody up back then, teenagers, fathers, guys with glasses or some medical conditions. A cousin of his, he said to my dad Curt, 'Curt, join the Navy. You'll sleep at night in a bunk, you won't be in a muddy trench, you'll have food three times a day, no cold rations, and no marching.' So he joined the Navy."

Gus rotated his cane twice. "Since he was so smart and quiet, he was assigned to some military evaluation team. He and a bunch of others were sent to Hiroshima and Nagasaki, to check on what the places were like after the atomic bombs had been dropped a month earlier. It was horrifying, he told me later, all these blasted buildings, the trees burnt stumps, and wounded and burnt people still stumbling around."

"That's war," Mike said.

Gus shook his head. "No, dad thought differently. It may have ended the war, but it also opened the door to something much more terrifying, something that could go beyond destroying cities to destroying whole peoples, whole countries, even the damn planet itself. He said every day and night there just sickened him. He said going across the Pacific, not once did he get seasick, but he was nauseous and threw up a lot when he was in Japan."

"That's why he didn't want you to join the military, do anything that had to do with defense."

"You got it. He only talked about it as he got older, and then, in 1962, he got lung cancer. Pretty funny, since he never smoked a cigarette or a cigar in his life. His doc told me privately that he probably kicked up a lot of radioactive dust when he was going through Nagasaki and Hiroshima, kept on breathing it in. By then I was married, to a nice girl called Sylvia, had two young boys, and I was working at the shipyard, making good money. My dad died that October. I was his only son, so I went through some of his things. That's when I found the movies."

"What kind of movies?"

"My dad, he told me that he and the others, they were forbidden to take photos at Hiroshima and Nagasaki unless it was part of their official work. But somehow dad got a hold of an eight-millimeter movie camera, even used color film. I think he went out on his own and took these short little movies. No sound, of course, but you didn't need sound to figure out was going on."

Michael let him sit quiet for a few moments, wind coming off the water flapping the loose ends of Gus's white zippered jacket. "What were the movies like?"

A heavy, drawn-out sigh, like the man next to him had just finished climbing an impossibly high peak. "I still dream about them, even though it's been thirty years. I found a projector and one night, hung up a white bedsheet in the basement and played them. The city...you see those TV reports, about a tornado hitting some city out in the Midwest? Just piles of rubble and debris. That's what it was like. Except the rubble had burned...there were places along the sides of bridges or cement walls, where the flash from the bomb had burned in shadows...and the last bit of the third film, it was the people. Still walking around in shock at what happened to them. One plane, one bomb...there were these two little boys...about the age of my own little fellas...looking at the camera, looking at my dad...they were barefoot...the clothes they was wearing was filthy...and each was holding a little ball of rice. And you could tell they was brothers, they looked the same... even were hurt the same..."

The old man's voice dribbled off. Michael cleared his throat. "How were they injured?"

"The right side of their faces. Scabbed and crisscrossed with burns. Like they were walking down a street, going in the same direction, when the bomb hit and burned them. Oh, I know they were the Japs, the enemy, and lots said they deserved it for what they did at Pearl Harbor and Bataan. But when I saw it, in 1962, the war had been over a long time. All I saw was two kids, all I saw was my two boys, burned and barefoot in the wreckage of their city."

Michael saw the emotion in the man's face, the tears coming up in his eyes, and it came to him. "You said your father died in

October, 1962. That's when the Cuban Missile Crisis was, when we almost got into World War III with the Russians. You put the two together, didn't you."

"Yeah," he said, his voice hoarse. "Had Sylvia take the two boys up to a hunting camp of ours, over in Maine, with food and supplies. She said it wasn't right to take 'em out of school, but I also said it wouldn't be right to have 'em vaporized or burned in Portsmouth, because, by God, we were a goddamn target for the Russians. That and the SAC base over in Newington. And a couple of times, I went out drinking in some of the bars in Portsmouth, and got drunk and pissed off, and said that damn fool Kennedy was going to kill us all, burn us and flatten our cities, because he got kicked in the nuts at the Bay of Pigs fiasco in Cuba, and had to prove he was a real man to his bootlegger daddy."

"Somebody heard you, then."

Gus said, "Oh yeah. Somebody heard something, who passed it on to somebody else, and one day, a guy came by and bought me some drinks. Said he was in the government, trying to work for peace, but he and the others were fighting against the hawks that were controlling JFK. He spun a good yarn, the bastard, and said if I was truly for peace, I could help things out. And I said, how? And he said, well, the *Thresher*'s being overhauled. If the overhaul took longer and longer, if problems cropped up, if things were delayed, that would help him and the others. Put things over budget. He and the others could help JFK rein in the defense department, help him work for peace with the Russians."

"And what did you say?"

"I told 'em to go to hell...but he was sly, he was wicked sly. Wouldn't take no for an answer. Showed me his ID, said he worked for the Department of Defense. Even took me to his office, just outside of the SAC base."

"All faked, wasn't it?"

"'Course it was," Gus said. "But I was too young, too dumb.

He kept on going back to Hiroshima and Nagasaki. He said look, back then, the Japs were our mortal enemies. Now we're best buds. We're buying their radios and soon we'll be buying their televisions. That's what happens in wartime. Your enemies become your friends. Look at Germany and us. So who can say what we and the Russians will be like, ten or twenty years down the line? But the big difference was the bomb. The next war would be fought with the bomb, and this guy—Chandler was his supposed name—said, you know what Einstein said, about World War IV?"

Michael said, "Beats the hell out of me."

"Einstein said, the fourth world war would be fought with sticks and stones. That's what he said." Another long sigh. "I watched those movies again, and I made up my mind. I told Chandler I'd help, but only to delay things. Not to hurt anybody. He gave me a tiny black box to smuggle in during my next work shift, which is what I did. A week later, the *Thresher* went out on a shakedown cruise, never came back..."

Gus coughed. Tears were rolling down his cheeks. "What was worse...I mean, the whole thing was bad. All those poor sailors, all those poor families. But what made it worse was knowing there were seventeen civilians on board, guys from my own shipyard, guys from companies like Raytheon. You think, hey, the military, they sign up to put their lives on the line, that's the risk. But these civilian techs...I'm sure they thought it was a thrill, to go along on this test dive, to make sure things worked...and then they sure didn't. Can you imagine that, you're a civilian, having a blast on this top-secret sub, thinking about bragging to your coworkers when you got back, figuring out what you could tell your wife and kids...and then alarms. Navy crewmen running around. Shouting. The sub tilting its nose up, sinking by the stern...knowing in your bones that the water wasn't shallow enough to hit bottom... only knowing you were going to be dead within seconds..."

Michael said, "The Naval inquiry said it appeared a pipe broke, releasing water that shorted out instrument panels, that led to the reactor shutdown...and they couldn't keep her up, until she went to crush depth..."

Gus said, "Sure it said that. What else would they say? Sabotage, at one of the most secure shipyards in the country? I went to that office building, where Chandler was supposedly hanging out. Empty. It was all a front. I thought about killing myself, about giving myself up...and I thought about Sylvia and the boys. And I tried to forget it...tried really hard."

"But here you are, Gus. Every Wednesday."

Gus leaned forward on his cane. "I lost Sylvia two years ago. Both boys are married, doing fine. One in Oregon, the other in California. I'm here by myself, and every Wednesday, I come here. Pray for them. Pay tribute to them. And ask forgiveness."

"For how much longer?"

Gus shrugged his shoulders. "Until the very end, I guess."

"Does anybody else know about you and...what happened?"

"God, not at all."

"Do you have any evidence from what happened back then?"

"Like what?" Gus shot back. "Pictures of me with that damn Russian? Written instructions on how to sabotage a submarine?"

Michael slowly nodded, and then Gus turned to him, eyes still watery, face flushed. "But what about me now, eh? You and the FBI, you know it all. What now?"

"What I promised," Michael said, taking out a little notepad and a ballpoint pen, which he clicked open. "That you'll never be bothered, ever again."

And with one practiced motion, he took the pen and jabbed it into the base of Gus's neck.

Gus looked stunned. He coughed, gurgled. A few words were whispered, the last one much quieter than the first.

Michael checked the old man's neck for a pulse.

Nothing.

He put the pen and notebook away, and walked back to his rental car.

* * *

Two days later, after his supervisor held a debriefing, his boss shook his head and said, "Misha, you need to know your history better."

"How's that?"

"Two things," the stern man said. "First, you told the American that your grandfather had fought the Germans for four years. Maybe your grandfather did, but the first time Americans fought Germans were in North Africa in 1942. That would be three years, not four. And you said your grandfather was proud to fight fascism. That's crap. Americans fought the Krauts, the Germans, the Nazis. They weren't fighting fascism."

He just shrugged. "Got the job done, though, didn't I?"

"But you didn't have to be sloppy. We can't afford to be sloppy. The damn Americans are in a loving and forgiving mood. Ready to lend us billions so long as we play nice. If they find out some of our old secrets—like that damn attack submarine and how we sank it—they won't be in a loving and forgiving mood. Got it?"

He sighed. "Heard you twice the first time."

The supervisor walked past the office window, which offered a good view of the Kremlin's buildings and where the white-blue-red flag of the new Russian Federation flew.

"Misha, you're a romantic at heart. You probably write poetry in your spare time...but stay focused. Now. What did you leave out of your official report?"

"What makes you think I left anything out?"

"Previous experience from that Swedish school teacher who helped Olof Palme's assassin escape."

He crossed his legs, shook his head, still in disbelief. "The shipyard worker, he managed to say something as he was dying."

"What did he say, 'go to hell, you bastard'?"

Another shake of the head. "No. He said thank you. That's what he said. Thank you. Like he was thanking me for ending his life, ending the guilt. Can you believe that?"

His supervisor sat down heavily in his chair. "When it comes to

Americans, I can believe almost anything. They spend fifty years threatening to burn us off the map, and now they offer us loan credits and McDonald's. What can you say about a foe like that?"

"Makes you wonder who really won the Cold War."

His supervisor, a sharp-eyed man named Vladimir, said, "Who says it's over?"

THE HONEY TRAP

BY BEV VINCENT

Anna picked up her latest target at Tempelhof shortly after he arrived on a Pan Am flight from New York via Frankfurt. She recognized him from the photographs in the dossier tucked under her arm. Though her handlers were in charge of surveillance, she always wanted to see her men in the wild, to get a sense of what they were like when they didn't know they were being observed. This helped her decide how to approach them. If she was too aggressive with a man who was awkward around porters and taxi drivers, she'd scare him off. If she was too timid with a blustery man who acted like he owned the world, he'd soon tire of her.

Her target was Donald Weatherly. He was fifty-nine and looked it. He wore a brown suit with the jacket unbuttoned, and no hat. He was taller than average, but only slightly. His hair, disheveled after his long journey, was receding at the front and thinning at the back. He wore black-rimmed glasses and had a small, neat mustache that was tinged with grey, as were his eyebrows. He was paunchy but not fat. All in all, not the sort of man a young woman would have typically afforded a second glance.

Older men, she had learned, were particularly susceptible to seduction because they thought their chances of ever being with a sexy young woman again were nearing an end. Not *at* an end, but almost. This gave them an unusual sense of optimism. They flirted with waitresses, cashiers, stewardesses, and any other pretty women with whom they came into contact. Deep down, they probably knew that their only real option was to pay for it—which many of them did—but they never stopped hoping. Eighty-year-old men flirted with her. She admired their spirit, in part because it made her job easier.

She made sure Weatherly didn't notice her. With over three million people in Berlin, it would have been too much of a coincidence to run into a person twice in different parts of the city. It happened, of course, but she couldn't risk making him suspicious. Weatherly wasn't a spy, but he had a degree from Princeton, so he wasn't stupid. Gullible, perhaps. Susceptible, she hoped. But not stupid.

She stood at a pay phone, smoking a cigarette and holding an imaginary conversation with the dial tone. A kerchief was wrapped around her dark hair, and she wore oversized sunglasses with tortoiseshell frames. She never looked directly at Weatherly after he came through the security checkpoint with his luggage—one suitcase and a briefcase—but she never let him escape her field of vision either.

A porter approached, offering to take his bags. Weatherly handed over the suitcase, but maintained his grip on the briefcase. He pointed toward the exit and let the porter take the lead. A professional exchange, she decided. The man was neither timid nor brash. Average.

As they drew near, she turned aside and crushed her cigarette out in an ashtray. Weatherly looked straight ahead, displaying little interest in his fellow travelers, the airport shops, or overhead signs. Neither did he look over his shoulder. Civil engineers weren't typical targets of espionage.

The porter led him through the exit doors to a queue of taxis. She followed at a discreet distance. The porter signaled a taxi driver and loaded the suitcase into the trunk. When Weatherly tipped the porter, the man smiled and touched the brim of his hat, an effusive display of emotion for a German, she thought. Weatherly got into the back of the cab. A few seconds later, the car merged with traffic and headed toward the nearby city center. She returned to the terminal and made a phone call.

Anna watched him discreetly for three days, getting a sense of his rhythms and schedule. Each morning, Weatherly entered the breakfast room in the hotel at seven thirty on the dot, poured a cup of coffee—black—and had a light meal of bread and jam, with a slice of cheese on the side. After eating, he returned to his room for fifteen minutes, then descended to the lobby, picked up an English-language newspaper from the front desk, and asked the doorman to hail a cab.

She didn't know where he went during the daytime—that was for others to worry about. He returned to the hotel at around six, and had a couple of drinks in the hotel bar before going out to a nearby restaurant for supper. After that, he retired to his room.

Starting with the second morning, she allowed Weatherly to notice her. She was a legitimate guest of the establishment, after all, and she wanted him to gradually become aware of her presence. That day she arranged to leave the breakfast room just as he was arriving. As they passed each other, she glanced at him with casual interest. The next morning she greeted him with a dazzling smile as he was leaving, as if she remembered him from before. She wanted him to carry the moment in the back of his mind as he went about his business that day.

She spent the morning window-shopping on Kurfürstendamm and had lunch at an outdoor café, treating herself to a glass of Riesling. She could see, in the distance, the Mercedes Benz star logo atop the new Europa-Center near the entrance to the zoo and, closer and to the left, the damaged spire of the Gedächtniskirche, which the locals called "the hollow tooth." A new bell tower had been constructed beside it a few years ago, but the ruins remained as a war memorial, even though the city seemed determined to ignore the past.

Anna had been in West Berlin for nearly a year, after proving herself in Moscow. She started out in Volgograd—known as Stalingrad until Khrushchev's de-Stalinization program—entertaining her father's guests. At first that simply meant bringing them drinks or plates of cold meats and cheeses. One of his colleagues noticed the way men responded to her and asked if she would be willing to go farther. When she did, and was amply rewarded for her efforts, she knew she'd found her calling. Between assignments, she became fluent in German and English, thereby increasing her value.

She enjoyed the relative freedom of living in this surreal city, where people partied as if there would be no tomorrow. Everything was bigger, brighter, and louder here, as if to deny the blighted scar that ran through it and the darkness beyond. The city was an island of Western culture a hundred and fifty kilometers from the rest of the free world. One of her targets had likened it to a head walking around without a body. Every way out of West Berlin passed through hostile territory. Every flight—French, British, and American airlines only; German airlines weren't allowed access to their own former capital—used one of three narrow corridors through East German airspace.

City walls were usually built to keep the outsiders at bay, but here the outsiders had built a wall to prevent their people from getting into the city. The mayor called it the Wall of Shame, but people in the GDR referred to it as the Antifaschistischer Schutzwall. She had gone to see it once, but had never returned. The guard towers and barbed wire reminded her that she wasn't truly free here, and the closer she got to the eastern zone, the stronger the feeling that everyone was up to something. Spies spying on other spies who were in turn spying on them. This city was the Cold War in a test tube, and she had a part to play in it.

She finished her wine, paid her bill and returned to the hotel.

Back in her room, she took a long, hot bath—a decadent Western luxury she had grown to appreciate—anointing herself with oils and perfumes. This evening, she would meet Weatherly officially for the first time, in the hotel bar. Generally, one encounter was all it took, but he wasn't scheduled to leave for several days, so she had time to defeat any defenses he might attempt to erect. In the end, they always surrendered. She hadn't failed yet.

She waited in the lobby, pretending to be engaged in a conversation on a pay phone near the bar. This time, she wasn't trying to hide from Weatherly—she wanted him to notice her. When she saw him approaching, she dropped her lipstick. The clatter of the metallic tube on the marble floor made him look in her direction. She picked up the lipstick and continued her make-believe conversation.

Anna waited until he found a place at the bar and ordered his first drink—two was his limit—before strolling in. American jazz played in the background. She was prepared to wait if there were no open stools around him, but she was in luck. While seating herself, she got close enough to allow her perfume to waft toward him. She ordered an old fashioned in her best Hochdeutsch, which was tinged with a Bavarian accent, not that she'd expect an American to notice.

In the mirror behind the bar, she saw Weatherly glance at her. She touched her hair and smoothed the bodice of her dress. Then she fumbled in her purse, pulled out a packet of cigarettes, shook one out and placed it between her lips. She continued rifling through the bag, pulling out cosmetics, change, and other bric-a-brac, strewing them on the bar in front of her. After several seconds she sighed, tossed everything back into the purse and pushed it away. She made a show of looking around before touching him gently on the arm. She smiled when he looked at her. *"Entschuldigen Sie, bitte. Haben Sie Feuer?"* she asked.

Weatherly furrowed his brow. "I, uh, sorry?"

"Oh, English," she said. "Never mind. I was asking for a light, but I'm sure the bartender—"

"No, wait. Allow me," he said. He plunged his hands into his pants pocket and came up with a gold lighter.

She inhaled deeply after he flicked the flame to life, and blew a cloud of smoke into the already hazy room. "Thank you," she said, and turned back to her drink. She took a sip, staring straight ahead, waiting for him to make the next move.

"I saw tanks in the streets today," he said.

Sometimes men wanted to talk about the strangest things, she mused. She took a measured sip from her glass and said, "This is your first time in Berlin?"

He signaled for his second martini. "No," he said. "It's been a number of years, though."

"Business?" she asked. "Let me guess. You're a banker."

He laughed. "No!"

"Politician?"

He shook his head. "You'll never get it. I'm an engineer. Don Weatherly."

She shook his extended hand and crinkled her nose, a gesture that most men seemed to find appealing. "You drive trains? Into the Bahnhof Zoo?"

Another chuckle. "Not that kind of engineer. I design things before they're built."

"Like a—how do they say? *Architekt*?"

"Sort of," he said. "They design buildings. I do just about everything else. Bridges, roads, things like that. Pretty boring stuff."

She nodded. Weatherly's dossier said that he worked for a company in Virginia. According to her handlers, he was in Berlin overseeing the construction of tunnels under the wall to assist defectors and to create spy stations. "Have you seen our great architectural achievement?" When he frowned, she said, "Our wall?"

"Oh, yes, of course," he said. "I've even been to the other side. Through Checkpoint Charlie—that was an experience. It's depressing over there. Smoggy and dark. No one would talk to me."

"You look too American," she said.

"Do I?"

"It's quite charming," she said.

"You've been across, of course," he said.

She shook her head. "Someone escaped over the wall several days ago. One of the guards. They shot at him, but missed. He went straight to a bar. Of course, he had no money, but everyone treated him to drinks to celebrate his bravery. They had to take him to the hospital afterward." She smiled and raised her drink. "*Willkommen in Berlin.*" He clinked his martini glass against hers.

"I think I saw you this morning at breakfast," he said. "What brings you here?"

"A trade show," Anna said. "Also boring. Mostly they just want me to stand in a booth and smile at the customers." It was her stock answer. There was always a convention of some sort going on. If he wanted to know more, she could fill in the details, but most men weren't interested. Their questions were gambits toward their end games. "I'm Petra, by the way."

By now, Weatherly had turned to face her, and she had done the same. Their knees brushed against each other from time to time. They talked a while longer about inconsequential things. He leaned forward when he spoke, as if they were part of a conspiracy, which in a way they were—only not the same one. He was trying to bed her and she was trying to trap him.

"Can I buy you another drink?" he asked. He blushed. "Or dinner, perhaps?"

She had to hold back a laugh at the eager-puppy look on his face. She waited long enough to make it seem like she was giving serious thought to the question. "How about room service instead?" she replied. Her hand went to the front of her dress, as if her audaciousness had taken her by surprise.

"My room is a little messy," he said. "I hope you don't mind." He signaled the bartender for his tab.

"Let's use mine instead," she said. And just like that she had him. From this point forward, everything was predetermined.

She let Weatherly kiss her in the elevator. His lips were soft. This was a job, but it had its moments. Now that he was on the hook, she could relax and enjoy herself.

She rarely allowed herself to think about the consequences of what she was doing. Life as this man knew it was about to end. Here he was, thinking he was having such good luck. In a way, he was, she supposed. His job had brought him to the attention of some very dangerous people, and she could just as easily have been preparing to slip a stiletto between his ribs. But killing him wasn't the plan. That would bring unwanted attention, and he wasn't irreplaceable. Her handlers wanted something to hold over his head so he would surrender information. Knowledge was the most valuable commodity in this city. The events of the next few hours would cause a subtle shift in power between two vast nations intent on expunging each other.

After they entered her room and started to undress, he reached out to turn off the lights, but she asked him to leave them on. "All the better to see you with," she said, but what she really meant was "all the better to photograph you with." He relented. They always did. The promise of sex turned them into overeager and compliant teenagers.

Later, she did turn the lights off, but by then the damage was done. She held him in her arms for a while—another of the job's benefits—and listened as his breathing slowed to a deep, steady rhythm. She quietly dressed and slipped out of the room. Her handlers would clean up in the morning, after they explained to Weatherly how things were about to change for him.

How many had stood up to them over the years? There was a Frenchman, she'd heard, who'd laughed and asked for copies of the photographs to share with his friends, but very few resisted, she suspected. Shame was a powerful weapon.

Two men she didn't recognize were waiting for her downstairs. It was nearly three o'clock in the morning and, though there were still distant sounds of revelry out on the street, the hotel lobby was quiet, the lights dimmed. Her new handlers, she assumed. They were changed out every month or two. None had ever met her after an assignation before, but they all did things differently.

They led her to a car waiting by the curb. One of the men held the back door open for her. He was young, bright-eyed, and eager. Not her type.

He was still in bed, admiring the patterns the morning light was creating on the ceiling and luxuriating in the afterglow, when the door burst open and two men stormed in. They wore dark suits, dark hats, and the grim demeanors of the oppressed nation they represented. One man held a gun. They dragged him from bed and shoved him into a padded chair in the corner of the room.

The gunman stood in front of him while the other man pulled the chair from the desk across the room and stood on it to remove something from a panel in the ceiling. A few minutes later, he handed it to the gunman, who held it out for Weatherly to see. A canister of film.

"If you're looking for money, I have a little cash," Weatherly said.

"He thinks we want money," the man with the gun said to his companion. He had a heavy German accent. The other man snorted but said nothing. "This," he said, waving the film in front of Weatherly's nose, "is your future."

Weatherly said nothing.

"It could be a dream, or it could be your worst nightmare." He paused. "Wasn't she beautiful, our little Anna?" the man said. "I hope she was worth it."

Weatherly maintained his silence.

"Our cameras are very good, you know. Crisp, clear pictures, every time. Imagine what your boss will think when he finds out what you've been up to." He winked at Weatherly. "Never mind him—maybe he doesn't care. But what about your wife? Or your kids. Your little boy and your daughter. We know everything about you, Donald Weatherly. Where you work. Where you live. Where you go to church, even. Everyone will find out what kind of man you are. We'll plaster your neighborhood with pictures. You'll lose everything."

Weatherly remained quiet but attentive. He licked his lips.

"Or we could just keep this little roll of film hidden away." He placed it in a pocket inside his jacket. He patted his chest. "Nice and safe. It's up to you."

"What do you want?" Weatherly asked.

"Only a little information. We understand you are designing some tunnels. Never mind how we know that—we do. Tell us where they are going to be built and when, and what they're for, and this can all be our little secret." He smiled. "There might even be a little money in it for you. If you provide satisfactory results." He paused. "Now, and in the future, of course."

It was a lot to take in. Another man might have been over-whelmed by the unexpected situation and the decisions he was being forced to make under duress. However, he'd heard the same threats at least a dozen times before, in Vienna, London, Washington, Helsinki, Oslo, Geneva, Bonn, and Paris. If his name had been Donald Weatherly and if he'd had a family in Norfolk, Virginia, he might have been concerned. He didn't say a word. He simply crossed his legs, folded his arms, and waited.

The gunman said, "Do you understand what I'm saying?" He moved in, holding the gun at waist level, close to his body.

The hotel room door swung open and several armed men swarmed into the room. The gunman dropped his weapon and raised his hands. The other man, taken equally by surprise, offered no resistance. Less than a minute later, he and his confederate were escorted from the room in handcuffs. Where they went and what happened to them—or to "Petra," who would have been scooped up as she was leaving the hotel—was of no real interest to him. His job was over, for the time being.

He wondered where Operation Apiary would take him next.

Somewhere interesting, he hoped. He would be given a carefully constructed identity and a background that would make him a prime target for foreign operatives. His impending arrival would be leaked through various back channels and double agents. If the other side didn't take the bait, he would enjoy a nice vacation in a city he might not otherwise have gotten to visit before moving on to the next job. Eventually the other side would catch on to the scheme and they'd have to try something else.

He'd been telling the truth when he told Petra—or Anna—he'd been to Berlin before. The previous time had been a decade earlier as part of Operation Stopwatch, building a tunnel into the Russian sector so they could tap into the Red Army's communications. A mole had revealed the presence of the tunnel to the Russians before it was even finished, although it was years before MI5 and the CIA found out. All part of the game. It wasn't often like chess, as many claimed. Opposing pieces were rarely removed from the board as the ones this morning had been, and they were mere pawns. It was more like the game of Reversi, where opposing players were surrounded and forced to change allegiances until one side controlled the entire board.

He'd been on the verge of retiring when he was asked to join Operation Apiary. They needed men of a certain age, and he fit the bill. Once his role had been explained, how could he refuse? The benefits were obvious—and they paid him, to boot.

He got dressed, washed his face and combed his hair before going downstairs to have breakfast. He found a seat at a table next to one occupied by a pretty young woman who was by herself. She glanced at him, then returned to her muesli and yoghurt. That was the way the world normally worked. What sensible young woman would be interested in an old guy like him?

HOUSE OF A THOUSAND EYES

BY KATIA LIEF

Berlin, August 1961

I

Conrad slipped his rifle off his shoulder and took aim the moment he heard the thud. Across the road from where he guarded the border, a woman had stumbled rather dramatically. He blinked away perspiration dripping into his eyes from beneath his helmet and saw that the woman appeared to be in her thirties. She was loaded down with shopping bags, and something seemed to have fallen from one of them. A knot of garlic shed its papery skin as it bounced along the cracked pavement, settling just short of the snake of barbed wire separating east from west.

The slope of the woman's cheekbones stirred something in Conrad, and for a moment he imagined touching her skin, its softness, even its taste. He thought fleetingly of Emilie. How long since he'd seen her? Swallowing the aching regret of her loss, he consulted his watch. It was nearly quitting time, and he was getting hungry. He reshouldered his rifle. He was about to fetch the garlic and toss it back to her when Hans, a fellow guard, beat him to it.

The woman was just out of sight when the explosion ripped Hans from the ground. Conrad rushed to his side along with Axel, his oldest friend and also a guard. As the smoke cleared, it was obvious that Hans was dead. The back of his head was crushed, threads of blood spinning lacework on the arid ground. His blue eyes, frozen, stared at nothing.

A siren wailed into the cacophony of panicked voices. Fellow East Berliners watched the scene through the dusty windows of apartments whose view had been radically transformed from open street to barbed wire. Conrad scanned the length of the street for any trace of the woman. Somehow, she had vanished into the havoc.

The next day, vultures appeared. The first three reporters came on foot, with notebooks, and the fourth on a rusty blue bicycle with a camera strapped across his back. Conrad refused an inner pull of jealousy; he'd had a bicycle as a child but it was stolen by the son of a neighbor who had been a Nazi. Conrad's parents hadn't dared complain. Axel would have remembered the bike, as he himself had borrowed it on occasion when they were boys. The friends glanced at each other now and in silent agreement refused to show any sort of response to the predators on the other side of the border. Hans had died a martyr for socialism, and if they couldn't figure that out themselves, it was their loss.

"Officer!" The reporter slid off the bike and uncapped his camera. "Give us a wave."

Conrad walked the border without changing his gait or even looking at the young man, who appeared to be twenty-one or -two, not much older than himself. He had to realize there was no way Conrad could reply. If he did, his commander would give him a severe talking-to; but worse, his own conscience would destroy him.

They hurled their questions like stones.
"How did it feel seeing your comrade die?"
"Has the bomber been identified?"
"Why did she do it? In your opinion. Why?"
"What will happen to her now?"

And then a ripple of laughter passed among the Westies. Journalists loved interpreting the German Democratic Republic for the benefit of the rest of the world, though what they came up with was predictable, generally something about Soviet imperialism, hypocrisy, tyranny.

Conrad ignored them. He had been raised well, and was proud of his work guarding the border. The two halves of Germany were too philosophically opposed to coexist. For the GDR to thrive, the capitalists needed to be kept out. As for the question of East Berliners being kept in, his father, a schoolteacher of some local renown, had explained that the resources of a new nation were vulnerable, and it was intolerable to continue allowing people to live in the east and work in the west, reaping the benefits of socialism while enriching themselves on filthy capitalism. "The soullessness of greed," his father had called this kind of dual citizenship in a broken Germany. Still, Conrad was as surprised as any when the coils of wire appeared overnight, the root of a wall that enforced new rules of nonemigration. Within days, though, he was used to the idea and signed on as a guard while a permanent wall was gradually constructed.

"Give us something," a reporter shouted. "Anything. A smile."

Conrad marched steadily along his route. It wasn't his problem if they'd missed the garlic bomb yesterday, if today their cameras were hungry for some sustenance. It wouldn't come from him.

When finally his relief appeared, he handed over his rifle, and saluted. He noted with some disappointment that Axel, with whom he often shared an after-work beer, was still on duty. Conrad started for home.

* * *

"I saw you admiring the reporter's bike." Herr Muller, an older man his sister, Gabi, had briefly dated, pulled to a stop on his own gleaming black bicycle. He patted the handlebars. "Want to take her for a spin?"

"It's a beauty. Where did you get it?"

"Bought it from a colleague last year." Conrad tried and failed to recall what it was that Herr Muller did for a living. "I'm thinking of getting rid of it. It takes up too much room in my apartment, and I never ride it."

"You're riding it now."

"Thought if I took her out, it would help me decide."

"And has it?"

Herr Muller shrugged, and suddenly Conrad remembered why his sister had broken up with him. It wasn't his relative age, but his inability to settle on anything, anything at all.

"Go on, try her out, I don't mind."

Conrad took her around the block, twice, waving to Herr Muller each time he passed. He enjoyed the sensation of gliding. It was exhilarating. He decided he wanted the bike.

"I'll buy it from you," he told Muller, thinking he could free the man from his indecisiveness by putting it bluntly. "Name your price."

When Muller smiled, a web of deep lines radiated across his temples. He was even older than Conrad had thought. His parents felt his sister had made a good choice marrying a man closer to her own age. They had two children now, and Lutz worked faithfully at the butcher shop where his own father had spent his life. He was your typical good man, or as his sister had put it, "a decent catch." But Conrad had his suspicions after hearing from a friend who spotted his brother-in-law on Normanstrasse, in Lichtenberg, walking in the direction of Stasi headquarters. It was one thing to work openly for the GDR like Conrad, in uniform, so everyone knew who you were and what you stood for. It was quite another to work secretly as an Inoffizielle Mitarbeiter, informing on your friends and family. It was impossible to know who was an IM and who wasn't. You had to watch your ground at all times, not that Conrad had anything to worry about. Even so, it was well known that when a Berliner was seen in Lichtenberg, chances were he was paying a visit to the House of a Thousand Eyes.

"*Name your price.*" Muller laughed. "You talk like a true Westy."

"I only meant that—"

"Relax, son. Can't you take a joke? I'll tell you what: keep her until tomorrow and we'll decide on a price. Same time and place. Who knows? Maybe I'll even give her to you for nothing."

Conrad rode off under the chalk-blue sky, eventually arriving home in Friedrichshain, circuitously, over an hour later than usual. His father was standing outside their building, banned from the apartment to smoke his cigar on the sidewalk. He was chatting with the grocer, who also smoked, when Conrad appeared, in his uniform, riding Herr Muller's bicycle.

The rage that spread across his father's face so startled Conrad that he almost fell off the bike. "Are you out of your mind?" his father hissed in a tone new to Conrad, who had always admired his father's even temper. "Get off that bike. Get off it now."

"Take it easy, Erich," the grocer advised in a low voice, practically a whisper. "You don't want to attract attention to the situation."

"What situation?" Conrad asked. "It belongs to Herr Muller. You remember him, Father—the one Gabi threw over for Lutz. He loaned it to me until tomorrow." For reasons Conrad couldn't decipher, it seemed like a bad idea to mention that he was in fact considering buying the bicycle.

The offending bike now stashed in the front hallway of the apartment he shared with his parents, he overheard them whispering frantically in the kitchen though couldn't make out what they were saying. Eventually his father appeared with a bottle of schnapps and two glasses, and sat his son down in the living room for a man-to-man talk.

"The Schumanns don't ride bicycles," his father began. Conrad noticed that, when his father ran his fingers through his thinning grey hair, a tremor shook his hand. "What's wrong?" Conrad asked. "Is it your health?"

His father drained his schnapps and poured another. Conrad hadn't touched his. "My health is fine, and so is your mother's. But please, listen to me. The bike has to go."

Conrad was nineteen. In two months, he would be twenty. He crossed his arms over his chest and waited for the explanation he believed he was due.

"It's like this," his father finally began. "These days, a bike is not a bike."

"Which means?"

"The woman who threw the garlic yesterday, has she been found? Have you thought about what will happen to her?"

"She's a traitor. She killed Hans. Why do you care what happens to her?"

"Let me explain something to you." His father spoke in the tone he used with his students, the same tone with which he had often enlightened Conrad and Gabi throughout their childhoods. His voice fell to a whisper and he leaned in, as if fearful of being overheard. "The bicycle is to get around more easily."

"Exactly."

"Don't interrupt. Let me finish." Agitated, he poured himself a third schnapps.

Conrad's throat tightened. There was something his father needed to say but didn't know how. Never before had he seen the man speechless. He laid his hand on his father's knee. "Don't worry. I'll return the bike to Herr Muller tonight. Gabi might still know where he lives."

"You don't know what a bike means these days. You don't understand." When his father's hand landed on top of his, the sticky heat was overwhelming, but he left his own hand where it was. "IMs ride bikes to get around quickly, and they're given clearance to pass through the checkpoints."

"But it isn't possible," Conrad argued, "that everyone with a bike is an IM."

"Who else can afford a bicycle these days?"

"You once said that, before the war, a lot of people had bikes."

"Conrad, do I have to remind you how little survived the war?"

Of course he didn't; it was a ridiculous suggestion. Almost nothing survived. Every building in Berlin was scarred with bullet holes. The Jews were all gone. Nearly everyone in the east was scraping by with what little was left after the Soviets cleaned them out, while the west rebuilt itself and snickered at them across the border.

"I've often wondered," Conrad ventured, curious what his father thought about the tender issue of informers, and questioning now the depth of his concern, "if IMs provide a necessary service, even if it makes us uncomfortable when we don't know who is..." How exactly to put it?

"Betraying you," his father spat.

"But is it a betrayal when it's for the good of the country? I don't like IMs any more than you do, but I've wondered about this. Mielke must have a good reason for needing them. It's no secret that splitting the country has been a tricky business."

His father's mouth tightened. A frightening clarity overtook his eyes. "IMs are scum. Mielke doesn't need them, he wants them. He's terrified of losing his grip around our throats."

It was the first time Conrad had heard his father speak so bitterly about the leader of the GDR. He was taken aback, and waited for the rest to pour out.

"You remember, when you were seven, and I went away for five months?"

"Of course I remember." Their mother had explained that their father was on a teacher-training expedition, which had seemed plausible at the time, but suddenly didn't.

"I was in prison, first tortured, then put in solitary. And what was my transgression?"

Transgression? His father? Never had Conrad known a more loyal citizen than his father, which is why he'd been trusted with the honor of educating the new country's youngest minds.

"I sat down for a cup of coffee one afternoon. At the table next to mine was a man. I'd never seen him before. I didn't know his name or anything about him, only that he was drinking a beer at the next table. I asked him the time. That was my transgression. I was picked up the next day, accused of subversion. Apparently, the man with the beer was a spy for the Americans. They wanted to know what we talked about. They wanted to know if he "recruited" me. They kept me awake for four straight nights. No sleep, Conrad, you have no idea how insane that makes you. No sleep at all, and very little food or water. I thought I would never see you children or your mother again. I was out of my mind."

"So you confessed?"

"They never broke me. Not like that, anyway."

"How, then?" Conrad knew as well as anyone that traitors, even perceived traitors, weren't released back into society without paying a price.

"A promise was extracted from me. I vowed to teach my students, all of them, year after year, the purest values of the GDR. If I wanted to see my family again, that was what I had to do. And I've done it, haven't I?"

"What were you teaching them before?"

"Mathematics. Science. History. Literature. To ask questions and to think critically. After, I kept my lessons to the benefits of socialism, and still do."

His father watched him, waiting for it to sink in: the new understanding that, for much of Conrad's lifetime, his father was not exactly whom he'd seemed to be. "I see now why you don't want me to appear to be an IM."

"Don't let them turn you into a monster," his father whispered, hands gripping his knees, eyes sharp as crystal, "like they did me. I can't live with that. Do you understand?"

"I'll go right now and find Gabi. I'll walk to her apartment, leave the bike here, and when I have Muller's address I'll wait until dark and return it."

Conrad rode shakily to Muller's, and in the twenty minutes it took to get there, he tried but couldn't digest his father's confession. All these years, his father, the man he loved and respected above all other men, the man he emulated, the man he'd hoped to make proud by wearing the uniform of the GDR, had sustained his loyalist persona under duress. Conrad felt trapped in a quicksand of bewildered disappointment.

Muller's elderly sister answered the bell by peeking through the curtains onto the street. In moments, Muller himself appeared at the door.

"What's this? I thought we agreed on tomorrow."

"I've already decided. Thank you, but I don't want it." Conrad leaned the bicycle against the bullet-scarred wall of the Mullers' building. In the moonlight, he was able to see that someone had left a thimble in one of the holes. It made no sense to Conrad. Nothing made sense tonight. He turned to leave.

Muller stepped forward and grabbed Conrad's arm. "I won't take no for an answer." In the strange shadows of night, Conrad noticed jowls on the man, who seemed to age rapidly with every conversation.

"I've made up my mind."

"I don't care about money. I'll tell you the truth." And here Muller leaned in to whisper in Conrad's ear. "It's my sister. She told me if I don't get rid of the bike, she'll toss me out. You'll be doing me a favor by taking it off my hands."

"I wish I could help you, Herr Muller. My father asked me to return it. Good night."

"When Emilie fled for the west, she was pregnant."

Conrad turned back to look at Muller, who stood now in a pocket of darkness, his face blackened. Behind him, the thimble glimmered.

"Who ended it?" Muller continued. "You, or her? Or did she leave you high and dry without mentioning she was going to the other side?"

Conrad stared at Muller, but the inscrutable thimble kept intruding on his attention. Why was it there? How did this man know anything of Emilie? He struggled to recall exactly when he had last been with her. How long now since she'd fled to the west? Fifteen months, he guessed, was the answer to both questions.

"I don't understand why you've mentioned Emilie," Conrad said, "when our business only concerns this bicycle."

"Your girlfriend's defection might look bad for you, don't you think so? Especially now that she's given birth to your child."

Given birth. Child. Was it really possible that he, at nineteen, was already a father? His gaze melted against the hard thimble in the bullet hole.

"It seems to me, Herr Schumann, that someone could think you'd have good cause to follow her over. Who wouldn't want to see his own child?"

"I'm not sure why I should believe you, Herr Muller."

"But are you sure why you shouldn't?" He stepped out of the darkness now, his old face pallid in the weak moonlight. "I can fix this problem for you, if you let me."

"I'm not yet convinced it's a problem, with all due respect."

"*All due respect.*" Muller laughed. "I'm not your father, boy. Trust me. Take the bike."

"No, thank you."

"I insist. You'll take the bike, and I'll protect you from the powers that be. One hand washes the other. You understand?"

Finally, Conrad did understand.

"And if I refuse?"

"I'll have no choice but to report that fact. How will it look?

KATIA LIEF

Someone could think that your uniform is just a costume to keep you near the border, giving you an opportunity to get to the other side before the wall is fully built. It could look very bad for you, Herr Schumann. Refusal to cooperate. Baby on the other side of the wall. If that isn't begging to be put under suspicion, I don't know what is."

None of that had ever occurred to Conrad. He guarded the border out of pride as the wall was constructed, to please his father, and himself. Never once had he considered his daily proximity to the west as a temptation of any kind. His father's words rang in his ears, "Don't let them turn you into a monster, like they did me." But his father was not a monster. Who was a good man, if not his father?

"You'll be better off if you accept the bicycle," Muller pressed, "as will your entire family. Your sister also has children now, I understand?"

The barely veiled threat against Gabi's children startled Conrad. Apparently he was to become an informer, or else. Without considering it another moment, he took the bike from the wall, got on, and rode home. He did not, however, bring it into the apartment. Instead, he leaned it against a tree around the corner, hoping that when he returned for it, it would be gone. But to his dismay, the next morning, the bicycle was waiting exactly where he'd left it. He decided he was better off riding it to work than chancing his father seeing it abandoned against the tree, or Muller intercepting him on his way home without it.

"Did you hear the news?" Axel greeted Conrad as they prepared to assume their posts.

"What news?"

"The woman bomber. She's been caught."

"And?"

"She's a baker's wife with three children at home. She'll be hanged."

Conrad wondered briefly what the woman's name was. He could still see the curve of her cheek. If he knew her name, he would mourn her, so he decided not to find out. Instead, impulsively, he asked, "Since you know everything, Axel, what can you tell me about Emilie?"

"Emilie?"

"Never mind. I don't know why I asked." Would anything Axel said to him now be fodder for the Stasi, that great iron ear that hovered above them and forgot nothing? Conrad tried not to listen to the answer, but found he couldn't resist.

"I heard she had a child. Didn't you know?" Axel stepped so near, Conrad was sure he caught a whiff of the currant and raspberry pudding Frau Bauer used to make them sometimes after school. The familiar yet distant fragrance sent a cascade of regret through him. He was to lose his friends, all of them, he was sure of it. He needed to keep quiet, say nothing, hear nothing, but there was one more thing he felt compelled to ask.

"Boy or girl?"

"I've heard both, so I can't tell you."

"Why didn't you mention this to me before?"

"Only to hurt you?"

The morning progressed, and for the first time he wondered what he was doing and whom he could trust. How was it, for instance, that Axel had heard about Emilie and the baby but Conrad hadn't? Was Herr Muller already an IM when he and Gabi were together, and if so, had he spied on his sister and perhaps the entire Schumann family? What, if anything, did Gabi know about it? Now, as the day passed, minutes mounting to hours, each one compounded his distress. It didn't help that the same band of reporters had taken up their usual spots, waiting for something new to happen.

"A baker's wife!" One of them tried to capture Conrad's attention. "What do you think of that?"

"Do you, in your opinion, think she could have done more damage by loading explosives into a loaf of bread? Why garlic?"

"In your opinion, was the baker's wife a traitor to the people?"

"What was her statement in throwing her little garlic bomb, in your opinion?"

Conrad's job was not to hold opinions. His job was to guard the border. But at the end of that day, when Herr Muller intercepted him, it fully sank in that he now had another job as well. Today Muller rode a red bicycle, and traveled beside Conrad along the avenues of the Mitte.

"So tell me," Muller began. "What were you and your friend discussing this morning, by the border?"

"You were there?" Conrad sped up, but Muller only followed.

"I'm asking the questions. So tell me. What's on Axel Bauer's mind these days?"

"Nothing. The weather."

"You mean to say that he didn't tell you about Emilie?"

"How would you know what we talked about?"

At that, Muller laughed and rode off in another direction. As he continued home, Conrad could hear the man's cackle far into the distance. Once again he propped the bicycle against the tree, and was disappointed the next morning when it was still there.

He no longer spoke to Axel; it felt too dangerous. And now, he found that when the reporters called out to him, provoking him with their questions, he sometimes listened ponderously. He wished he could take his new concerns home to his father, but could see his parents had made a heavy peace with their past choices and only hoped that their children would follow the path of least resistance. A path Conrad believed no longer existed for him.

As he walked the border one afternoon, his attention kept landing on the black bicycle propped against a lamppost, *his* bicycle, with its menacing gleam. He hated it. Muller waited for him every evening, asking what the guards had discussed on their breaks. As if he spoke to anyone these days. There, in the distance, was Axel. He remembered bunkering under a homemade tent with his friend when they were children, late at night, bending their fingers to make shadow puppets dance on the glowing white sheet they had pilfered from the hall closet. He blinked away the reminiscence. Axel was lost to him. Any sort of intimacy would be impossible now; no one could be trusted, including him. And Emilie. Someday, when he looked back, would she glimmer in his memory as his one and only love? When he thought of the rumor of their child, blood pumped wildly at his temples, deafening him against the usual discipline of his thoughts. Hans was dead. Axel was a stranger. His father was heartbroken. Emilie had vanished into a world he staunchly refused to imagine.

Suddenly, without thinking, Conrad turned to face the lens of a photographer... and heard a click.

"Come on," the man shouted. "Give us something to look at."

Before he knew what was happening, Conrad was flying over the barbed coil, dropping his rifle on the eastern side and landing, suddenly, in the west.

The chaos that followed was instantaneous. Axel and another guard ran to intercept him, but were too late. The photographer's camera clicked mercilessly, capturing Conrad's every move. Others joined in. The mechanical clacks and whirs sounded more voracious than any of the excited voices. People were shouting but he heard nothing of substance. It happened fast: suddenly, without thought, he was over. For a moment his body felt light as a feather, though when he landed he experienced the full force of his weight. He thought of his father's disappointments, the open sore of his own uncertainty, and ran.

II

Emilie's Kreutzberg building would have been visible from Conrad's side of Berlin, if he had known where to look. It turned out she hadn't made it very far, but west was west and east was east whether you were an inch or a mile from the border.

Her window was open. From the street below he saw stained white curtains billowing on a lackadaisical summer breeze. A couple of books were piled beside a crusty-looking glass half-full with water. The high wail of a baby crying followed a breeze onto the street, landing painfully in Conrad's ears.

The building's front door was unsecured so he walked right in. He took the steps in pairs until he reached the third floor, breathless, and knocked three times.

Emilie's porcelain face, stiff as a doll's, held its composure when she opened her door and found him. "I saw the papers." She wore the same crimson lipstick she used to.

"May I come in?"

"What took you so long?"

"I've been busy." He didn't have to explain why it had taken him nearly a week to find her. Defectors were always held and questioned by the Allies until their motivations were fully understood.

She was dressed for the office, in a skirt and blouse, and was barefoot; the red polish on her toenails was badly chipped. Conrad stood at the entrance of her small living room and listened for a baby. The tepid silence unnerved him. He was sure he'd heard it crying.

"Where is it?"

"What a nice greeting." She plopped down on a tattered couch, bundling her knees in front of her. There was little furniture in the place other than the couch and a table with a single chair. There was no sign of a child. On a mantel across the room a pair of bricks served as bookends, with a single book lapsed sideways between them. This was the Emilie he remembered: haphazard, improvisational, a reader. Often selfish. "Why are you here, Connie?"

She had once whispered that in his ear at the height of passion. *Connie.* Teasing him, calling him a woman's name, just at his moment of release. She had been his first and only lover. He had assumed they would marry, and was devastated when she disappeared across the border without warning.

"Just tell me: Is it true you had our baby?"

Her eyes were black scythes in a white face. A new pageboy hair-cut made her severe. Finally, she answered, "I gave it up. I had to. I couldn't make it on my own with a child."

"Why didn't you tell me you were expecting?"

"I didn't know until I was already here, and then it didn't matter anymore. I wasn't going back, and you weren't coming over. You were always too good a comrade for me."

"And yet here I am."

"Why?"

It was an excellent question. "The truth is, I'd rather be home."

"But you defected."

"It was an impulse. I wanted to..." Words failed him. It wasn't as simple as finding her and learning the truth. He'd wanted to get away from Muller, and from the black bicycle. "Was it a boy or girl?"

"I don't know."

"How can that be?"

"They were instructed not to tell me at the hospital. I never even saw it."

"So you don't know where it is now?"

"How could I?"

She had walked away from her newborn, just as she'd walked away from him. Her mercilessness was electrifying. He wondered if she was telling the truth; if there really had been a baby. A shiver of cold passed through him. Why *was* he here?

"Want something to drink?"

He sat down beside her. "Why not?"

They drank beer until midnight, after which it was agreed that he should spend the night on her couch. By the second night, he was in her bed. It quickly made no sense for him to leave at all.

"The wall will be finished soon," Emilie whispered in his ear. "They say it's going to seal off West Berlin completely, turn us into a little island unto ourselves."

Conrad thought of his father and mother, trapped on the other side. He'd written to them several times, but doubted any of his letters had gotten through. "I need to see my parents."

The sheet slid off when she propped herself on an elbow, exposing her small breasts. "I know a way we can both go back."

"You said you'd never make a good socialist."

"That's not what I mean." Without her lipstick, the wild self-assurance of that slash of vivid red, her smile betrayed a rare vulnerability. He kissed her.

"What do you mean?"

"You'll see." She lay back on her pillow and closed her eyes. A blue shadow from yesterday's makeup lingered in the relaxed folds of her lids. Wetting a finger, he smoothed away the color. He disliked it when she became mysterious.

"Explain," he insisted.

"Do you really want to go back?"

"Yes, but only if you come with me." He kissed her, and she threw her arms around him.

"Someone very special is in town," she whispered in his ear. "He can help us. I'm told he's willing to meet with us today."

A slender man in a suit and tie reclined in an easy chair in the back room of the construction outfit where Emilie worked. His dark hair was brushed neatly off his forehead, and his fingernails were conspicuously clean. There was no denying his elegance. He held a tiny espresso cup on a saucer, balanced on his knee.

"This is Mischa," Emilie told Conrad, the moment they walked in. He wondered why she hadn't introduced him, as well. Did the man already know who he was?

"A pleasure to meet you, Herr—"

"Wolf." His voice was as unimpeachable as his manicure, without tone. The name Mischa Wolf rang a distant bell in Conrad's mind. And then it struck him like a thunderbolt.

Markus "Mischa" Wolf was second in command of the Stasi, the notorious spymaster who ran the Hauptverwaltung Aufklärung. It was rumored that the HVA sent its tentacles worldwide, and well known (if rarely discussed) that the East German secret police recruited far and wide, and greedily. It had to be some kind of absurd dream, finding Wolf in the dusty back room of a minor capitalist enterprise in West Berlin. Unless of course this business was a front. Conrad glanced at Emilie's pretty face and saw nothing different from before.

Wolf set his cup and saucer on the arm of the chair, and stood. He was tall, with a guileless manner that commanded the room. "It took some time to figure out how to get you here."

"I can't imagine why you'd be interested in me, Herr Wolf."

"It was Emilie's idea. I'm told you're trustworthy."

She nodded, earning a small smile from Wolf. That they addressed each other on a first name basis made Conrad wonder how long they had been acquainted.

"Trustworthy? I myself crossed the border I was guarding."

"You behaved exactly as we anticipated."

"I don't understand," Conrad lied.

In fact, he understood perfectly. Finally, things made sense.

Herr Muller has been just the beginning. The bicycle. Muller's threats against his family. That spin around the block had always led right here. For a frantic moment Conrad even wondered if the woman with the garlic bomb had also been arranged by the HVA, to attract the press, to bring the bicycle, to spark his reminiscing and make him susceptible to Muller's offer of a bike. The story of a baby. How had they known precisely how to tunnel into his mind?

He felt the urgent need to speak with Emilie privately. How long had she worked for Wolf? Was her defection to the west always part of the plan? When had Conrad been factored into it? If this was the case, perhaps she'd been in love with him from the start, in her own strange way. Her face revealed nothing. As his mind awoke, he recognized another fact of life: There was never any baby. It was merely a lever to bring him over, as planned, because Emilie asked for him. But it was Emilie they really wanted. Emilie, with her looks, her brains, her confidence, her inscrutability, would doubtless make the perfect spy.

Light-headed, Conrad turned to leave. But when Emilie's hand landed in his, with its blast of warmth, he found he couldn't get to the door.

"What exactly do you want from me?"

"Eyes and ears," Wolf answered. "Keep us up to date."

"How long have you been doing this?" Conrad asked Emilie.

"Connie, you've got to understand. The wall is just the beginning. Once they're isolated, once they're hungry, the wall comes down again and the GDR will run the entire city. No more separation."

"What do you mean, hungry?"

"There's a plan for how it's all going to work. All we need to do is pass along information that could be helpful."

"What kind of information?"

"Anything. Anything we might notice. Whatever we might overhear."

"You told me we could get back to the east. Is *this* what you meant?"

Emilie looked at Conrad with a spark in her black eyes. He hated what she had done to him, and yet he loved her. "We'll get back home by staying here and working together. We'll have each other. It's going to be perfect, don't you see?"

Thoughts crashing, Conrad did the political math. If he agreed, they would work for the east against the west, while appearing to have defected to the west, as all the while Wolf and his team surveyed and manipulated them. Double agents, if he'd done the puzzle correctly. And if he didn't agree? He thought of the bicycle, leaning against the tree outside his parents' building every morning without fail, and knew he'd never get away.

"How can you be so sure we won't be caught by the Allies?" Conrad asked them both.

"I'll protect you," Wolf answered.

"How? What makes you think that *you* of all people can keep us safe in the west? And what about my parents? How can I know nothing will happen to them if I'm caught?"

Wolf smiled, his teeth slightly yellow in the dim light. "You're right, no one can trust anyone these days. But even so, young man, you'll have to make a choice."

A NEIGHBOR'S STORY

BY VICKI DOUDERA

My name is Rachel Hirsch, and here is what passes for my life: I reside at the Stone Coast Home for Seniors, along with a dozen other old souls in various stages of decline. I'm sharp-tongued and silver-haired, five-foot-two, and Jewish, even if I have not practiced my religion since childhood. At sixty-one I am still fairly spry, and have the dubious distinction of being the youngest resident, although nobody knows my true age.

Every morning for the past month I have woken at dawn, read for an hour in my room, and then pulled on a jacket to hike down the hill to my old house and Roy's. I watch the sun rise as the lobstermen visit their traps, I hear the shriek of the gulls winging beside the boats, and I breathe deeply of the cold, spruce-scented air. Thoughts of my prior life flit in and out, and, for a few seconds anyway, I feel something akin to peace. Turning, and taking the hill with slow steps, my spirit seems serene in a way that I suppose only the very wicked can understand. Perhaps the snowfalls to come will make these morning pilgrimages impossible, but who can say when—or if—that will happen. I've found that winters on the coast can be capricious.

I take my breakfast with the other denizens of the Home. Seated in the stuffy salon where we consume our meals, I spoon oatmeal from a big bowl, sprinkle raisins and chopped walnuts on top, and listen to the memories of my housemates.

Each of us has a story. There's Frank, a former surgeon from New York, tall, white-haired, and wobbly; Rita, raised up in a restaurant-owning family in a small Vermont town; and Betty, a martini-drinking, summer-stock-singing beauty. I pass the oatmeal to Willis, once the owner of a sardine packing plant Down East, who controls both the conversation and seating arrangement. He hasn't lost the bullying demeanor of one who single-handedly ran a factory, no more than Frank has forgotten a certain air of medical arrogance, nor Betty the lyrics to songs from *South Pacific*. Seated beside Willis is Evelyn, dressed as if she's headed to a disco, even though it is 1989 and the disco craze is dead.

My own story will never be told, not unless the dementia that is gradually gripping my mind loosens my tongue in a way that torture never could. Every day I look for signs that I've become a slack-lipped, crazy woman like Mavis, who was removed from Stone Coast Home for Seniors last week because she'd begun shrieking profanity. I wonder whether I'll know when the time is right to take the cyanide pill I've so carefully concealed in an antique locket. I ought to remove it from my jewelry box tonight, pour a glass of Riesling and be done with it, and yet my spirit is such that I cannot help but hang on to this life. Perhaps my tenacity—or cowardice— springs from an inability to imagine a reality beyond the one I now know. Visions of heaven, angels, and welcoming white lights do not ring true for me. Unlike Roy, I believe that the end is The End.

I tell myself that I am curious, that I cling fast to my meager existence because, even after all these years, my story is still unfolding and I long to see where it goes. I hope and pray that is my truth. But there is a terror lurking beyond even the bleakness of death: I fear I am already lost in the fog of forgetfulness, and do not know any better, that I am closer to being like Mavis than I really know.

There are a few things I can say with certainty, and here is one: Roy Mahoney was my next-door neighbor, and a good one at that.

For close to twenty years he performed a laundry list of little acts that bespoke friendship and kindness. Each fall he'd prune the rambling *rosa rugosa* that bordered my land and the beach, cutting the canes nearly to the ground so that the following June's blooms would be riotous. Every spring he rustled up a rototiller to turn over the garden, mixing in the aged manure he'd hauled from a neighboring farm. In return, I baked zucchini bread, lent him Tom Clancy novels, and helped pick out presents for his grandkids. My contributions to our friendship seemed small in comparison to his, and yet the man never once made me feel guilty.

Roy brought over a tuna noodle casserole on the day the dog died.

I'd pulled into the driveway in my Civic, and there he stood, wearing jeans and an LL Bean chamois shirt, an aluminum-foil-covered pan in hand. I'd just left the vet, the feeling of the old retriever's coarse fur still fresh in my mind. My hands trembled as I yanked the keys from the ignition, hot tears threatened to spill from my eyes.

"Cancer?" he asked as he followed me to the door.

I nodded. "Tumor as big as a grapefruit." I blinked back the memory of Dr. Pease and his assistant carrying Sadie's still body out of the examining room.

"Putting down a friend is hell." Roy said. He plunked his casserole on the counter. "Comfort food. Figured you could use a little."

Roy stayed for supper that night, something he'd done once or twice a week since we both became widowed. I tossed a green salad and uncorked a bottle of Burgundy, while he ripped the foil from his Pyrex pan, letting the smell of tuna waft up and around us.

We talked a lot about the past when we were together. My late husband Henry met Roy while serving at the American Embassy in Vienna, and they were colleagues and friends. Roy liked to reminisce about waltzing in the fancy palaces of *alt Wien*—old Vienna—especially the elegant dress balls held at the State Opera House. Dressed to the nines, young, and confident, Roy and his wife, Sally, made a handsome, happy couple, a light around which Henry and I fluttered like moths.

In addition to Austria, our chats centered on Connecticut, where we lived in neighboring towns and the men rode the commuter train into New York City each morning. Back then, we met most weekends for bridge. Sally would catch me up on the growing Mahoney family, and the men would smoke cigarettes and discuss politics. This was the tumultuous time from the mid-1960s to the late '70s, before we'd sold our homes and moved up north to Maine, before Roy went into real estate, before our spouses passed away: first Sally, from breast cancer, and then Henry, from a heart attack.

Never once did we discuss Berlin. It was as if the five years between posts in Austria and New England did not exist.

Instead, we focused on pleasant memories, or kept our conversations firmly rooted in the present. A safe topic was the never-ending list of chores that went hand-in-hand with old-house ownership, like maple syrup and pancakes.

Alone, I never could have handled the work my antique Cape required, but with Roy's assistance even the most arduous tasks were manageable.

He was ready to help with the roof when Hurricane Gloria tore up the coast back in '85. I remember the morning after: a sky scoured clear of clouds, an August day so blindingly beautiful it made seeing the storm's wrath obscene. Damage and destruction were everywhere. The Mahoney's little dory was smashed into jagged chunks, and up the street a mobile home had been flipped and gutted like a carp. An old apple tree that still bore fruit lay ripped from the ground, the tiny nubs of Northern Spies now stillborn on the branches. In the front of the house, a gaping hole the size of a man now graced my porch ceiling.

Roy patched the roof that afternoon while quizzing me about other storms.

"Doria was back in '71, right? That one did a heck of a lot of damage." It was later in the day, and Roy had filled his pockets with roofing nails and climbed back up the ladder. He was sixty-six at the time, agile enough to do any chore. A cool breeze blew in suddenly from the water, a reminder of fall weather to come. I'd hugged my cotton cardigan closer to my body while shaking my head.

"I wasn't here for that storm."

"Right." Roy had held the hammer ready to strike, a thoughtful look on his face. "You went home to see your father."

"Mother."

He tacked down a shingle and reached for another. "She lived in Germany."

"Yes." The pinched face of the woman I knew only as *Mutti* flitted through my brain. She had lived in Germany, and, although I took orders from her, she was not my parent.

There was often this type of teasing element to our conversations, as if Roy was trolling for information. That day I'd met his questioning eyes and we'd regarded each other for several seconds. What had I said next? Probably something light, like, "I'm not paying you to gab, Mahoney."

And what had he answered?

"You're not paying me at all."

Because Roy seemed to enjoy this banter, and was in fact the one who initiated it time and time again, I was unprepared for his comments last month. It was Thanksgiving, and we were washing dishes from dinner in his steamy kitchen.

"It was all a game," he'd said suddenly, stopping in the act of drying a piece of china.

"The Cowboys over the Eagles?" I said, even though I sensed he wasn't talking about football.

He shot me a look. "Three weeks ago the wall came down," he said, carefully placing the gravy boat back in the cabinet. "Did you ever think you'd see that in your lifetime? The Berlin Wall is history. If your relatives were still alive they could go back and forth freely."

I shrugged. The times they were a-changin'. "True."

"The Cold War is over." He took an oval platter from my soapy hands. "I keep asking myself why it seemed to matter so much." He dried the platter, set it on the counter, and draped the dish towel over one arm. "Remember that Thanksgiving we were detained?"

"Yes." I turned off the water and faced him, my hands on my hips. "How could I forget?"

It was 1960 and a cold autumn had settled on Berlin. The four of us decided to visit English friends in Salzburg for a holiday dinner. It was snowing, hard, and Henry's car, an ancient Lancia, broke down in the middle of Berlin's Soviet zone.

"Were you frightened?"

"Of course," I answered. "We all were." But not for the same reasons.

I pictured Sally and me, waiting in the military police station, flanked by the men. I saw the watchful eyes of the little Soviet private, his AK-47 aimed at us as we sat on the hard wooden benches. I suppose that Sally feared imprisonment or death, and I assume the men did as well. But I dreaded being exposed, my carefully fabricated life destroyed by one stupid blunder.

"Sally was pregnant," he said hollowly. "I don't know if you knew that."

"No."

"She lost the baby the next day."

I thought back. Sally had shared no news of her condition. Apparently she had kept secrets as well.

"You went on to have other children." As if on cue, the voices of Roy's grandchildren reached us from the backyard. They were returning from a walk to the little beach.

"Yes, but that was her first. It mattered."

I untied the faded checked apron and hung it on the back of the kitchen door. I'd seen Sally wear it, dozens of times, when baking chocolate chip cookies for the children, or stirring batches of Chex Mix for our bridge games. "I'm sorry."

"Yeah, well it was a long time ago." He looked up at me. "Another

Thanksgiving has come and gone. I'm grateful for your friendship, you know. Along with the kids, you've kept me going."

I nodded. A shriek from the other room made us both smile.

"You and Henry—you never wanted children." Stated like a fact, but I knew he was probing. Roy's interrogation style was nothing if not smooth.

"There were medical issues," I hinted, pursing my lips together as if the whole subject made me uncomfortable. Let him think Henry had been to blame, when in truth I'd swallowed pills surreptitiously to prevent conception.

"I'm sorry, Rachel—I don't mean to pry." He paused, changed the subject. "Sometimes I think you've hardly changed from our Vienna days. Those same blue eyes—just like when you came to work for us at the Embassy. What did Henry call them? Danube Blue? I don't think I've ever seen a man fall so hard for someone."

I turned my blue eyes on him and fluttered my lashes. "That's me—irresistible."

He chuckled. "Apparently."

Truthfully, it hadn't taken much more than a little flirting to get hired by Henry as an errand girl. Once I'd gained his trust, I'd secured a marriage proposal and shown *Mutti* and my superiors that I was serious about undercover work.

Roy brought us back to the present by brandishing a folder. "Ready to sign that offer?"

I'd come to a decision in the early fall: I was tired of taking care of my old house. I reserved a spot at the Home and hired Roy to list the property in September. Two months later, we had an offer from a New Jersey nurse. A good offer.

"No time like the present." I sat down at the kitchen table while Roy pulled papers from his file. The children flicked channels in the other room.

"As we discussed, the buyer is willing to pay cash and meet your price. You sure you can clear out of here in two weeks?"

"I can't wait." I took the papers from him and initialed several pages.

"Come on, you'll miss living on the bay, won't you?"

"I can walk to the water whenever I want. Where do I sign?"

Roy indicated the last page. "Right here."

I scrutinized the buyer's signature, a messy scrawl of unrecognizable letters. "Is this supposed to be her name?"

He nodded.

"But her handwriting...I can't even read it. Is this legal?"

"Sure. You can sign your name with an X and it's legit."

"How insulting," I continued. Proper penmanship had always been a thing with me, perhaps because my schools had been so strict when it came to writing. "I'll admit it, I'm offended."

"Come on, Rachel—who cares? So Miss Julie Lamont from Lyndhurst has a messy signature. All that matters is her bank account, and I assure you, it's strong."

I signed and handed him the papers. "I hope I don't meet her," I said. "Because if I do, I'm going to say that she ought to be ashamed."

"Really?" He gave me an odd look.

"It's rude and disrespectful, that's all." I gathered my jacket. "Is that all you need? I'm going home."

I stomped out of Roy's house, barely saying goodnight to his children and grandchildren.

The next day I called to apologize. "It's a strange quirk with me," I said. "You're right—getting upset about a signature is ridiculous."

He was silent for a few seconds.

"I'll forgive you—if you make goulash with some of this leftover turkey."

"Yes, but only if you'll join me to have some."

Roy brought a plateful of turkey over that afternoon and returned in the evening for supper. His company had gone back to southern Maine, and we were enjoying a glass of wine while our dinner simmered on my stove.

"I was thinking about Vienna," Roy said, swirling the ruby red liquid in his glass. He was seated at the table, a big man who was comfortable in his skin. "I guess that's why I craved the goulash, huh?"

I smiled. "Hungarian food always was your favorite—Henry's too—and it certainly was plentiful there."

He nodded. "What a fabulous city. I don't think you've ever told me what brought you to Vienna in the first place?"

"Curiosity, I suppose," I gave a little shrug to add credence to my lie. I had been sent to Vienna: there had been no choice about it. "It was such a lively spot once the war was over."

"Yes." He knocked back the rest of his wine. "It was a wonderful listening post, too."

I stood, reached for the bottle, and refilled his glass. "What are you talking about?"

He chuckled. "Rachel, you know what I mean. Certainly Henry told you the real reason we were stationed in Vienna. It was fertile ground for information...for espionage."

I moved to the stove and stirred. "Don't tell me you and Henry were spies?" I kept my voice very light. "I can see my exposé now: I Slept with an Agent."

"Rachel." Roy rose from the table and walked to me. Put his hands on my shoulders. "Henry told me that you knew about our cover."

I turned and regarded him with wide eyes. "I would have been a total dummy not to suspect something, especially once you both got transferred to Berlin. What about Sally? She must have known, too?"

He shook his head. "I don't think so. Sally had a very trusting nature."

"And you're saying I don't?"

I watched as he walked back to the table and picked up his wine glass and seemed to study it. "We had a mole in the Berlin office," he said quietly. "Lost several good men because of leaks we couldn't plug." He paused. "I always suspected Henry."

"That's ridiculous! Henry would never have betrayed his country. He didn't have the..." I stopped. "He wasn't like that."

"What were you going to say? That he didn't have the nerve? The imagination?"

"No, I—"

"You're right, you know, Henry didn't have the guts. He was the type that followed orders to the letter. You, on the other hand—"

"Me? Now you're making no sense at all."

"I've speculated about you for years."

"What?" I faked a lilting laugh. "Roy, I think your days of drinking burgundy are over. Of all the crazy things to say! It's the nonstop stories about the Berlin Wall. It's put you into some kind of fantasy land."

"Come on," his voice was soft, cajoling. "After all this time, after everything we've shared, you can't keep pretending. Not to me, Rachel. Admit it: you were an East German spy working right under our noses."

"I see."

"I'm not going to do anything about it, so why not come clean? It's not like anyone would care at this stage of the game."

I felt the bottom drop out of my stomach. I knew people who would care very much. "I don't know what you're talking about."

His eyes were boring into mine, his jawline taut. "Who was your contact?"

I turned, removed the lid of a pot, and slammed it down on the stove with more force than I intended. "I'm not talking about this anymore. You're accusing me of terrible things." I stirred the noodles for the goulash and hefted the pot to the sink. Steam rose as the water poured out and they drained, fogging the window that looked out to the bay.

I carried the noodles back to the stove and added them to the turkey mixture. "Set the table, Roy," I instructed him in a quiet voice, "and stop talking nonsense."

He turned to the cabinets, opened one, and pulled down plates. They clattered as he placed them on the table.

"I've never had any real proof," he said, opening a drawer for silverware. He pushed it shut with his hip. "That is, until yesterday."

I reached up to a shelf where I kept spices. "Oh really? What gave me away, the type of cranberry relish I ate for Thanksgiving?"

"Signing that contract. Your strange reaction to the buyer's signature."

The house was silent except for the bubbling of the goulash. "I don't understand."

"I didn't either, at first, but then I remembered a man Henry and I interrogated."

"This gets more and more complicated." I sprinkled the contents of a jar into the goulash and stirred.

"Bear with me. This guy told us about a spy who was extremely fastidious about penmanship."

"Nothing wrong with that." My voice sounded flat.

"He described a young German woman whose father was a Jewish doctor. In 1933 her family fled the Nazis for Switzerland, eventually settling in Moscow."

I swallowed, and he went on.

"She was educated at elite Party schools and trained for undercover work. After the war, she went to the Soviet-occupied zone of Berlin, becoming part of the East German foreign intelligence service. Sound familiar?"

"Yes." I carried the pot of goulash to the table. "It sounds like a John le Carré novel." I struggled to keep my voice light. "Sit down, Roy, and let's eat."

He pulled out my chair with a flourish. He was enjoying himself, demonstrating just how clever he was. "Don't you want to hear the punch line?"

"You mean there's more?" I gave a gay little laugh and spooned goulash onto his plate and then mine. I took my napkin, spreading it carefully onto my lap.

"Yes. The best part, you might say." He put a forkful of the steaming noodles up to his lips and blew on them. "The agent we were questioning said that the German spy was known to be ruthless, with a strange trait: an almost sadistic hatred of poor penmanship." He paused. "I'll never forget what he did, Rachel. He held up his hands, like this," Roy spread his fingers out, palms toward me, "and he was missing the middle finger from each. The agent had hacked them off to teach him a lesson."

"Quite the story."

"Isn't it? Now you can see why I thought of you."

"I see—my flair for the dramatic? My skills with a butcher knife?" I tried to smile.

"Your reaction to that signature yesterday."

"I'm flattered that you think I could have been—could still be—a notorious spy." I took a gulp of my wine. "Try the goulash."

"Sure smells heavenly." He peered down at his fork. "These mushrooms remind me of the ones we ate in Austria, the heaping basketfuls you gathered in the Vienna woods."

"Yes," I said. The same mushrooms I'd picked as a girl in Hechingen, and later in the forest outside Moscow. The ones often confused with deadly *Amanitas*, a small quantity of which I kept dried in a jar among the spices.

He took a bite, chewed, and gagged violently.

I watched him slump to the floor. Several moments later I would take his pulse, grind up the goulash in my garbage disposal, and carefully wash and dry the dishes. I would put dessert on the table, compose myself, and phone for an ambulance. But first, I bent down and kissed his cooling cheek.

"It's over," Roy rasped. "Can't you see that it's over?"

I knew he was referring to the Cold War, and I gave a sad smile. "Not for me, Roy. It will never be over for me." A thin trickle of spittle seeped from his mouth as I sat back on my haunches. "*Auf Wiedersehen.*"

How often in the weeks that have followed have I wished for a different ending to Roy's story? Wished that he had never made the connection exposing me, wished that he had not been the one to list my house, wished with all my heart that he'd anticipated my lethal nature? Even as I watched the emergency responders try to restart Roy's heart, I pictured the way a different scenario might have played out. I saw Roy, raising a hidden gun, firing, and my world going black. Roy, realizing that my cover had to be protected at all costs because it was the only world I had ever known.

My wishes all vanished when they wheeled him away.

Now I rise at dawn to take my walks. I listen to stories, eat oatmeal. I keep my secrets and save my memories, especially those of good friends who were hell to put down.

EAST MEETS WEST

BY JONATHAN STONE

Yes, sure, joy, celebration, jubilation, dancing in the streets, standing atop it triumphantly with upraised fists for the world's photographers, rock music blasting from open apartment windows, spray painting the dirty grim brick and stone in exuberant neon red and orange and blue, happy vodka- and schnapps-fueled reunions and toasts and excitement and tears of gratitude, yes, sure, but now there is also the jurisdictional nightmare, the integration of Berlin city services separated for almost three decades, subway line and bus line confusion, new hospital assignments and emergency vehicle routes, new patrol zones and a new public safety management grid, and that is why I am striding, in cold November, two days after the fall of the Wall, to meet one Inspector Alexander Grimmenkauf at one of the old checkpoints, because the investigation's thin trail of evidence so far winds a path on both sides.

Because amid the joy and jubilation and celebration, a young woman has been murdered.

And if you were to observe this meeting—say, from one of the celebratory open apartment windows—you would laugh at the cliché of it, because I am so West German—from my leather jacket and moptop black hair (an indirect legacy of the Beatles' famed

Hamburg stint), to sloppy mustache, to my jazz CD collection, to my sweet blond American girlfriend, Susie (dozing this morning at my pad on Tiergartenstrasse), and Grimmenkauf (whose reputation precedes him) is so Eastern bloc—stepping out of the past and out of one of those noir American films Susie and I have been seeing—trenchcoat, collar turned up, black fedora. Short, squat, compact, and powerful beneath it. Classic Stasi. As schooled in torture and coercion and confession as I am schooled in forensic techniques and databases. As steeped in enforcement's murky ugly past as I am in police work's best practices and weekly white papers. And the idea of our working together—of my selection for the case, and of his—with our methods so utterly separated by technology, culture, style, police law—is someone's idea of a joke. A lab experiment assembled by our respective departments. Even our ages conspire in the metaphor—I am just thirty, looking forward in career and life, he is past sixty, looking back at both.

"Herr Grimmenkauf."

"Herr Bunder."

He shakes my hand, glances up at me merely dutifully, and allows only the briefest ironic smile—just enough to tell me that he knows too, what a joke this is. Some administrative committee's hasty response to sudden shifting conditions. Symbolic. And ridiculous.

And then—no preliminaries, no chat from him. "We can walk to the crime scene and the morgue," he says flatly. "In that way, a very convenient murder." He turns, and begins leading me.

Making it clear. *I'm not going to be a poster boy for détente. For Western victory and normalization. Let's figure this out, and go our separate ways as quickly as possible.*

Cops don't walk on the Western side, we'll take our Mercedes sedans even two blocks. But Grimmenkauf walks, I learn. And as I fall in silently behind him, I notice the limp, of course. Trenchcoat, turned-up collar, gruff monosyllables—and he's even got the grim limp. Noir on noir. You couldn't make this guy up.

* * *

We walk in silence. And it is walking through the past. Floating through an alternate universe existing alongside my own. Through the trash, and the crumbling, and the decades of sorrow and isolation and imprisonment, and two days later there is still jubilation and smiling and energy from the people, but the buildings around them, the crumbling infrastructure and roadway beneath them, are the vision into what their lives have been. The stunning events of the last two days don't suddenly erase the last thirty years.

The morgue is as primitive as I expected. Slabs in a basement room, indecipherable paperwork and record-keeping, grumbling resentful functionaries who recite the rules mindlessly and unbending. A dead woman on a slab in a basement morgue: to me, a perfect summation of East Germany.

"Anna Hoppler," Grimmenkauf says, as we stand over her. "Twenty-four. Graduate student in pharmacology. Found at 31 Strasse Aussenlander. Multiple blows to the skull with a blunt instrument," he recites with what must be an Eastern bloc sense of irony, because we are looking at a thoroughly crushed-in cranium. Just about enough, coupled with the displaced cranial and facial bone, to obliterate the vision of her original beauty—but not quite.

"Pretty." I correct myself. "Once."

He leans closer to her, as if trying to see for himself. He shrugs.

Her body—pale, deflated, now a mere used vessel—is nevertheless taut and supple. Nights dancing, and in the small hours, spreading those long legs and with them, languorous joy. A good-looking grad student. What a waste.

"Pharmacology? Sounds ambitious and practical."

Grimmenkauf smiles grimly, briefly.

"What?"

He wipes the smile away, still looking at her. "Anna was a prostitute."

I look at him questioningly. He shrugs again. "On this side, it's a way of life. To get cigarettes, booze. To save some money. To barter for a little joy." Then his steely blue eyes go hard again, professional. "We know the prostitutes. We know the trade, the traffic. That's our research. Our database." And he taps his head.

He is teasing me, of course. On our side, it's computers, national databases, interagency cooperation, orderly electronic files. On this side, it's a more traditional method of information storage.

I ask the obvious. "So where are you on her johns? Any regulars?"

"One in particular. American military boyfriend. With all the access, plus goodies and treats to bring her. That's why she was with him." The Allies moved relatively freely between East and West, papers issued by embassies a required but quick and painless formality. They are the kings; the chosen; the Americans.

I'm already getting the sense—the instinct. This could turn out to be very easy—and very hard.

"And what do we know about the boyfriend?"

"Corporal Chad Miller. Chicago, USA. Good looking." Adding, after a pause, so the thought can stand on its own, "Entrepreneurial."

"Meaning…?"

"You name it…he traded it. We know of Chad. A very industrious young man. An American love of commerce," he says with a smirk.

It's clear that I can ask a former Stasi directly, cop to cop; no intervening nicety or formality required. "Was it him?"

"Oh, it was him." He points to his belly, still impressively tight, disciplined, from what I can see. "I know it here." And then to his head. "But not yet here."

Grimmenkauf's initial "fieldwork," let's call it, has already informed him how Ms. Hoppler's pharmacology studies put her exactly where she needed to be. In the hospital supply rooms. At the medical lockers. Access—and privacy. "So they each were bringing something to the dance. On his side, he was dealing the drugs. Selling to other soldier dealers in Western Europe. Trading them for drugs and other products that he would bring to the East German side. Making money in both directions." He looks at me mournfully, his face hanging. "And we'll never get him for it, and he knows it."

"Why not?" I'm already building the case in my mind. "Relationship to the victim. Establish movement on the night of the crime. Trace the money trail. Testimony from recipients of stolen goods in exchange for avoiding prosecution..." Seems straightforward enough.

He shakes his head, starts to explain. And I quickly come to understand that Chad is not only one enterprising bastard. He is lucky beyond belief. And lucky, perhaps, beyond justice.

In the East German judicial system, a murder case comes before a panel of three administrative judges—no jury of one's peers, nothing so egalitarian. They are appointed by the state, and in the pocket of the Communist Party—career Party stooges—who normally would convict on the flimsiest of circumstantial evidence. It was a systematized corruption that would make an African warlord blush. Mock trials—invented here.

But now, according to Grimmenkauf, with the prospect of a real system of law being established in short order, all these corrupt East German judges were suddenly facing lawsuits against them from countless unjustly convicted defendants. West German lawyers had filed cases already, literally thousands, in the past forty-eight hours. And these judges would now be looking to demonstrate an understanding of such subtle and previously unexercised concepts as due process and reasonable doubt in order to curry favor with their new West German colleagues who would soon be sitting in judgment of them, and especially with the Americans—who would have significant influence in the new judicial policies of a united Germany. These corrupt career jurists were angling to avoid prison themselves. They could see the handwriting on the Berlin Wall—and they would do what they could to hastily rewrite it.

Grimmenkauf smiled, explaining the irony. How previously it would delight them to convict an American serviceman dealing contraband on the Eastern Bloc side. (Would the American military intervene? If so, it would appear as if *they* were trying to manipulate the system.) But now, these judges would only convict if a case was utterly proven. The testimony of informants, the mere say-so of local cops, circumstantial evidence, would never cut it. There would need to be an unbroken chain of evidence, certainly including a murder weapon. In an environment of leniency, of liberation, of enlightenment, they would do everything to not appear as the force of darkness they had always been.

"These are political appointees, these judges, political creatures. All their lives, their verdicts have had nothing to do with evidence or justice, everything to do with politics. Now, they feel the political wind shifting, and they will shift with it—it's all they know."

Politics. Bringing the liberation of millions of East Germans. And one American corporal who doesn't deserve it.

Justice—a blunt instrument, at best, behind the iron curtain.

And now apparently, no weight to the instrument at all.

One more aspect of the joke Grimmenkauf and I are inhabiting.

"This Corporal Miller. I assume I'm going to meet him shortly?"

"Our next stop," smiles Grimmenkauf. "We can't hold him. But the military has made him available to us..." he grunts, raises an eyebrow, "as a witness."

The rest of the world hears about the Wall, sees the photos, the barbed wire, the sections made broader and thicker over the years, as if the Wall itself is growing into grim, gray adulthood, and the world knows the stories of those shot trying to cross, their bodies left to bleed out, for those on both sides to see. But in fact, it's a sieve. How could it not be, with a border of over 100 kilometers between the countries; 43 kilometers in Berlin alone. Thousands have made it across successfully over the years. A remarkable brave few evading the guards above their heads (by glider and balloon), and many more under their feet, in the leaky maze of the subway tunnels—those subway lines that cross the border officially sealed off, but the network of repair tunnels still there. And in fact, in the years since the West Germans were allowed to cross in and out daily with the right paperwork, it became of course even tougher to police.

Hence, Corporal Miller.

He is in uniform camos. Black wavy hair grown out a little, as the U.S. military now allows. He has a smiling, cheerful, upbeat way, practically a spoof of the guileless American character. There is also a U.S. military advocate in the interview room, which the U.S. military always provides. In fact I know him, Captain Laughton, and I know the type, from dealing with soldiers stationed in West Germany who get themselves into some bit of trouble over the years. I can see that Grimmenkauf is a little surprised and annoyed by this bit of procedure. I've seen the soldiers inevitably get off with a slap of the wrist, with good relations maintained and unjeopardized between Western powers. Not always, but generally.

"Corporal Miller, I'm Inspector Bunder of the Berlin police department," I tell him. Grimmenkauf has decided to listen from outside the interview room, muttering to me that his anonymity might be useful later. "We have a few questions for you."

"Go ahead," says Captain Laughton. Puffing out his chest. As if to say, *This all goes through me. I have authority here.*

"Did you know Anna Hoppler?"

"Sure," Miller says. "Everyone knew Anna." A slippery little smile.

I feel a twinge of anger at this. At its rudeness, at its casual, insolent carelessness. Corporal Chad Miller, operating with impunity. The American military moved liked kings. Immune. Lofty. Unassailable. Heroes, unscarred and untested. "What does that mean, everyone knew Anna?" *Does that mean everyone slept with her?*

"A group of guys from the base used to party with her and her friends."

"Regularly?"

He considers. Cocks his head. "Off and on." That slippery little smile again.

Off and on. I leave it alone for now.

"Were you partying with her on November ninth?" The night the wall fell. The night Anna died.

"Everyone was partying with everyone, man." He smiles. "It was some wild shit."

And though he is pretending to be a regular American dumbass GI—and doing a passable job at it—I am picking up more. And here is what I already feared, and what Chad is already confirming. *It was such a wild, confusing, crazy night over here, you'll never be able to sort out who was where, who saw what, who was doing who.* Generalized insanity—the perfect cover for murder. As the murderer would know in a premeditated way—or get extremely lucky with, if it was a crime of impulse or passion.

"Do you know where Miss Hoppler worked during the day?"

He shakes his head. "Nah." Still playing the dumb soldier.

"You don't know she worked at the hospital pharmacy?"

He shrugs.

I look at his wrist. "That is an awfully nice wristwatch, soldier," I said.

The arrogance, the insolence, to wear that wristwatch to a meeting like this. Or perhaps, not to even think about it? It could not have been more apparent. Chad the black marketeer. Casual or big time, remained to be seen.

There is probably no more vibrant black market in the world than Berlin's. No surprise. All the abundance of the West on one side of the wall, all the want and need of the East on the other. It creates an irresistible vacuum, a spinning vortex of goods and desire, with everything imaginable swirling in it—jeans, TVs, computers, cell phones, watches, cigarettes, liquor, jewelry. Even chocolates and candy. And, at the center of the swirling vortex, of course, its common currency, its constant rate of exchange—drugs.

"American goods. And with them, American values," Grimmenkauf mutters summarily, as we watch Chad saunter out of the stationhouse with Captain Laughton. "And now all of Germany can have those American values. *Wunderbar.*"

I look at Grimmenkauf, and stay silent, not wanting to be lured into a political argument. Is he needling me, commenting on my own values, on my American girlfriend? He seizes my momentary silence as a chance to go further.

"American-style freedom," he snickers. "Freedom of choice. Sure. The freedom to choose who you kill, and kill who you choose." He broods. He warns. "You watch. East Germans won't know what to do with freedom. Won't understand it."

And Anna, did she want, admire, lust for, those American values too? Commerce? Freedom? Did she want to better herself, lift herself up? Did she want just a little piece of Chad's business? To be a capitalist? To be free to choose?

And maybe Corporal Miller didn't like that. Didn't like it one bit.

Corporal Miller—earnest witness, thanked for his time and testimony—goes blissfully, ignorantly on with his life, full speed ahead, in the wide-open, post–collapse party atmosphere. People are celebrating, rules are changing or suspended outright, it's Chad's time to shift into high gear; to shine. Over the next several days, Grimmenkauf tracks Chad everywhere—limping after him, unseen, invisible, serenely and superbly professional and adept, unsuspected by the arrogant Chad, who is blind to all but the profit motive. And Chad, it turns out, is dealing everything. Swapping jewelry for pharmaceuticals, pharmaceuticals for cocaine, cocaine for cash, cash for cigarettes. Born richer and more privileged, he would be peddling institutional bonds and trading insider tips on Wall Street, but the kid is Army, so he's doing the next best thing. He is a one-man supermarket. Operating with the impunity, access, and mobility of his U.S. citizenship and the implied might and threat of his armed military pals behind him. It was every confirmation of Grimmenkauf's hard-line, right-wing, cynical view of the world. And worse, it could turn out to be exactly right.

Chad—what kind of name is that anyway? Has no meaning. American meaninglessness. American blandness. It itches at me, annoys me. And I realize: Grimmenkauf's anti-American sentiments are rubbing off on me.

Grimmenkauf had recently lost both his wife and son to cancer—larynx, bladder, one year apart. He presses on alone. As if fairly certain that cancer can't ever touch him. Can't incubate in him. That nothing can. He is too hostile an environment, too harsh, too forbidding, for cancer. Cancer will have to nestle somewhere else.

I only learn about the cancer deaths from my own comrades on the West German side, who ask how it's going with bemusement. Not from Grimmenkauf. He never mentions it.

We are building a case step by laborious step—as if with a limp. We have turned up some eyewitnesses who will place Chad and Anna together, alone, on the night of the murder, who can put Chad in Anna's apartment, but can they prove themselves coherent enough amid the partying, if they're put on the witness stand? They are all kids; all jobless. And Grimmenkauf grumbles, reiterates the politics, that the panel of judges won't convict on merely a logical chain of connection, they'll need proof, irrefutable. Proof as blunt and unforgiving as whatever killed Anna Hoppler.

Anna's dark, drafty apartment has been picked over thoroughly. The West German police have swept it carefully, professionally. The East German police swept it brutally. And Grimmenkauf and I inspect it ourselves afterward—look at every chipped corner of furniture, every pot handle, every hairbrush, every book, every closet top, every toilet tank, every fireplace implement—for blood, for anything, and find nothing.

Chad's apartment is clean—mockingly so. Nothing stashed. It is a spoof of the bachelor pad—sleek and clean, burnished and expensive, polished gleaming surfaces, utterly unused kitchen utensils, shiny sinks, way out of line for a soldier (he spends scant time in the barracks, only the two nights a week he is required to). As if the apartment says, *Look all you like. There is nothing here.*

And as we search it, Grimmenkauf won't let the beer garden politics go. "An apartment like this—this is what the typical East German thinks freedom will mean. An existence of sleek modern surfaces with no history and no past. They long for freedom, because they think it comes with accommodations like this. Because that is the sales job that the Western media has done on us. Freedom as Western goods, as American lifestyle. No wonder the Americans are such champions of freedom. Because they know deep down that it is really a matter of untapped markets, of economic potential…"

Grimmenkauf's hatred of American values only finds more expression as the days go on.

He is still dutifully limping after Corporal Miller when Miller wanders into a West German post office branch.

A fact which, when Grimmenkauf mentions it, catches my interest—and my instincts—much more than it does his. Because I know, as Grimmenkauf doesn't, that Corporal Miller can ship and receive at no cost, overnight, any cargo, any freight, through the PX at the military base. The faster, cheaper, far superior way for him to ship. So why the German post office?

"Obviously," says Grimmenkauf, "to avoid the risk of his packages being inspected by the American military."

He's right. It is obvious. Safety. Anonymity. And there I would have left it. But something is beating at me; something feels odd. *No cost. Overnight. Ship and receive for free.* Lower middle-class Army kid from the wrong side of Chicago, out hustling the world. The transactional personality. The trader. Wouldn't he gravitate to the most profitable method? Figure out an arrangement, as he apparently had with Anna? Wouldn't he find a way to make a deal?

On a hunch, I checked with authorities on the base, with whom we West Germans have a good working relationship and who saw no reason not to cooperate, and it turned out that Colonel Miller was shipping *plenty* of goods through the American PX. He clearly felt a high degree of safety and confidentiality in using the American PX. Clearly he had his own contacts there, partners he could trust, cut in on some profits, and thereby blackmail and control.

A little digging and prodding, and we get the full picture: Pharmaceuticals. Untracked duty-free timepieces. African pelts. Monkey brains. Rhinoceros testicles. Freeze-dried poppy seeds. Corporal Miller is a one-man transfer station. A one-man import-export center. We could bust him on any of these, of course. But it will be another slap on the wrist; a tortuous legal process. We want him, we need him, for Anna.

So—a robust use and enjoyment of the American PX advantages.

Except, maybe, if you're sending something you *really* can't risk. Only then do you turn to the official, anonymous, utterly reliable German postal system.

Anonymous, that is, until we persuade the postal service for an inspection exemption. Circumventing privacy rules with the reluctant assistance of none other than my brother Siggy, a long-standing, dutiful postal employee, who nervously, grudgingly, locates the appropriate confidential shipping waybills for us. A little family connection. A little back-scratching. A little arm-twisting. A little East German tactics on my part, I guess. My nod to my partner of the moment, Herr Grimmenkauf.

We find only a couple of receipts. The bare minimum disclosed on them. Including the shipping date.

A package sent the morning of November 10th, 9 a.m. Contents undisclosed, as is permitted. But the date stamp is clear.

The morning after the Wall fell. The morning after the partying.

The morning after Anna Hoppler was murdered. Just as the post office opened.

Giving me a thin hope, the sliver of a sense, that Chad didn't hide the murder weapon, didn't bury it, or throw it in the river.

That he shipped it.

Remember I said it was a joke, this East West partnership of Grimmenkauf and me? Well, the joke now accelerates. Gets straight to the punch line. Because the German police—as if to have the full belly laugh out of this—happily pay to put us both on a flight from Berlin to London to Los Angeles, California. To Grimmenkauf's fabled, beloved America. To Los Angeles, no less, the belly of the beast. To an address in West Hollywood, where some particularly large cartons sent by Corporal Miller have made their way before us.

Grimmenkauf in Los Angeles. The trenchcoat, the squat form, hunched against the unfamiliar sunshine, the gleam off buildings. Squinting out the rental car's passenger side window as we wind our way up into the Hollywood Hills. Looking at the gleaming, buffed, immaculate ostentation. Disgusted, dreamily, fascinated, silent, as if he has arrived in heaven and hell simultaneously.

I am fully expecting one of Grimmenkauf's anticapitalist diatribes. *Look how precarious, Herr Bunder. Look where they build, on outcroppings of rock, on shifting land. It is irresponsible. Arrogant. A statement of impermanence. Beautiful homes built on the backs of Mexican laborers. Who tend their green lawns and picture-book shrubbery for them. These hills themselves like a Hollywood set.*

Of course, these are my own observations. Grimmenkauf never utters a word. Are his anti-American views infecting me? Or perhaps, convincing me?

We cruise now along Mulholland Drive—a street name I recognize from the noir movies with Susie—but on this Los Angeles morning, sunshine bright and bouncing against the rental car sheet metal, against the bright clean road bed. It is the polar opposite of East Berlin, I'm thinking. In weather, appearance, attitude, in past and history (or lack thereof), in atmosphere both literal and metaphoric, in every possible way, its opposite. Grimmenkauf stares out. Blue eyes soaking it in.

The woman's name is Elaine Markham. The home is beautiful, of course. A big glistening swimming pool, overlooking the Los Angeles valley. Bright colorful abstract paintings on the wall. Ms. Markham greets us in her red tracksuit. Early forties. Bronzed. Gleaming smile. Plastic surgery on her upturned nose, her high cheeks, and her ample and equally upturned breasts. A Hollywood liberal. I once thought that Grimmenkauf and I were opposites, but I have been significantly trumped—as I see polished, sunny Elaine Markham and wrinkled, trenchcoated Grimmenkauf regard each other—from across the globe, from across the universe, divergent species passing unexpectedly close.

We see it on display in the bright living room at the same time, Grimmenkauf and I. Presented beautifully on a pedestal, with a pin light on it. She sees us both looking, and smiles.

"That's right," she says. "A piece of the Berlin Wall. To us, it's so symbolic," she says, eyes glistening, still visibly moved by this recent triumph of the human spirit. "Such a powerful political moment. Such a statement of freedom." She looks at it with awe. We step closer to it.

It is amusing, entertaining, to see a piece of the wall we have lived with, dull obtrusive brick, part of our lives like roadway or culvert or drainage pipe or curb, enshrined like this. Worshipped. Like bowing down to a roll of toilet paper.

"This is what Corporal Miller shipped to you?" I ask.

"Yes. Isn't it wonderful?"

Chad the black marketeer.

Another product. Another sudden lucky way to make a buck.

Grimmenkauf then asks her, in his hesitant English: "He sent you more pieces, yes?"

"Oh yes," she says proudly.

"We can see?"

"Sure."

"Each one you will sell?"

She looks offended. "Fund-raising. To promote the cause of freedom."

"How much for a brick?"

"Each goes for $3,000 dollars."

We stare at her blankly—both of us imagining what $3,000 dollars U.S. would mean in our pay envelopes and in our lives.

"It goes to charity," she explains. "A charity in West Germany to benefit sick and disabled East German children, called Liberation."

Liberating you from your cash, I thought. Grimmenkauf and I both knew who we would find behind said "charity." We knew its founder and sole proprietor.

Grimmenkauf takes the other bricks out of the big open cartons in Elaine Markham's huge walk-in storage closet.

Ordinary bricks, though most with splashes of vibrant celebratory spray-painted color, all of them still wrapped fully, carefully, in tissue paper.

He finally comes to—unwraps—the last brick in the bottom of one of the cartons.

One side of the brick is completely covered in red.

Merely more paint, graffiti, to the untrained eye. The running joyful color of protest, the bright vibrant evidence of the human spirit.

But to Grimmenkauf and myself, it is obvious.

The West German lab will confirm the blood type. I will guide Grimmenkauf through the new process of DNA matching.

A blunt instrument.

Symbol of freedom.

Though Corporal Miller's has finally come to an end.

But they have no legal stature to impound the brick

A brick from the Wall. All the weight, heft, and consequence a panel of skittish judges could ask for.

The carefully bagged brick is between us now, as we wind our way back down out of the Hollywood Hills.

In the celebratory chaos of that Berlin night, wouldn't it be easy for Corporal Miller to simply dispose of it? Drop it in a river or stream? Leave it by the side of a road in the dust and rain? Crush it into pieces, bury it in one of the growing piles of Berlin wall rubble? Yes, he is a risk taker, with a risk taker's personality, but doesn't this go foolishly beyond that?

"Why ship it?" I ask. "Why take the chance?"

Grimmenkauf narrows his blue eyes. And the old Stasi—lifelong student of, and witness to, human behavior under duress—smiles thinly, and soon shows he has given up none of his acuity. A limp, yes—but he has not lost a step.

"Panic, Herr Bunder. Panic shipped in a cardboard box." His steely blue eyes stare out, unblinking. And then, more quietly: "It is one thing to be a cool, confident young entrepreneur. Party drugs, contraband, fancy watches, exotic pelts—sure, why not? But when you kill someone?" His blue eyes squint. "You suddenly enter a new terrain. You cross a border," he says, pausing, looking at me, and speaking, I realize, from a place very distant from this California sunshine. "And when you first cross this border, everything changes. You are no longer cool and confident. You don't think clearly. You miscalculate. Make poor judgments. You have fuzzy, childish thoughts—get the bad object as far away as possible, as fast as possible." Now he looks away. "A twenty-year-old kid who murders someone, someone close, in cold blood? Trust me—you are shaken. You are no longer the same."

Trust me. You are no longer the same. And I see that Grimmenkauf is speaking from that same far side of the border. From the dark side of that wall.

"For that brick to end up in some unknown wealthy American home—the ultimate hiding place, you think, yes? Forever anonymous among the other bricks. But that is the West German way to see it—a brilliant, inspired twist of commerce. Now look at it the East German way—a desperate act, terrified and impulsive, and in the end, futile." He turns back to me, blue eyes swimming. "So which is it, Herr Bunder?"

Brilliant? Or desperate? But the verdict is already in. Miller is caught. Grimmenkauf is right.

Smiling a little now, feeling expansive, suddenly enjoying California, the sunshine on his pale craggy face, Grimmenkauf settles back in the passenger seat, and sums it up for himself. "In a panic, Colonel Miller resorted to capitalism," he says. "But capitalism, Herr Bunder, can't solve all life's problems." A pause. A chuckle. "Especially murder."

His worldview confirmed—and basking in a rare, brief moment of justice and order—my partner Alexander Grimmenkauf turns his pale face to the passenger window, and rolls it down for one last blast of California sun and air.

But East will never meet West.

SHOW STOPPER

BY GIGI VERNON

The dress had a recklessly full skirt, nearly eight meters of hand-painted silk, and was the most capitalistically decadent garment Ludmila Blatova had ever designed. Every time she set needle or shears to it, a shock, a combination of adoration and apprehension, rippled along her spine and tightened her abdomen. She still couldn't believe the dress was permitted. But Khrushchev himself had directed that no expense or extravagance was to be spared for the 1959 Soviet Exhibition of Science, Technology, and Culture in New York City. There, the USSR's superiority would be demonstrated in every aspect of life, from Sputnik to rugs. They'd already beaten the Americans in the race to outer space. But they'd always lagged behind in fashion. Until now. The clothes shown in New York would epitomize the socialist aesthetic—simple, modest, and functional. Even Westerners would want them.

Ludmila was one of four designers brought to the center of Soviet fashion, the Moscow ODMO, the All-Union House of Prototypes, but she was the only one plucked from a provincial garment factory. The others came from GUM, the state-sponsored department store. For months, all of them had worked long hours on the collection of daywear and evening gowns that would represent the

Soviet Union in New York. None of them complained. To handle such luxurious materials and patterns was a dream. And a nightmare. One misstep or accident—a clumsy drape or silhouette, the wrong length, crooked or puckered seams, a smear of blood from a pricked finger on a priceless textile—might mean a Siberian gulag, or so Ludmila feared.

They were to be steered clear of such disasters through the close supervision of a senior ODMO designer, Vladlena Gribkova. Not only was her father a high-ranking Party member and Deputy Commissar of the Ministry of Light Production, but also she'd had the benefit of visiting Paris, twice. Her advantages showed in the brilliance of her work. Every design in the collection showed her creative stamp. Ludmila was as jealous of her position and spotless pedigree as of her talent.

Ludmila was the only designer allowed to contribute an entirely original dress to the collection, an honor which both thrilled and terrified her. As she feverishly worked, nausea alternated with light-headedness. She could scarcely sleep and had no interest in food. The only hunger she felt was for the chance to realize more of her ideas. She hoped her cherished dress was just the beginning of a dazzling career. If she could impress Gribkova, Ludmila might gain a permanent position at ODMO, advance, and maybe, one day, become senior designer herself. She tried her best to win over Gribkova, but the senior designer rebuffed all attempts with chilly resentment and mistrust, or so it seemed to Ludmila.

"Is it finished?" Gribkova asked, standing over Ludmila.

All afternoon Ludmila had labored over the skirt's hem, which required thousands of tiny invisible stitches. "Another minute or two." She didn't look up and kept sewing, hoping the anxious tremble of her fingers escaped the senior designer's scrutiny.

The only soft thing about Gribkova was her generous curves. Everything else was cold and sharp—her voice, demeanor, and scathing criticism, her elegant spiked heels and cat-eye glasses. She was tireless and seemed to see and hear everything. No one dared pilfer fabric scraps or extra buttons, or indulge in anticommunist jokes.

Out of the corner of her eye, Ludmila saw the pointed toe of Gribkova's black pump impatiently tapping the floor. Ludmila had been so proud of her own new flat sandals from Poland, which she'd procured after standing in line for hours. Now, compared to Gribkova, the shoes made her feel as sturdy and practical as her homemade button-down dress.

At last, Ludmila made the final stitch, cut the thread, and handed Gribkova the skirt for her inspection. "There. Done."

Gribkova took it, her lips pursed, ready to disapprove. Holding it up to the light, she examined it centimeter by centimeter. When she'd finished, she called, "Inessa."

Inessa was the model assigned to the dress. A twenty-two-year-old redhead. She and the other models lounged in their underwear around a scarred wooden table in a corner of the workroom, smoking, gossiping, and turning dog-eared pages of *Zhurnal mod* and *Modelt zesona*, while they waited to be fitted. At her name, Inessa stood and melodramatically threw off a blanket draped around her shoulders. "Yes, Comrade Gribkova," she said, hiding a giggle behind her hand. She was always giggling. Tall and stick-thin, her best feature was her almond-shaped eyes and long eyelashes. From certain angles, she might have looked like a giraffe, but on the runway she walked like a goddess.

"Put it on so we can check it again," Gribkova ordered.

Inessa bent down and held her skinny arms over her head like a child so Ludmila could slip the dress over them.

"The petticoat too," Gribkova said to Ludmila.

She helped Inessa climb into the layers of stiff netting.

The dress became a frothy confection that took Ludmila's breath away.

"Walk," Gribkova ordered. She peered critically at the model as she pranced up and down the workroom.

Ludmila peered too, chewing her lower lip.

Inessa stopped and whirled, showing off, as vain as if the dress belonged to her. It was sleeveless with a form-fitting bodice that ballooned into a full skirt. The cream colored silk was tissue-paper fragile, like moth wings. From a distance the fabric appeared to be spotted with fashionably large, multicolored polka dots. Closer, the dots resolved themselves into a pattern, each dot a traditional Ukrainian motif delicately rendered in shades of azure, carmine, teal, and sunflower. The tones suited Inessa's bronze freckles, and the fit was perfect.

The dress was to be worn at cocktail parties, which were apparently common in the West, or so Ludmila had been told. Couples and young single professionals held them at their big suburban houses in the early evening before dinner. Everyone dressed up. Martinis and other fancy mixed drinks and appetizers were served. She herself had neither attended nor heard of any Russian attending or hosting such gatherings, but her social circles were limited to a few seamstress friends.

"Stop. Don't move," Gribkova ordered and picked up Ludmila's razor-sharp shears. Holding them like a weapon, the open blades glinting in the light, she walked over and cut a dangling thread. Then she stood back.

She and Ludmila studied the dress looking for more flaws. Ludmila could see none.

"All right," Gribkova said, with a curt nod. "You can take it off."

Ludmila helped the model wiggle out of the dress, gingerly, so very gingerly. A ripped seam and they might find themselves both convicted of sabotage and sentenced to ten years' hard labor.

Gribkova clapped her hands and addressed them all. "Workers. That is enough for today. Tidy up and then go home. Get some rest. It's another early day tomorrow."

Dutifully, Ludmila began to straighten up her workstation.

"Ludmila," Gribkova said.

"Yes, Comrade Gribkova?"

"Stay behind. I want to speak to you."

Ludmila swallowed. Had the senior designer changed her mind? Gribkova didn't like the dress after all. It was to be purged from the collection. She might even censure Ludmila for individualistic tendencies and send her back to Minsk. Not trusting herself to speak, Ludmila nodded.

Once the others filed out, Gribkova wearily sank onto a stool. "I congratulate you. The Deputy Commissar has seen your dress and is satisfied that it is far superior to any American party dress. It will be a centerpiece of the New York City show." She pronounced this news in the same stark tone that she denounced something as an utter and disgusting failure. "It embodies the style and comfort Comrade Khrushchev envisions for the modern Soviet woman."

This wasn't what Ludmila had been expecting. Her face turned hot, which she knew resulted in unbecoming blotches. "Oh," she said, the word squeaky with relief. "Thank you, Comrade. That is very kind of you." She realized she was babbling but couldn't stop herself. "And him. Comrade Khrushchev. And all of them. Too kind. Of everyone."

Gribkova seemed unmoved by gratitude. In the same icy tone, she continued, "Furthermore, when we go to New York, we will need a hard worker who's skilled with a needle, someone able to handle any last-minute crisis that might arise. The deputy commissar has agreed. You will come to New York City."

Ludmila's face became even hotter, and no doubt even more blotchy, and her vision blurred. "Oh, thank you, Comrade Gribkova."

"Just make sure I don't regret my decision," Gribkova said meaningfully.

Outside of the workroom, the lightbulb was burned out and the corridor deserted, but someone loitered, hidden by darkness.

"What do you want?" Ludmila asked, her tone more openly frightened than she intended.

Inessa stepped out of the shadows. "What did she say to you?"

she asked conspiratorially, her eyes shining with excitement. "Whatever she said, she's wrong. She's just jealous. It's the most beautiful dress I've ever worn. It's as good as anything from the Paris salons. I was in Paris last year, you know."

Despite her lack of respect for Inessa or her opinions about fashion, Ludmila flushed again. "Thank you," she said stiffly, not wanting to encourage the girl's familiarity. Inessa was half her age and flighty. Ludmila turned to go down the stairs, abruptly aware of a deep fatigue. Her eyes burned and her back ached.

Inessa linked arms as if they were old friends and accompanied her down the stairs. Ludmila's short legs and Inessa's stilts made a disjointed clatter on the scuffed wooden steps. Why this sudden friendship?

"I can't wait to get to New York City," Inessa continued. "What's the first thing you're going to buy?" Without waiting for an answer, she said, "Soviet Customs will turn a blind eye when we return if we slip them a little gift, you know. As long as we're not too greedy. Not too much or too big. I'm going to buy a cashmere twin set at Saks Fifth Avenue. It is one of the best American department stores, you know. It will be violet or perhaps crimson. Which shade do you think would suit me better?" She batted her eyelashes at Ludmila.

"Either," Ludmila said gruffly. How did Inessa know Ludmila would be going to New York City? Was it a guess? Or had she been eavesdropping?

"Or maybe silk pajamas. Igor would go wild. Igor's my fiancé, you know. He might even set a wedding date under their influence. Or I could get a Maidenform brassiere," Inessa chattered on, not seeming to expect responses.

They'd reached the street which was deserted at this late hour except for a porter on duty who was obviously KGB. Ludmila turned toward the Metro, which would take them to the Moscow State University dormitory where they'd been provided with temporary rooms. Inessa turned in the opposite direction.

GIGI VERNON

"Aren't you going back?" Ludmila asked.

"Not yet," Inessa said with a coy giggle, and began to walk backward. "A friend is having a little birthday party. I want to drop in."

Where did the girl get the energy? The young. Ludmila could barely keep her eyes open.

"Would you like to come?" Inessa asked. "Some very nice looking boys—men have been invited."

"What about your fiancé?" Ludmila searched her memory for his name. "Igor?"

"He can't come," Inessa pouted. "He has to work late. He's always working. He never wants to have any fun."

Ludmila remembered he was some kind of scientist, a physicist, involved with missiles. If you could believe what Inessa said.

"Come with me. Live a little," Inessa said.

"No, I can't. Thank you. Another time perhaps." Ludmila intended to fall into bed and sleep like the dead.

But later, when Ludmila tossed on her lumpy dormitory cot, she wondered if New York City was more curse than opportunity. If anything went badly, if the Party were unhappy with any aspect of the fashion exhibit or show, she would be a convenient scapegoat for Vladlena Gribkova.

Or was that Ludmila's paranoia surfacing again? It never left her for long. All her life she'd been haunted by her parents' fate. Her mother had been a tour guide and her father a translator of newspapers. One January night during Stalin's time, when Ludmila was just a girl, both had been arrested by the secret police. Eventually she learned they'd been convicted of espionage and sent to a gulag, where they died. They'd both been innocent. Their only crime had been contact with foreigners and a knowledge of English. Such activities and skills might not currently be construed as treason, but that could change. Ludmila remained cautious and kept her own knowledge of English to herself.

* * *

The remaining seats of the Aeroflot flight were filled by their escort of hatchet-faced KGB men and one lone woman with the hard expression of a prison matron, who must also be an agent.

They landed in New York at Idlewild Airport and were directed to U.S. Customs. Gribkova pulled Ludmila aside. "Help me."

But an army of American officials, all disconcertingly friendly and apologetic, whisked them through Customs. Not a single piece of luggage, trunk, box, or garment bag was opened. Not a single person was searched. A professional and diplomatic courtesy, it was understood. A gesture of goodwill toward the staff of an exhibition intended to foster warmer relations between the two superpowers. Besides, the Americans didn't care if they brought in illegal goods. A suitcase full of caviar, vodka, or furs? All relatively harmless. No, contraband would be the issue on the return journey, and Soviet Customs would not be so accommodating.

Outside, they were blinded by white sunshine. It was blistering, American hot. The only smell was exhaust; the only sight a desert of glittering automobiles, pavement, and ripples of rising heat. Ludmila was glad to be ushered into one of a waiting fleet of shiny black limousines, the interior dim, cool, and enormous. Several KGB men squeezed into the rows of seats with them.

On the drive into the city, the models gaped and exclaimed at the skyline. Ludmila wanted to do the same, but she didn't dare when she saw Vladlena Gribkova's impervious disdain. Instead she risked sideways glances out the windows. An assembly line of cars, all of them sounding their horns, inched through the granite crevices of Manhattan. Not only was it louder than she expected, it was also grimier and much darker, even on a sunny June afternoon. The flight had been long, and they were tired, but they were not taken to the hotel.

Instead they were driven to the New York Coliseum, where the exhibition was to take place. They pulled up to a white block of a building that looked like a futuristic flying saucer or a frosted cake. Protesters gathered in front holding signs, "Russkies Go Home."

Inside, they were met by a group of Americans, five or six men in gray suits and two women. They greeted the Russian delegation warmly as if they'd been the best of friends for many years. Polite introductions were exchanged, the Americans making a valiant effort to pronounce Russian names.

Ludmila was disconcerted by them and their smiles. Their teeth so white. Their shoulders and jaws so square. They seemed as unreal as mannequins.

The exhibition hall was an echoing cavern so large it could have contained whole airplanes. Air conditioning made it artificially cold and clammy, and Ludmila shivered. They were cocooned by an escort of KGB and Americans. An area had been reserved for fashion in the Culture section. There, workmen were constructing platforms, a stage, a runway, and dressing rooms. When Gribkova saw what they had done, she announced, "It's all wrong. Completely wrong. Who gave you these instructions?" She glared at them. "Wrong. Who told you to do it this way?" she repeated in careful, heavily accented English.

Most of the American workers assembling the exhibition were Negroes. They were the first Negroes Ludmila had ever seen. None of the men were actually black. Each man's skin was a slightly different color, rich, satiny shades that recalled chocolate, earth, coffee. They in turn stared at Vladlena Gribkova, trying to comprehend the Russian woman.

Two American women pushed their way to the front. Miss Bennett and Miss Johnstone, they'd called themselves. They wore summer suits, stylishly cut, one lilac with black trim, the other navy, both with half sleeves, and Ludmila could scarcely wrench her gaze from them. Both had pulled their hair into smooth buns at the base of their skulls. It turned out they were translators, and Gribkova began to lecture them about the problems with the layout.

Meanwhile, the models clustered in a corner, smoking, Inessa at the center. Ludmila joined them to escape the legion of forbidding gray-suited men. "Why so many KGB? Do they think we're conducting espionage?" she murmured.

"They must show Soviet superiority by outnumbering the CIA agents," Inessa whispered, with uncharacteristic sarcasm. At Ludmila's gasp of surprise, she giggled and added, "But they can't compete with the Americans on looks. Especially the one on the left. Dreamy."

Ludmila saw nothing remarkable about the man. Without much enthusiasm, she agreed, "Yes, very handsome."

After a moment, Inessa continued, "And those are only the KGB that are not undercover." She inclined her head slightly toward Vladlena Gribkova.

Of course there were informers, there were always informers, everywhere, but Ludmila hadn't suspected Gribkova. Informers were rarely subtle. They usually tried to entrap people, but Gribkova spoke only about fashion. How would Inessa know? "I don't believe you," she said aloud.

Inessa shrugged. "Just watch yourself around her, okay?"

Why would Inessa warn Ludmila? Just because she was wearing Ludmila's dress? No. It was more likely Inessa thought Ludmila had a future; that Ludmila would design clothes for her, help her build a modeling career. Ludmila was flattered, but had no intention of worrying about someone else. She had her own career to think about.

And then there wasn't time to think about anything. First, the garments had to be unpacked, pressed, hung up. One of the evening gowns was misplaced and panic ensued. Instead of joining the hunt, with breathless anxiety Ludmila looked for her own dress. Inessa was uncharacteristically helpful. Together the two of them located the box, which had been mislabeled "sewing tools and supplies." Inessa even helped her unpack it and found a place for it on the clothes rack.

Then, showroom exhibits had to be installed as well as the final preparations for the fashion show made. The evening before the opening day, a special preview and reception would be held, which would be attended by Deputy Premier Kozlov and other top Soviet officials, Vice President Nixon and his wife and daughter, the American and Soviet press, and many other illustrious dignitaries of both nations. It all had to be perfect. The order of models had to be adjusted. Last-minute alterations had to be made.

Days at the Coliseum sped by in a frenzy of pressing, trimming, cutting, and stitching. Vladlena Gribkova never asked for advice, and Ludmila never offered it. Ludmila just watched and learned, and little by little, it seemed, Vladlena came to trust her and rely on her.

In contrast, the models were useless, too giddy and lazy to be delegated the simplest task. When they didn't manage to slip out to tour New York, trailed by KGB, they loafed, drinking Cokes, smoking, and looking at the *Vogue* magazine they'd bought from the corner newsstand. They also flirted with the Americans, or at least tried to.

They stopped when one of the KGB men looked their way. Except for Inessa. She paid the KGB no mind and they, miraculously, didn't seem to harass her.

As Ludmila watched, Inessa blatantly waved at one of the American CIA men who seemed particularly taken with her.

Ludmila resolved to distance herself from the girl even more.

"Where is she?" Vladlena screeched. "The devil take that girl! I should never have brought her. Where is she? I'll send her back tomorrow, so help me."

It was the morning dress rehearsal before the evening preview. It had been decided that Ludmila's dress would finish the show, a position of great prestige. Ludmila might have been ecstatic if Inessa wasn't missing. She'd been on the bus with them from the hotel, but once they'd reached the Coliseum, she'd disappeared. Off on some stupid lark, Ludmila thought, numb with frustration and despair. When the girl finally turned up, she'd probably charm the searching KGB men into not reporting her, too. But by that time it might be too late.

Vladlena was beside herself with a rage that struck them all dumb with terror. They'd never seen her like this, and Ludmila feared she might use Inessa's absence to strike her cocktail party dress from the show entirely.

Ludmila wanted to plead for her dress, but she was afraid if she opened her mouth, she might vomit. She shivered in the air conditioning, and hoped.

To her relief, Vladlena ordered, "Put Alla in it!"

It would be too tight and too long on Alla, but Ludmila hurried to obey.

At the last minute, as Ludmila was about to help Alla change, Inessa dashed in, all smiles, as if nothing were wrong, her cheeks rosy with summer sun.

There was no time for lectures now. They blotted the perspiration from Inessa and slipped her into the dress. Vladlena glowered at the girl, but said nothing.

But on stage, Inessa was the best of them all, walking with an insouciant confidence that none of the other models could match, and Vladlena was mollified.

When the dress rehearsal was over, Vladlena led them in a round of applause. Before they dispersed, she delivered a speech detailing all the many errors that would have to be corrected before the next day, but they knew her well enough to see how pleased she was. Ludmila now realized just how nervous Vladlena had been, that the senior designer had just as much to lose, perhaps even more to lose than Ludmila herself if the show was a failure.

The tension drained from Ludmila. Calm descended on her as she headed backstage, and she allowed herself a smile when the models congratulated her.

In the changing area, Alla asked, "Cut this thread, will you?"

The model lifted her hair above her neckline. "It's been tickling me all morning."

Ludmila picked up a pair of shears, found the offending loose thread, and snipped it.

"Ah, that's much better. Thank you," Alla said.

Ludmila looked for Inessa to help her change. She glimpsed the model still in the dress exiting through a back door. The anger that Ludmila had been too afraid to let herself feel earlier at Inessa's tardiness welled up. Would the girl never learn? Furious at Inessa's disregard for her garment, Ludmila followed, a harsh reprimand forming on her tongue.

Behind the stage was a service corridor, its light dim and sickly green. Inessa scurried down it and into the women's toilet. A man, an American, followed her in.

This was too much! Wearing Ludmila's creation to some sordid romantic rendezvous!

Ludmila burst in on them.

The man knelt before Inessa, the skirt in his hands. At first Ludmila thought he was lifting it, before she realized he was picking at the fabric. They both were.

The man turned toward her and exclaimed, "Hell."

"Ludmila, give me a moment's privacy, please," Inessa begged. She didn't giggle.

"What are you doing?" Ludmila choked out. But she knew, even as she asked. She saw it on the man's fingertip. A dot, a microdot. According to Soviet propaganda, spies used them, American spies. She'd never believed such things existed. But here was the evidence before her eyes.

How long had the microdots been in place? The tiny dots blended with the fabric, indistinguishable from the pattern. She handled the garment daily and even she hadn't noticed them.

The man stood, uncertainly glancing at Inessa.

In a flash, Ludmila understood. The girl had used *Ludmila's* dress, *her* beautiful creation to smuggle out secrets. With or without her fiancé the physicist's connivance. The invaluable information wouldn't be lost or go astray if it was attached to a carefully tended dress. Inessa must be hoping to buy defection to the U.S. with such a delivery. And if the microdots were discovered, Inessa could claim she knew nothing. Inessa would get away with it as she always did. It was Ludmila's dress. Ludmila would be the one condemned as a traitor and spy, not Inessa.

"In my dress?" Ludmila rushed forward, hearing herself roar, "You used *my* dress!"

"Your precious dress is fine. It hasn't been damaged. I was very careful. Go away for a moment," Inessa said, and pushed her gently back toward the door. "You never saw any of this."

Ludmila held her ground. "My dress! You filthy little slut!" she shrieked. Her vision clouded, and a scream filled her ears, reverberating on the lavatory tiles. She struck Inessa, punched her, forgetting she still clenched a pair of shears. Rather than a blow, it was a stab.

Too late, Inessa flinched. The blades glanced over her jawbone and tore open the fleshy part of her long neck.

Ludmila pulled out the shears and stabbed again, harder, deeper.

Blood spouted from Inessa's throat and poured down the front of the dress, drenching it, painting it a bright and terrible red.

The sight stopped Ludmila. "My dress," she croaked, her voice raw.

Inessa went white and her ankles buckled. Her eyes rolled up into her head, before she crumpled to the ground, the skirt spread around her.

Ludmila couldn't move, couldn't take her eyes from the blood seeping across the silk.

The American shoved by her.

People poured in behind her, the KGB, the other models. Vladlena was there, shaking Ludmila, turning her head forcibly to get her to look away, to focus on something other than the lifeless model. "What is the meaning of this? Have you lost your mind?" Vladlena slapped her.

"She was spying. Using my dress…" Ludmila managed, her voice hoarse and painful. Her knees went weak and her whole body began to shudder convulsively.

She hadn't realized she was sobbing until Vladlena pulled her head down to her shoulder and murmured, "My dear."

Conversations happened, but Ludmila couldn't understand the words. Vladlena spoke too, but it was as if Ludmila were far far away. Disjointed phrases were spoken but they had nothing to do with her.

"She must have slipped and fell."

"Scissors."

"Dead. She's dead."

"A dreadful accident."

"Traumatic. Too much for her. A breakdown."

Ludmila wasn't aware of leaving the Coliseum or returning to the hotel or going to the airport the next morning at dawn with Vladlena in a limousine. Her body felt heavy, her mind dull, her eyes unable to focus. Vaguely, she understood she was to be put on a flight to Moscow.

At the gate, Vladlena held her hands, squeezed them, and kissed her warmly on both cheeks in farewell. "You've done the Soviet Union a great service, my dear. You're a hero of the revolution." Then, apparently overcome with uncharacteristic emotion, she embraced Ludmila and said in her ear, "You're fine. There's nothing to worry about now. In gratitude for your services the Party will reward you well. Your career is made."

"But my dress," Ludmila whimpered into the collar of Vladlena's elegant black suit.

DEEP SUBMERGENCE

BY JOSEPH WALLACE

Monterey Bay, California. October 1968.

A thousand feet down. Water pressure: About 435 pounds per square inch.

The creature hung outside the porthole, fragile and crystalline as a chain made from blown glass. Lit only by the gleams of sunlight filtering down from the surface far above, and by the dim glow of the submersible's running lights. Not bothered at all by the cold, the dark, or the pressure.

Jack Harbison put his face up to the porthole's three-inch-thick window to get a closer look.

"What do you see?" one of the other two men in the cabin asked.

Harbison didn't reply, though he could have. He was no scientist, but if you worked as a sub pilot for long enough you couldn't help but learn something.

He was looking at a giant siphonophore, a whole mess of little individual organisms—each of which had its own job, hunting, digesting, excreting—that had joined together to form one huge animal. Working as a unit to scare away predators that would gobble up any one of them on its own.

Harbison could see only a portion of this one, but he guessed it might be fifty feet long. He knew he wouldn't take it on, not if he were on the other side of the glass.

Not even if he could survive out there.

As the Deep Submergence Vehicle *Alvin* sank through the midwater, the siphonophore drifted away. Harbison craned his neck to keep it in view, hoping for the show, knowing it would come.

And then it did. Something startled the enormous creature. A stray current, perhaps, a touch from one of the sub's two robotic arms, or merely some electrical impulse transmitted through whichever individual comprised its brain. All at once, the entire chain flared with light. An unearthly blue-green outlined its shape, and at its core, jagged crimson webs like lightning.

Even though Harbison had seen such things many times before, his breath caught. Nearly everything out here in the murky midwater could light up, glow with cold fire, but the sight always awed him.

He watched till the siphonophore, dark again, drifted out of sight. The view outside the window was empty...except for some shadowy forms that never came close enough for him to make out. Sharks? Giant squid? Something big and dangerous, most likely.

It didn't matter. Nothing was breaching the submersible, not from outside. The three of them were safe inside the personnel sphere. Cramped—the capsule was less than seven feet in diameter—but protected by its reinforced steel walls.

Harbison straightened, checked the instruments. They'd passed two thousand feet, and everything was fine.

Everything was always fine with *Alvin*. In public, Harbison always called it "the tugboat," as if he found its tiny dimensions absurd. That twenty-three-foot-long hull, the spindly arms with their Erector-set claws, thruster propellers that resembled nothing so much as the ones that you wound up with rubber bands to make your toy ship speed across the bathtub. Ridiculous.

But the truth was, though he never said this out loud, Harbison thought that in some strange way *Alvin* was alive. Sentient. After dozens of dives aboard the diminutive sub, he felt he barely had to give it orders. The slightest touch on the controls would take him wherever he wanted to go.

Harbison shook his head. Stephens, the older of the two other men in the sphere, looked up. His lips thinned, and the furrows on his cheeks, like matching dueling scars, deepened.

"What's wrong?" he said.

Harbison said, "Nothing."

"You want the kid to take over?" Stephens asked.

The kid, Michaels, the third one in the sphere. The youngest, at twenty-five, more than a decade younger than Harbison. The back-up pilot on this crucial mission.

"No," Harbison said. "I'm fine."

A lie.

Woods Hole, Massachusetts. August 1968.

It's happened again.

The word had run through the cafeterias, dorms, laboratories, and offices of the Woods Hole Oceanographic Institution, just as it had two years earlier. Like some vast neural pathway linking everyone's brain. A human hive mind, like the one bees used.

Harbison had just left Bigelow Laboratory when someone told him. Without thinking, he'd turned his head and looked down Water Street. Seeing, as almost always in this season, the horde of summer people gathering around the shops and restaurants or just wandering aimlessly as they waited for their ferries to carry them to Martha's Vineyard and Nantucket.

At the best of times, Harbison felt like the tourists were a different species. He spent months each year out at sea, while for them the staid forty-five-minute ferry ride to the Vineyard was an ocean adventure. He journeyed to depths and saw things they could not imagine, while they stayed on the surface, oblivious.

He knew when the United States lost a nuclear weapon, as it had now. Again. He knew when it happened, and what it meant, and what the consequences could be.

If the government had its way, the rest of them, the world's innocents, never would.

"Where?" he asked when they were all together. Eight of them around a conference table. Fewer than Harbison would have guessed, given how the military usually worked. It looked like this was going to be a quick and dirty operation.

The director of the Oceanographic Institution, who was Harbison's boss. A representative of the U.S. Navy and one from the Air Force, in elegant suits, not uniforms. Two men from the Defense Department, in slightly less spiffy suits. Harbison and Michaels, the pilots.

And the old man, Christopher Stephens. The minute Harbison saw him in the room, he knew what was going to happen. All he needed were the details.

"You hear about that incident in Monterey?" one of the Defense guys said.

Harbison nodded. Of course he had. Everyone had. It had been in the newspapers just a few days earlier. "Sure. That B-52 out of Travis AFB. A bird or something got sucked into the engine—"

"Or something," the Air Force guy said.

Michaels blinked. "You talking sabotage?"

Harbison kept his gaze on the table before him.

The officials all frowned, and the Air Force guy went on. "It went down. Three of the crew ejected safely, but the pilot's seat malfunctioned and he went down with it."

Harbison raised his eyes, sat up a little straighter. "And they were carrying hydrogen bombs, like last time."

"Just one," the Defense guy said.

"Bet you're planning on handing out medals for that," Harbison said. "I mean, last time it was four."

The Oceanographic's director looked sorrowful, but the military guys all fixed Harbison with identical steely stares. He might even have been intimidated, if he'd cared.

"How big was this one?" he asked.

The Air Force guy grimaced. His face was suddenly gray, weary. "Bigger payload than the last time. A hundred kilotons."

"How far offshore?"

"Something like three miles."

"You might not have read this page in the search-and-recovery manual," Harbison said in a lazy voice, "but parts of Monterey Canyon go down two miles or more out there. That bomb is likely way out of reach."

More glares. They really hated him. Hated having to clue him in.

Only Stephens, the old man, seemed amused, looking down at his gnarled hands linked on the table before him. His lips twitched, causing the lines on either side of his mouth to deepen.

It was the Navy guy who spoke. "According to estimates taken from the testimony of witnesses, we don't think it went down into the canyon." He frowned. "We are having difficulty confirming that with sonar, though."

"The deep scattering layer is getting in the way," the director said.

Harbison nodded. Of course it was, in a place like Monterey Bay. Wherever there was nutrient-rich water, countless masses of zooplankton—tiny plants and animals—gathered. Every day, the enormous assemblage rose and fell in the water column, moving toward the surface at night, into deeper water during the day. Scientists called it the largest migration of life on earth.

Though you could pass through the deep scattering layer in *Alvin* without even noticing, it played hell with sonar. From the surface, you could look at the screen and think your sound waves were bouncing off the sea floor, when they were actually reflecting off the mass of plankton in the midwater.

Made searching for something little, like a crashed plane and a nuclear bomb, nearly impossible from above.

"How many ships you got looking?" Harbison asked.

"Enough."

"And you're hoping to keep that under your hat?" Harbison laughed. "In Monterey? You must have turned into a tourist attraction already."

"It's a search and recovery for the pilot, that's all," the Navy man said. "All anyone needs to know. And it's no lie. We don't leave anyone down there if we can avoid it."

If we can avoid it. That was the important phrase. Truth was, countless pilots and officers and grunts lay in unmarked graves all over the planet, and plenty of them were American.

And not just members of the military, either. Civilians, too. Collateral damage.

Harbison looked at Michaels, who looked back at him and spoke. "Which one of us goes?"

"Both of you," the guy from Defense said. "Just in case."

"And Stephens here, he comes along for the ride," Harbison said, shifting his gaze. "Like last time."

Everyone nodded. Stephens would form the second half of the search-and-recovery mission. He was the guy who had created and built the CARV, the Cable-controlled Aquatic Recovery Vehicle, an unmanned submersible that would bring the bomb to the surface after *Alvin* found it.

Alvin had its robotic arms, but they'd been designed to grab comparatively lightweight scientific specimens, and (though Harbison disagreed) the military didn't trust them to be strong enough to haul the bomb back to the surface. The CARV, on the other hand, had but one purpose: To retrieve lost torpedoes and bombs from the sea floor.

Plus, it had one other advantage: A camera that could transmit along a cable back to the surface. Once *Alvin* had pinpointed the bomb's location, the CARV could swoop down, take a look, and do the rest.

Harbison had seen it in action once before, the first time he'd worked with Stephens. He hadn't been impressed. If *Alvin* felt like a living creature to him, the CARV was more like a mechanical dog, programmed to fetch.

He raised his gaze and saw Stephens looking at him. There was a glint in the old man's eyes, but it was buried deep, and no one else saw it.

The second guy from Defense, who'd been silent till now, was the one who said what they were all thinking.

"Well, gentlemen, this is a colossal fuck-up," he said. "But we dodged a bullet that the thing didn't hit land. Can you imagine the consequences if that had happened?"

They all could. Harbison snorted.

"I've been stationed out there," the Navy man said. "The California coast. The wind always blows onshore. East."

Everyone nodded. They all knew the direction of the prevailing winds out there.

"What's the population within a radius of fifty miles?" Harbison asked.

No one answered. But the Navy man said, "Not to mention the Central Valley."

Harbison thought about it. The steady winds blowing out of the west, sweeping through the mountain passes of the Coast Range and heading east into the valley.

Some of the most heavily farmed land on the continent.

He looked across the table, and saw the hidden glint again in Stephens's eyes.

Harbison's boss asked him to stay after the meeting ended. His expression mixed confusion, anger, and sadness.

"What on earth is *wrong* with you?" he asked.

Harbison was silent.

"You keep yanking on their tails, eventually they're going to turn around and bite you."

"Let them." Harbison spoke in a savage tone. "Let them bite, and then they can go out and find another pilot as good as I am and ask *him* to find that bomb."

"Jack," the director said, raising his hands. "Listen. I was just—"

But Harbison had already turned his back and was heading out the door.

Twenty-two hundred feet. Still descending.

While they'd been heading down, the sun had set up above. The recovery was being carried out at night, in secret, as everything about this mission had been. Only two Navy ships on the surface, along with the CARV on its tender, all waiting for *Alvin* to reach its destination.

They were traveling through a dead zone now. *Alvin*'s lights barely penetrated the black water, illuminating only a multitude of tiny white and brown and red flecks drifting slowly downward themselves. Harbison knew what these were: The organic remains of leaves, fish, whales. Humans. Whatever had died up above.

It was a constant, endless organic snowstorm that provided a feast for the creatures that inhabited the lightless environment of the ocean floor below. The blind eels, giant white crabs, bulbous-eyed fish with shining fleshy lures where their tongues should be.

"How long?" Stephens said.

Harbison took a deep breath. Even though he was wearing a wool jacket, his skin felt cold.

"Soon," he said.

Too soon.

The last time it happened.

Another thing the innocent tourists waiting for their ferries didn't know: The skies above them were filled with B-52s carrying nuclear weapons. These jets crisscrossed the earth at all times of the day and night, preparing for—or forestalling—the next world war.

There was one big problem, though: a B-52 couldn't fly all the way from the U.S. to Europe on one tank of fuel. It had to refuel in mid-air, coordinating with a KCF-135 tanker jet and connecting its gas tank to a boom dangling from the tanker.

This was a delicate operation at a couple hundred miles an hour, a test of piloting skill. Two and a half years earlier, in January 1966, a B-52 pilot flying over Spain had failed the test. He'd run into the KC-135's fueling boom, ripping his plane apart and causing the tanker jet to explode.

Everyone on the KC-135 died, as did three of the seven men on the bomber. However spectacular, none of this would have been worth remembering—military pilots and crew died all the time, after all, even when the war was cold, not hot—if it hadn't been for the B-52's cargo.

Four 70-kiloton hydrogen bombs had gone down with the wreckage. One of them had fallen into the Atlantic Ocean off the coast of Palomares, a small fishing town on Spain's coast.

The Navy had sent thirty-three ships to try to locate the wreckage. But it was *Alvin* that finally succeeded in finding the bomb more than half a mile down.

Alvin and the CARV, and their pilots and designers, had their moments of fame. But what Harbison remembered most about that time was all the weeks of waiting in Palomares while the Navy narrowed down the search area.

And meeting Adriana, of course.

Depth: 4,260 feet.

They had landed on a ledge protruding from a cliff face. Lit by the beam of *Alvin*'s harsh floodlights, the cliff was a steep gray expanse. Here and there rocky spires emerged from the murk, looking half-melted, protean.

This was the midnight zone, where sunlight never penetrated. No plants grew. Nothing photosynthesized. Everything that lived down here ate meat.

Harbison and Michaels had located the B-52's wreckage, half-buried in silt, three days earlier. It lay on the ledge amid half a dozen outcroppings that pointed like twenty-foot-long stony fingers toward the canyon just beyond.

Now they were back, with Stephens, to watch and wait as the CARV descended, controlled by an operator on its tender. Its cameras would allow it to spot them and then the bomb, and to do its job.

Harbison bent over the controls, maneuvering *Alvin* between two smokestack-shaped rock promontories. The little sub could easily get caught here, trapped, turning within a few hours into a tomb.

The downed B-52, hidden from his sight for a few minutes, came back into view. Harbison could see the tailfin of the bomb emerging from a tangle of what had once been the jet's fuselage.

They'd been lucky. Another fifty yards or so west and the ruined jet—and its cargo—would have fallen another mile or more to the bottom of the canyon. And stayed there forever.

Stephens was staring through his porthole. "There it is," he said.

"Yeah," Michaels said, "we know."

He sounded bored. There was no role for a copilot on *Alvin*, and there was no pilot born who enjoyed being a spare tire.

"How long till your boat shows up?" Michaels asked Stephens, "I want to get the hell out—"

He never finished the sentence. His words turned into a harsh cry of terror and pain.

Harbison couldn't turn around. Not immediately. First he had to shut off the thrusters, or else risk running *Alvin* into a rock wall.

But he didn't need to look. He knew what had just happened.

When had Harbison figured it out?

That was easy: The first time he and Stephens been together, heading down to retrieve the hydrogen bomb that had been lost off Palomares.

The seas had been rougher than usual, and the bomb, located a little more than half a mile down, was not deep enough to avoid tidal surges and strong currents.

Stephens had gotten seasick.

In the tiny cabin, this was never pleasant, either for the man suffering or for his trapped companions. The smell alone could make seasickness contagious, if you were a greenhorn.

But Harbison had seen—and smelled—it all by now. It happened often enough when scientists came down on their first descent. He didn't particularly enjoy the experience, but he was used to it.

After twenty minutes of explosive vomiting into the sick bags *Alvin* always carried in abundance, Stephens fell into a doze that was more like semiconsciousness. This was typical, too, and Harbison, feeling a little sorry for the old man, let him rest as they descended. He wasn't needed yet.

During both descent and ascent, *Alvin*'s journey was almost entirely silent. It used no engine in either direction. Weighted with steel ballast, it fell through the water like a stone. After its mission was complete, it dumped the ballast and popped back to the surface like a slow-motion cork.

Its only engines were the thrusters, designed for short-term maneuvering and keeping the sub in position.

After a few minutes of silence broken only by the musical sound of the water buffeting the submersible as it fell, Stephens started muttering. At first it sounded just like nonsense, random syllables, and Harbison paid it no mind.

Then the old man's voice rose and he spoke more clearly. Harbison felt himself grow still, and inside his chest his heart thumped. He still couldn't understand the words, but he had no problem figuring out what language the old man was using.

No adult living and working anywhere around the United States military could fail to recognize Russian when he heard it.

Especially when it was coming from the mouth of a man who was about to be in close proximity to a hydrogen bomb.

A few moments later, Stephens came back to awareness. Harbison watched as his eyes went from hazy to sharp, and only looked away as the old man fixed him with a sudden, sharp stare.

But neither of them said a word. Soon afterward they got busy recovering the bomb, and it was as if the incident, the revelation, had never happened.

Except it had.

By the time Harbison was able to shut off the thrusters and turn away from his porthole, Michaels was lying on the floor. In the tight space, his kicking legs collided with the seats and thudded against the metal walls. His pale, red-rimmed eyes were glassy, and spit was flowing from his stretched-wide mouth. He was gasping loudly, the sounds echoing off the metal walls.

Stephens had a gun in his right hand, something silver, with a long barrel.

"Great idea," Harbison said, "using one of those in a pressurized cabin a mile down."

Stephens smiled and shrugged. "These darts won't penetrate the walls."

Now Harbison saw the metal shaft emerging from Michaels's neck. The spasms coursing through the dying man's body had diminished to deep shivers.

"That wasn't the plan," Harbison said.

Stephens shrugged. "He was too noisy."

"And me?"

Stephens raised the weapon. Harbison could see the tip of the arrow resting in the barrel.

Then the old man let his arm fall. "You I trust," he said. "Enough."

He sat down on his stool and placed the gun on the floor beside his foot. "Fire up those thrusters again," he said, "and I'll tell you what we do next."

Harbison took another few seconds, then turned back to the instrument panel.

Alvin rose from the rock face and moved forward.

Harbison had spent months after returning from Spain asking questions, making inquiries, calling in favors. Never saying exactly what it was he was looking for, or why, but learning all he needed to know by the end. Doing what he did for a living, he'd met a lot of people who could answer his questions.

Finally he knew enough to pay a visit to Christopher Stephens.

The headquarters and laboratories of Vision Industries, the company that built the CARV, were located in a corporate park near the New Jersey Turnpike. Just another set of long, low buildings made of yellow-gray stone and glass, with the future being created inside.

You never knew what was going on inside those anonymous buildings. Or wanted to know, if you were most people.

When he walked in the door of the corner office, its windows overlooking a pond with geese floating in it, the old man looked up at him but did not bother to stand.

"I heard you've been sniffing around," he said. His voice was deep and gravelly, his eyes cold behind the fleshy ridges that bracketed them. "Now I'm guessing you've come to threaten me."

Harbison glanced around. "Anyone listening in on us?"

"Of course not." Stephens steepled his fingers. "So talk."

Harbison talked. He told about what he'd overheard when Stephens had gotten sick onboard *Alvin*, what he'd suspected, what he'd learned since coming back home. What he believed Stephens's ultimate plans were.

As he listened, Stephens relaxed, tension leaving the line of his jaw and the furrowed skin above his cheekbones. "Ah," he said at last. "I see. Not threats. Blackmail."

"No," Harbison said. "Teamwork."

At last the old man seemed surprised. His gaze grew cold again. "You want to...work with me?" he said cautiously.

"Yes."

"Why should I believe that?"

"Because if I didn't want something, I would just have turned you in."

Stephens shrugged, though his expression was angry. "I'm not afraid of that. I'm...well protected."

"Maybe you are. But it would be a terrific pain in your ass, wouldn't it?" Harbison drew in a breath. "You're right. I'm here because I want something in return. But it's not money."

"What, then?"

Harbison didn't answer directly. "If something like Palomares happens again—"

"Oh, it will." The old man's eyes gleamed. "There's always a next time."

"Bring me in on it."

For a long moment Stephens stared up into his face. "If it's not for money," he asked again, "then why?"

Harbison didn't reply.

Stephens straightened in his chair. "For me to believe you, you must tell me."

Still Harbison hesitated. Then, at last, voice harsh, breath short, he began to speak.

Telling the story he'd never told to anyone before.

In Palomares, the only bomb Harbison had cared about was the one that had fallen into the water, the one he waited weeks to retrieve.

The three that hit land didn't concern him.

It was only later that he heard what had happened to them. None had been fully armed, meaning they couldn't explode with five times the power of the bombs that had flattened Hiroshima and Nagasaki just twenty-one years earlier. The bombs that had started the arms race and the Cold War.

Small favors. But that didn't mean that the citizens of Palomares were free and clear. The reason: Every nuclear weapon came packed with conventional explosives as well as nuclear material. When two of the Palomares bombs hit the ground after a six-mile free fall from the doomed jet, their explosives detonated.

The military claimed that no one was killed by the explosions themselves. What came out later was the fact that a cloud of radioactive material—plutonium dust—was blown hundreds of feet in the air by each exploding bomb and dispersed by the wind over the surrounding farmland.

While farmers, unaware of the dangers, unprotected, continued to till their poisoned fields, teams of American scientists and soldiers in hazard suits dug up countless tons of tainted dirt, which was then shipped to a plant in South Carolina for decontamination.

Of course the residents of surrounding areas were alarmed. Who wouldn't be? But scientists claimed that the level of exposure couldn't possibly be harmful. To prove it, the Spanish minister for information and the U.S. ambassador even went swimming off a nearby beach for newspaper and TV reporters.

By the time the first reports of radiation sickness came in, it was too late.

Harbison had met Adriana in the café where she worked in Palomares. Perhaps thirty, she was dark, pretty, lively, with a mass of black hair that she wore pulled back, revealing her high forehead and eyes full of intelligence and merriment.

Adriana knew enough English that, alongside his workmanlike Spanish, they could converse. And she seemed to like him, a rare enough occurrence to be worth noticing.

If he'd told anyone about her, they would have laughed. A summer-camp romance, they would have called it. A fling. Something to enjoy, then forget as soon as you went home.

But for the *Alvin* pilot, condemned to spend eight or nine months a year out at sea, it was much more.

Day after day, waiting for his mission to begin, he hung around the café, drinking coffee, watching the people come and go, and grabbing Adriana's few free moments to chat. As the days passed, she took to spending her breaks with him, and then they started to meet in the evenings as well.

They never spent a night together, though. Not once. Every evening she went home to her parents' farm outside of town. A farm located just two miles from where the explosives on one of the hydrogen bombs had detonated, spewing a plume of radioactivity into a stiff wind.

By the time the lost bomb was found, and Harbison was called to work, Adriana was looking thin and feeling unwell.

By the time he returned, she was in the hospital, already a grotesque scarecrow version of the plump, talkative girl she'd been.

And by the time he was called back to the United States for debriefing, she was dead.

No one ever made the news public, or took responsibility.

Harbison guided *Alvin* closer to the wreck, which lay between two of the twisted spires. The floodlights showed that its nose, still mostly intact, was pointing upward, while the rest, a jumble of jagged shards, lay around and beneath it.

Something caught his eye. Motion. A human arm and hand, the bones of the fingers and forearm protruding through gray ragged skin, waving in the slight current. Below lay the white blur of a half-skeletal, eyeless face.

The B-52's pilot.

Harbison saw a sudden, slithering movement. A hagfish rose into the light, the heavy slime that coated its snakelike body catching *Alvin*'s floodlights. It stared through the porthole with eyes like holes, and its nightmare mouth, a black cavern ringed by gleaming teeth, gaped at him.

Other hagfish moved in the shadows beneath it. Perhaps a dozen more, writhing in the dead pilot's midsection, gorging on the unexpected deep-sea bounty of flesh.

Alvin moved forward, leaving the feast behind. Ahead lay the rest of the wreckage and the bomb. It was shaped like a torpedo and composed of black steel that absorbed the light and reflected nothing.

And beyond it, behind one more line of rocky spires, lay the black abyss of Monterey Canyon.

"Okay," Stephens said, gesturing. "Pick it up."

But before Harbison engaged the thrusters, he felt an odd vibration tickling the front of his spine. It grew stronger, still not quite a sound, more like the throbbing at the onset of a migraine headache.

"Ah," the old man said, lifting a hand. "Wait."

Ten seconds later there came a muffled thud and a brilliant flash of light, just as quickly extinguished, in the middle distance. *Alvin* jolted where it stood. When it settled, the vibration was gone.

Harbison said, "That was your baby?"

"The CARV, yes." Stephens gave a shrug. Then he smiled. "Easy enough to plant a limpet mine on it, designed to go off at depth."

Harbison understood. "Without its cameras, they're blind up top now."

The old man smiled. "Yes, blind and panicking. Scrambling around, trying to figure out what happened to their robot sub... and us, too. Blind, deaf, lost."

Harbison thought about it. "With the deep scattering layer, they won't even be able to find us on sonar."

Stephens nodded. "Right now they just think they're in the middle of a fiasco. By the time they figure out what really happened, we'll be long gone." He made a delicate gesture with the fingers of both hands, like a bomb exploding. "And they'll have plenty of other things to worry about."

That had been the part of the plan Harbison had heard, though he'd been spared the details. Pick up the bomb. Return unseen to the surface, where they would be met by two boats run by Stephens's compatriots. Once they'd taken the bomb aboard, they'd sink *Alvin* over the depths of Monterey Canyon, where it would never be found.

One boat would then head inland to launch the attack. The other, with Stephens and Harbison onboard, would head west, into international waters, to meet up with the larger ship that would carry them to safety.

It was guaranteed that at first the military would have no idea where the two of them had gone, or even if they were still alive. There would be a search, but it was likely that in the long run Harbison would be declared dead, a captain gone down with his ship.

And, as Stephens had said, once the conventional explosives on the hydrogen bomb had detonated, sending a vast cloud of radioactive material over densely populated northern California and across into the fertile Central Valley, the U.S. government was going to have plenty on its hands. By the time the search resumed, their trails would have gone cold.

As close to a foolproof plan as you could devise.

Though, of course, no plan was completely foolproof.

At the end of their conversation in Stephens's New Jersey office, Harbison had said, "Why?"

The old man had raised bushy gray eyebrows in an answering question. But Harbison knew he understood, and merely waited.

Finally Stephens said, "Fear."

Harbison was quiet.

"Fear," Stephens said, "is powerful. Yet you Americans have never felt it here, not real fear, not on your own soil. For you, it's always someplace else. Everyplace else." His mouth twisted. "Fear loses wars, especially the ones that last for decades."

Still Harbison didn't speak.

"And you?" the old man said.

Harbison was ready for the question. "Revenge," he said. "Of course."

And kept his gaze steady.

On a typical mission, his next step would have been to dump ballast and head for the surface. But this time, the bomb securely clasped in *Alvin*'s claws—up to the task, as he'd known they'd be—he followed Stephens's instructions. Using the thrusters to move north, then west, then north again, maneuvering into position over Monterey Canyon in preparation for making their rendezvous at the surface.

Following instructions, that is, for every move but the last one. That one he took on his own.

When Stephens said, "Fifty meters south," he set the thrusters on idle instead. The submersible hung in the water, quivering.

In the sudden stillness, Harbison looked out the porthole at the pitch-black void that lay below them. A strange current like the flat of a huge hand tried to push the submersible down into the canyon.

But he wasn't staring at eternity. In his mind he saw only Adriana, the way she'd looked in the hospital, the last time he'd seen her.

Stephens glanced over. His expression showed only annoyance, as if he thought his orders simply hadn't been heard correctly.

Then his eyes widened at what he saw in Harbison's face.

"I couldn't do it," Harbison said, reaching for the inside pocket of his wool jacket. "I never could."

Stephens went still for an instant. He stood just a few feet away, but that moment's hesitation was enough. Had Harbison had a gun, he could have put a bullet through the old man's head.

Yet it wasn't a gun that Harbison pulled from his inside pocket. It was a hammer.

With his left hand he shut off the thrusters. With the hammer in his right he smashed their controls, at the same time bracing his legs for the jolt.

Alvin fell into the darkness.

I'm sorry, Harbison said to it. *I'm sorry.*

He heard Stephens curse, lose his balance, stagger against the far wall. A sharp metallic sound as his gun slid across the floor.

A second blow of the hammer, and the switches that released the ballast, that allowed the sub to rise to the surface, were damaged beyond repair.

Alvin fell.

By now Stephens had regained his balance. With a wordless grunt, he threw himself across the small space and brought his hands down in a clubbing motion on the back of Harbison's neck.

Late. Too late. One last swing before the hammer went clattering away, and all the sub's lights, inside and out, were extinguished.

Carrying its lethal cargo with it, *Alvin* fell, spinning end over end like an out-of-control satellite plunging to earth.

Stephens screamed, a guttural sound swallowed up by the darkness. His body fell away from Harbison and slammed against the far wall. His scream cut off, leaving no echo behind.

Harbison had been ready for the freefall. He clung onto the sub's ruined controls, put his face up against his porthole, and stared unblinking into the abyss. He felt calm. He'd long accepted that his world would end this way.

A light flared just outside the window. A sudden blue flash illuminated the porthole and let him catch a glimpse of his own face. Then another flare, this one a fiery green, and a third as warm and yellow as the sun.

They accompanied him the whole way down, creatures no one had ever seen before and no one was likely to again. Tracing his path until their beautiful lights merged with the ones inside his skull, and he closed his eyes.

SPARKS TO
THE BEAR'S HIDE

BY ROBERT MANGEOT

In Budapest the streetcars were painted yellow. Sometimes I believed that was all the color left in Hungary. Margaret, my foster mother, said that the cars had been painted yellow before the communists took over and would be yellow after the communists fell. To her, the color was a spark.

We jerked and swayed along with the other people crowding the line out to Little Pest. At each stop the January wind cleared the air thick with body heat and drying wool.

"See?" Margaret said, a smile on her leathery face. "The men drool over my sweet Helena. Saint Jerome is with us."

Margaret was Roma and a closet Catholic. For her the world was as piled up with signs as the snow against her farmhouse. After knowing her eighteen years, I found that she had a way of creating the signs she credited to her saints. On a streetcar full of workers heading back to their tenements, I was the only young *Budapesti* wearing an Italian overcoat and with my hair styled for evening. I was the only girl in a floral dress, one Margaret had me sew tight to catch Typhon's eye.

We pushed our way off at Üllői Avenue and into a light rain.

Around us drab lines of apartment blocks rose like grave markers over Pest.

Her contact's building looked no different from any of the gray slabs scored with balconies. The elevator was out of service. Despite her years I struggled to keep up with Margaret on the ten-story climb. She had fought the fascists and later the Russians, but how the British found her, as with any of her clients, I never dared to ask.

A tidy man introduced as Braintree ushered us into the flat. Margaret had me remove my coat and turned me toward him standing beside the window. Braintree fidgeted like someone uncomfortable with planned housing, either this one or of tenements in general.

"So this is your student," Braintree said. "She's pretty enough. Bit older than requested though, isn't she?"

Margaret lifted my skirt to the thigh and turned me into a profile. "Twenty-three. Not too old. Tall like requested. Brown hair. Typhon does not miss my sweet Helena. Face of a girl, body of a woman."

"Quite."

A week earlier I had managed to find a copy of *Beggar's Banquet*, and wearing out Margaret's turntable with the Rolling Stones somehow left me expecting my first live Englishman to resemble a wild-haired and languid Brian Jones. There was no "Street Fighting Man" in Braintree.

I was a street fighter's daughter. Out the window was a view west, to where the river wrapped around Csepel Island. There the Allamvedelmi Osztaly murdered my father in the last hours of the Revolution and first of the reprisals.

"Still," Braintree said, "we rather hoped for a professional."

Margaret lit a pipe and watched him through the smoke. "Tell me when you discover how to get a working girl into a Party social. Helena is Communist Youth, monitored for membership. Smartest girl I have."

"I relay messages for her," I said, speaking up to impress. I had finished top of my English class despite the Party elite's children spending their summers in Britain. "I gather information. True, I am not one of her Mata Haris. Margaret is happy with what I bring even so."

"Admirable accent, dear girl," Braintree said. "They'd have you at Selfridges. But as I understand you round up café blather from drunken underlings. Typhon is somewhat up the food chain. And acting on a different set of expectations."

"She will get Typhon alone," Margaret said. "Sweet Helena, so pure, but gypsy in her heart. She keeps her head always. She shows you now if you like."

"You Magyars must have taught the Russians their tricks," Braintree said. He turned toward me, something not quite benevolent about his grin. "Very well then. Not the first large rabbit Margaret has pulled out of a small hat. Understand, dear girl, that learning Typhon's name means you leave Hungary tonight."

I understood that and more. I understood Hungarians smuggled records in and the West smuggled defectors out. I understood that Hungary had few men so special as to lure Braintree from London, fewer still with a weakness for university girls. For Margaret to send me, there was but one. Zsigmond Irinyi, deputy head of Central Control and the AVO's Butcher of Csepel, packed his bags for the West.

"When you have Irinyi alone," Braintree was saying, "absolutely alone, deliver this message: 'Cicilia.' He will provide a confirmation word. Return here with it straight away. We close up shop at three tomorrow morning. Mustn't be late for your flight west, not with the great bear and her cubs nipping at your heels."

"Then you find me a warmer new home?"

Braintree nodded. "I believe we've still a few of those about."

Margaret followed me down as far as the lobby. "Sweet Helena," she said, grasping my hand. "Tonight I lose my Helena."

I did not cry. Margaret punished any tears, saying Hungary did not need more silly girls. "You will leave first."

"Second if you are careless," Margaret said. "Braintree follows protocol, moves early before the Butcher is found out. Tonight they give us the Butcher on his wrong foot. Tonight, we must be the spark."

I stepped off the streetcar at the Oktagon and crossed People's Republic Street—what the people called Andrassy Avenue—for the Party social. Scattered in the shop windows were sun-blanched propaganda posters, American jeans, and French foods. I remembered the morning Russian tanks rolled down the boulevard. The West had been nowhere on Andrassy then.

At the club entrance a guard brushed me away. He made a show of flashing his holstered gun. "Workers' Party only."

I gave this toy soldier my KISZ card and invitation letter.

"Helena Szabo, Communist Youth," the guard read aloud. He put on an oily grin. "You know why they invite the young girls, Helena Szabo?"

"I hoped to dance."

"You can call it that. Come home with me, Helena Szabo. I'll be your first dance, huh?"

I reminded him that those the Party invited to recruiting events ranked some levels higher than those tasked with standing in the cold and rain.

"I'll think of you come the first dance," I said as I passed inside.

I checked my coat in a grand art deco foyer. Neglected repairs had left the gilded designs scuffed and dingy. Such places were like embers to me, the faded reminders of what Hungary must have been in my father's time.

Do not move first on Typhon, Margaret had said. *That brands you an amateur. Be the liveliest brunette, and Typhon will find you.*

Hungarian pop warbled over the sound system, György Korda and Kati Kovács. Soon though, Margaret had promised the curmudgeons would leave for their beds, and the younger bosses would permit uncensored records, the Beatles or Elvis Presley. I longed for anything by the Rolling Stones.

Typhon was ensconced at the bar and chatting over drinks with his retinue. The old man was as bald as a whale, his polished dome gleaming in the light. I angled through the smoky club and found a stretch of open bar to order mineral water.

A middle-aged apparatchik sidled up to me. He smelled of must and looked of unloved husband. "Cigarette?"

I shook my head. Typhon did not like his girls to smoke. I smiled and said to my lonely bureaucrat, "But I love to dance."

For the next hour I danced with every man who asked and every man who cut in, a parade of faceless political officers with tobacco and vodka on their breaths. Some were bolder than others, but none too bold. When the folk music stopped and the newer records began, we changed to whatever fast dance went with the song. I twisted, I ponied, I did the loco-motion, I thrilled at the heat of it all, and when the men tired the other girls and I go-go danced for them.

It was after the go-go dancing that Typhon approached. He brought with him two coupes of sparkling wine.

"You must be thirsty," he said over The Byrds. He reached out the wine as if completely certain of my accepting, kissed my offered hand, and said, "The Socialist Workers' Party appreciates your contributions to dance."

I saluted him with a sip. The wine tasted of green apples, but not so much to pucker my face. I puckered anyway, Helena the innocent.

Typhon chuckled. "*Sovetskoye Shampanskoye.* It is what happens when a central committee plans wine. But not so bad for cheap, eh little bird?"

Typhon will expect you to know of him, Margaret had said. *And to be flattered by his attention.*

"Champagne for everyone," I said, and fanned my sweat. "Thank you, Comrade Deputy Secretary."

"No anonymity in office. This is not good, I fear. Please, you must call me Zsigmond."

Zsigmond Irinyi. Enforcer, traitor, murderer. Despised at home but to be welcomed in the West. "Comrade Zsigmond," I said.

"And you are Helena Szabo, Youth Party. It concerns us at Central Control that we did not know all the beautiful Party candidates in Budapest. Helena, the beauty of Troy." Typhon gulped down his champagne and chewed my name along with the wine. "Come, I introduce you to friends. Maybe you start a war."

He will suspect a rival sent you, Margaret had said. *Possibly the KGB. Convince him otherwise.*

At our corner of the bar, Typhon was content to drink brandy and listen as his cohorts tested me with oblique questions. Yes, I knew this or that KISZ official. I proved it with personal details that an acquaintance would know. Yes, I heard the Óbuda school superintendent had been sacked. For being spotted at a Lutheran service, I added, feigning shock at clerical reactionists lurking near our children. Ideology tickled the graybeards. No, I did not see General Secretary Kádár speak at my university, because Kádár had spoken not to the students but later, to a private gathering of *nomenklatura*. One by one the lesser graybeards moved off, leaving Typhon and me a bubble of privacy.

Once Margaret had sworn on her taped-up saints that Satan would be irresistibly handsome. This devil looked fat and tired. In his late fifties, time weighed on Irinyi—*think of him as Typhon*, Margaret had said—and left him a sagging belly. Crow's feet etched his temples.

I wanted a turn asking questions, and the ones I fought back were direct. How could anyone send so many to waste away in prison camps? How could he order the deaths of countrymen fighting to free Hungary? He bore the guilt for Csepel more than those he had pull the trigger. The killing was his idea.

Perhaps the devil's trick was to appear as what we expected least. Perhaps that made me a devil, too.

"You are not drinking," Typhon said.

"I am sorry, Comrade Secretary."

Typhon pushed my wine toward me. "Zsigmond, little bird. Do not apologize. Drink! A Magyar does not trust a teetotaler."

"I cannot drink like you and keep my head."

"Sip, sip, sip. What good is drinking if we keep our heads? Clear heads are for morning."

I grinned for my devil and drank the glass down.

"There you are," Typhon said. "Magyar after all."

On the record player was a slow song, Dusty Springfield. Typhon showed no inclination to dance, nor did he touch me other than careful brushes with his fingertips. Instead he shared with me secrets of the others around the club. He started with who was whose patron or who was going places in the Party, but after another brandy he began to point out those he derided.

"That man there," Typhon said, nodding to a prim apparatchik on the dance floor, "should someday join the Central Committee, like his father. But he is homosexual."

"He is?"

"Thinks we do not know. He should thank his father he is not disgraced. Or worse."

Irinyi—*Typhon, call him Typhon*—struggled off his barstool. "They always think we do not know. Do not fly off, little bird. An old man must see to—well. Do yourself a favor. Stay young forever."

When Typhon wants you alone, Margaret had said, *Typhon will leave alone.*

None of the men who had danced with me approached after Typhon left. Nothing happened for some time except that the crowd thinned and the records changed to older songs, Bobby Darin and Connie Francis. The new music had been exhausted.

Eventually a man in police officer uniform appeared with my coat over his arm. He had a callow face and crooked teeth, someone who fed off the fear he inspired. I extended my hand for him, but the callow man did not take it. Instead he tossed me the coat and turned on his heel. That I was to follow went unspoken, both the order and the threat.

They will search you, Margaret had said. *Stand through it like a girl, tense and ashamed.*

The callow man took me down a flight of stairs to a rear door. He stopped me and placed his hands on my ribs.

"Excuse me," I said, though to me his body search and added grope of my breasts were mere pressure. "I am no criminal."

"Comrade Irinyi is a cautious man."

"More expert than you, I should hope."

The callow man gave me a jaundiced glance. "Not so gentle."

He led me into the back of a dark Mercedes and slid in beside me. A junior officer drove us through Pest, deserted at one in the morning. The radio was kept off and none of us spoke, the only sounds our breathing and the wiper blades squeaking against the drizzle. The streetcars had shut down for the night.

Soon the Mercedes whisked us over the Danube. Out my window the towers of Fisherman's Bastion stood like impotent knights watching the river flow. Buda Castle slumbered atop its hill. Further out were the shards of my childhood: Csepel, where my father was found dead in an alleyway, and Budafok, where the AVO came and dragged my mother off to die in a camp.

We drove through quiet neighborhoods and up into the hills, past vineyards and wooded estates. Soon we pulled off at a private gatepost, and a guard stepped out to search the car. He grunted a laugh at me in my floral dress and nylons. I lowered my head, ever the embarrassed girl. He would choke on his laughter if he knew how many Roma eyes watched him from the forest.

A dirt track cut through evergreens and linden trees and ended at a patch of land cleared for a cottage house. No cars were parked in front, but lights burned from the ground floor windows.

The callow man took me inside, into a parlor furnished with volumes of bound books, silver trays, and crystal glassware. A large painting of a hunting scene hung over the mantel. A newly started fire had done little to warm the cottage.

"Upstairs," he said.

"I have to pee."

"Do it fast."

He left the door open and watched me the entire time. That told me what I wanted to know: he was thorough. The callow man would leave no opening to palm a knife or sneak his gun. He would respond quickly to any hint of trouble. I finished in the bathroom, and he showed me to a cramped stairway off the kitchen. "Work hard to earn a patron, Comrade Szabo."

I took the stairs slowly to keep up appearances. Really it gave me a chance to slow my breath. In the bedroom Irinyi was waiting in what light reached up from below. He poured two shots of brandy.

"Come in, little bird. Cheer an old man with a kiss."

Somewhere Typhon will have a gun, Margaret had said. *Be the first to use it.*

I closed the door behind me and crossed through the soup of shadows. Then I gave the devil his kiss. When as hollow as he, there was nothing lost by it.

Irinyi laughed. "I was not sure you would do it."

"Why not?"

"There are two types of pretty Helenas, I find. The merely pretty and the too pretty to be true. You were invited tonight after a late recommendation from an officer of suspect loyalty. You wanted my attention but did not use it. You did not tease like the schemers or coax me off like the professionals. Now it is just us two, no bugs, no tapes. We drink to plain speaking, then you state your purpose."

I let the shot burn down into my belly.

Irinyi contemplated me over his brandy. My eyesight had accustomed enough to catch a frown crease his ample cheeks. "Who do you work for?"

"Hungary."

"Central Control knows the Hungarian spies. Tell me or I give you to Gyuri downstairs."

"A man named Braintree sent me. He has a message: 'Cicilia.'"

ROBERT MANGEOT

Irinyi went still. "One word. One simple word you could have delivered at the club."

"Braintree insisted we be alone. At the club someone might overhear. Or be recorded."

"Probably true." Irinyi braced himself on the dresser and stood. "Time is short. As is trust. You must come with me as far as Budapest, little bird. Braintree tells you where to fly?"

"The British lie the same as the Russians, but in nicer suits. They have made a habit of abandoning Hungarians. Please, make them take me with you."

Irinyi waved away the suggestion. He opened a closet, turned on its bare bulb and hefted out a suitcase. Age had robbed the devil of strength, the brandy of his balance. I would kill him with a lamp cord, a broken bottle, with my bare hands if necessary.

"Trust can be demonstrated," I said, and where I placed his hand on my body left no doubt of my meaning.

"I prefer never to risk what Roma girls plan during such demonstrations. Flying to the West is no simple matter, little bird. We fly as the British say, no variation."

"They will not take me without a confirmation word."

"'Echidna,'" he said. "Tell them 'Echidna' and they see that my bird flies."

Irinyi opened his bag and shuffled through travel documents and stacks of American money. Tucked in the suitcase lid was a pistol, its aluminum polish catching the closet light. Aluminum meant a PA-63, its loaded magazine holding seven shots.

"How will we get clear of your men?"

Uncertainty flickered in his eyes, and he began rummaging through his case faster.

"Hit me." I grabbed my dress at the collar and tore it open to expose my brassiere. "Hard. For us both it must look like I fought you. Otherwise, why leave now, unsatisfied? Just please, get me back to Budapest alive."

Irinyi nodded. He swung a flabby hand at me, weak but catching my lip with his ring. I screamed and tumbled bawling across the bed. My skin burned where he struck me. I tasted blood, felt it dribble down my chin.

Heavy feet pounded up the wooden stairs. Irinyi spun toward the sound, preoccupied readying his story for the guard. He did not see me reach for the gun.

The callow man burst through the door and turned on the overhead light. "Comrade Deputy?"

"Little bitch likes to bite," Irinyi said. "Take me to—"

I rolled off the bed and fired twice at the callow man. Both bullets hit the center of his chest. Any noise he made before dying did not carry over the ringing in my ears.

"Fool!" Irinyi said. "You have damned us! If all the hills did not hear, the guards will—"

I turned the gun toward Irinyi. "More likely they are already dead."

The rage drained out of him. My devil rubbed his face while he collected his silver tongue. "The West pays far better than terrorists. Come with me. The British want me badly enough to grant anything. I can see you are more than comfortable."

There never was much in me to charm. "The British can rot as they let us rot."

Irinyi gave a resigned grimace and stood up tall, seeking more dignity in death than ever he had granted. "They do not stop hunting those who cross them. Hope they find you before my friends do. The British kill faster."

"Not so fast as a Hungarian."

I put three bullets into Irinyi. The first was for Csepel, a shot to his bald forehead. The last two I put in his heart, one for each of my parents.

I shut off all lights except the front room. Next I unlocked the doors and raised a shade one-third off the windowsill. From the woods a flashlight blinked its reply.

A minute later Margaret slipped inside the house. She inspected the pistol and wiped it over her coat. "Show me."

Upstairs I let Margaret pace the bedroom and prod both dead men. She spat on Irinyi's corpse.

"The saints make us their sparks," Margaret said. "My Helena, brightest spark of all. One hour yet to reach the safe house. Flash the light twice and head for where I signaled. Braintree will be hard on you. Be just as hard."

"Margaret—"

"Do not go stupid on me now. What did I ask when you first came to stay with me?"

"If I wanted to fight."

"Then fight," Margaret said. "Play out your part. Swear you left the Butcher alive. Spare the others Braintree comes for if he is not convinced. See he gets you out before the bear is awake. Go, and someday Saint Jerome leads my Helena back home."

I waited until out of the cottage before crying, my tears mixing with the soft rain. Margaret deserved more than to see that from me. I was halfway to the tree line when she pulled the trigger and returned her spark to Hungary.

SIDE EFFECTS

BY T. JEFFERSON PARKER

W e're down in the bomb shelter alphabetizing the canned foods so we can find what we're looking for during an invasion or nuclear attack. Not bitchen on Labor Day weekend. The shelter is a long rectangular room with fluorescent lights, a bathroom at one end and a sink and small stove/oven at the other. Surplus military cots, blankets, pillows, and flashlights everywhere you look. No windows because it's underground. The ceiling is low, and the lights flicker and hum and make you squint. Mom and Dad have a small record player set up down here for Tijuana Brass, Engelbert Humperdinck, and Andy Williams. If we get bombed I'll take in my Cream and Doors. Amazing, the music old people would want to hear during a nuclear attack.

We've already reviewed the Batteries/Drinking Water/Perishables Rotation Schedule, which is written out on graph paper in Dad's perfect handwriting and tacked to the corkboard below the Radiation Exposure Do's and Don'ts. The whole family is here— Dad, Mom, Max, Marie, and me. I'm Mike, sixteen and the oldest. I can't wait to finish up the work so I can get to 15th Street in Newport Beach, where there's a south swell and waves running three to five feet, glassy conditions, water temp of seventy. Of course Dad has other ideas.

"Take your time and do a good job here, troops," he says. "Chicken noodle before clam chowder and so forth, right on down the line. When this is done we've got some reloading to do in the gun room. The forty-five brass is really piling up! Then, the rest of Saturday is yours. But remember we've got the chapter meeting here tonight."

Again, not bitchen. Fully not. The meeting is the South Orange County California chapter of the John Birch Society. Which means monthly atrocity films about the World Communist Conspiracy, programs on how to detect drug use in young people, plenty of cocktails and cigarettes, moms in short skirts, and dads with skinny ties and flat-tops. Dullsville. Me and Max steal almost-finished drinks when the grown-ups lose track of them. Which is easy when the living room is dark so they can see the atrocity films. Piled bodies, executions, maimed survivors. The speakers all agree that these things will happen here in America if we let them take our guns away. Or negotiate with the Russians. Or if we let the government put fluoride in our water. Fine, but I'm a member of the Newport Beach Bodysurfing Association, and Newport's three-to-five and I've got the keys to the Country Squire.

It's more like six to eight feet by the time we get to 15th Street that afternoon, a blow-out, the waves just mountains of chop. Some of the other club members are there. We wear white water polo caps to distinguish us in the water from nonbodysurfers, whom we call "goons." We meet once a month and talk about contests, techniques, and trips to other breaks. I catch a right and stay tucked up high in the pocket as long as I can hang there, trimming along, palms and swim fins vibrating on the wave, which catches up and breaks over me. I could stand in that cylinder it's so big. It's *loud*, too—a full-on roar. I'm blinded by the spray, the brine grinding away under my eyelids for my short, sweet ride. Then the usual bodysurfer's exit—a lip-launched freefall. Gravity tilts me downward but I try to maintain my elevation. Like a falling jet. I'd scream but I'll need the air. Soon. The wave drives me straight to the bottom, where I flatten, rake my fingers into the sand and hold what's left of my breath while the wave thunders by above me. Fireflies in my eyes. Finally I shove off and wriggle upward, break the surface in the oddly smooth and spreading wake to gasp in sudden red sunlight. Fully bitchen. So bitchen I swim back out and do it again. Several times. Later Max gets a great ride but comes up under a jellyfish and when we're riding home his face looks like a stewed tomato. Marie, who has worked hard on her tan, thinks it's hilarious.

When I turn onto our street I slow way down and casually look at the Lamm house. Adlyn is nowhere in sight, which is a bummer. Neither is her older brother, Larkin, which is fine with me. His van is in the driveway. The house is all concrete and glass, curvy and science fictional, nothing like the tract houses across from it, where we live. The Lamms moved in six months ago. On the last day of school I got brave enough to talk to Adlyn. Dr. Lamm is an important officer at the Tustin Naval Air Station, says Dad.

"Adlyn is nowhere, nowhere, nowhere to be found," singsongs Marie from the back. "She's too mature for you, *Mike.* You're too chicken to call her so she has to call *you.*"

"Shut up, Marie."

"My whole face is burning. Mom's going to make me soak it in vinegar again."

In the darkened living room the eight-millimeter projector clicks along, showing a mass grave and soldiers looking down into it. The black and white film makes all of it look even more freezing and bleak than it must have been. More doomed. Some of the soldiers still have their rifles unslung. There's a mist in the air, but you can't tell if it's fog or gunpowder or the cigarette smoke in the living room.

My brother and sister and I sit three-across on the piano bench in the back. Max smells like vinegar. Mom and Dad make us sit through these things, the atrocity film and guest speaker, anyway. Mom will give us a quiz on Tuesday evening after dinner to make sure we paid attention. The next footage shows a man sitting on the edge of a big pit, stiff with bodies. He's dressed in a beat-up suit of all things, and his hands are folded over a small suitcase on his lap, apparently something he'll need for his coming journey. His face is sad and dirty, and he reminds me of Charlie Chaplin. A soldier steps up beside him and shoots him in the temple with a pistol, and the man slumps back against the pit side and slides in.

"Latvia? Lithuania? Estonia?" asks this month's speaker, State Senator Brock Stile. "Do you think the World Communist Conspiracy simply stopped in Europe? How naive can you be? What do you think happened in Korea? What's going on in Vietnam right now? Do you think the U.N. will protect us from this? I urge you to take steps to prevent this from happening here. First...become informed by joining the Society tonight. Second..."

I sip a stolen cocktail medley over fresh ice with plenty of root beer poured in. The projector clatters along, and I look at Max and Marie, the images playing on their faces, their eyes fixed to the screen. I look at Dr. Lamm, trim in his golf shirt. His mustache is brief, and he stands beside Mrs. Lamm. Mrs. Lamm is half a head taller, slender and mini-skirted, a Barbie doll with a chocolate bouffant. I spring one, hope it goes away. Why now? Why should an important part of me be outside my control?

Between Dr. and Mrs. Lamm stands their son, Larkin, a husky guy with a strong face, a cleft chin, and calm gray eyes that don't blink. His hair is short like the grown-ups', but he looks just a few years older than me. Smile lines at the corners of his lips. He seems amused by the film. He's been to a few of these. He walked by the house yesterday wearing a beret and sunglasses, then came past the other way a few minutes later. Now he turns slowly and looks at Marie, then me, then back to the screen. *Click-click-click-click* goes the projector. Mom says Larkin attends a prestigious private liberal arts college in the Midwest, so he's only around holidays and some weekends.

As soon as Senator Stile's presentation is over I wander out to the back patio, where the picnic table is loaded with chips and dips, beer, and soft drinks. When no one's looking I stride to the side yard, march past the trashcans to the gate and let myself out to the driveway. Half a dozen gleaming police motorcycles are parked in formation on the front lawn, local law enforcement always welcome at our Birch Society meetings. The streetlights shine off their black-and-white paint, their chrome, and their civic emblems, but I hardly notice them. There's a flagpole in the middle of the lawn, too, one of Dad's and Mom's patriotic projects. There's a toilet float spray-painted gold bolted to the top of the pole. As a family, we hoist the flag in the mornings before school, and take it down at sunset. Humiliating.

A minute later I'm halfway down the block, and I can see the Lamm home, fortress-like and glowing at the end of it. As I trot toward it, I look to Adlyn's large bedroom window for a vision of her. No vision, but the light is on. Her room is an upstairs corner on the west side of the house. I let myself through the side gate and stand under her balcony. Leaning my back to the high concrete sidewall, I see the railing and the beam ceiling, from which all kinds of glass-enclosed candles and potted plants dangle in macramé slings. It's like a jungle. Suddenly she's standing amid long tendrils of Wandering Jew and Creeping Charlie and Boston fern. She looks down at me and gathers two handfuls of greenery then holds them to her breasts.

"How you doing down there, little Romeo?"

"Groovin', Adlyn. And you?"

"Oh, fine I guess."

"Far out. I was pretty stoked when you called me."

She looks at the plants in her hands with what appears to be mild wonder. "Mike, I've seen the way you look at me. Like in class and at the beach and at that party at the end of school. And I've made some difficult decisions. I want to tell you some things."

"Uhhh..."

"Sorry I couldn't go to the beach today."

"I looked for you. It was blown out."

"Larkin's back for a whole week. So we had to do cultural stuff. Went to lunch in Pasadena, then the Huntington Gardens."

"I'm glad you're back now. Larkin's over at our place for the chapter meeting."

"He likes that kind of thing. He always has. Wherever we live."

"Freaky."

"That's nothing!" She giggles, lets go the foliage, and leans over the railing. Her beautiful red hair drops forward into the light. She's wearing a lacy white top that there isn't much of. "Would you like to come in?"

"Bitchen, Adlyn. Fully boss."

"Would you mind climbing up? The house has alarms on the doors and windows and I don't know the code."

"Alarms?"

"Silly. But Mom and Dad never quit trying to keep us safe and sane."

The round columns supporting Adlyn's balcony are concrete and ivy-covered, and I manage to bear-hug my way to the balcony floor, swing one knee onto it, then get my hands on the railing and pull myself over. I've got ivy juice on my favorite Hang Ten shirt and jeans, but Adlyn is smiling. I can smell her strawberry perfume. Under the white lacy top she wears a two-piece swimsuit, pink-and-orange swirls. Her legs are tan and smooth.

Her room is three times the size of mine and Max's, with a tall ceiling. There are lights built up into it, not like in my room, where there's only one ceiling lamp in the middle of the popcorn, with an opaque shade that collects dead moths. She slides a button on the faceplate and the lights dim and brighten. "It's called a rheostat."

"We don't have those."

"On our way home from Pasadena today, Ronnie Feurtag was on the news. They found her in a drainage ditch in Huntington Beach."

"That's good news."

"Not for her it isn't. She was dead. They think murdered."

"Oh, Geez." Ronnie had disappeared from the beach on the Fourth of July, and it was front page of the *Register* for a week and even made the L.A. TV news. She lived a few blocks away. First they thought she ran away to Knott's Berry Farm or Disneyland, then police said it could be foul play. I didn't know her but I'd seen her around, always roller skating down the block. Ten years old— same as Marie.

Adlyn takes my hand and leads me from her room down a wide hallway. We pass one closed door on the left, another on the right, then on the left another closed door that has steel bars across it. The bars run horizontally across the door, from top to bottom, spaced approximately six inches apart. They look like stainless steel, and I think at first this is some science-fictional design flair for advanced, sophisticated people like the Lamms. "Larkin's room," whispers Adlyn, stopping and running the backs of her fingers up the rungs. Sounds like steel alright. "You can only open it from outside and guess who has the key? *Mom*."

She smiles, pecks me on the lips, and takes my hand again. Bitchen! I smell the strawberry perfume very strong on her. I spring one again and as we walk down the wide marble staircase I put my hands in my pockets and shove it up and to one side where it won't show as bad. It always happens at the worst times, like catching some rays at the beach, like watching TV, like now. Somehow Dad seems to know, warns me about becoming "a bathroom idiot."

We sit side-by-side on a black leather-and-steel sofa in their living room. The room is very large and high and it has more of the hidden lights up in the ceiling. The walls are plain white, and the carpet is white. There are paintings hung everywhere, huge things that don't look like anything I've ever seen. No frames. I wonder if some of them are hung upside down then wonder: how would you know?

"Would you like to try a confession pill?" asked Adlyn.

"I don't know what that is."

"It makes you want to confess."

"A pill does that?"

"Pills can make you do anything."

"Hmmm. What's it called?"

"Just X62-13. There's no name for it yet because it isn't approved. The X means experimental. The 62 means it was first formulated in nineteen-sixty-two, and 13 makes it the thirteenth drug created in that year. Nineteen sixty-two was a good year, so far as numbers go. The number of drugs created, that is."

"So, drugs like pot or speed or downers?"

"Oh, no! X62-13 is not recreational. Although not-real-smart people might think so."

"Your mom or dad work at a pharmaceutical place, then?"

"Well. Let me just take the pill first. Then I'll tell you everything you need to know. Probably more!"

She runs across the carpet, up the stairs. Her legs are beautiful and the bottoms of her feet are white, like the carpet. I try to distract myself by making some sense of the paintings, but they make no sense. I look out the windows, but it's dark and there are no streetlights nearby. The Lamms' big, unreal house seems to sit in a nest of darkness. It's on a slight rise. I go to one of the big windows and can see our tract below—Heritage Acres—huddled in orderly fashion, gridded off by the streetlights that lie in perpendicular rows and burn strong, none of them flickering, none of them out. There are orange groves surrounding Heritage Acres, though some of them are being cut down to build houses. Out there, beyond the streetlights, where the groves and partial groves are, it's very dark. A new moon.

Behind me Adlyn clears her throat. When I turn she's got a glass in one hand and a large white pill in the other, which she holds up to me like a treat for a dog. She's wrapped a long, airy, green scarf around her neck. She smiles and sits primly back down on the big black sofa and I stride over, beginning to spring again. Damn. I sit near but not close to her, and cross my legs. She drops the big pill down into her mouth and swallows half the glass of what looks like water.

"Larkin discovered what Dad does years ago," she says. "Which is, he's a doctor and he works for the military. He creates tactical drugs. Helps create them. It's extremely top secret, but Larkin figured it out anyway. Larkin's kind of talented like that, and Dad's very absentminded and careless sometimes. Dad's fundamental belief—I read this in a top secret paper he wrote—is that drugs are a better way to win a war than bullets. He wants to have wars without any killing. Or hardly any. He says that 'targeted malfunctioning of the human organism' is the goal of his drugs. On a battlefield, that will probably have to be a gas. But there are pills too. This one, the one I just took, was developed to make prisoners confess. Larkin gave me my first one of these when I was six. I spent the next four hours confessing *exactly* what kind of horses I had dreamed of having, and *every* detail about my ranch in the mountains, where the horses and I would live. I confessed things I didn't even know I *knew*. And then I confessed the name and gave a full description of *every* boy I had ever had a crush on, and *every* person who had ever scared me, which turned out to be really only one—him, Larkin."

I look hard at Adlyn then, harder than I'd ever looked before. Yes, she's a pretty, lightly freckled, suntanned redhead with green pools for eyes, wearing a bikini and a white lacy top and a bright green scarf around her neck. But she also seems...compelled? Driven? What I mean is, when I look into those really bitchen green eyes they are really, really *eager*. Like she can't wait to get there, can't wait for the next thing. So I wonder where she thinks she's going. And what the next thing might be.

Adlyn shudders then, as if a cold blast of air has come through the room. She twists the green scarf tighter and holds it over her eyes. "Would you please tie it?" She turns her back and wriggles closer to me. You know what that causes. I manage to tie the scarf in a loose knot. The green ends fall across her back. In the strong light I can see the fine golden hairs dusting her suntanned shoulders showing through the lacy openings. Because she can't see me I lower my right elbow to my zipper area and grind down *hard*.

"It's hitting me strong now," she whispers. "The 62-13. One day Larkin found drug samples Dad had hidden in the garage. Later we found out it was because Dad thought there was a Soviet spy in his research lab. This was back in Bethesda. Larkin started sampling the pills. There was X59-11, X61-14, and X62-13—what I just took. The first one put Larkin in a coma for eleven days and he woke up feeling happy and relaxed. The second one gave him seizures and he broke out in red measles-like triangles. The third one made Larkin confess to me his very…scary fantasies about, well…me, and other girls my age. In the garage Larkin also found some things Dad had written. Larkin slipped some 62-13 into Dad's vitamins then demanded to know what Dad did, and where, and when, and for whom. Everything. Of course Dad told him without a fight, because the drug can't be defeated. Larkin tape-recorded it and said he'd play it to the *Washington Post* unless Dad brought home plenty more samples—he wanted everything Dad had because Larkin enjoyed trying them out. He also demanded a fifty-dollar per week allowance and a new car, even though he was only fourteen. It was a Roadrunner."

"Why did Larkin take all the drugs?"

"He craves sensation. He's sensational."

"You're shivering, Adlyn."

"It's one side-effect of 62-13."

"I'm kind of mind-blown by this stuff about Larkin."

"Oh, that's nothing. It started getting really scary. It…Mike… it still *is* really scary. Can you get me a blanket from my bedroom closet, the pink one with the unicorns on it?"

"Be right back." And I am.

"They found her in the woods near Bethesda."

"Who?"

"Tammy. Our neighbor. Ten. Strangled. Two months later Dad got transferred to the Edgewood Arsenal up on the Chesapeake Bay and guess what? It happened again. In the woods, our neighbor, Kathleen. I knew her. Then Dad got a big promotion that took us way out to Missoula, Montana, and guess what?"

"Another neighbor girl strangled and left in the woods."

"Forest, actually. Our next door neighbor. That was when Dad finally put two and two together. So did the police. The detectives interviewed Larkin for hours. Several times. Of course he wouldn't tell them anything because before the questioning he'd taken X62-15, which Dad designed to prevent captured Americans from confessing. It was intended as an antidote to X62-13. It raises your pain threshold to almost nothing and gives you a gigantic but completely logical imagination. You can make up convincing lies and follow them up with irrefutable details. Even a lie detector can't tell. You get real calm. Larkin told me one night, in tears, after taking 62-13, that he had taken 58-37 before he killed the girls. That drug was supposed to be a waking-hours sedative but instead it causes dissociation and violent behavior, and Dad and his partners considered it a total failure. Larkin told me he cased the girls' houses by daylight but always went out and took them on new moons, so he'd be harder to see at night. Afterward, he felt so bad about what he'd done, when he took 62-13, that is. So bad.

"Well, then the Pentagon generals came in and met with Dad and Larkin and the local police and the next thing you know we're living in Albuquerque, where they've got another government pharmaceutical research facility. But not Larkin. He gets sent away to a prestigious private liberal arts school in the Midwest and only comes home on holidays and some weekends. Mom and Dad put bars on Larkin's door and windows, and alarms on all the other doors and windows, for when he visited. So he couldn't get out. Mom would be his jailer-nurse-cook. They never let him outside the house unless they were both with him. Never. But? He still gets another girl in New Mexico, from her own house around the corner, Christmas break. Left her in the desert. So we packed up and headed out to California. Everything was fine until the Fourth of July, when Ronnie Feurtag disappeared. And until tonight, because it's a new moon and Larkin took the 58-37 about an hour before he left for your house."

"Marie!"

"I genuinely like you, Mike. Can I say one thing before you go?"

"No!" I'm already to the door. I hesitate at the keypad on the wall, lights blipping red, red, red.

"Mike, I took a lot of those pills with Larkin. I helped him but only a little. That's why Mom and Dad lock me in, too. I'm more prone to shoplifting, burglary, and self-destructive behavior. But I have residual goodness. I hate what those drugs did to us. They broke down our souls then built them back shapeless and black. Sometimes I can smell them. Our souls. I can't wait to die."

I throw open the door and the alarms shriek. Adlyn yells out that she's sorry. She's confessing her sorrow in very emotional detail, raising her voice higher and higher. But it only gets fainter as I run across the lawn toward Heritage Acres, faster than I've ever run before.

The chapter meeting is just breaking up. People stand out in the yard by the flagpole and the police motorcycles. Some of them are the cops who ride them. A station wagon sweeps away from the curb. Mom stands on the porch, saying goodnight and handing out the red-white-and-blue John Birch Society ballpoint pens that litter our entire house. No sign of Dad. *"Where's Marie?"*

"What's wrong, Mike?"

But I'm already past her and into the still-darkened living room where through the smoke I see Dad in close conversation with Mrs. Lamm, and Ken Crockett pounding out "Battle Hymn of the Republic" on the piano while Mrs. Crockett slow-dances alone, and my brother Max using the beam of projector light to cast shadow figures on the wall with his hands: rabbit head, flying bird, devil with horns. But no Marie and no Larkin Lamm. The sliding glass doors are open to the back patio and the curtains sway. I fly through the house, room-to-room. In the master bedroom Mrs. Frantini and Mr. Dale are kissing. Back in the living room I throw open the slider and spill onto the back patio by the snacks-and-drinks table, where a few last guests are smoking and loading up paper plates. I can see the whole backyard: no Marie. And the side yard: no Marie. But I see the lights on in the gun room and the door slightly ajar. Suddenly, Dr. Lamm bursts out, looking left and right, searching everywhere, fast as his eyes can focus—just as I am. He sees me and throws his arms wide and cocks his head like *I'm supposed to know* where Marie and his homicidal pervert of a son are.

And then I remember. The woods, the forest, the desert, the drainage ditch.

I yank open the back gate and run to the flood control channel. I hear Dr. Lamm behind me. At the edge of the channel I see the trickle of water at the very bottom. And in the faint patio lights from my house I can see the still-dripping footprints—just one pair—leading up the opposite side of the concrete canal toward the orange grove. In a blink I'm down the near bank and through the little stream and up the far side. When I get to the grove the light is too dim for footprints so I have to go right or left and I choose right because I always do, automatically, I always choose right because I'm right-handed, and because Dad and Mom choose right, the right wing, because the right leads to freedom and liberty but the left leads to communism and death. I run a few yards then stop. I hear footsteps behind me and turn to see Dr. Lamm catching up.

Suddenly, back in the trees, Marie is screaming. It's more of a snarl—a throttled grunt made while biting or tearing with your teeth, though her two front top teeth are missing. She has a ferocious temper. The trees are dark, the oranges just faint dabs of color. The earth of the grove is big-clodded and firm. I run toward her like in a dream—slowly, laboring so hard but moving so little. Some fool inside me thinks: this *is* a dream. Wake up. Wake up!

Marie has stopped screaming. But I see them, Larkin Lamm crouching with his back to me, wrenching her wrists, pushing her against the trunk of a big orange tree, pulling her back, slamming again. I hear her breathless huffs. It takes time to get there. Minutes. Hours. But some dreams come true some days, and mine comes true that day. I jump up and drop my arms around Larkin Lamm's neck and choke him as hard as any sixteen-year-old has ever choked another person in the history of this Earth.

He's strong. He stands, but I stay on. He tries locking his hands on my arms then pulling on my hair but I can feel the start of his panic. He spins away from Marie and crashes me into another tree trunk. The same fireflies buzz my eyes as when I held onto the bottom of the ocean while the wave went over me. I do not let go. I will not let go. Then Larkin straightens and jumps and lands on his back, crushing me between himself and the ground. Lights out. I'm gone, completely.

But just for a second or two. I open my eyes to Larkin above me, his hands outstretched. He's moving backwards, like a lunging dog held by a leash. I roll away and get to my hands and knees and I see the belt around his neck, and Dr. Lamm, holding on with both hands, arms taut and legs braced, pulling Larkin back.

Marie runs up behind me, grunts, and a good-sized rock sails past Larkin's head, barely missing Dr. Lamm. Larkin gags and tries to get his fingers under the belt. "I am responsible!" calls out the doctor. "I...take...full..." Marie's next rock hits Larkin smack in the middle of the forehead and a spurt of black blood appears.

When I look back I see our patio lights still on and the open gate and flashlight beams crisscrossing in the darkness toward us. Then voices: Dad's and Mom's, higher-pitched than usual, voices calling out for Marie and me, voices full of fear and hope. Dr. Lamm has gotten the belt into a branched "V" of a tree trunk and he's pulling hard. Larkin stands levered against the tree, arms in a reverse hug of it, his head raised in order to draw breath. His face is smeared with blood and tears, and his gray eyes are calm as always, and, as always, unblinking. Marie throws her small light body against me and I lift her and trudge back toward the light.

THE EVERYDAY HOUSEWIFE

BY LAURA LIPPMAN

The summer that she was a newlywed, Judith Monaghan watched *The Newlywed Game* almost every day, except when it was preempted by the hearings. She watched those, too, marveling at Senator Ervin's eyebrows and Maureen "Mo" Dean's outfits, but she preferred *The Newlywed Game*, despite the fact that she had once been vitally interested in politics. Actually, maybe that was why she preferred the game show to the hearings; it seemed more real to her.

The Newlywed Game came on at 2 p.m. on Channel 13, and Judith set aside the next two hours to accomplish whatever could be done while seated in the living room—darning socks, shelling peas, whipping in hems, teaching herself to knit. She was sure that she and Patrick could answer every question correctly, as they had known each other for six years before they married. But how would they get to California from Baltimore? Would her mother be upset about the inevitable "Making Whoopee" questions? And was it possible to angle to be on the show when the top prize was a washer-dryer? Judith didn't like the look of the furniture sets given away as prizes—too shiny new for her tastes—and the Monaghans already had a perfectly good television, a wedding gift from her second-oldest brother, who owned two electronics stores.

The Newlywed Game was followed by a show called *The Girl in My Life*, about women who had made a difference to others. Judith didn't care for it as much. She usually switched to *The Edge of Night*, which led right into *The Price Is Right*, where she won almost everything. Or would have, if she had been in the studio audience. Judith was a very focused shopper, paying attention to prices, calculating the per unit cost among different brands.

Judith did have a washer, but no dryer, a problem during that clammy, damp summer, when the sun rose every day only to disappear until 4 p.m.—the time that Judith tied an immaculate apron over one of her pretty, hand-tailored dresses and began to prepare dinner for her husband, who arrived home at 5:30 p.m. and expected his food at 6. (He spent the intervening half hour with a beer and the evening paper, the Orioles pregame show on WBAL.) She liked making Patrick dinner. She liked doing things in general. Judith was as restless as a hummingbird, and the small brick duplex required so little of her. She cleaned the woodwork with a Q-tip, vacuumed the Venetian blinds, scrubbed the long-discolored grout with a toothbrush, and still she ended up with time on her hands. She even started ironing the sheets when she changed the linens on Fridays and she might have washed them more often, but they took so long to dry on these strangely overcast summer days. She tried to bake her own bread, once. The loaves were flat and dense; Patrick said he preferred store bread, anyway. He liked Wonder Bread, and Judith liked Maranto's, the fresh, paper-wrapped Italian loaves.

"Those only taste good the day you buy them," Patrick said. "Wonder Bread tastes good all week long."

They had only one car, and of course Patrick took that every day; the bus stop was four blocks away and he would have been required to change buses on Route 40. Besides, he needed the car for his job, which involved driving from bar to bar, doing inspections. Judith didn't mind. She did a big grocery shop on weekends and could do any daily marketing on foot—vegetables, last-minute items—at the High's Dairy Store on Ingleside, or even the grocery stores on Route 40 if it came to that. She knew if she shopped efficiently, she wouldn't have to do these daily runs to High's, but the walk down Newfield Road was another way to fill the long days.

Married life was lonely, which seemed strange to her. Shouldn't marriage be the end of loneliness? She tried to find a neutral way to express this thought to her mother, who called every day at 9 a.m., despite the fact that Judith told her repeatedly that was when she cleaned the kitchen.

"The days seem so long that I find myself cleaning even more than you did."

"I," her mother said, "had four sons. No one could clean more than I did."

"I cook a lot, too. I'm getting pretty good." Judith was proud of her cooking, the meals she put together for Patrick. She would never be like the woman in the Alka-Seltzer commercial, the one who made heart-shaped meatloaf. "Sometimes I wonder if I should have kept my job until I got pregnant."

A quick laugh at her own expense, as if what she was saying was silly. But she did miss work, the intrigues of an office, being around others. She had lived at home until she married. She had wanted to take an apartment with another girl after she finished college, but her parents wouldn't hear of it.

"Marry in haste, repent in leisure."

Judith adjusted the phone, which she had cradled between her ear and shoulder, thinking she must have misheard. For one thing, no one could call Patrick Monaghan's courtship hasty.

"I didn't catch that," she said. "I'm washing the breakfast dishes." Patrick liked to start the day with eggs, bacon, toast, and juice. She had made the juice fresh until he told her he preferred Minute Maid concentrate. That was okay, she used the empty cartons to set her hair after he left in the mornings, the best way to get the smooth look that he liked.

"Mrs. Levitan died that way. She was washing the dishes and the phone slipped in the sink and she was electrocuted."

"I don't think that's what happened," Judith ventured.

"You're right. Mrs. Levitan is the one who died while talking on the phone in a thunderstorm. It was Irene Sandowski who dropped the phone. Although I think it was in the bathtub."

"Oh, Mother, how could someone drop the phone in the bathtub? The Sandowskis aren't the type of people to have a phone in the bathroom."

"She thought she was so clever, that one. And grand. She had her husband find an extra-long cord—I think he had to call Bell Atlantic special—and she hooked it up to a princess phone, pink, a birthday gift, and she would take it into the bathroom and prop it up on the toilet and take bubble baths like she was Doris Day or somebody, talking the whole while. Well, one day, the whole thing fell in." A pause. "I just realized—I never did understand why she got a pink phone, when her bedroom was all gold and white, but the bathroom was pink."

"Irene Sandowski is alive," Judith said.

"Are you sure?"

"She was alive as of last week when I got the invitation to Betty's wedding. Irving *and* Irene Sandowski request your pleasure, et cetera, et cetera."

"I didn't say she *died*. But that's why she has that white streak in her hair and now she has to be careful when she gets her teeth cleaned because her heartbeat is irregular. So Betty is getting married? Someone nice, I hope."

Nice meant *Jewish*. Nice meant *rich*, or at someone who might be rich, some day. It also meant: *Not like your husband, the Irishman, the Mick, who took you to the far side of town, where I suspect you are eating HAM every day.* Yet the Weinsteins didn't keep kosher and ate pork when they had Chinese carry-out, while crabs were okay as long as they were eaten outside on newspaper.

However, her mother had never tasted lobster, a fact of which she was strangely proud.

"It's nice over here," Judith said. Sometimes, saying a thing could make it true. It wasn't *not* nice. It just wasn't where she had expected to live.

"It's tacky, sharing a wall with another house," her mother said.

"You grew up in a rowhouse."

"*You* didn't," her mother said. "I'll talk to you tomorrow."

"You don't have to call every—" but her mother had already hung up.

Judith thought maybe she should spend less time talking to her mother and more time with her brother, Donald, the one closest to her in age. A bachelor who worked for a state senator, Donald was used to listening to people. Plus, he liked Patrick, had helped get him the job with the liquor board. Donald had lots of connections, lots of pull.

"Maybe you should get a job, Judith," Donald said. "I can help you if that's what you want."

"Oh, no," she protested. "I'm a married woman now. And the babies will start coming any day. I'd just end up quitting."

Those wished-for babies were the reason for the house on New-field Road, which Patrick had rented without consulting her. "With three bedrooms, a yard, and a washing machine—no dryer, but it has one of those umbrella like things to hang the clothes on and the yard gets good sunlight, I made sure to check that. And a garbage disposal, Judith. Plus an unfinished basement, which we could make into a rec room, the landlord said improvements were fine. Of course, we probably won't be there long enough to care. I mean, it's okay for one kid, but once we get past that—"

Patrick had never said so many words at one time in all the time Judith had known him.

"Newfield Road? I don't even know where that is," she had said.

"Edmondson Heights. Over by Social Security, but closer to

Route 40. You know Mr. G's, where I used to take you for soft ice cream when we started dating? And the drive-in where we saw that movie together the night we met? Sort of between those two places."

Judith had fond memories of both Mr. G's and the drive-in. But Judith had considered those exotic adventures, akin to going on an African safari. *Observe the Baltimore Irish Catholic in his natural environment, eating soft ice cream and onion rings after a movie.* The boys Judith knew congregated at diners, after dropping their dates at home. Edmondson Heights was seven exits away on the Beltway from where she grew up in Pikesville. It might as well have been seven hundred miles.

"I don't know people who live over there."

"You'll meet some. I have lots of cousins in the neighborhood, if it comes to that."

"I mean, I mean"—But she could not say: I don't mean people, people. I mean *my* people. Your people are not my people. How could she point out that there wasn't a single temple along the Route 40 corridor? Patrick thought she wasn't going to go to synagogue any more. They had thrown in their lot together, Romeo and Juliet, vowing to disown their disapproving families and live their own lives, by their rules. Only it turned out their families would not be disowned so easily and what were supposed to be their rules, Patrick's and Judith's, were turning out to be Patrick's rules. He chose where they lived. He chose how they spent their weekend hours. She suspected, come December, he would choose to have a tree in the living room. At which point, should Judith's mother visit, she would drop dead on the spot.

But, so far, her mother had inspected the rowhouse only once. She had walked through it without comment, unless sniffs could be counted as comments. In which case, she had made roughly forty, fifty comments, five to ten per room. The thing that seemed to bother her the most was the umbrella-like drying line in the backyard that Patrick considered such an asset. She had placed a hand over her heart and shook ever head ever so slightly, the way she did when she watched the war coverage on TV.

Certainly, her mother could not be surprised that Judith didn't have an automatic dryer, and she had to admit the washer in the duplex was a step up from the coin-operated machines in the Bonnie Brae Apartments. Louise Weinstein, as a newlywed, had pinned clothes to a line strung behind a Butchers Hill rowhouse, not that far from where the Monaghans lived in Fell's Point. Both families had moved up and out, of course, but the Weinsteins had headed northwest, while the Monaghans marched due west. Judith and Patrick might never have met if they hadn't ended up on a double date together, and it wasn't even with each other. Judith's date, Harold, asked to find a boy for her friend Thelma, had suggested Patrick Monaghan, an enthusiastic volunteer in the governor's race. Thelma was a pretty girl, but Judith could feel Patrick's eyes on her neck throughout the entire film, *Sweet Charity*. The next day, Patrick called and asked if she was really as interested in politics as she had claimed over soft ice cream at Mr. G's because the Stonewall Democratic Club was always looking for volunteers. Oh, she was *interested*. She was interested in politics and interested in this stoic Irish redhead. Go figure—the man was trustworthy, but politics broke her heart. Patrick's, too, if it came to that. They never quite got over what happened in that governor's race. The Watergate hearings, as far as Judith was concerned, were just an opportunity for the rest of the nation to learn what they already knew. It was all a shuck, a game, business as usual. Patrick and Judith had presented their youth and idealism like a burnt offering to pagan gods, then comforted each other when it came to naught. At least they had a marriage to show for it. Lots of young couples were marrying early if only because of the lottery numbers the boys had been assigned. But Patrick had a high number. Judith knew he really loved her.

Besides, whatever the pace of their courtship, she was not *repenting*. She didn't regret her marriage. The house was fine, just fine, especially for a place to pass through. The neighborhood was—

There, her resilience failed her. She hated Edmondson Heights, the blocks and blocks of brick rowhouses just like her own, thrown up in the '50s to address the shortages after the war. She could and did walk for miles, but the scene seldom changed. Sometimes, she walked all the way to the Westview Mall, but it was a dark, jerry-rigged place, an open-air shopping center that had closed itself in to keep up with the times. Besides, she had no money to buy the things she really wanted, clothes and shoes and books, so she ended up at Silber's Bakery, eating those abominations known as pizza rolls, hunks of white bread with tomato sauce and cheese smeared on top. She would probably weigh an extra ten pounds if it weren't for all the walking.

Over the summer, she gradually began to see the small distinctions from block to block along Newfield Road, which had initially looked all of a piece to her. She could tell, for example, where the neighborhood changed over from renters to owners. The tiny front lawns were better-kept and often had shrubberies, the ones hung with bright red berries that Judith had always heard were poisonous, but perhaps that was just a story told to scare children. The doors and shutters were painted in glossier colors, and the houses had storm doors. Renters kept iridescent globes on pedestals in their yards. Owners nailed ceramic cats to their brick facades. Some even had those hitching posts that looked like jockeys, although the faces had all been whitewashed. There were more children, too, in these blocks. Judith's block was almost childless. Two blocks over, the Lord Baltimore diaper truck was a daily presence. Go another five blocks and it was the Good Humor man.

Walking as she did, day in and day out, Judith felt like a spy in her own life. She looked like the other women she saw, she lived a life like theirs, and yet she was not one of them, she was sure of that. Was it merely being Jewish in a neighborhood where almost everyone else seemed to be Catholic? Her face burned with the memory of her humiliation when she served pot roast to one pair of neighbors on a Friday night, only to have Mrs. Delaney say quietly, "We go meatless on Fridays."

"Oh, who gives a crap, Frances?" said Mr. Delaney, who took seconds. It was a good pot roast; Judith couldn't help preening a bit. Mrs. Delaney limited herself to potatoes and the Jell-O salad, said she was considering giving up red meat anyway.

"Frances would be a hippie, if I let her," Mr. Delaney said. "But I'm not going to be married to a hippie. And I'm not going to live on rabbit food. She'd grow her own vegetables if I let her."

Judith's face had burned at that, too, thinking of the plot that Patrick had planted in their backyard.

Frances Delaney was young, younger than Judith, yet Judith still thought of her as Mrs. Delaney, perhaps because Mr. Delaney was so much older, in his 40s, closer to her parents' generation than hers. He had been career military until a year or so ago, and Judith was unclear where he had met his bride. His attitudes, too, made him seem old. Gruff, bossy. He worked at the Social Security Administration, as did many in the neighborhood. At the dinner table that night, he placed his large hand over Mrs. Delaney's and said: "No hippies and no women's libbers for us, right, Pat? Our wives stay home and take care of us, as it should be."

"Judith worked at her father's variety store before it went bust," Patrick said, missing, as he often did, the point beneath the actual words, words not being something he used very much. "She was a secretary at Procter and Gamble when we met."

"*Before* you married," Mr. Delaney said.

"Yes."

"That's okay. Frances here was a nurse."

"And you met—" Judith began.

"Oh, it's such a boring story," Frances Delaney said. "Don't bore them with it, Jack. Where did you two meet?"

"The movies," Patrick said. No one would ever accuse Patrick Monaghan of telling long stories. At night, when Judith tried to share her observations about their neighborhood, he would say: "I'm not much of one for gossip, Judith."

But Judith didn't mind that Patrick was the strong, silent type. She had come from a family of big talkers. Patrick was her Quiet Man. She loved his silences. Except when she didn't and then she locked herself in the bathroom, wishing she had a phone cord that stretched all the way in there. Only whom would she call? Her mother, who would repeat the line about marrying in haste? Her girlfriends, who had married proper Jewish boys and were living proper Jewish lives in the northwest suburbs? Judith might be able to find a cord long enough to stretch into the bathroom, but she wasn't sure that there was any phone line long enough to take her back to the life she had known. She was a spy. A spy in what her mother called the land of Mackerel Snappers and Shanty Irish.

She did not look that different from the other women. Her hair had a reddish cast and she was given to freckles, even in this sun-less summer. She was often asked, in fact, what parish she had grown up in, a question she eventually realized was meant to suss out whether she preferred St. William of York or St. Lawrence. There was some confusion in the neighborhood about which par-ish to join, and the choice was considered a tip to one's ambitions. Would you be moving southeast, to the larger houses in Ten Hills and Hunting Ridge, or west, closer to Social Security, where Jack Delaney worked? It was all very complex, a mathematical equa-tion made up of the husband's ambitions and prospects, the pace at which the children arrived. Even if Judith managed to sidestep that first question, the other questions were still lying in wait. Patrick had a good job as an inspector for the city liquor board. Safe, solid. But how high would they rise? How many children would they have? And when those children arrived, how would they be raised? All very well to say love was all when it was only the two of you, but baby makes three and some very difficult questions, as Judith was now realizing. Who was she? Who would her children be?

So while others might call what she did on her walks snooping or spying, Judith believed she was simply trying to find a way to be. Would she move toward Ten Hills or Woodlawn? Would she have an iridescent globe on a pedestal in her yard? (Probably not; they struck her as tacky.) She definitely would not have one of those whitewashed hitching posts. And she didn't know what to make of the people who affixed those two pairs of kittens to their brick-fronts, always a white one and black one. What was that about? Who were they? Who was she?

The summer continued cool and damp. Good for sleeping and good for walking, but not for much else. Judith imagined this was like summer in London, not that she had been there, or San Francisco, not that she had been there, or—well, she really hadn't been anywhere. She had grown up in Northwest Baltimore, the youngest of five, the only daughter. Spoiled, she saw in retrospect, but does anyone ever realize they're spoiled until the spoiling ends? Yet spoiled as she might have been, she could put her little house shipshape by 11 a.m. and then what? She could have stayed in and watched soap operas, but she was more interested in the soap operas playing out in the neighborhood. In plain sight, once one knew where to look. The battling Donovans. The literally bursting-at-the-seams Kate O'Connell, who had just given birth to her fifth child in five years. The Horton hooligans, as they were known, a brood of terrifying brothers. Judith took to walking down the narrow lane that led to the carports behind the houses of Newfield Road. This was where real life could be glimpsed. Almost no one here had a proper garage and some didn't even have carports, only concrete pads. She saw Betty Donovan sitting on her back steps, which could use a coat of paint, smoking a cigarette and holding a frozen package of succotash to a swollen eye. She saw the Horton boys trying to burn ants with a magnifying glass, which made her glad that the sun was weak and fitful. She saw Katie O'Connell tie one of her children to the useless umbrella drying rack in her backyard. "He tried to run away," Katie said when she saw Judith looking. "What else can I do?"

And Judith saw the Lord Baltimore diaper service truck parked in the carport behind the Delaney house, despite the fact that the Delaneys had no children.

"They do shirts," Frances Delaney said one July morning as Judith headed out again for a walk, thinking she might do a little marketing, or even have an ice cream cone at High's for lunch. She always left by way of the street, then returned via the alley, her bag of groceries a cover of sorts, a legitimate reason for being in the alley. It would be natural, with a bag of groceries, to want to enter the house through the kitchen door.

"Excuse me?"

Frances Delaney was on her knees in her front yard, tending to a small flower bed. The men did the lawns, the women did the flowers. Judith did not have a green thumb, perhaps because her own mother did not, so her lawn was just lawn.

"Lord Baltimore Diaper Service," Frances said, rising to her feet, brushing off her knees. She was wearing short shorts and a halter that left a strip of her midriff bare. A good outfit for tanning if the sun ever came out again; Judith just didn't feel comfortable in such clothes since she married. She thought the whole point of being a wife was to look polished, grown-up. To look as if you had some place to go, even if it was only High's Dairy Store. *She* was wearing Bernardo sandals and a hot-pink shift that she had made from a remnant at Jo-Ann Fabrics, a coordinating scarf over her hair, which she would wash and set later today in the loose straight style that Patrick liked. "They do shirts, too."

"You send your husband's shirts out?"

"Jack's fussy in his way."

Judith thought about Mr. Delaney. *Jack*. He had come to her home for Friday night supper in a Banlon shirt. He wore his hair very short, even shorter than Patrick wore his, practically a crew cut. He had picked his teeth at the table and touched his wife a lot, stroking her, patting her. He reminded Judith of the fairy tale in which a Chinese emperor kept a nightingale to sing for him.

"His work shirts," Frances Delaney continued. "They're particular at Social Security. Always looking for something to hold against a man, Jack says. He liked the Army better, he says. The rules were clear. He even liked Germany when we were stationed there."

"Is that where you met? Germany?"

Frances laughed as if the idea were absurd, meeting someone in Germany. "Anyway, he likes his shirts just so, and I like Jack to be happy."

"Isn't that expensive? Sending out shirts?"

"Jack doesn't know I send his shirts out. He just knows that they're ironed and starched to his standards, which are very high." She smiled shyly. She looked like a gypsy to Judith, but Patrick said Frances Delaney was pure black Irish—dark hair, blue eyes so pale that they were barely there. But there was something in her voice, a suggestion of an accent that had been vanquished, or was being kept in place through strict discipline.

"Where did you go to high school?" she asked Frances. It was usually the first thing Baltimoreans asked of one another.

"All over," she said.

"Army brat?"

"Of a sort. My father's work took us to Asia and Europe."

That probably explained her accent, although it wasn't so much an accent as a complete absence of accent, unusual here in Edmondson Heights, where almost everyone, except Judith, spoke with the exaggerated *o*'s and extra *r*'s that marked what people called a Baltimore accent.

Judith knew she shouldn't ask more questions, that part of being a good neighbor was to respect all the little boundaries—the cheap white pickets that people placed down the middle of their shared lawns, the invisible lines dividing the parking pads, the shouts and sounds heard through the paper-thin walls late at night.

Yet she pressed, curious: "Don't you get an allowance? Doesn't he go over the checkbook?"

"I'm clever with money. I economize on the groceries—I'm a good cook, if I do say so myself. No one's ever left my table unhappy." Was Frances Delaney suggesting that she had left Judith's table unhappy? That was so unfair. It wasn't Judith's fault that she forgot most Catholics didn't eat meat on Fridays. "And I use what's left over for the laundry. What he doesn't know won't hurt me." She clapped a hand to her mouth. "I mean what he doesn't know won't hurt *him*. I always get that wrong. Would you like to come in for a Tab?"

"Sure," Judith said.

Over the next two weeks, she stopped at Frances Delaney's house almost daily, enjoying Tab or Fresca and, sometimes, a white wine that was quite unlike anything Judith had ever tasted. They talked about everything and nothing. They complained, in the self-deprecating code that was allowed, about their husbands' foibles. Silent, oblivious Patrick. Gabby, grabby Jack. They watched the Watergate hearings and made fun of Sam Ervin's eyebrows, talked about Mo Dean's style, which Judith admired but Frances thought drab.

"If my husband had that kind of job, I'd look better than that," said Frances, who almost always wore cut-offs and halter tops. "She looks dowdy to me."

"I worked in politics," Judith confided in Frances. "I thought I was going to change the world."

"The world never changes," Frances said, smoking a Virginia Slim. Judith yearned to join her, but she had worked too hard to give it up.

"That's what I found out."

Inside the Delaney house, she saw enough evidence of money to believe that Frances Delaney did have a household budget with considerable fat in it. The appliances were new, unusual in this block of renters. The dining room set could have come straight from the grand prize package on *The Newlywed Game*. Mahogany, shiny. Tacky, but expensive, and Frances seemed to loathe it, too, neglecting to use coasters beneath their sweating glasses. The television set was color and huge, a Magnavox with a stereo built in.

"Do you own or rent?" Judith asked one day.

"Own." Frances made a face. "It was his mother's house. She died, left it to us, so we moved here. We could afford something nicer, but he says there's no point in moving until we outgrow it."

"So you're going to have a family?"

"Of course." She looked—insulted, that was it. As if Judith had given offense. "Why wouldn't we? Jack's only forty-two."

"My oldest brother is forty," Judith said, a peace offering. "I'm the youngest of five, the only girl. I grew up in Pikesville."

"Pikesville. Isn't that all Jews?"

"Yes," Judith said, thinking it the most tactful way to reply. If she knew anything about her new friend, it was that she was delicate and sensitive, not at all like her coarse, belligerent husband. She would appreciate the chance to avoid hurting Judith's feelings.

"Wow. How did you stand it?"

Judith thought very hard about what to say next.

"Hasn't it been the worst summer?"

"Yes, but it's a blessing in a way," Frances said. "These houses get so hot, you have no idea. The second floor is usually unbearable during the day." Frances stuck out her bottom lip and blew a few errant tendrils from her face. "You know, I suppose we should have you over to dinner, in return. I should have thought of that sooner."

"Oh, please—don't worry about that."

A rumbling noise from the carport. From where they sat, in the dining room, Judith could see a white truck pulling to a stop. The Lord Baltimore diaper truck.

"I should go."

Frances didn't protest. "Friday night," she said, not rising from her chair. She dangled a hand between her thigh absentmindedly, then across her collarbone, caressing herself. Judith left behind a half-full can of Tab, desperate to be out of the house before the Lord Baltimore Diaper Service driver crossed the threshold.

When she returned from High's forty minutes later, the truck was still there.

The next day was Thursday. It rained all day, and Judith decided not to walk anywhere, but to stay inside and watch the hearings.

Friday night Judith and Patrick walked down their front walk, traveled perhaps fifteen yards, and went up the Delaneys' front walk. Judith carried a loaf of zucchini bread, although the Delaneys had come to her dinner empty-handed. But proper people, truly mannerly people, did not come empty-handed in her experience.

"I wonder what they'll serve us," she said.

"Probably fish sticks," Patrick said mournfully. "I thought I was leaving this behind when I married you."

They were both surprised—Patrick happily, Judith ambivalently—to learn that Frances Delaney was an outstanding cook. Yes, dinner was fish, but poached salmon, served with little potatoes unlike anything Judith had have ever tasted, something called "fingerlings." The salad was served *after* the main course, which Frances said was how the French ate.

Her husband rolled his eyes. "Judith studied cooking in France. I promised not to bitch about her pretendions as long as her grub is good."

"Pretendions?" Judith couldn't help asking. "France?"

"You know," Jack said. "Putting on airs. Pretendions."

"Oh, pretensions," she said, then hated herself for it. She was trying to show Frances Delaney, by example, how a well-mannered person behaved, but Frances Delaney seemed to be one step ahead of her. She was even better dressed than Judith tonight, in a modest, knee-length lace shift that exposed only her arms. As she moved back and forth between the dining room and the kitchen, serving dinner with an ease that Judith had yet to master, Frances seemed not to notice Jack Delaney's proprietary pats on her rear end. Judith did, though. She also noticed, with a sinking heart, Patrick's approving looks at the house, the furniture. He probably thought this dining room set was classy.

"What the fuck is in my salad?" Jack Delaney held up a fork with a yellow blossom on the tines.

Judith had wondered the same thing, but would never have questioned it and would certainly never have used *that* word, which she did not remember ever hearing spoken aloud before, except through the walls late at night, when the Mulcahys were fighting. At least, they started out fighting. Where they ended up was more shocking still.

"Nasturtiums," Frances said. "They're edible."

"They're flowers," her husband sputtered. Patrick looked hopeful, as if his host's temper tantrum might get him off the hook.

"Don't forget your promise to me, Jack," Frances said, her tone even and polite. "To try anything once."

"And don't forget yours to me," he said. "Try *everything* once."

Frances seemed paler than usual, but she said nothing, not even when he patted her rear end again, leaving a grease stain on the white lace that she had managed to keep spotless while preparing and serving this meal.

"Hey, Pat, do you know what they call the alley behind our houses?" Jack Delaney did not wait for an answer. "Bonk Alley! Could there be a better place to live? *Bonk Alley.*"

"I don't get it," Judith said. She didn't. She looked at Patrick. Patrick busied himself, making a little pile of flowers on the side of his plate. He was a polite man, but he had his limits.

"Bonk—it's slang for screwing." In some ways, Judith found that Jack's use of that word even more shocking. "Something I picked up from the Brits."

"Brits?"

"You know, when I was in London. God, that city is a shithole.

307

They're pre-verted, too, the Brits. Think they're so superior to us. But they're the preverts."

"Perverts," Frances said quietly. "The word is pervert."

"Well, you would know honey. You would know."

Jack fondled his wife's rear end again as she collected the salad plates, making way for dessert. "Coffee?" she asked brightly. She made it in a Chemex, Judith observed. Judith and Patrick normally drank Nescafé. He said he preferred it, yet he had seconds of Frances's coffee.

Frances did not serve Judith's zucchini bread for dessert. Judith could not fault her for this lapse, as Frances had prepared something called tiramisu. "Could you get the recipe for this?" Patrick asked Judith.

"I'm not sure I could make something like this," Judith said. She couldn't even spell it.

"It's not so hard," Frances said, "if you use store-bought lady fingers."

"Do you?" Judith asked.

A slight pause. "Sometimes I do, sometimes I don't. I made these. But then, I like to bake. It fills the long afternoons."

Judith felt she had lost a contest, although she wasn't sure what it was, or who she was playing. She was almost tempted to make a crack about long afternoons, but she knew the women were in this together.

At least Judith could help clean the kitchen. She scraped the plates into the trash—the Delaney house did not have a garbage disposal, score one for her—and tried not to think about the white Silber's bakery box she saw in the can, a box that clearly had held something nowhere in evidence. Lady fingers?

They parted, promising to do it again, knowing they never would.

The next time Judith walked to High's, she did not return via what she now knew was Bonk Alley. She did not want to see the white Lord Baltimore truck coming and going, did not want to risk being taken into Frances Delaney's confidences, confidences she sensed would be too heavy for her to bear. August passed. The gavel came down on the hearings and the country went on, as Judith knew it would. Everything goes on. The weather turned glorious around Labor Day, just in time to mock the children returning to school. The days were shorter, technically, although they still felt long to Judith. The vice president resigned, and while some Marylanders felt ashamed of their native son, Judith and Patrick, Stonewall Democrats, toasted the news, he with a beer, she with vermouth, which she had bought under the mistaken belief it would taste like the white wine that Frances Delaney had served. But the two couples, the Monaghans and the Delaneys, did not socialize again. Nor did the two women. Judith kept to the street, eyes straight ahead, trying not to see or hear the secrets all around her.

But it was impossible to miss, ten days before Halloween, the ambulance parked outside the Delaney house, lights twirling, Jack Delaney being carried out in a gurney, face covered. All the women of the neighborhood gathered to watch, somber yet excited in some horrible way. At least something was happening.

"Is he okay?" Judith asked Katie O'Connell, who may or may not be pregnant with number six under her shapeless coat. Probably better not to ask.

"He's dead," she said. "They don't pull the sheet up over your face unless you're dead, Judith."

"But how?"

"Who knows? Heart attack probably. That's what a man gets, taking up with a younger woman."

"You mean they—in the afternoon?" The O'Connells shared a wall with the Delaneys. She shrugged.

The news would not make its way up and down the street for several days. Frances Delaney, in her quest for culinary sophistication, had harvested the yew berry bushes at a neighbor's house a block over, asking permission before she did so. She had researched the berries carefully at the Catonsville library—or so she thought. It turned out the berries themselves were not poisonous if prepared properly. But everything else about the plant was so toxic that any preparation was risky. She had made her husband a tart. The only reason she hadn't eaten any was because she had given up desserts, worried about her weight. He had awakened with a stomachache and called in sick to work, but Frances hadn't thought it could be that serious. He was dead by the time the ambulance arrived.

Within a week, a for-sale sign went up in the yard. Within a month the sign was gone, and the neighbors, who had felt sympathy for the young widow, were incensed: Frances Delaney had sold to the first Negro family in Edmondson Heights. The gossip flew up and down the street. Who did she think she was? Where was she from, anyway? Not here. She hadn't even gone to high school in Baltimore.

A week after that, Judith saw a moving truck pull into Bonk Alley. Not a regular moving truck, a Hampden Van Lines, or a Mayflower. A U-Haul. Not even a U-Haul, just a gray, no-name thing.

But it was driven by the dark-haired man who used to drive the Lord Baltimore Diaper Service truck. Frances Delaney came out with a box of things, caught Judith watching, gave her a cheery wave.

"I'm moving to San Francisco," she said. "Isn't it exciting?"

"Is that where you're from?"

"I'm not really from anywhere."

"Army brat, right?"

"Something like that."

A week after that, the men in black suits came to Newfield Road. They walked up and down, up and down, knocking on doors. They said they were insurance investigators. They asked questions about the Delaneys. Nice people? Friendly people? Did Jack Delaney talk much about his work? Where had Frances Delaney said she was going? These conversations were reported along the back fences and the sidewalks of Newfield Road. More gossip, Patrick sighed, when Frances tried to talk to him at night, when he just wanted to watch *Kojak*. Katie O'Connell, who shared a wall with the Delaneys, had the most to share and tell.

Until the day the men in the black suits knocked on Judith's door.

"Did Mr. Delaney talk about his work much?"

"Just that he worked for Social Security."

"Doing what?" There were two men, one named Simon, the other Arthur.

"Oh, goodness, what does anyone do at Social Security? Make sure all the checks go out, I suppose."

"But did he ever say what he did?" pressed Simon. Or Arthur.

"No. I remember his wife said he liked it better in the Army. That the rules were clearer."

"He said he was in the Army."

"Yes, in Germany, I think. Although he also said he spent time in London. I guess things are awfully close over there."

"And the wife, Frances—she cooked with plants a lot?"

"I wouldn't say a lot," Judith said. "There were nasturtiums in the salad, the one time we ate over there. She was a good cook. Still, I would have known she wasn't from here, once I heard about the yew berries. No one who grew up in Baltimore would ever touch a yew berry."

"Anything else?" The two men, Simon and Art, looked at her with so much hope that she felt obliged to try.

"She said she made her own lady fingers from scratch. But she didn't."

They left, clearly unimpressed by this intelligence, but Judith thought it meaningful. Why had Frances lied about the lady fingers? Later, when Judith relayed the story to her brother Donald, who liked to talk in the way that women did, she asked what insurance company they represented. She went to look for the card, only to realize she didn't have one. But she had seen one, surely. Something State? State something? Something State Something?

"Jesus, Judith, don't you even know who you let into your house?"

"Don't be so paranoid," she told her brother.

"Everyone's paranoid," Donald said. "It's in style, like sideburns."

A few days later, her brother dropped by, looking serious. "That neighbor of yours. What did you say his name was?"

"Jack Delaney."

"And he worked at Social Security? That's what he told you? Do you know what he did there?"

Hadn't Simon and Arthur asked the same thing? Judith gave the same answer. "What does anyone do there?"

Donald's question turned out to be rhetorical. "He was developing computer programs, Judith. Computer programs that don't have anything to do with senior citizens getting their checks every month. Yeah, he went to Woodlawn every day, parked his car in the lot. He worked at Social Security, but not for them."

"I don't understand."

"Judith, have you ever heard of a guy named Oleg Lyalin?" He didn't wait for her answer. "KGB. Defected two years ago in England, in part because he fell in love with his secretary. The Russians don't like that, in-house adultery. They think it makes you vulnerable. So he defected, got to be with the love of his life, in return for whatever information he had."

"I guess it sounds familiar." Judith used to be so up on things. What had happened to her? A summer of *The Newlywed Game*, walks on Newfield Road, ice cream cones from High's Dairy store, Frances Delaney's brief and baffling friendship.

"You don't get it, do you, Judith?"

"Get what?"

"The Delaneys—I have an old friend working for Mac Mathias. This guy, your neighbor. He's a computer whiz. He was married to someone else. He wanted to be with his secretary. Someone made it happen. Not officially, not like Lyalin. But Jack Delaney—or Boris Badunov, or whatever his real name was, and maybe he worked for the East Germans, not the Russians—this guy, he came in from the cold on the condition that his girlfriend could come, too."

"The house belonged to his mother. Frances told me that."

"Yeah, *she* told you that. Did she tell you where they met?"

It's a long boring story. "No."

"Did you tell you where she was from?"

All over. Asia. Europe. An Army brat? Something like that. "No."

"They brought her over, thinking they were going to make him happy. Wanting their computer whiz to be happy. But I guess the KGB, having lost one agent to his secret love, had a better plan. She killed him. Killed him and took off."

"Took off with the Lord Baltimore diaper truck driver."

Donald laughed. "Where did you hear that? He was her handler. CIA. And he was found dead in St. Louis three weeks ago."

"He used to be parked in her driveway. For long stretches. I thought—"

"That's probably what they wanted all you gossipy housewives to think, Judith."

They were sitting at the little built-in breakfast nook in Judith's kitchen, drinking coffee from the Chemex she had bought a few weeks ago. It really did make better coffee. She looked at the clouds forming in her half-empty cup, glanced up at the kitchen clock. Almost 4 p.m., time to fix Patrick's dinner. Then it would be time to clean up. Two hours of television after dinner. Tonight was a Wednesday, which meant *Adam-12* and the *NBC Mystery Movie.* She hoped it was the *Snoop Sisters* tonight and not *Banacek,* although George Peppard was very cute.

"Donald, how is what you do—talking to people, finding out stuff, then telling other people—how is that different from what housewives do? Isn't it all just gossip?"

"You have a point there, Judith. I guess it's a thin line between gossip and espionage."

"Do you think your boss could help me get a job, the way he did with Patrick? Given that he knows Mathias?"

"You want a job with the feds, not the city or the state? I suppose I could swing that. What are your qualifications? What type of job are you looking for?"

"I type eighty words per minute. And I see things. I want to work at the CIA."

"You didn't see two spies under your own nose."

"I will," she said. "You see what you look for. Once I start looking for spies. I'll see them."

She did not tell him everything else she had seen that summer, things that no one thought mattered. She saw Katie O'Connell, worn down by a baby-a-year and a husband who was never going to advance in his career. She saw Betty Donovan, smoking and weeping on her back steps. She saw the Horton boys, who had stopped trying to burn up things and moved on to suffocating cats in milk crates, cats that Judith freed. She saw ceramic cats nailed to walls, iridescent globes on pedestals, whitewashed lawn jockeys. She saw a laundry truck parked for hours behind the Delaneys' house. Donald was wrong. Judith wasn't just seeing what someone wanted her to see. The Lord Baltimore driver may have started out as Frances Delaney's handler, but Frances Delaney had learned how to handle him before long. He probably knew about the yew berries, thought they would end up together.

"You know I'll ace the civil service exam," Judith said. "And with two salaries, we can move up and out of here."

"Not sure you need to take a test," her brother said. "Anyway, I'll see what I can do."

The CIA meant a two-hour commute to Langley, so Judith settled for NSA, just down the parkway in Fort Meade. She accepted a clerical position, but even that demanded absolute nondisclosure on her part. When her neighbors, soon to be her old neighbors, asked what she did, Judith smiled and said: "I can't tell you. But I can assure you that we are not involved in *domestic* spying. NSA is forbidden by law to spy on our own citizens. So domestic spying is just my hobby."

Then she winked, as if it were all a big joke. The women of New-field Road—talking over back fences, drinking Tab during the soap operas, running into each other at High's Dairy store, tying their children to the clothes line, holding frozen vegetables to their bruised eyes, pretending not to see the little boys who tortured living things—the women of Newfield Road said to each other: "Did you hear? Judith Monaghan claims she's a spy. A spy in Edmondson Heights. Did you ever hear of anything so ridiculous?"

CUBA LIBRE

BY KATHERINE NEVILLE

Just because you're paranoid doesn't mean
they're not out to get you.
—1960S MAXIM

Rochester, Minnesota: 1961

*He felt them rubbing the cold grease onto his temples. He kept his eyes
shut against what he knew was coming. They were doing it again; no
one could stop them, the shock of volts would slam through his head
like a railroad car—and then, oblivion. They'd got him good now,
hadn't they? Sucker punched, and down for the count. How had this
happened? It was his own fault. He should have been warned, all the
signs were there, he should have seen it coming: Mea maxima, maxima
culpa. But whenever he said "they" were after him, they were following him, they were spying on him, it was dismissed as paranoia. Well,
paranoia or none, he knew what they were after: they were after his
memory. He knew what men could do, what their actions could lead
to. And now they wanted to erase his memory, kill it. They could kill
him too. They would kill him. They were killing him. His job, his only
job now—before the next deadly lightning bolt hit—was to hold on*

to what he knew. Hold on to truth. He forced himself to go down into those dangerous, dark pools of his past, descending deeper and deeper and darker, moving down until all the muted light surrounding him was slowly swallowed into darkness, despairing, despairing... then suddenly he thought he glimpsed it—just a quick flash!—like that trout lurking against the pebbled bottom of a riverbed.

And then he knew what he must communicate; he just prayed it was not too late.

Big Wood River, Idaho: The Present

My name is Paloma Perez. I am twenty-three years old, I'm so-called "mestizo" (part Anglo/Spanish, part Native American), of the Catholic faith, born in New Mexico of parents who separated shortly after my birth. I am a graduate student in History of Journalism. I am currently on an exchange grant between New Mexico State and University of Idaho. The latter place has an archive containing many very important papers of the famous writer who is the subject of my dissertation. I've been working on this project for almost two years. Though all my professors except one think it's a humongous waste of time to cross that tundra again.

I'm sitting in the living room of my cabin along the Big Wood River, hundreds of miles south of the campus at Moscow, Idaho. The Big Wood is a fast river that runs from the Galena summit, 9,000 feet up in the Sawtooth Mountains, down to the reservoir below my cabin, where it joins other rivers. It is a great trout-fishing stream. I decided to live in this cabin, on this river, because it is just across the river from the place where, fifty years ago, my subject took his own life.

I mention these facts about myself and my project, because two months ago I took leave from the university and moved here so I could get closer to resolving an enigma about this man that I still cannot quite understand. One way to understand it, I thought, was to try to bond with him in some way. To understand the role that his later journalism played, I believed I needed to figure out what he was thinking just before he died. But now I'm not so sure.

Because tonight, as I was sitting here with a cold plate of uneaten macaroni on the coffee table before me and my notes scattered around me on sofas and chairs, something unexpected happened: I was browsing my subject on my laptop and I somehow got pulled into the back door of a website, where I read something that frightened me. On a black screen background, these words came up: *"SECURITY, CONFIDENTIAL: Apply through the Freedom of Information Act through proper channels."*

It was a scam, I thought—so I shut down for the moment.

But that was when I got my first inkling, a premonition that something in my factual research didn't fit, that something was very wrong. And that little idea, that small piece of doubt, began to rub at me like a burr under my saddle; it was making me more than uncomfortable, more than wary. I felt like I just had to dig it out.

Still, I always take all the security precautions that Leo taught me: I've switched my computer onto "private browsing," so no one can follow my path, trying to track my train of thought; I've glued a sticky star onto my laptop's camera aperture so no one can see me at work; I've stripped off the cookies that were left there as tracers by others; I've checked the antivirus data...though I cannot shake the certain conviction that I'm being watched. Maybe I'm getting as paranoid as *he* was. I don't really care.

I flipped open my laptop and started to write down the facts of what I actually knew. That was four hours ago. And I'm still writing. And it still irritates me, and it still doesn't fit.

It's midnight now, I can hear the crickets chirping along the river, a twig snaps outside and I flinch; I go to the window; my motion-detector light is on, flooding the band of guilty culprits that are nightly huddled there at the edge of my gravel drive. A small cluster of white-tailed deer: undeterred by the glaring light, they are peacefully munching my landlord's blueberry bushes.

I take my cold macaroni plate to the kitchen and I make a pot of black coffee—just the way my subject once famously described doing it, where you boil the grounds and water together right in the pot. (Leo says I'm sick to try to bond with my subject this way, but I hope that maybe tonight, drinking this sludgy muck will clear my brain.)

I get back to the sofa and shuffle my papers into a stack—stuff that I'd earlier culled from the web and half-covered with my own scribbled notes—and I leaf through these as I look on my screen at what I've just written tonight:

> *He was born in 1899 in the American midwest; barely got out of high school, no college; went to World War I, got wounded; came home, became a newspaper reporter (over his life he would cover four wars: three hot and one cold); got married, went to live in an icy flat in Paris; filed periodic nondescript newspaper articles for a pittance of cash; hung out in bars with other expats, who convinced him to focus on fiction rather than facts; went daily to Luxembourg Palace ("on an empty stomach") to study the Cézannes, these gave him an epiphany about writing; inspired by hunger and painting, he invented a new way of seeing, the "Iceberg Theory," using slashes of words like paint to suggest hidden depths without using description; one day this revolutionary technique would win him the world's top prizes, it would re-create American literature, and would make him the most famous living writer (and one of the richest) in world history. At the absolute pinnacle of his success— when he was living in a house just across the Big Wood River from my cabin here—he put a 12-gauge Boss double-barreled shotgun in his mouth and pulled the trigger.*

His name, of course, was Ernest Hemingway.

Even though thousands of books and essays and dissertations have been written on Hemingway's life and literature they mostly stress the influence that his early journalism training had on him, and how it in turn created his breathtaking impact on American fiction. These are the "facts" that everyone knows. My thesis is very different:

Though Hemingway claimed to despise journalism, he never stopped being a journalist. He wrote hundreds of thousands of words on current events for magazines that paid him very well, scribbling his observations on every conceivable topic from barbershops to boxing, from bullfights to bullshit, from picadors to pecadillos—while decade after decade, he produced less and less fiction, and even then, only under "literary duress." In the end, if you weighed his fiction against nonfiction, on word count alone, fiction was less than that one-eighth of his total output: the "tip of the iceberg" syndrome.

There was one place that my subject—over a period of thirty years, almost half his life span—had visited, frequented, and finally lived in. Yet he never wrote much about it until late in his life. And even then, it wasn't reportage, it was just a sketch, a short story, a simple vignette that he crashed out in a matter of weeks, and which he somehow with effort managed to stretch into a brief novel.

It sold five million copies in magazine form, and another million in books. It was made into a movie, it landed him a Pulitzer and a Nobel Prize. It's still found in libraries all over the world and taught in schools. It made him rich. Maybe it also made him dangerous. It was—oddly, for a man who hated symbolism—the only allegory he ever wrote: *The Old Man and the Sea*.

If that simple allegory was the tip of the iceberg, then what exactly was the vast, deep mass of "subaquatic facts" lurking beneath the surface?

It was the place where he'd set the allegory, the place that was almost a character in the story—the place where Hemingway lived from World War II to the very height of the Cold War—the place he loved so much that he refused to leave it, even when he knew he had to, even when his property was about to be seized by the local State, even when he had been warned repeatedly to leave by the U.S. State Department, even when he was being haunted by the FBI, had been threatened by the CIA.

Cuba.

Less than a year after his return to the U.S.—to his house here across this very river, near Ketchum, Idaho—the world's most famous living writer, Ernest Hemingway, was dead.

That was precisely the burr I'd been struggling to dislodge all night. But now I thought I knew: all the signs had been there all along, hadn't they? All the numbers now added up. I knew that if *I'd* figured it out, then whoever was watching me (and I was sure by now that it was not just my imagination) was not likely to hit the "pause" button any time soon. And it really terrified me.

I checked the clock: it was four o'clock in the morning. Yanking some tiny digital memory cards out of a plastic bag I always carried in my jeans pocket, I frantically jammed these, one after another, into my laptop and started downloading my data with links. I left a little jingle as my own calling-card on each. If I couldn't reach Leo, maybe he could reach me. I would hide these each in ways that he'd be sure to find them. Then I would hit the road just before dawn, and cover my tracks—as he'd taught me, so long ago, to do.

For I'd suddenly guessed why Ernest Hemingway took so long to leave Cuba—even after the revolution was over, after the Castro takeover—why he'd never written about it, why he'd felt he had to encrypt what he knew in an allegory, why right afterward, he'd been in two plane crashes in a row that looked like accidents, why he was so depressed by the huge success of his book—the awards, the money, the spotlight of fame—that he couldn't go to the Nobel ceremony, could barely bring himself to write his brief acceptance speech.

Less than six months after Hemingway moved back to America, he was secretly flown out of Idaho and slapped, by surprise, into the

Mayo Clinic in Minnesota, where he was submitted to electrocon-vulsive shock therapy: month after excruciating month, over and over, they'd fried his brains. Whatever it was that Hemingway dis-covered at the height of the Cold War, was something deadly dan-gerous that had to be erased from his mind—a process that quickly and surely drove him to suicide. The cold, frightening thought even entered my own mind, that he may have been murdered.

This was why I had to reach Leo at once: whatever it was I'd stumbled onto involving Cuba—whatever I was being watched for, paranoia or not—was something that seemed about to raise its ugly head again. Right now.

Most people never listen. Nor do they observe.

—ERNEST HEMINGWAY

Santa Fe, New Mexico: Leopold's Observations

When Paloma vanished, I was the one who was in trouble with everybody.

Our parents were livid—the only thing they'd agreed on in years was that it was my fault Palo was missing. After all, I'd encouraged her in this crazy idea about Investigative Journalism. Didn't I know that *those* kinds of journalists got themselves killed? (Actually, though our dad taught History of Journalism, it involved nothing more recent nor dangerous than Carlyle's reports on the French Revolution. While mom couldn't figure out how her gorgeous daughter, at age twenty-three, was still in school and unmarried.)

Not to mention that The Company, my employer, was equally miffed with me. My sister had apparently stumbled in the back door of an "eyes-only" website, sending up incipient-terrorist flags. They thought I'd given her the link (I hadn't) and they put me on temporary leave, saying I was mucking about in the wrong backyard: *Who do you think you are, Leo?—you're an analyst, not a field operative.* (Well actually, I *am* a field operative—been one for ages—my employer just doesn't know it!) This break in my routine, however, afforded me the opportunity to do some investigations of my own.

In this entire scenario, my beautiful and brilliant sister, Paloma, seemed to be the only one with a grain of sense in her head. At least, she had the sense to get out of town before the yapping dogs got on her trail. (Well actually, they don't use yapping dogs in the Rocky Mountains, that's the Deep South, I believe.)

And she had the presence of mind, just before decamping, to send me that frozen trout: the one with the teeny digital card embedded inside its head. As soon as I got it, I knew she was gone, and why. Despite her fears she'd expressed on that disk, I felt sure my sister was okay. I did not yet know what had spooked her so much that she'd taken the drastic measure of using a dead cutthroat trout as bubble wrap for her communiqué. But since I was now on leave, I didn't feel it necessary to share that communiqué, at least not yet, with my employer.

I waited with bated (or was it baited?) breath to learn more.

Meanwhile, I dropped by New Mexico State University in Santa Fe to pay a visit to Professor Livia Madachy—"PM" as Palo called her—Palo's advisor, the one who'd first encouraged her to branch out and study something other than (what everyone else had voted for, due to Palo's good looks) being a weather girl or a TV anchor.

PM was a middle-aged Anglo lady with tanned skin and leathery wrinkles that outdid even Georgia O'Keeffe's. Soon, I gathered that Professor Madachy had also received a frozen trout. But hers just had a note that said thanks for supporting an unusual thesis: seems everyone *other* than PM was down on Hemingway as a topic altogether, and not just here at the university.

According to PM, the Hemingway bashing was nearly universal throughout all of Academia, e.g.: the feminists said he was a machismo misogynist for having four wives he cheated on with each successor, and mistresses on the side; the gay professors called him a sexually insecure homophobe with a penis-gun fetish; the sociologists said he used the "N" word for black persons, and looked down on folks of Indian roots, like Palo and me. In psychology classes they said he suffered from depression exacerbated by alcohol and a long history of familial suicide; even in Palo's journalism courses they played podcasts from a noted "literary" writer, harping on how boring Hemingway was, and how he'd destroyed American literature. While in literature departments, Hemingway was apparently *total* anathema. And why not?—after all, the guy got to be a Nobel laureate, while packing nothing by way of credentials but a midwestern public high school diploma.

I could certainly see how Palo had a problem finding a thesis advisor who had accepted her general concept. Now I just had the problem of finding Paloma herself.

Maybe a wolf always returns to its known haunts, but my sister had only one haunt that I ever knew of. And that was the late, great Ernest Hemingway. He seemed the one and only key to my next move.

My little sister was perhaps Hemingway's first official girl "camp follower." Palo had been obsessed with Hemingway even as a child. By the age of ten, she'd read everything he ever wrote—his fiction, nonfiction, journalism, letters—and she hankered to go everywhere he'd ever been, so she could experience him in the three dimensions of Life with a capital L, as the legendary, larger-than-life writer had experienced it himself. I confess, whatever one thought of his work, Hemingway was one of the best-looking bastards who ever graced a page of literature.

Because our parents were separated, Palo knew how to torture them into her service in different ways, and she marked them out accordingly: Mom got to suffer through the "Two-Hearted River" phase, where, for month after month, Palo would eat nothing but sandwiches of raw onion slabs, washed down with canned apricots in syrup, and she'd make coffee by boiling the grounds right in the pot, because that's how Nick Adams, Hemingway's alter ego, ate when he went fishing alone in the wild, just after the Great War.

Then too, Palo tagged along with our dad at every conference he'd allow—from Venice to Paris to Wyoming—even to Lago Maggiore—consuming along the way everything that our Great White Hunter had eaten, from roast baby pig in Madrid to wild marlin in the Florida Keys.

There was only one place she couldn't get to, due to "Cold War Hangover" as she put it: the restriction printed into our passports against travel to Cuba. But now—based on her cryptic notes on that fish-scented flash drive she'd sent me—I was pretty sure that was right where Palo would be headed. And though restrictions had started to lift, of late, she'd still need my help and connections to get there. I knew of some private strings I might pull, and I was just checking flights through Miami and Mexico, when the message popped up on my screen from a private, unlisted server. A missive that changed everything.

> *Your sister dead in drowning; remains found in Magic Reservoir; contact Sheriff of Blaine County, Idaho. See contact info below.*

It was signed simply: The Company.

When it came to "family," The Company usually got there first: cowboys to the rescue and all.

But apparently, not this time.

Big Wood River, Idaho

I was absolutely miserable. Okay, I'd flunked a major intelligence test, and in doing so, I had maybe killed my own sister. Because one thing was as transparent as a martini glass right now: Palo's death on that river could be no "accident."

And yet, during all my rickety flights through the Rockies, from Albuquerque to Salt Lake to Ketchum, and with as many times as I'd read and re-read Palo's notes on that digital card plugged into my cell phone—again and again and again—they still didn't add up to her death.

Where was the underbelly of the iceberg? What was I missing?

Even now, out here on the Big Wood River, as the Blaine county sheriff and I moved against the icy current to reach the spot where my sister had last been seen before she vanished beneath the waters, it was all pretty tough for me to visualize. What was she doing on this river all by herself before dawn? Especially since, by now, her paranoia seemed to have had a strong basis in reality.

I had to get to the bottom of it. And fast, before this wild river claimed me, too. Why had I even asked to see this place?

I was wending my way around the downed cottonwoods along the shore, struggling to keep my balance on the slippery, rocky floor wearing these unwieldy rubber suspender waders that the department had loaned me; they encased my lower body and came all the way up to my chest.

Over the rush of waters, the sheriff—I'll call him "Ted"—was asking me: "You or your Sis ever come hereabouts, before, to visit our 'fly-caster's paradise'?"

"Idaho, yes; Ketchum, no," I told him.

Despite our disdain toward the exotic technicalities and trappings of fly-fishing that Palo and I had historically shared, at the moment I thought it prudent to try a bit of fish-bonding, myself:

"As kids, though," I added, "our dad used to take us to a place on Redfish Lake, to watch the Rainbows hatch out."

"So you're from fishing stock! I thought so!" Ted beamed appreciatively, as he navigated his bulk along the shoals with surprising ease. "It's our biggest Idaho industry, you know: fishing and hunting. We got 26,000 miles of rivers in our state, almost more than anybody on the planet, I guess..."

As I followed Ted downstream to the place where Palo had last been sighted, he launched into a verbal tangent, casting details back to me over his shoulder about rods and reels, bait and tackle, hooks, lines, and sinkers...until I tuned out.

I realized glumly, with my legs stuck in these unwieldy waders and my butt bashed by fast water, that this scenario was destined to go on for quite awhile with no possible chance of escape.

Palo would be laughing her ass off at my predicament—that is, I thought in abject misery, if she weren't dead as a minnow, and washed ten miles downstream by now. And worst of all, I was still no closer to finding out exactly what happened to her. Palo was right, she had been in danger, and I kicked myself for not seeing, much sooner, how real it was.

Ted had worked his diatribe all the way up to the esoteric dangers posed by "ghost gear"—those yards of line and hooks strewed around by irresponsible Out-of-State fishermen, which had endangered the local sturgeon population nearly out of all existence—when all at once I thought that I'd caught an important non sequitur:

"...until we found your sister's waders, where they were floating..."

"My sister's what?" I said, as calmly as possible.

"Well, not real *waders* like you got on now, but her foot gear, you know—them lightweight-type wading booties, more like rubber shoes, that the ladies all wear..."

Now my heart was thumping. This bit of news gave me my first glimmer of hope: what was wrong with this picture? A gaping hole had just appeared smack in the middle of the jigsaw, and I thought I knew exactly what was missing.

Sure, Paloma knew how to catch a fish—as her recent frozen-trout "messenger" had demonstrated. But when it came to the *art* of fishing, she was a Nick Adams girl: simplicity before all. Her "technical equipment" of choice was a safety pin for a hook, a grasshopper for bait, a pair of dungarees for attire, and a boardwalk to sit on. She'd always left the rest—the "ties and flies and waders and wrist-posturing"—to the "Weekend Sportsmen," as she liked to call them.

No, if those shoes they'd fished out downstream were indeed Paloma's, as I very much doubted, she'd certainly never have worn them; the very idea was against her religion. She'd tossed those "booties" into the drink herself: a messenger wending its way downstream into my waiting arms—just like that trout—and likely bearing the very same kind of message.

"Where did you find those wading boots?" I asked Sheriff Ted, adding carefully: "And how were you able to discover, so soon and with such certainty, that they belonged to my sister?"

"The right boot was found yesterday, stuck in a trap," he told me. "They cleaned it out down near the Magic Reservoir. The other was hung up, upstream here, on a cottonwood branch—right near the accident. At least, near where your Sis was last spotted. But as for how we knew that them booties was *hers*—that part was a real no-brainer: the shoes had her name printed on them, each one—in waterproof ink!"

I tried not to show a reaction. I just hoped to God I was right. It would fit more than neatly into that hole in the jigsaw puzzle. And it would explain something else, as well. So I had to risk it.

"Which of these boots that you located was found the nearest to the spot where you found my sister's body?" I asked the sheriff.

Though by now, I'd guessed what his answer would likely be.

"Oh, the body, as to that we're still waiting," Ted told me. "We figure she hit a deep pool and got sucked down under the current. And here's the place, right here." He tapped one of the large, downed cottonwood trees along the bank, its dead branches drifting out into the river, and he added,

"It was right here on this spot that your Sis was last seen. That's where the trout always like to hole up, down in those hollows under all them trees along the banks; them downed cottonwoods been there forever, all along the river; that's why we call this river the 'Big Wood.' When folks goes down in spots like that, there's no way we can troll, the current's too fast and those hollows are too narrow and they go too deep: sometimes we don't find the missing for months or years. Might even be never."

"Ah, I see. Well, many thanks for explaining all this, sheriff," I said politely, retaining my sober expression, while privately I was doing cartwheels in my head. How amazingly perfect! I had to give Palo credit for more brains than I ever realized.

There was no body around, and Palo had left the "handwriting on the wall," on a pair of shoes. Why would she do that, unless she was planning on remaining alive and in hiding—camouflaged like a trout holed up beneath the cottonwoods—just as, after all, she'd told me she would do, hadn't she? Now I was dying to crawl out of the icy water myself, rip off this damned rubber skin, and go try to find her.

But there was one thing that I'd nearly overlooked.

"I'd like to see those wading boots that you found," I told sheriff Ted, "and also any of my sister's other effects you can show me. And by the way, Sheriff," I added casually, "who was it that actually sighted Paloma out here on the river that morning? Was it a local resident? Someone who knew her?"

Sheriff Ted was clambering up the bank by now. Perhaps it was my imagination, but he seemed to be avoiding a reply. He got to the top and stuck out his big, meaty mitt to help pull me and my rubber casing out of the water. Once on dry land, I still felt like I'd been embalmed.

"Sheriff?" I repeated, with a raised eyebrow, once we stood eye-to-eye.

Sheriff Ted looked down and shuffled his big foot in the pine needles.

"Not sure I can tell you that," he said. When he glanced up and saw my expression of innocent surprise, he added, "I'll check with the department as soon as we get back there. But even though you're kin of the dead woman, this may be too confidential..." He tailed off with a look of uncertainty.

"My, this *is* turning mysterious," I said. And I waited.

But when it came, I was really unprepared.

"I can tell you this much—but when we're back at the department, you never heard this from me," the sheriff said under his breath, glancing around, though no one was within miles of this spot. "You won't find any 'other effects' of your sister's, except maybe her clothes and whatever food was in the fridge. *He* confiscated the rest—her papers, computer, and everything—from her cabin. The fella who saw her wading out on the river that morning did know her, but he was no fisherman. He was Official, showed us his government badge, said he'd been keeping an eye on your Sis for her own protection. Seems like your little Sis was doing something important, up here in these parts, for the U.S. government. Mine not to guess at just what, naturally."

I swallowed hard. I felt dizzy. My mouth had gone drier than the pit of the seventh olive. This was worse than I thought. Confiscating Palo's possessions before they even found a body? What on earth could she have been up to, that might call for such swift action to suppress it? Who *was* this "Official" lying bastard, who'd grabbed her stuff?

"Sheriff," I said, choosing my words as carefully as possible, so they wouldn't come back later to bite me in the butt, "I'm sure you'll understand if I say that I, *also*, am not at liberty to share everything about this affair nor to speculate about my sister's untimely death. But I thank you for your confidence, which will remain safe with me. Since we are speaking in confidence, though—could you tell me what 'official badge' it was that her colleague showed you, which has inspired your department to support those actions of his?"

But before the sheriff could reply, or even blink, I had whipped out my own ID from The Company, which I knew trumped most others in the security field, and I flashed it before him.

Now he could blink. And he did.

"Yes sir, Officer Perez," he said. And he actually saluted me, as if I were his military superior. "I can tell you, though, that fella's badge was genuine: from the FBI. But it wasn't no straight FBI case that he was on, none of that 'Safe House' witness protection stuff, he said. He told us that your sister was involved doing research in a case involving Homeland Security..."

I went down to the sheriff's office in Hailey. The wading boots weren't needed by the sheriff as evidence, since the FBI had trumped everyone and taken charge of what they wanted. But thanks to that spurious cover, no one (except me!) suspected foul play in Palo's "accidental death." I tucked the bag with the boots under my arm, accepted the keys to Palo's cabin, and I hit the road in my rental Jeep, heading back up Route 75, toward Ketchum and Sun Valley.

I needed one more piece of the puzzle. This time, I knew where to find it.

Even before I'd had the chance, alone, to pull those wading shoes from their plastic bag, I'd already glimpsed the clue she'd left me (in addition to plastering her name on the sides of the floaters in indelible ink, so that everyone would know they were hers.) I kept glancing at the bag lying beside me in the Jeep.

On the top tab of each rubbery shoe, she'd tightly glued a cute little plastic sticky label that was hard to miss: a tag, about an inch long, in blue, green and yellow, with a stylized drawing of an exotic young woman with ruffled sleeves, sporting a basket of fruit on her head; she seemed to be dancing a samba. At the top, the label read: ORGANIC. And beneath the young woman's lithe, dancing form, in large letters, it read "CHIQUITA."

Where had I—quite recently—seen that reference?

I pulled my jeep off the road, yanked out my iPad, powered it up, stuffed Palo's stinky, fish-smelling digital card into the port, and clicked it open. There it was, it had been staring me in the face all this time, even before I'd ever left New Mexico: A jingle!

I clicked the black box with the cheery musical quarter-notes on the front, and out blared the opening bars of one of the oldest, and at one time, most famous advertising jingles. Hearing it now made my blood run cold:

Hello Amigos! I'm Chiquita Banana, and I've come to say…

I turned it off at once, before I got to the end. I knew that in this newer version of the jingle, they'd modernized the lyrics to stress nutrition and heath, but I still remembered how the jingle used to go, back in the old days. Mom liked it so much that she used to sing it to us when we were little.

That memory was what Palo was counting on.

And I knew where my sister had hidden the goods that she needed me to find.

> *I'm Chiquita Banana and I've come to say—*
> *bananas have to ripen in a certain way…*
> *bananas like the climate of the very, very tropical equator—*
> *So you should never, never put bananas in the refrigerator.*
> —"Chiquita Banana," 1945, Shawnee Press

I found the critical mass—the bunch of bananas. Naturally, they were tucked into the vegetable drawer of the refrigerator in my sister's abandoned cabin. Inside a single banana that still had its symbolic label affixed to it, I located the digital chip that Palo had buried there.

Once again, smelly fish and browning bananas seemed to have triumphed over state-of-the-art security forces (or whoever they were) and their much vaunted superiority in data harvesting through space-age digital technology.

Now that I'd gotten back inside my Jeep with the loot, and I'd powered up my iPad again, I could begin to connect the previous links she'd sent me (in the fish) with the conclusions she had drawn from them (in the banana). It didn't take as long as I thought it might, for me to piece together the following:

1. What Palo had found out that had lit up somebody's mega-Bunsen burner.
2. What it all had to do with Ernest Hemingway's rapport with icebergs, fish, bananas, Cuba.

And more importantly:

3. Where my sister was hiding out—which, if my intuition was correct, was not very far away.

Now that I knew, though, I needed to get to the Horse's Mouth and let *him* know that I knew. I pulled out my Company-issued satellite phone and dialed the personal private number I'd learned by heart.

It didn't take long to get the Director himself on the line. Word must have gotten out pretty fast, that I was asking strange questions for a bereaved guy whose sister was in an accidental drowning. The first words out of the Director's mouth confirmed this.

"Sorry about your sister, Leo," he said. "But you're supposed to be on leave. Now I hear you're mucking about in Idaho, crossing swords with our close compatriots in the FBI—even trying to dig into your sister's attempt to resuscitate the image of late Nobel laureates. While others, as you know, might prefer to leave the past under the ground."

"You got a false report on me, sir," I said. "Exhumation from the grave, even for noted writers, would seem tasteless, especially this near to Easter. But as I recall, that Nobel guy did dub those compatriots of ours in the Bureau: 'Franco's *B*astard *I*rish' for their support of the right-wing Spanish fascists who'd infiltrated the Americas, all throughout World War II."

The Director sighed.

The message: he was a nice guy with a tough job, and I—the loose cannon—was making it tougher.

"Leo, you're an analyst, and a good one," he informed me. "But what you're regurgitating here, that was all in the Dark Ages. Long before even the Cold War. May I ask you, what is the purpose of this call?"

"Well gee, let me bring things more up-to-date for you then, sir," I said. "I have a proposal I'd like you to consider…"

"A proposal?" the Director cut in, with ice in his voice. "Your tone makes it sound more like an ultimatum. Leo, may I remind you I have a pretty full plate right now. Please don't try to yank my chain."

"Far be it, sir," I said. "I'll get to my point at once. But first, I wanted us to discuss that second fish."

The Director had the grace to be silent.

So I pressed my full court advantage:

"You remember," I told him. "The fish with the 'note' attached? The fish that poor, innocent Professor Livia Madachy received in Santa Fe? Paloma didn't send that one, did she? You knew I'd go there first. You sent it yourself, to use as bait and trawl me in. That was right after you trawled for my sister Paloma—luring her into that spurious 'Freedom of Information Act' website; and then you turned around and used her 'blunder' as an excuse to send me on leave from my job."

"And your point would be?" asked the Director. Though his tone now was more guarded than icy.

"It's not a *point*," I said. "It's just an observation: but it appears that 'Homeland Security' is not quite as chummy between agencies as it's supposed to be. You set me up, and you endangered my sister's life—you used us as bait—just so you could find out exactly how much the FBI knows about what's about to happen down there."

After a long pause, the Director said, "All right, granted. But tell me, Leo: if you're not our analyst or working undercover for the Bureau, then who *are* you working for?"

"It's 'whom,' sir," I corrected him. "I'm working 'for whom' I have always worked. If you want to know the truth, I'm working for my tribe."

"Tribe?" said the Director, as if he'd never heard the term.

"The locals—the Indians, the Hopi, Zuni, Apache, Navajo—the Mestizo, whatever you call us: the natives, the indigenous, the peasants. Your Cold War means nothing to us. Whether communism or capitalism is better is something of a moot point to folks who've been used as fodder for your ongoing battles, these past fifty or sixty years. That's really what it's all about—that's what is just about to happen—isn't it?"

The Director was silent again; after awhile, he sighed.

"Yes, that's what it is all about, Leo. And you've demonstrated that the Bureau does not yet know as much as they'd wish to: that's clear. Otherwise they would hardly have been watching your sister and appropriating her files the moment she vanished—before we could get at them. So tell me, Leo: what's this proposal of yours?"

I was relieved that he couldn't see my smile from two thousand miles away.

"I think the Company needs to fund an important fellowship program," I told him. "One that would encourage young scholars to share their research. Not a surfing exercise or 'leaks'-type thing, but something officially sponsored by us, along with others. It would aid the State Department by consolidating our historical wisdom to help focus on specific events, even dangerous events, that are about to repeat themselves.

"And," I added casually, "I believe I know just where to begin, and who might write the first of such reports, based on events set in motion more than one hundred years ago..."

impossible dialogue

Sawtooth Botanical Gardens: Ketchum, Idaho

I found Palo seated beneath the pagoda in the "Garden of Infinite Compassion," just outside of Sun Valley.

I'd guessed she'd be here, when I learned that this part of the Sawtooth Botanical Gardens, just downstream from her

naturally

bloody marvelous

disappearance, was created for the Dalai Lama's 2005 visit, here to Sun Valley. What with prayer wheels and water wheels silently spinning, it seemed the perfect spot to recall what peace and harmony once must have looked like in the world.

She was pretty unrecognizable, with her waterfall of silky black hair all twisted up and tucked underneath her baseball cap, the dark mirrored glasses, and her bulky sweatshirt covering layers of padded clothes. I sat down beside her on the bench and put my arm around her shoulders.

She took off her dark glasses and looked at me seriously with those silvery eyes. "Leo, I think maybe you saved my life," were her first words. "I don't know who was watching me or what their motivation was. But since you found me, I'm assuming you've figured it out."

"I can answer that," I said. "The FBI was watching *you*, and The Company was watching *them*. But lucky for you, I was watching them both."

"And were you able to figure out from my cryptic notes and links why Hemingway was so hunted and haunted?" she said. "Why they wanted to blot out his memory altogether, before he remembered too much?"

"Yep," I assured her. "He was Mr. antifascist, and he'd figured out what was going to happen, at any moment, in Cuba. Just as *you* figured out how it's connected with what is about to happen right now, just next door."

She looked at me for a moment, then she grinned a wide grin. I was so happy to see her smile like that.

"So were you able to do it—what I suggested?" she asked.

"The Company seems to think it's a real peachy idea," I assured her. "You'll get the first fellowship grant. So you'd better get it written from those notes pretty fast. After all, the trials are going to begin next week."

"I don't have equipment to type it on," she said. "The asshole took my computer."

"There's a new invention called pencil and paper," I told her. "If you play your cards right, I think I can get you some. From what I can tell of your prior efforts, it seems safer than surfing the web. Why not try it? After all, my dear sister, as Santayana said, 'Those who cannot remember their own past are condemned to repeat it.'"

When she agreed, I added:

"But tit for tat, my dear Paloma. I just want a couple of answers by way of payment. A symbolic translation: If, as you say, Hemingway wrote *The Old Man and the Sea* at the height of the Cold War, and if it really was an allegory about Cuba—then who was Santiago, the old man who was named for a saint? What does the marlin, the giant fish that got eaten by sharks, represent? And who were the sharks?"

"You'll have to figure it out when you read my report," she told me, still smiling.

And I did.

> I am trying to make, before I get through, a picture of the whole world—or at least as much as I have seen.
>
> —ERNEST HEMINGWAY

Report to the Secretary of State on Genocide in Central America: by Paloma Perez (generously funded by a research grant from numerous U.S. Security Agencies)

1899 was a very big year:
- The Spanish-American War has just ended: The U.S., having helped Cuba attain independence from Spain with the rallying cry "Cuba Libre," now occupies Cuba.
- The United Fruit Company is incorporated, merging with several other importers; it now controls 75% of banana imports to the U.S.

- The first dictator to take over Guatemala with a gun, Manuel Estrada Cabrera seizes control of that country.
- Ernest Hemingway is born in Illinois.

1901: Guatemala hires United Fruit to manage its postal service.

1903: Guatemala grants United Fruit a ninety-nine-year concession to build and maintain a railroad, with land in exchange; U.S. intervenes in Panama; U.S. intervenes in Honduras; U.S. intervenes in Dominican Republic.

1904: Author O. Henry coins the term "Banana Republic" for countries with one main product like bananas, ruled by a small rich military-elite of landowners at the tip and a vast impoverished populace crushed beneath like an iceberg.

1912: U.S. intervenes in Cuba, Panama, Honduras. United Fruit now gets land concessions in Honduras to build another railroad; the poor are pressed into service as banana workers, the cash crop.

1914–19 WWI

1917–1933: U.S. Army invades and occupies Cuba until 1933.

1928: "Banana Massacre" in Columbia: United Fruit workers pressed into service now strike and are killed by government militia.

1936–39: Spanish Civil War against elected government (loyalists) and General Franco (fascists); Hemingway sides with the former, but the latter prevail.

1937: Hemingway speaks against fascism at Carnegie Hall (1937) while his Spanish friend in Paris, Pablo Picasso, paints *Guernica* to protest the fascist bombing destruction of the small Basque city (1937); both men are labeled by Western governments as possible communists for their antifascist stance.

1941–45 WWII: German submarines in the Caribbean reduce United Fruit banana exports; Hemingway and his "Crook Factory" of ex-Loyalist Spaniards hunt German subs off the coast of Cuba; "Chiquita Banana" icon styled after Carmen Miranda, invented to use after war.

1942: J. Edgar Hoover has the FBI open a file on Hemingway as possible communist; file remains active until Hemingway's death in 1961.

1945: Chiquita Banana jingle copyrighted; bananas promoted as the healthiest and most useful food as breakfast for babies, women.

1947: Guatemala begins support of labor laws to protect peasant workers against foreign multinational firms.

1951: Jacobo Arbenz elected Guatemala president, begins agrarian reform; Hemingway writes *The Old Man and the Sea* in Cuba, about a fisherman from Canary Islands, Spain, living in Cuba, who captures a huge marlin, fights it for days, calls it "brother," defeats it, and ties it to his boat, and it is eaten by sharks before he returns to port. The old man dies.

1952: Guatemala Decree 900 passed, a reform act to redistribute unused land that had been given in ninety-nine-year leases to foreign companies like United Fruit; young Argentine med student Ernesto "Che" Guevara assists in reform moves; *The Old Man and the Sea* published to universal success and acclaim.

1953: Guatemala president redistributes 210,000 acres of United Fruit's unused land to peasants for cultivation; pays United Fruit their own appraisal value (low for tax-free purposes) for land; John Foster Dulles (U.S. Secretary of State) and brother Allen Dulles (director of CIA)—both shareholders of United Fruit—back a successful coup against Guatemala; Eisenhower instantly recognizes new military government; Che Guevara, appalled, vows to retaliate; *The Old Man and the Sea* wins Pulitzer, Hemingway's first major award.

1954: Banana workers strike across Honduras, U.S. investigates United Fruit's monopoly; Che joins Raul and Fidel Castro to launch revolution against U.S.-backed Cuban government;

from Cuba, Hemingway opposes U.S. Senate hearings on
un-American activities, says the only thing to stop senator
Joseph McCarthy is "a .577 Solid" (Elephant bullet);
Hemingway in two successive plane crashes in Africa, wins
Nobel prize in literature, returns to Cuba.

1958: Fidel Castro takes power in Cuba, U.S.-backed president
Batista leaves; Castro seizes United Fruit properties, says
"Cuba is no Guatemala."

1960: Banana workers strike in Panama; Hemingway leaves
Cuba for Ketchum, Idaho (July); John Kennedy elected U.S.
president (November); Hemingway sent to Mayo Clinic
in Minnesota, undergoes two months of electroconvulsive
shock therapy (December–January), while still privately
being investigated closely by the FBI. Guatemala begins
civil war between (U.S.-backed) military governments and
(Cuba-backed) peasant-guerrilla fighters; the war will drag
on for thirty-six years.

1961: John Kennedy inaugurated (January); CIA Bay of
Pigs invasion of Cuba (April); Hemingway receives two
more months of shock therapy (April–June); FBI follow
Hemingway inside the hospital for observation and tap his
phone; Hemingway commits suicide (July)

1962: Cuban Missile Crisis (October); USSR agrees to
withdraw missiles if U.S. agrees not to invade Cuba (again);
United Fruit creates small blue Chiquita sticker to promote
its bananas.

1967: Che Guevara killed in Bolivia, backed by U.S. Special
Forces and CIA.

1972: FBI director J. Edgar Hoover dies in Washington, D.C.;
his secret files are removed from FBI headquarters, and some
destroyed, by his longtime assistant and confidante, Helen
Gandy; Miss Gandy immediately retires from FBI.

1974: FBI finally closes posthumous file on Hemingway.

1988: Former FBI employee Helen Gandy dies, and her knowledge of Hoover's secret files dies with her; the *Washington Post* reports that Miss Gandy's "favorite passion" was trout fishing. *So?*

1996: Guatemala civil war ends after thirty-six years; the conflict has resulted in 200,000+ persons missing or killed—"disappeared"—in what is later called genocide against the indigenous Mayans and rural peasants.

2013: In Guatemala, genocide trials have just begun against the military, former government officials, and powerful landholders; it is unclear whether the recently elected president of Guatemala will support their continuation, or what the official U.S. stance will prove to be.

Really boring

HIS MOTHER'S SON

BY J. A. JANCE

I t was decades ago, a bright Saturday morning in August of 1978 when my then teenaged granddaughter, Alyse, dropped the bomb that would forever change our lives.

"Nana," she said, absently dunking the marshmallows that topped her freshly made cup of hot chocolate, "what would happen if Daddy turned out to be a spy, you know, the bad kind?"

Lloyd, my husband, was sitting in the kitchen with us, but he was mostly oblivious to the ongoing conversation between Alyse and me. Once he disappeared behind the pages of his copy of the *New York Times*, the world could have come to an end around him without his paying the slightest bit of attention. This time, how-ever, Alyse's offhand comment managed to penetrate his concen-tration on the day's news. He had just taken a sip of coffee. He choked on it and had to get through a coughing fit before he could respond.

"Your father a spy?" he asked. "How utterly absurd! I can't imagine how you came up with such a preposterous idea!" Then, dismissing the whole idea, he folded his newspaper, slapped it into the basket on his walker, and then stalked off into the living room, in search of peace and quiet.

I remember standing by the kitchen sink for a long moment,

staring down into the depths of the cup of coffee I had just poured for myself. There were any number of issues at work in the kitchen that morning, not the least of which was the fact that Lloyd had answered a question that had been addressed to me. But after being married to Lloyd Anthony Creswell for more than forty years, I had learned to pick my battles. The real problem in the room that morning was that my husband had been entirely confident in dismissing Alyse's stated concerns. Unfortunately, although Lloyd could allow himself the luxury of regarding her accusations as preposterous, I could not.

Yes, Alyse's father, Gunnar Lloyd Creswell, was my son, my only son. And yes, as his mother, I should have been shoulder to shoulder with my husband in leaping to our son's defense. And yet I couldn't be, because something in Alyse's innocently asked question spoke to me and touched a nerve I didn't even know was there. My first instinct was to look that question in the face and say the whole idea was out of the question. The ugly truth of the matter is, not only did I not like my son, I didn't think he was that bright either.

My husband's people came from England, not on the Mayflower, but shortly enough afterward. Lloyd always told me that his family referred to those early female immigrants as GARs—Grandmothers of the Revolution—whose female descendants were fully entitled to membership in the DAR.

My forebears came from Denmark nearly two centuries later. My name, Isadora, comes from my great grandmother; Gunnar bears my father's name. Lloyd's family has always believed in the English tradition of "keeping a stiff upper lip." Mine came with a full dose of Scandinavian-bred stoicism. Between us, neither one of us believed in being overly emotional.

So it was in keeping with family tradition that I picked up my cup and saucer from the counter and returned to the kitchen table without spilling so much as a drop of coffee along the way. Another child might have had her feelings hurt by Lloyd's curt dismissal, but Alyse has spent enough time with us the last few years, especially during the summers, that she's learned to shrug off her grandfather's occasional grumpiness the same way I do.

I sat down next to her. "Calling your father a traitor is a rather serious allegation," I said quietly. "What would cause you to come to that kind of conclusion?"

"I saw him," she said quietly. "I saw him in the park with a woman when he was supposed to be at work. She was very beautiful, and she must have been rich. She was wearing a fur coat."

Lloyd Creswell is true blue and always has been. When we got married in 1936, he swore to love, honor, and cherish, and I have no doubt—not a single one—that he kept those vows. Even when he was overseas during World War II or afterward, when he found his calling in the world of banking and we came back to Altoona to live, I'm sure he never strayed. Not once. I wish I could say the same for me. Or for Lloyd's son, for that matter. Maybe that's part of why Gunnar bugs me so much. Looking at him is too much like seeing myself in the mirror.

But the idea of Gunn having a woman on the side? That made perfect sense to me, because he always had a woman on the side. That was certainly true when he was married to his first wife, Alice—Alyse's mother, and I saw no reason why it wouldn't be true now with his second wife, the eminently regrettable Isabelle.

Alyse takes after her mother—in looks, brains, and temperament. Alice was a lovely girl. Why is it that nice girls always feel obliged to tie themselves to bad boys? Is it some ingrained need to fix the scalawag and make him into something better? Good luck with that. All I know is that Alice Goodwin was a beautiful bride. As she walked down the aisle on her father's arm, she was nothing short of radiant, smiling at Gunn who was grinning back at her from his place next to the altar. And what was I thinking when I saw that shit-eating grin? Was I happy for him and for her? No, there was a part of me that was thinking, *What a lovely girl. Please don't break her heart, Gunn. Please.*

Which he did, of course, in short order. Alice came to me in tears only a month or so after Alyse was born. Someone at work had sent her an anonymous note saying that Gunn been carrying on a passionate affair with someone at the office most of the time she was pregnant. What did I think she should do?

My advice would have been to throw the bum out, but Alice wasn't one to make hasty decisions. She would want to have all the facts at hand, but the real problem was this: Alice didn't want a divorce. She wanted her husband back. She wanted Gunn to grow up, shape up, and be a decent husband, father, and human being. That left it up to me to do the only thing that seemed reasonable to do at the time. I ran up the flag to Lloyd. I told him what Alice had told me and turned him loose to have a fatherly chat with his son. According to Lloyd, he gave Gunn a stern talking to—not that it did a bit of good.

Two months later, in the middle of an ice storm in upstate New York, a semi jackknifed in front of the vehicle Alice was driving and slammed into the driver's side of her car, killing her instantly. Alyse, swathed in a cocoon of blankets and lying in the back seat, was left unscathed. Within months, Isabelle—the girlfriend from work, a gorgeous babe who had once been Miss Indiana, was the new Mrs. Gunnar Creswell and Alyse's stepmother besides. I believe it's safe to say that I hated the woman on sight, and I'm pretty sure the feeling was mutual.

I didn't tell Alyse any of this. It wasn't my place, but the idea of her father Tom-catting it around with someone from work made more sense to me than anything else. But my first thought was that if he was, it would serve Isabelle right.

"When was this?" I asked casually.

"Last winter," Alyse said. "I was with one of my girlfriends. We were taking a short cut through Book Hill Park when we saw them. Since I wasn't supposed to be there, I made sure Dad didn't see me, but I got a good look at her. She was very beautiful."

"Your friends saw them, too?"

"I was with Crystal. I ducked back out of sight behind a tree. She's the one who saw the briefcases."

"What briefcases?"

"They had matching briefcases, brown ones. Dad always carries one like it back and forth to work. Crystal said that when the woman got up to leave, she took Dad's suitcase instead of the one she brought. You know, an old switcheroo like they do in the movies."

"That's not much to go on, now is it," I said kindly. "It might have just been a mistake."

"I guess," Alyse said. She bit her lip and shrugged. "I was just thinking if he got in trouble or something, maybe I could come live with you and Grandpa all the time instead of just for a few weeks during the summer."

Alyse said the words with such heartfelt earnestness and innocence that it broke my heart. Long before Alyse's little brother, Jimmy, was born, Isabelle treated her like so much excess baggage. As soon as Isabelle appeared on the scene, baby Alyse was shuffled off into the care of a series of mostly non-English-speaking nannies. Later on, she was packed off to various daycare facilities for long hours every day even though Isabelle had by then given up all pretense of holding a paying job.

Over the years it was clear that as far as Isabelle was concerned, Alyse was tolerated rather than loved. Once Isabelle and Gunnar's child came along, it got worse. Jimmy is an obnoxious kid, your basic spoiled brat, and Alyse is expected to spend her weekends, afternoons, and evenings serving as an unpaid babysitter for the little demon while her mother goes off to do whatever it is she does with all that spare time.

Because Lloyd and I were fairly well to do, Isabelle assumed that meant Gunnar was, too. Supposedly, Isabelle comes from an impoverished background, but once she and Gunn tied the knot, she started making up for lost time. She wanted to live in the best neighborhoods, drive the best cars, wear the best clothes. And if

Gunn's paycheck didn't pay the freight, she figured they could come to us with their hands out to get whatever was needed to make up the difference. Isabelle was willing to be chummy with us as long as the money kept flowing. When Lloyd finally put his foot down a few years ago and turned off the money spigot, Isabelle stopped making any effort to be pals, and so did I. We've tried to stay in touch with the grandkids. That's been easy to do with Alyse but not so easy with Jimmy.

I finished my coffee. "Let's not give this another moment's thought," I said. "I told you we were going to go shopping for school clothes for you today, and that's exactly what we're going to do."

We were parked outside the Logan Valley Mall by the time the first stores opened at 10 a.m. I stayed on the sidelines while Alyse tried on clothing. Just because we were no longer talking about her father's outside interest didn't mean I was no longer thinking about it.

It was the fur coat that Alyse had mentioned, the one the woman in the park had been wearing, that piqued my interest and ate away at me. For one thing, I knew far better than Alyse that Gunn and Isabelle were still deeply mired in money troubles, enough so that only a few months earlier, Gunn had once again come crawling to Lloyd, begging for a loan to keep from losing the house. Lloyd claims to be a tough guy, but he knuckled under one more time— more out of concern for keeping a roof over the grandkids' heads than to help Gunn or his money-grubbing wife.

And now there might be a new woman in Gunn's life, one presumably that Isabelle knew nothing about. If that wasn't just deserts, I didn't know what was. And since the woman was wearing a fur coat, that made me wonder if it was possible that my two-timing son had found himself the female equivalent of a sugar daddy.

At the time I set out to find out who that woman was and what she was about, I told myself I was doing it for Alyse's sake. If some kind of marital scandal was about to tear that poor child's world apart, I wanted to know about it before it happened rather than after the fact. But the truth is, it was for Alyse's mother's sake, too. There was nothing that would make me happier than being able to rub Isabelle's nose in the same kind of mess she had made for her predecessor.

That was why, the following week, when I drove her back to D.C. in time for school to start, I made an unscheduled stop in my present that took me back to my own, less-than-exemplary past.

Even now I won't put the man's real name to paper because it is one too many people would recognize. Yes, it's more than thirty years in the past, and the brief affair I had with him—a man I'll call Alf—happened twenty years before that, while Lloyd was off fighting for God and country. At the time, I was a young, attractive woman with a husband who was far away, a young child to care for on my own, and an aching need to have some fun in my life. Back then Alf, an aide to a longtime senator, had a wife back home in Dixie and more money than sense. From my point of view, he was perfect. That had been true in the forties, and he was still perfect for what I needed now—now that Alf was a senator in his own right with the same wife who was a mover and shaker in the city's inner social circles. I had watched the couple's rise to power from the sidelines without ever thinking I might want to contact Alf again, but now I did.

I played the "old family friend" card when I gave my name to the receptionist out front, and it worked. Within minutes I was ushered past a roomful of waiting lobbyists into Alf's private office. He came around to greet me, hand outstretched, as though I were some kind of visiting constituent from back home. He leaned over and kissed me hello, but I could see he was worried about what I was doing there.

"To what do I owe the pleasure?" he asked, leading me over to a pair of comfortable leather armchairs.

"I'm here about my son," I said.

Alf frowned. "Forgive me," he said. "I remember he was a cute little kid, but what was his name again?"

"Gunn," I answered. "Short for Gunnar. He's a military analyst who works for the Pentagon."

A shadow seemed to fall across Alf's face. "You need to know that I have very little influence over what goes on inside those walls," he said. "Promotions, pay-raises, that kind of thing are totally outside my realm of influence these days."

"What if Gunn were a spy?" I asked. I didn't really believe that at the time. The words were only a means to an end—bait meant to get Alf to bite and do what I wanted him to do.

Alf's jaw dropped. "You're saying you suspect your own son of being a traitor to his country?"

"It's a possibility," I said with a dismissive shrug. "Gunn and his second wife, Isabelle, have lived beyond their means for years. I also have reason to believe that he's become involved with some other woman. There are children involved, of course, and I was hoping you might be able to put him under some kind of surveillance to let me know exactly what kind of scandal our family is about to be up against."

"You want me to investigate your son?"

"Yes, if it's just another case of skirt-chasing, so be it."

"And if it turns out to be something worse?"

Gunn was a womanizer and had always been a womanizer. It didn't seem possible that it might be something worse. Besides, in this battle, Isabelle was my main target. Whatever happened to Gunn as a result would be collateral damage, but it wouldn't be undeserved.

"Then he gets what's coming to him," I said. "My husband didn't put on a uniform and go to war so his son could grow up to be a traitor to his country."

"What about Lloyd?" Alf asked. "Does he know anything about this?"

I was surprised that Alf remembered my husband's name, but I don't suppose I should have been. After all, Alf is the consummate politician. For politicians, knowing people's names means money.

"No," I said. "There's no reason for him to, or for anyone else to know about it, either."

I was thinking of Alf's very pretty wife, whose surgically maintained good looks kept thirty years or so off her face. Alf must have been operating on the same wavelength. Up to that moment, he must have been worried that I had turned up at this late date intent on making trouble for him over our long-ago indiscretion. My last words caused a visible look of relief washed across his face.

"So we understand one another?" he asked.

"Completely," I said, gathering my things and standing up. "It's good to see you again, Alf, but I don't expect we'll stay in touch. Once I know who the woman is, we're done."

Was it blackmail? More or less. I made my way back to where I'd parked the car, thinking about how Alf was one of the most powerful men in the country and how I was now the power behind the throne. It was oddly exhilarating. On the long drive back to Altoona, I wondered how long it would take for me to hear from Alf again. I never did.

In fact, I hardly gave the matter another thought. For one thing, two weeks later, Lloyd landed in the hospital for triple bypass surgery. The surgery was followed by postsurgical complications that kept him in intensive care for the better part of three weeks and hospitalized for another two weeks after. He was released to a rehab facility for a month after that before he finally came home.

In all that time, Gunn drove up exactly twice to visit. Alyse came along. Thankfully, Isabelle and Jimmy stayed home. The first time he came, Lloyd was still so out of it, I doubt he knew they were there at all. The second time, he was in rehab. After Gunn left, Lloyd wanted to know if he'd asked for money.

"Nope," I said. "And I wouldn't have given it to him if he had."

Lloyd gave me a wan smile. "That's my girl," he said, then he added, "So they must be doing better."

While Lloyd was in the hospital and rehab, it took all my energy to keep the house running, the bills paid, and get back and forth to visit him each day. I thought my life would get easier once he was home, but it didn't. After someone has been a patient for that long, after he's been used to having nurses at his beck and call at all hours of the day and night, it was a big shock to both our systems to have him come home with only me to take care of him. Neighbors pitched in and so did people from church. That was the time I could have used Gunn to show up and help out—to rake leaves and put up storm windows or even answer the damned telephone, but true to form, he didn't, and I was too busy to worry about what my useless son was or wasn't doing.

What I remember most about that winter was the snow. It came in early November and it never went away. If it hadn't been for the guy next door who used a snowblower to keep my driveway clean, I have no idea how we would have made it out to doctors' appointments or to buy groceries.

By the time we were approaching the end of March, I was more than tired of snow and tired of being locked up in the house with an often disagreeable and impatient patient. With another snowstorm predicted, I had made a quick trip out for groceries. I was in the kitchen putting them away, while Lloyd snoozed in front of Walter Cronkite and the CBS *Evening News*. When the phone rang, I answered it in the kitchen.

"Grandma," Alyse said breathlessly. "It's true."

"What's true?"

"Dad's a spy. The FBI was just here. They arrested him, put him in handcuffs, and took him away."

I didn't have to pretend to be surprised. I was surprised. I had a hard time catching my breath. I staggered over to the table and dropped heavily onto one of the kitchen chairs.

"Are you sure?" I asked. "Is it possible there's some mistake?"

"There's no mistake," Alyse said quietly. In the background, I could hear Jimmy wailing as though his heart was broken.

"Where's Isabelle?" I asked.

Between us Alyse and I never referred to Isabelle as Alyse's mother because she wasn't.

"She went out," Alyse replied. "She said she was going to talk to a lawyer."

"Have her call me when she gets back," I said. "I need to go talk to your grandfather."

As I walked into the living room, I realized what I had done. I had been aiming for Isabelle, but the person I had hit—the one who deserved it least—was my husband, Lloyd. I walked over to the TV set and switched it off.

"Wait," Lloyd said. "It's just a commercial. The news isn't over yet."

"It's over for now," I said, and then I told him.

Lloyd heard me out, listening stone-faced as I repeated what Alyse had told me. When I finished, he wanted details I didn't have.

"Spying for whom?" Lloyd demanded, his face contorted with grief. "And what kind of information could Gunn possibly have that would be of use to anyone?"

"I don't know," I said. "I have no idea. But try not to get so upset, Lloyd. It's bad for your heart."

"Not knowing is bad for my heart. I want to talk to Isabelle, and I want to talk to her now. Where the hell is she?"

"According to Alyse she went out to talk to an attorney."

Lloyd leaned back in his chair. I could see he was making an effort to get himself under control, and while he fought with his emotions—looking for his stiff upper lip—I battled my own, because I knew without a doubt—without a single doubt—that I was the one who had put this train in motion.

For the next half hour, we sat there in silent misery, waiting for the phone to ring. "If it's Isabelle," Lloyd said when it rang, "put her on speaker."

It was, and I did.

"It's Gunn," she said breathlessly. "He's been arrested by the FBI. I don't know what it's about. We have a friend who's an attorney—a criminal defense attorney. I didn't know what to do, so I went to see him. He says he'll take the case, but he needs a $50,000 retainer."

"No," Lloyd said.

"What do you mean, 'No'?" Isabelle wailed. "This is your son. Are you saying you won't help him?"

"I've helped him before," Lloyd said, "but not this time. This time he's on his own, and so are you."

"Hang up the phone, Isa," Lloyd said, shortening Isadora to the pet name he hadn't used in a very long time. "You've already talked to Alyse?"

I nodded.

"Then take it off the hook. If anyone else calls tonight, we don't want to hear from them."

I didn't sleep that night. Neither did Lloyd. Maybe women are more realistic than men. I had understood my son's shortcomings all his life. Lloyd had not, and now the idea that his son had betrayed his country had broken my husband's heart. By the next morning the story was headline news on the local television stations and on the national networks as well. When Lloyd went into the bathroom to shower, I tried calling Alyse. Naturally, Isabelle was the one who answered.

"What kind of parents are you?" she screamed at me. "You're just going to let your son rot in jail? You're not going to lift a hand to help him?"

Lloyd came out of the bathroom. "Who is it?" he asked.

"Isabelle."

"Let me talk to her."

I handed him the phone. He listened to her in silence for the better part of a minute. I could hear her voice screeching into the earpiece, but I couldn't make out any of the words. When he was finally able to get a word in edgewise, he said in a tone I had never heard from him before, "I'm very sorry to hear that."

Then he ended the call and handed the phone back to me.

"What did she say?"

"If we don't help, she'll see to it that we never see our grandchildren again. That she'll take them back home to her folks' place in Indiana."

I was aghast. I didn't care that much about Jimmy one way or the other because I didn't know him that well. But Alyse?

"Can she do that?"

"Of course she can," Lloyd replied. "She's the mother."

By the middle of the day, friends and neighbors were showing up with covered dishes, almost like it was a funeral. I'm not sure why they do that when no one can stand the thought of eating, but they do and they did, and I tried my best to be grateful. Lloyd had been one of the premier bankers in town. Gunnar had been one of the best-known graduates from the high school, one people had pointed to with a certain pride of ownership. People didn't talk about that very much as they sat quietly in our living room, commiserating with us. They talked about the weather. They talked about our health.

And then came Sunday morning and the worst call of all, and it wasn't Isabelle who broke the news. It was Alyse. "He's dead," she sobbed into the phone. "Daddy's dead."

We were sitting at the kitchen table, drinking our coffee. I had put the phone on speaker so we heard the news together.

"How is that possible?" Lloyd asked.

"They found him in his cell," Alyse answered brokenly. "They say he committed suicide."

I heard Isabelle's voice, shouting from somewhere in the background. "Are you talking to them? Damn it! I told you not to. Get off the phone right now!" The line went dead as she disconnected.

Lloyd put down the phone. "He was guilty," he said quietly. "Otherwise he wouldn't have taken his own life. And someone wanted to spare the country the ordeal of taking him to trial. That's why they left him the means to do it."

It was amazing for me to see that in the face of this disaster, Lloyd was the one who was dead calm while I was falling apart.

"I still have some friends in high places in D.C.," he said. "Let me see what I can find out."

I had friends in high places, too, but I wasn't about to call on Alf. Not now. Not ever.

While Lloyd worked the phone, I emptied the refrigerator of casseroles, dumping out the food I knew we would never eat, and arranging the clean dishes, marked on the bottoms with their owners' names, on the dining room table to await pickup.

It was hours later when Lloyd finally put down the phone. "It was the Russians," he told me. "Gunn was working for the Russians. He evidently provided them with plans for a new top secret spread-spectrum military communications system. The woman he was working with has already been spirited out of the country. They're trying to establish her identity."

"That must have been the woman Alyse saw. Remember? She told us about seeing them together. In the park."

Lloyd gave me a long look. "If Alyse is in a position to identify a Russian spy, then we have a major problem on our hands. Does anyone else know that?"

"I certainly never told anyone."

"Neither did I," Lloyd said. "But if security people from both sides of the Iron Curtain are looking into this matter, then Alyse could be in real danger, especially if she can identify someone the Russians don't want identified."

The next few days were a nightmare that had to be lived through. The sun came out and the snow turned to mud and muck. We sat glued to the TV set, hoping for snippets of news. No one called to let us know when Gunn's services would be. No one invited us to attend, but we heard about it from a local news reporter. The funeral would be held at their Georgetown church on Wednesday afternoon.

"Are you going?" I asked Lloyd.

"No," he said. "I won't go where I'm not welcome."

"I want to see Alyse," I said. "I want to talk to her and Jimmy at least one more time before Isabelle spirits them off to God-knows-where in Indiana."

Early Friday morning, I set off on my own, driving Lloyd's lumbering Lincoln. As the heartbroken widow, Isabelle was the star of the show, and she was making the most of it. I sat near the back in the crowded church and spoke to no one. When the service was over, I went back to the house and let myself into the reception where I hoped to find a chance to speak to Alyse alone.

The house was crowded with people I didn't know. We weren't part of Gunn and Isabelle's circle of friends, so there was no danger of my being recognized. At least I didn't think so. I stayed in the background, and made sure that when Isabelle moved from one room to another, I stayed one room away.

Jimmy was up to his usual tricks. I saw him sneak a sip from someone's abandoned glass of wine. Then when his mother approached, he knocked it over and blamed Alyse, who was half-way across the room when it happened.

"You stupid girl!" Isabelle yelled at her. "Didn't I tell you to watch him? This is all your fault!"

I'm sure Isabelle meant that the spilled wine was all her fault, but I saw the look on Alyse's face, and I knew how she was taking this—that her father's death was all her fault. And of all the people in the room, I was the only one who knew for sure that was true.

When Alyse fled upstairs, I followed her and found her sobbing into the pillows piled on her bed. Standing there looking at her, listening to her, I knew exactly how her life was going to turn out with an impish half-brother and a stepmother who was prepared to blame her for every little thing. And in that moment, I made up my mind. It didn't matter if I was going to be guilty of kidnapping or custodial interference or whatever, I was going to get her out of there, no matter what.

"Alyse," I said gently, placing a hand on her shoulder. "Tell me something. Do you want to go to Indiana?"

She stopped sobbing. She didn't look at me, but she shook her head.

"I know you know your father was a spy," I said softly. "You told me so last summer."

She nodded again, into the pillows, without raising her head.

"And you know who his partner was," I added. "The woman in the park. You can identify her."

"I guess," Alyse mumbled.

"That means people are going to be looking for you. Bad people."

"Russians you mean?" she asked.

"Yes," I said, "And maybe some of our people, too. I don't know—the CIA maybe or the FBI. But if the good guys can find you, that means the bad ones can, too."

"Will they hurt me? Am I in danger?"

"Grandpa thinks so," I said. "And so do I."

"So what should I do?"

"Write your mother a note," I said. "Tell her you're running away. Grandpa's car is down the street. The doors are unlocked. It's almost dark now. No one will see you if you slip out now and hide in the back of the car."

"Isabelle will kill me if she finds out," Alyse said sitting up. "And if I'm gone, who'll look after Jimmy?"

"That's his mother's problem," I told her. "It's not yours."

"But I'm just a kid, Grandma. Where will I live? How will I find food to eat? What will happen to me?"

"First we have to find a safe place for you to stay," I told her. "As to how you'll live? Let Grandpa and me worry about that. We'll take care of you, Alyse. I promise. Will you do it?"

Alyse squared her shoulders. "Yes," she said. "Yes, I will."

I went back downstairs. I was through the dining room and

halfway through the living room on my way to the front door when a voice behind me inquired, "Mrs. Creswell?"

I froze, thinking Isabelle must have realized I was there and sent someone to eject me. When I turned around, however, a man in a suit was holding up an FBI badge for my scrutiny. "I'm Agent Holloway," he said. "I believe you're Gunnar's mother, correct?"

It made sense that the FBI would be a presence there. If there were a conspiracy, they would be looking at all of Gunn's connections to see who else might be involved. Still it spooked me that a complete stranger had successfully spotted me in a crowd when I had been making such an effort to remain invisible.

I nodded as cordially as I could manage. "I'm Isadora," I said. "And yes, I'm Gunnar's mother."

"I'm very sorry for your loss." Agent Holloway said mechanically. At the same time, however, I caught him surveying the room behind me. "Is Mr. Creswell here by any chance?"

"Our family has some estrangement issues," I said, making a show of dabbing at my eyes. "Under the circumstances, Lloyd thought it best to stay away. I only came in hopes of seeing the children. In fact, I was just looking for Alyse. You haven't happened to see her anywhere, have you?"

"No," he said. "I haven't."

"I need to find her," I said, "because I'm going to be heading home in a few minutes. Now, if you'll excuse me."

I bustled off and spent the next little while making an obvious effort of searching for someone while continuing to stay out of Isabelle's way.

When it seemed reasonable to do so, I made my exit. By the time I reached the car, Alyse was already huddled invisibly on the floorboard of the backseat. We left D.C. and drove for hours. Only after I had stowed Alyse safely with a friend who ran a parochial school in upstate New York, did I go home to face the music. I thought Lloyd would be furious. He wasn't. In fact, he was the one who came up with the idea of creating an entirely new identity for her. I never asked him how he did it. Maybe he had a friend of his own in high places, one I knew nothing about. Then again, maybe he didn't.

Strangely enough, Isabelle never questioned the idea that Lloyd and I might have had something to do with Alyse's disappearance. As far as she was concerned, her stepdaughter was nothing but an ungrateful teenager who had run off in her family's hour of need and good riddance to her besides. Within weeks of Gunn's funeral, Isabelle and Jimmy moved back to Indiana. For a while I tried to stay in touch with my grandson, but eventually I gave up on that. My letters and gifts were all sent back marked RETURN TO SENDER.

Once Alyse became Debra Highsmith and left for Albuquerque, we never saw her again. By then I suppose I had convinced myself that what I had told her in her upstairs bedroom was true—that the Russians would never stop searching for her. I was wrong about that, of course. I know that now.

Lloyd died two years later. I know the loss of Gunnar and the humiliation surrounding our son's death contributed to and hastened my husband's death. I've accepted my responsibility for that. If I hadn't sent someone chasing after Gunnar, maybe he would have gotten away with it. Maybe he could have been more like me and never been caught. Maybe things could have been different. Maybe my life could have been different.

But I doubt it.

For more about Isadora Creswell and her granddaughter, Alyse, read J. A. Jance's *Judgment Call.*

GHOSTS

BY RAYMOND BENSON

They call us spooks.
You know—spies, agents, operatives—whatever.
Spooks.

But I'm here to tell you that it's not just spooks that occupy the darker regions of the intelligence field. Ghosts reside there as well. Lost souls that somehow fell through the cracks and disappeared into a black pit of secrets and lies, as if they'd vanished into thin air.

Ghosts.

I know this firsthand. It's the only justification for what happened, for I now believe it's a mystery that will never be deciphered. For years I wanted to think there was a reasonable and logical solution to the puzzle. For a so-called easy diplomatic mission, it has haunted me ever since that bizarre night. And because I couldn't properly explain it at the time, my career took a hit. I was removed from the field and brought home to the States. The pay was slightly better, surprisingly, but the new job was most definitely a demotion. Instead of working in an exotic European locale, such as the glorious city of Vienna, Austria, I found myself behind a desk at CIA headquarters.

What really happened on the night of November fourth, nineteen-fifty-six?

The crazy thing about it is that somehow it involves the Ferris wheel. The same one used in that spy movie, *The Third Man*, the one that starred Joseph Cotten and Orson Welles. I love that picture. I was in Vienna during filming, and I saw it three times when it played in the city. It was amazingly true to what was going on then, except I never really heard much zither music playing in the streets. You might know the scene—Cotten and Welles meet in one of the gondola cars for a clandestine rendezvous in the sky. The gondolas have roofs; like little wood cabins with windows, and large enough for fifteen people. The *Wiener Riesenrad*, at the time the world's largest Ferris wheel, already had a lot of mystique since it had been built before the turn of the last century. That movie gave it even more of an air of mystery, and subsequent films and stories added to it. Today the wheel is a major tourist attraction in Vienna.

I'm ninety-four years old now. I think I've outlived most of the guys I knew in the Agency. Hell, I can remember when our offices were spread around D.C., long before the Langley campus was built. I spent most of my life in the CIA and, before that, with military intelligence during the war. Getting into that was easy—I had an advantage. My grandmother was from Frankfurt and she lived with us in Texas when I was growing up in the thirties, so I learned to speak both English and German fluently. The Military Intelligence Service snatched me up when I was drafted and I was stationed first in France, then Belgium, and finally Germany. I didn't see any action. I analyzed intelligence reports. When the war was over, I had the choice to become a citizen again at the age of twenty-six, or join the organization that would eventually evolve into the Central Intelligence Agency. With the state of Europe being what it was—everyone was scrambling for pieces of divided countries—I figured that at the very least the work would be interesting. So I became a political analyst for a living.

And lucky me—they sent me to Vienna. Lovely Vienna. What a fascinating, gorgeous, vibrant place. Full of spirit, history, and the arts. It was an ideal posting, and I loved it. Officially, my job title was "Ambassadorial Assistant." I worked in Vienna's American sector until Austria was granted sovereignty in nineteen-fifty-five. After the war, Austria, being on the losing side, was divvied up between the U.S., France, Britain, and the Soviet Union. The capital city itself was also split into four sectors. Surprisingly, the system actually worked during the years it took for Vienna to be rebuilt and repaired. Even the Russians displayed no desire to occupy Austria the way they had other Eastern European countries, like Hungary. That was admirable, given that the Iron Curtain already dissected Berlin and was laying foundation from north to south across Europe. When Austria became its own boss again and the four superpowers dissolved their pieces of that pie, I stayed in the city and worked at the U.S. Embassy.

And that brings me to the question at hand. At my age, I know I could die tomorrow. Hell, I could kick the bucket tonight during dinner. Of all the memories I possess from my long life, there are indeed many treasured ones and also some I'd prefer to forget. And then there's the one I wish to God I could understand before I close my eyes for the last time.

What happened to the Szalay family that fateful evening of November fourth, nineteen-fifty-six?

It was a busy morning at the embassy. A lot was going on in the world that day. I was at my desk tracking the Suez crisis, because we knew the Brits were going to join the Israelis in the war with Egypt. That whole shitstorm began during the summer, when Nasser declared the Suez Canal belonged to Egypt alone and kicked out the Brits, with whom the Arabs had already fallen out over the existence of Israel. I imagine the Brits' colonial attitudes also had something to do with the feud. France got into the act and it was shaping up to be a war between Israel, the U.K., and France on one side, and the Arabs, in particular Egypt, on the other. Everything grew tense for the next couple of months, and finally, just six days prior to November fourth, Israel attacked Egypt.

After the fact we found out the Brit operation was called "Project Telescope." On the fifth, the Brits dropped paratroopers into the country. Royal Marines landed on the sixth. At that time, the U.S. position on it all was to discreetly favor the Arabs. It was in America's best interests to keep peace in the region. The Suez Canal was a major artery for the efficient flow of oil to the West. We also knew that the Soviet Union was backing the Arabs in the cause, and we didn't want to piss *them* off. Eisenhower didn't want to escalate the thing into World War Three. So America would end up trying to broker peace, which we eventually did, perhaps by dangling the possible fluctuation in value of the pound sterling over Prime Minister Eden's head.

Anyway, *that* was all going on in the Middle East. In Vienna, we were mostly concerned about the situation in Hungary. Although things had been quiet in that country for a week, the Soviets were going to invade the country *that morning*, the fourth. Needless to say, our phones were ringing nonstop. We had Hungarian refugees pouring into Austria from across the border—the first time since the war that citizens could do so. We had no idea how bad it was going to be in Hungary, but we knew it could get ugly. The Soviets were probably going to clobber the revolutionaries and punish the rest of the country for the rebellion.

Today it's called the Hungarian Uprising of nineteen-fifty-six. The Hungarian people got fed up with being ruled by the communists. On October twenty-third, students led a protest in Budapest that became violent—and suddenly it seemed that the entire country took up arms against their overseers. In five days, all Russian troops had been pushed out and back into the USSR. The Hungarian government failed, and a coup went into effect led by the "New National Government." Imre Nagy was appointed their first prime minister. The revolt was bloody and frightening to the rest of the world. Of course, the U.S. was on the revolutionaries' side, but we couldn't say so publicly.

For nearly a week, there was calm. It looked like the Soviets were going to leave Hungary alone. Hordes of Hungarians left while the borders were open.

But we knew that on November fourth the Soviets were going to strike back. In fact, we learned about it that very morning and did our best to get the intelligence where it was needed. In another week, though, the Soviets crushed the Hungarians and punished them, too. Thousands were lost. The arrests, kangaroo trials, and executions of hundreds of people went on for years. The country was under communist rule until the fall of the USSR in nineteen-eighty-nine. Today the Uprising is remembered as something akin to a Hungarian Holocaust, and the date is a national holiday.

As I was going over the latest cables from our station in Egypt, Ambassador Thompson called me into his office. As I assumed, it was about the Hungarian situation.

"The Soviets are encircling Budapest as we speak," he said in his typically calm, soft voice. "By tonight the city will be cut off. We understand the Soviet Eighth and Thirty-eighth Armies were deployed to boost the divisions already posted in Hungary. It's going to be a bloodbath."

"What are we going to do, sir?" I asked.

"Nothing, of course. What *can* we do? Unless the rebels hold out—which I seriously doubt will happen—Hungary will once again be under Moscow's control. I give them five days. A week, tops."

"I'm afraid I agree."

He shook his head and made a *tsk-tsk* sound. Then he took a manila folder that lay on his desk and opened it. "I have a small task for you. We received a coded cable from Dulles this morning with the request that we handle the matter." Thompson handed me the transcribed signal, along with a photograph of a middle-aged man with eyeglasses and a mustache. To me he looked like a college professor. His name was handwritten at the bottom. I had never heard of Tamás Szalay before that moment. Apparently he was a high-level guy in the Hungarian Working People's Party, someone with access to all the Soviet puppet big shots like Münnich and Kádár.

The instructions, which used Dulles's own code identifiers, said that Szalay and his family were among the refugees rushing to get out of Hungary, and the man wanted to defect to the West. He possessed extremely valuable information about the Soviet Union's plans to aid the Arabs in the Suez Crisis in the event that the U.S. entered the conflict. It was the kind of intelligence for which men were killed.

"Szalay is already in Austria," Thompson said, "and he will be in Vienna tonight. The problem is, the Soviets were unaware he had fled the country until yesterday. They know what he knows. They want him back. Failing that, they'll kill Szalay to prevent him from defecting."

"You said he's with his family?"

Thompson nodded. "A wife, a teenage daughter, and a young son."

"Christ. That's not conspicuous, is it?"

"Right. Now they're in hiding, but we have to get them out as quickly as possible. Would you mind being their contact tonight?"

"Me?" I wasn't an operations man. I should point out that my expertise in intelligence lay in strategizing and analyzing data. I wasn't the type of field agent who got his hands dirty. I never carried a gun. Fiction has often exaggerated what we did during the Cold War, especially those of us who were stationed in foreign cities. The spy game was mostly played on paper, or by interpersonal interaction with assets, or by observation. The cloak-and-dagger stuff was strictly for the movies and the novels of John le Carré and Ian Fleming. Thus, up to that day, my years in the CIA, while filled with many tense and worrisome moments, had never brought me face-to-face with violence.

"I'm afraid there's no one else. Really, it's just an easy diplomatic mission. You can handle it."

"What am I supposed to do?"

"Our Austrian friends will deliver the family to you tonight at the *Prater*. You'll babysit them for an hour or so, and then they'll be picked up by one of our men. That's it."

"Why the *Prater*?" The *Wiener Prater* was Vienna's long-standing amusement park, where *The Third Man* Ferris wheel was located.

"I have no idea. Maybe somebody decided that if they were going to appear in public, then the park would be the safest place. After all, they have children. Unless the Soviets know where they're hiding, they can't track them to the park. At least, that's what we're hoping. At any rate, extreme discretion is a priority. An Austrian asset will have all the details by lunchtime. You're to meet him at noon."

Thompson gave me the Austrian's info and sent me on my way. On the surface, the assignment seemed straightforward. As long as the Szalay family could get to the *Prater* safely, then I could get them out of Austria with no problems.

Or so I thought.

I met the asset at Trześniewski's, one of my favorite cafés. They served small rectangular open sandwiches of fresh bread and various spreads. It was a Viennese mainstay since before the First World War. The man gave his name as "Ernst." It probably wasn't real. He looked about my age, had blonde hair, and was as Austrian as they come. Being in public, we spoke German.

"There has already been one attempt on Szalay's life," he told me. "It happened last night in District Twenty-Two. Two assassins attempted to shoot into the car they were in while it was stopped at a street light. Luckily, our man in the car behind them engaged the attackers in gunfire. Szalay and the family got away safely."

"Jesus," I said. "How come we didn't hear about that?"

"I'm sure the police are trying to figure out what really happened. All they found were two dead men lying in an intersection." Ernst shrugged. "Vienna's a rough town these days."

We talked about the logistics of getting the family out of the park and into an unmarked van that would take them immediately to Salzburg, and from there, into West Germany and the American Zone. Since the *Riesenrad* was in the southwest corner of the park, near the front entrance, I thought it best that we meet in that vicinity. Just across from the attraction, on the other side of the circular *Riesenradplatz*, stood a small pavilion containing restrooms, a snack bar, and an ice cream parlor. Ernst thought that was perfect. *Ausstellungsstraße*, a major east-west avenue, ran just north of the *Prater* main entrance. At the given time, the van could pull up to the curb and I could herd the family into it quickly.

"As long as you're not seen by the opposition, that should work fine," my Austrian colleague said.

"One last question. Why are we doing this at the *Prater*?" I thought it was a reasonable question.

Ernst shrugged. "It's what I was told. Maybe the family wants to ride the carousel and eat some cotton candy."

The temperature outside was nippy but not terribly cold. The park would soon close for its regular hiatus through winter. On the fourth it would close at seven, and that's when the van would arrive to pick up the Szalay family. Ernst promised to have them at the designated spot at six-thirty, just as it was becoming dark. He didn't think that thirty minutes of exposure was too bad, but unfortunately that was the way the timing had to work. That was fine, or so I thought.

That afternoon, I did as much fact-finding as I could regarding the presence of Soviet hit squads in Vienna. All I found out was what we already knew. They were indeed in the city, but I had no idea how many or who they were. Nevertheless, I was confident the handover would go smoothly. It sounded easy enough: collect the family from Ernst at the amusement park, maybe have an ice cream with them, and then walk them to the street corner to catch the van. My part would take less than two hours of my time, including the travel to and from my home and the *Prater*. Easy.

I was at the park by six-fifteen. It wasn't very crowded due to the chilly weather. Much of the place had been hit by bombs during the war, and it had taken a while to rebuild everything. The big wheel had been damaged, too. The *Prater* reclaimed its former glory around the same time as Austria reentered the global community as a sovereign nation. Most of the attractions were back, along with newer things. The *Riesenrad* looked brand new, although they'd reduced the number of gondolas in order to spread them out more around the wheel. Part of the attraction was a small building that housed an exhibit telling the park's history. Passengers had to buy tickets, go through the minimuseum, and then climb the steps to the platform where they boarded a gondola.

Taking my position by the ice cream parlor, I lit a cigarette and stood as if I was waiting for someone—which I was. There's no entrance fee to the park itself; it's only if you want to go on the rides or play games that they charge you money. The wheel was right in front of me, as big as the sky. Unlike most Ferris wheels, this one rotated very slowly, so that riders could stand in the gondola, look out the windows, take pictures, or whatever. It was also possible to arrange to rent the "dining car," which was decked out with a tablecloth-covered table, candles, and waiters. Perfect for a special occasion.

I kept my eyes moving, noting the faces of the people as they strolled through the *Riesenradplatz* on their way in or out of the park. Some went straight to the Ferris wheel. By the time I'd finished my cigarette, it was six-thirty. And, right on time, Ernst appeared from behind the pavilion. He spoke German again. "I have your package."

I didn't see anyone but him. "Oh?"

He jerked his head toward the trees that lined the park behind the pavilion. "I wanted to make sure everything was okay. I'll be right back."

Ernst left me and I waited another minute. Then, the man I recognized as Tamás Szalay came around the corner of the building with his wife and two children. He was shorter than I'd imagined, but he was definitely the same man. The wife was even smaller, but she was pretty in a conservative Hungarian way. Her head was wrapped in a scarf to ward off the chill. Szalay's eyes darted fervently around the *Riesenradplatz*. The daughter appeared to be fourteen or fifteen, but I knew from the file she was only twelve. Her eyes were wide with excitement at the lights and colors of the amusement park. The boy, probably six or seven, was just as fascinated. Now standing near the base of the *Riesenrad*, he pointed to it and set off a string of Hungarian at his parents. He wanted to ride the wheel.

"Hello," Szalay said to me in English. We clasped hands. His was moist from nervousness. I asked him if he spoke any English. He shook his head. I tried German. Szalay made the universal sign with his fingers—"a little." His Russian was much better than my Hungarian, so we settled on that.

"Long journey?"

"Yes."

"Everything okay?"

"I think so, but we're being followed."

"Oh?" I looked behind the family. I didn't see Ernst. "Where is…?"

Szalay turned and motioned back to the trees. It was dark back there. "He…he's with the other man who brought us."

That didn't sound right to me, but I figured Ernst knew what he was doing.

The boy continued to jabber about the wheel. He was nearing tears as his mother tried to comfort him. Szalay turned to him and shook his head. No, they were telling him. No time to ride the Ferris wheel. The boy became hysterical. He started to scream and cry and throw a tantrum. We were attracting a lot of attention.

I looked at my watch. "Actually, you have some time, if you'd like. It might be better than standing here." I glanced toward the building at the base of the *Riesenrad*. There wasn't much of a line to buy tickets. "My treat."

He spoke to his wife in Hungarian, and then they decided to take me up on my offer. It would be a nice present for the children. After all, they didn't know when they'd ever be in Vienna again. When they told their son, he immediately settled down and was happy.

I walked them to the other side of the *platz* to the ride's box office, pulled out my wallet, and handed over enough Austrian schillings to buy four tickets. I gave them to him and said, "Here. Wrap yourself good. It might be cold up there."

Luckily, there weren't many people waiting. When business was slow, the management allowed small parties to take over an entire gondola rather than stuffing the car to the maximum. I went up the stairs with them and watched the Szalays get in gondola number four by themselves. The couple sat, but the girl pressed her nose to the window. Because the boy couldn't reach it, Szalay stood and picked up his child. He stood in plain sight through the pane. I didn't want him to do that. I waved at him to sit down, but he didn't see me. The operator started the ride. Gondola four jerked and then rose slowly along the circle to its next position before the wheel was stopped to let on more passengers.

There was nothing more to do for twenty minutes, so I left the structure and went back to the *platz*. Gondola four glided to its next position. I thought the timing would work perfectly. It would have been nice to be able to communicate with Ernst the way field agents could later with increasingly sophisticated radio devices. But that was not yet possible in nineteen-fifty-six. I lit a cigarette and stood in the same spot where I was before, watching the Ferris wheel go round.

Curious about my Austrian asset, I eventually turned and walked around the pavilion toward the park's perimeter, where the trees created a shadowy, more inconspicuous area. It was from there that Ernst had escorted the family to me. I couldn't see him, so I threw down my cigarette and strode closer. Once I was already amid the trees and didn't find him, I figured Ernst had already left the premises. He hadn't been required to stay, but I remember thinking he probably should have made sure the completion of the handover went smoothly.

When I moved to return to the *platz*, I saw a man lying on the ground, curled around the base of a tree. I quickly ran to him and saw that his throat had been slashed. Ernst. In the shadows his blood appeared black, and it was everywhere. I swear I felt my stomach jump into my throat. It was the first time since the war I'd seen something like that. Staying crouched, I snapped my head around in all directions, fearing that I was to be the killer's next victim. But no one else was in the proximity. No car idled at the curb on *Ausstellungsstraße*, the avenue on the other side of the trees. I was alone with Ernst's corpse.

Though I never carried one, I wished I'd had a gun. The so-called easy diplomatic mission had turned into something else entirely.

Once I was confident my own life wasn't in immediate danger, I remembered why I was at the *Prater*. I stood, ran back to the *platz*, and gazed at the wheel. Gondola four was at the very top, high above Vienna, where the passengers could look out and see almost the entire city laid out on both sides of the ride.

I spied a pay phone near the front entrance arch, where guests obtained maps and information about the park. There was time, so I trotted to it, inserted the correct amount of coins, and called the emergency number I'd been given. The *real* personal assistant to the Ambassador answered. I told him I needed to speak to Thompson, but he said I was to tell him whatever I had to say. He knew all about what was happening that evening. When I relayed the news of what had happened to my Austrian asset, he said, "For God's sake, where is Szalay now?"

I explained about the wheel.

"Christ. All right, stay there. Wait for the family and proceed with the plan. Your driver will be there in...what, ten minutes?"

"That's right. About when the family gets off the ride."

"Take them right to the rendezvous point. I'll try to get a field officer there immediately."

I hung up and went to center of the *platz* so I could check the wheel's progress. Gondola four was at the three-o'clock position. It wouldn't be long now. I went into the *Riesenrad* building and maneuvered my way to the staircase used by passengers exiting the ride. From the foot of the steps I could see the lower gondolas as they approached the loading platform. I'd be able to see the family as they disembarked.

Despite the brisk evening air, sweat soaked my shirt. Somewhere in the park was an assassin, maybe more than one. I told myself there was the possibility that murdering Ernst had nothing to do with the Szalay family, but I doubted it. The killers were Soviet agents sent to terminate the Szalay family. Somehow they had gotten wind of Ernst's plan. That meant they could be anywhere in the park. Did they know what I looked like? Did they see him hand over the family to me? It was possible. They got rid of Ernst first, and they were merely waiting for me to reappear with the Szalays. I thought that if I hadn't moved to a spot where other people could see me, I might have been dead already.

Gondola four was in sight now at the five o'clock position. It was next to reach the loading platform. My watch indicated we had five minutes before the van arrived. I noted the wheel operator staring at me. When we made eye contact, he asked in German, "May I help you?"

I pointed to gondola four and answered, "Waiting for them." Then I noticed the windows. I didn't see the daughter or Szalay holding his son. Despite the twinge of panic, I figured they must have all sat after a while. The operator waved me up so that I could stand on the platform and greet my friends. I stood in place and watched the gondola inch closer.

The ride came to a halt, and the operator opened the doors.

The gondola was empty.

I immediately repositioned myself so I could again examine the car's number on the front to make sure I had the right one. Sure enough, a white number four was painted on the exterior. I went back to the operator and asked, "What happened?"

"What?"

"Where are the people that were inside this gondola?"

He seemed confused. "Some gondolas are empty."

"I saw the family get in. I was here! A man, woman, girl, and a boy."

The operator shrugged like it was none of his business. He shut the door and started back to his controls.

"Wait! You can't move the wheel. There's been—"

"What?"

My first thought was that I should try and shut down the Ferris wheel and find out what the hell just happened. Then I remembered the instructions—extreme discretion was a priority. I couldn't let *anyone* know that I'd been there to help spirit away a defecting Hungarian family that the Russian death squad wanted to kill. And then there was the complication of Ernst's body lying in the trees not a hundred yards from where I stood. So I stammered, and said, "Maybe I'm mistaken. They're in the next gondola." The operator shook his head and then pulled the lever to start the sizable motor that powered the behemoth. Gondola four began its journey around the circle again.

I hoped perhaps I *had* made a mistake. The Szalay family *would be* in the next car. But I knew it was a futile dream. I'm really good at numbers, and I remember it was unequivocally gondola number four that the Szalays boarded.

The next car held six teenage couples, who laughed and carried on as they bolted out and ran down the stairs. The operator looked at me, and then *I* shrugged. "I guess they already got out. I'll look for them in the park." He nodded and went back to his job. I went down the stairs and through the museum to the *platz*, dazed and frightened. I spent the next minute circling the *Riesenradplatz* to make sure I hadn't missed them after all. Of course, they were nowhere in sight.

I stared up at the huge Ferris wheel, moving now against a starry sky. The park would be closing soon.

Where did they get out?

There was the other platform where passengers booking an extended stay in the dining car boarded, but it was closed and dark. The strutted structure that supported the wheel would be no way down. Climbing the exterior would be extremely hazardous. Children couldn't possibly do it.

Where did they go?

My God, they had vanished.

But that was *crazy*. I told myself over and over that it simply wasn't possible. There was a logical and reasonable explanation for what happened.

I noted I was panting, desperately trying to catch my breath. I looked at my watch. Seven on the dot. I moved out of the park and tried to walk nonchalantly to the corner of the entrance and *Ausstellungsstraße*. The van was there. The driver saw me coming alone and frowned. I opened the passenger door and stuck my head in. I'd never seen the man before.

"They're gone. I lost them somehow."

"What?"

I got in the car and closed the door. "Drive and I'll tell you. You can bring me back for my car."

So I told him the story and he said, "They've got to be there. They are somewhere in that park!"

"Maybe so, or maybe they're already out of it. I am. They could have been shoved into a vehicle in the amount of time it took me to find you. I swear, I put them in that gondola, watched it go all the way around, and then the thing was empty when it reached the bottom. I have no idea what the hell happened. It's like some kind of Houdini trick."

The driver was silent. He took me back to the parking lot, where I found my car and went home. I dreaded going to the embassy the next morning. I knew how my story was going to sound. I had really blown it. My first and only field operation and I screwed it up royally. In the end, it was acknowledged that I shouldn't have been sent to do such a delicate diplomatic task, but that I was to get a slap on the wrist. Hence, the move back to the States.

The Szalay family was never heard from again. They truly had disappeared into one of the black holes that existed all over the map in those days. You never knew when you were going to step into one of them, and there was no clue what happened to you when you did. I chalked it up to the nature of the beast—the world of spooks and ghosts. With denizens like that, you have to expect the unexplainable.

The rest of my career was uneventful. I was a good analyst. I did solid work. I retired with a pension. I often thought about the Szalays, though. My dreams of the *Wiener Riesenrad* turned into nightmares. All I saw were horrific images of the boy crying. Ernst's slit throat. The number four gondola. The excruciatingly slow-turning wheel. The faces of that hopelessly lost family.

Ghosts.

That was the Cold War for me. It was an enigma that haunted me the rest of my life.

And I never watched *The Third Man* again.

ABOUT THE EDITORS AND AUTHORS

A former journalist, folksinger, and attorney, **Jeffery Deaver** is an international number-one bestselling author of thirty-two novels and two collections of short stories. His novels are sold in 150 countries and translated into 25 languages.

His *The Bodies Left Behind* was named Novel of the Year by the International Thriller Writers Association, and his Lincoln Rhyme thriller *The Broken Window* was also nominated for that prize. He is a three-time recipient of the Ellery Queen Readers Award for Best Short Story of the Year and has been nominated for seven Edgar Awards from the Mystery Writers of America. He's won both the Steel Dagger and the Short Story Dagger from the Crime Writers Association in the U.K.

His most recent novels are *The Kill Room*, a Lincoln Rhyme novel, and *XO*, a Kathryn Dance thriller, for which he wrote an album of country-western songs, available on iTunes and as a CD.

Readers can visit his website at www.jefferydeaver.com.

Raymond Benson is the internationally acclaimed author of thirty published titles. The fourth book in his most recent thriller series—*The Black Stiletto: Secrets & Lies*—recently appeared, preceded by *The Black Stiletto*, *The Black Stiletto: Black & White*, and

The Black Stiletto: Stars & Stripes. The fifth and final chapter in the saga will be published late 2014. Raymond was the fourth— and first American—author of the official James Bond novels (1996–2002), and his work is currently collected in the anthologies *Choice of Weapons* and *The Union Trilogy*. His "rock 'n' roll thriller" *Dark Side of the Morgue* was a Shamus nominee for Best Paperback Original P.I. Novel of 2009. Raymond is also a prolific tie-in writer, the most recent work being *Homefront—The Voice of Freedom* (cowritten with John Milius) and *Hitman: Damnation*. For more information, you can visit www.raymondbenson.com or www.theblackstiletto.net.

Joseph Finder is the *New York Times* bestselling author of ten novels and whom the *Boston Globe* has called a "master of the modern thriller." A Russian Studies major at Yale, he did graduate work at the Harvard Russian Research Center and wrote widely on Soviet politics and intelligence before publishing his first novel, *The Moscow Club*, which was named by *Publishers Weekly* as one of the ten best spy novels of all time.

Killer Instinct was named Best Novel of the Year by the International Thriller Writers, and a major motion picture based on *Paranoia* was released in 2013, starring Harrison Ford, Gary Oldman, and Liam Hemsworth. His novel *High Crimes* became a hit movie starring Morgan Freeman and Ashley Judd. A member of the Council on Foreign Relations and the Association of Former Intelligence Officers, he lives in Boston. His most recent book is *Suspicion* (Dutton, 2014).

John Lescroart is the author of twenty-four novels, fifteen of which have been *New York Times* bestsellers. Libraries Unlimited places him among "The 100 Most Popular Thriller and Suspense Authors." With sales of over ten million copies, his books have been translated into twenty-two languages in more than seventy-five countries, and his short stories appear in many anthologies.

John's first novel, *Sunburn*, won the Joseph Henry Jackson Award. *Dead Irish* and *The 13th Juror* were nominees for the Shamus and Anthony Best Mystery Novel, respectively; additionally *The 13th Juror* is included in the International Thriller Writers publication "100 Must-Read Thrillers of All Time." *Hard Evidence* made "The Complete Idiot's Guide to the Ultimate Reading List." *The Suspect* was the American Author's Association 2007 Book of the Year. John's books have been Main Selections of the Literary Guild, Mystery Guild, and Book of the Month Club.

Gayle Lynds is the *New York Times* bestselling "Queen of Espionage." Her recent novel, *The Book of Spies,* was named one of the five best thrillers of 2011 by *Library Journal.* Her novel *Masquerade* is among *Publishers Weekly*'s Top Ten Spy Novels of All Time. She is a member of the Association for Intelligence Officers and the cofounder (with David Morrell) of International Thriller Writers, I.T.W. Gayle interested **John C. Sheldon** in fiction after they married in 2011. John, a former Maine state judge and Visiting Scholar at the Harvard Law School, had published frequently in legal journals. He now prefers writing fiction because "you can blow things up and grease people." They live together on fourteen wooded acres outside of Portland, Maine.

Sara Paretsky grew up in Kansas during the Cold War, when anticommunist fears were at their height. Her father, a cell biologist, went to Bratislava to meet his Czech counterparts in 1964. On his way home, he injected himself with their strain of Rickettsia. Paretsky loves Golden Retrievers, hates ideologies, and is also the author of the V. I. Warshawski novels, and holder of both the Diamond Dagger and the Edgar for lifetime achievement as a mystery writer.

Gary Alexander has written thirteen novels, including *Loot*, fourth in the mystery series featuring comic Buster Hightower. *Disappeared*, the first in the series, has been optioned to Universal Pictures.

He has written 150+ short stories and sold travel articles to six major dailies.

Dragon Lady, his Vietnam novel, is being published by Istoria Books, available both as an ebook and print-on-demand. His website is www.garyralexander.com.

Alan Cook writes mystery/suspense novels, including the Carol Golden amnesia series. Carol Golden isn't her real name. She gives herself that name in *Forget to Remember* when she gets hit on the head and can't remember who she is or anything about her past. In *Relatively Dead* she has recovered her identity but not most of her memory. While trying to connect with cousins, she discovers they are targeted for death and she may be next. *Dangerous Wind* finds her working with a shadowy group of government agents and traveling to all seven continents to apprehend an ex-boyfriend she doesn't remember who is supposedly trying to foment world chaos. Alan has also collaborated with illustrator Janelle Carbajal to create the children's book, *Dancing with Bulls*.

Brendan DuBois of Exeter, New Hampshire, is the award-winning author of nearly 130 short stories and sixteen novels including his latest, *Fatal Harbor* (Pegasus Crime), part of the Lewis Cole mystery series. His short fiction has appeared in *Playboy, Ellery Queen's Mystery Magazine, Alfred Hitchcock's Mystery Magazine, The Magazine of Fantasy & Science Fiction*, and numerous anthologies including *The Best American Mystery Stories of the Century*, published in 2000 by Houghton-Mifflin, as well as *The Best American Noir of the Century*, published in 2010. His stories have twice won him the Shamus Award from the Private Eye Writers of America, and have also earned him three Edgar Allan Poe Award nominations from the Mystery Writers of America. He is also a *Jeopardy!* game show champion. You can visit his website at www.BrendanDuBois.com.

Bev Vincent is the author of three books: *The Road to the Dark Tower* (nominated for a Bram Stoker Award), *The Stephen King Illustrated Companion* (nominated for a Stoker and an Edgar), and, most recently, *The Dark Tower Companion*. He has published over seventy short stories, including appearances in *Ellery Queen's Mystery Magazine*, *Thin Ice* (for his Al Blanchard Award–winning story "The Bank Job") and the MWA anthology *The Blue Religion*. He has been a contributing editor with *Cemetery Dance* since 2001, is an original member of the Storytellers Unplugged blogging community, and writes book reviews for Onyx Reviews. His website is bevvincent.com.

Katia Lief is the author of several internationally bestselling crime novels. Her latest is *The Money Kill*, the fourth installment of her Karin Schaeffer series, which was published in 2013 by Harper-Collins. She teaches fiction writing at The New School in Manhattan and lives with her family in Brooklyn. You can visit her at katialief.com.

Vicki Doudera is a top-producing real-estate agent at a busy firm in coastal Camden, Maine, and the author of the Darby Farr Mysteries, published by Midnight Ink and featuring crime-solving, deal-making real estate agent Darby Farr. Her debut novel, *A House to Die For*, was chosen as a Best Read of 2010 by *Suspense Magazine*. Her latest and fifth in the series is *Deal Killer*.

When she's not writing, Vicki enjoys cycling, hiking, and sailing with her family, as well as volunteering for her favorite cause, Habitat for Humanity. She has pounded nails from Maine to Florida, helping to build simple, affordable Habitat homes, and is currently President of her local affiliate.

In addition to MWA, Vicki belongs to Sisters in Crime and the National Association of Realtors. You can read more about her at vickidoudera.com.

ABOUT THE EDITORS AND AUTHORS

Jonathan Stone does most of his writing on the commuter train between the Connecticut suburbs and Manhattan, where he is the creative director of a midtown advertising agency. His fifth and latest novel, *Moving Day*, was published in March, and has been optioned for film by Nick Wechsler and Steve Schwartz. A graduate of Yale, Jon is married, with a son and daughter in college. His previous short story, "Hedge," appeared in last year's MWA anthology, *The Mystery Box*.

Gigi Vernon grew up in the Washington, D.C., area. As a child of the Cold War, she's always been fascinated by our so-called enemy Russia. She studied Russian language and history at Georgetown University, and earned a PhD in history from the State University of New York. Her short stories, set in a variety of historical time periods and places, have appeared in *Alfred Hitchcock's Mystery Magazine* and elsewhere. Currently she resides in upstate New York, and has always thought it criminal her closet isn't full of beautiful designer clothes, purses, and shoes.

Joseph Wallace is old enough to remember 1966, when the United States Air Force lost a hydrogen bomb in the ocean off Spain—the incident that inspired him to write "Deep Submergence" for this collection. He is the author of two novels: *Diamond Ruby* (2010), a historical novel set in his hometown of Brooklyn, and *Invasive Species* (2013), an end-of-the-world thriller. His short stories have appeared in *Ellery Queen's Mystery Magazine, Baltimore Noir, Bronx Noir, Hardboiled Brooklyn,* and a previous MWA anthology, 2009's *The Prosecution Rests,* edited by Linda Fairstein. "Custom Sets," his story in that anthology, went on to be selected by Lee Child and Otto Penzler for *The Best American Mystery Stories 2010*. Joe lives north of New York City with his wife and children, an overexuberant dog, and a put-upon cat.

Robert Mangeot has published short fiction in various journals and anthologies. His work has won contests sponsored by the

Chattanooga Writers' Guild and Rocky Mountain Fiction Writers. He is married and lives in Nashville, Tennessee. You can visit his website at www.robertmangeot.com.

T. Jefferson Parker is the author of twenty crime novels, including *Silent Joe* and *California Girl*, both of which won the Edgar Award for best mystery. His novel *Laguna Heat* was made into an HBO movie, and his books have been translated into fourteen languages. His last six books are a "Border Sextet," featuring ATF task-force agent Charlie Hood as he tries to stanch the flow of illegal firearms being smuggled from the U.S. into Mexico. Parker enjoys fishing, hiking, and cycling. He lives in Southern California with his family.

Laura Lippman has published nineteen novels, one novella, and a collection of short stories. Her work includes the Tess Monaghan series and several stand-alones, including *Every Secret Thing*, which has been adapted for the screen. Her work has won the Edgar, Anthony, Agatha, Nero Wolfe, Quill, Barry, Macavity, and Gumshoe awards. She lives in Baltimore and New Orleans.

Katherine Neville, *New York Times* bestselling author, has been called the female Umberto Eco, Alexandre Dumas, Charles Dickens, and Stephen Spielberg. *Publishers Weekly* and *Library Journal* have credited her groundbreaking first novel, *The Eight*, with paving the way for adventure-quest books like *The Da Vinci Code*.

Neville's previous twenty-year career as an international computer executive for the likes of the Department of Energy, IBM, OPEC, and the Bank of America took her to live in six countries on three continents; she had colorful stints along the way as a professional portrait painter, photographer, busboy, waiter, and fashion model. She draws on these experiences to enrich her fiction. Her award-winning books are translated into forty languages, in eighty-eight countries.

ABOUT THE EDITORS AND AUTHORS

J. A. Jance is the *New York Times* bestselling author of forty-seven contemporary mysteries in four different series—J. P. Beaumont, Joanna Brady, The Walker Family, and Ali Reynolds. Born in South Dakota and raised in Bisbee, Arizona, she now divides her time between homes in Tucson, Arizona and in Bellevue, Washington.

77 122 229 321
               322
80   324
82 129 248   323
89   251-52 324

         258   333
    153
    163
    164

    171 293